DEJA BREW

Also by Celestine Martin

Witchful Thinking
Kiss and Spell

DEJA BREW

Celestine Martin

FOREVER

New York   Boston

Forever
Hachette Book Group
1290 Avenue of the Americas, New York, NY 10104
read-forever.com
@readforeverpub

First Edition: October 2024

Forever is an imprint of Grand Central Publishing. The Forever name and logo are registered trademarks of Hachette Book Group, Inc.

The publisher is not responsible for websites (or their content) that are not owned by the publisher.

The Hachette Speakers Bureau provides a wide range of authors for speaking events. To find out more, go to hachettespeakersbureau.com or email HachetteSpeakers@hbgusa.com.

Forever books may be purchased in bulk for business, educational, or promotional use. For information, please contact your local bookseller or the Hachette Book Group Special Markets Department at special.markets@hbgusa.com.

Library of Congress Control Number: 2024936152

ISBNs: 9781538754450 (trade paperback), 9781538754443 (ebook)

Printed in the United States of America

LSC-C

Printing 2, 2024

For Emily

Acknowledgments

So, this book was freaking tough to write, but it was the book I needed to write.

Thank you to the following people who helped and supported me during the writing process.

My agent, Lauren Bieker, you changed my life that fateful August, and I'm so grateful that you believe in me. You deserve all the happily-ever-after endings in the world.

To my editor, Madeleine Colavita, thank you for being forever kind and generous with my work. I owe you a Costco-sized box of chocolate.

Gratitude to the production team at Forever, with special thanks to my copyeditor Lori Paximadis and production editor Anjuli Johnson. You two fabulous peeps were my lighthouses signaling my book to shore.

For my husband, Matthew, thank you for being my guiding star and my own personal romance hero. You're so wonderful, you are my dream come true.

To Poppyseed, who sat and wrote next to me on your toy typewriter when I was revising. I love and adore you to Saturn and back.

To Mama, who taught me how to shine, who makes sure that

libraries know who I am, and who is one of my biggest supports. I love you something awful.

To Brother, thank you for checking in on me and reminding me who I'm writing for and why I'm writing. You're an awesome person; keep it up.

To Emily, who heard and listened to me when I was struggling with this book. I adore you and love you beyond words.

To the readers, bloggers, reviewers, booksellers, and librarians who have uplifted and celebrated my books and this magical series with me across social media, I'm so absolutely grateful. If you've sent me a supportive email, text, or direct message, thank you so much for giving me sunshine when I needed light.

To Molly Harper, thank you for letting me be the remora fish to your awesome shark self.

Seriously, this book is in your hands because of the support and love my family, friends, and readers have shared with me.

DEJA BREW

Halloween Lore

by Lucinda Caraway

Those who are fortunate to be born on October 31 are believed to be born with good luck on their side.

Place an ivy leaf under a pillow to dream of a future lover on this day.

An apple buried in the ground on the last day of October will attract unicorns.

October

Pumpkins are considered symbols of protection and prosperity.

Chapter One

It was official.

Sirena Rachel Caraway just broke the world's record for having the weirdest month ever. Fate seemed determined to give her nothing but tricks and no treats during these thirty-one days of October. Sirena, having been born and raised in Freya Grove, expected silly scares and whimsy mayhem. When you formerly attended high school with ghouls and werewolves, you adopted an anything-goes attitude super quick about this time of year. However, Sirena was embarrassed, shocked, and just plain annoyed by the series of events that unfolded. Tonight, on Halloween, she wanted to be in a place where for once she felt in charge and learned how to hone her magic.

Sirena, in her fluffy robe and slippers, stood in the Caraway kitchen.

The hanging rack with copper pots and pans had a thin layer of dust on them. The stainless-steel appliances were pristine, and the ceramic jar was filled with untouched spatulas and wooden spoons. Just looking at the stove gave Sirena a stomachache. Bad things happened when she touched the stove. Even now, she could still smell the lingering aroma of burnt scrambled eggs and toast.

It was the last meal she had attempted to cook in her kitchen. She just didn't cook anymore, but rather put deli meat, sliced cheese, and grapes on a plate to eat after work.

The hand-painted moon-and-star wall clock Nana Ruth purchased years ago remained on the wall next to said stove. Its steady ticking filled the emptiness of the kitchen and gave Sirena a small sense of comfort. It felt as if Nana were still standing at Sirena's side, telling her to either make a cup of tea or take her sleepy behind back upstairs.

"This month needs to end," she murmured. "Right now."

The clock *tick-tock*ed in response, and the minute hand moved forward.

It was a good time for tea. Sirena filled the electric kettle with water, placed it back on the base, and flipped the switch. It began to burble. Her fingers played with the ends of her braids, which were coming undone. She leaned against the counter and recounted six events that made October a time of regrets.

First event: Sirena rolled her ankle while she was delivering a meal order for Empty Fridge. It was her fault, since she hadn't been paying attention and hit an uneven patch on the sidewalk. She had a choice: save her phone, or save the milkshakes and burgers that a start-up company ordered for lunch. Sirena saved the order from hitting the sidewalk, but her phone was cracked and barely functional.

She delivered the meals unscathed to the office manager.

The manager said, "Thanks, Sheila!"

Sirena's ankle hurt so much that she didn't even bother to correct her. Eventually, she had to dip into her meager savings to buy a new phone.

Second event: Sirena ruined Callie's Halloween decorations.

She hadn't even seen the pumpkins on the floor and ended up accidentally kicking a hole into one of the gourds. There were pumpkin seeds and guts everywhere, and the living room smelled earthy. Their cat, Shadow, got caught playing in the guts and needed a bath. Callie looked as if she was going to cry at the scattered seeds all over the carpet. This pumpkin incident led to Sirena missing out on a huge delivery bonus and limiting her cooking demo budget.

It had taken her two months to land an interview for Lighthouse, one of the Jersey Shore's best-reviewed award-winning restaurants in the last five years. Sirena wasn't going to cancel because her favorite fungus was super expensive. She slapped down her credit card and bought the porcini mushrooms, packed up her plastic tub of culinary items, and drove over to the premier beachfront eatery. After Ad Astra let her go as their head chef months ago, Sirena worked two part-time jobs to make ends meet. It was her goal to lead another world-class kitchen one day, and it was going to happen for her. Last month, Ursula helped Sirena make a whole vision board, and she even wrote her intention in permanent gold marker—the color that invited success and prosperity into one's life. Even now, she envisioned her intention, *Find Your Path*, in her mind, guiding like a shining neon sign. Sirena pushed away the wiggle of doubt in her stomach as she parked outside Lighthouse. So, her dishes were a little off, and her food didn't quite hit right the way it used to. It would be fine. She had magic on her side. Kitchen witches always brought the heat.

Third event: Sirena completely fumbled the big interview at Lighthouse.

Anyone could make an egg explode, but it took a special talent to make the hiring manager spit out their food into a napkin. Her stomach jumped into her throat the moment the entire dish was scraped into the plastic bin. Her second chance to run a professional kitchen just went up in flames—or rather went into the trash. Goodbye to another dream.

The manager spoke gently as she walked Sirena out after the interview.

"Your dish was...interesting. We're still looking at candidates. We'll call you."

Fourth event: Sirena went semi-viral after a Halloween prank at work went bonkers.

It wasn't her fault that she accidentally punched that terrifying trash clown; she just instinctively reacted to someone jumping out at her from behind the dumpster. What hurt more than Sirena's fist was the fact that her coworker Beckett set her up and filmed the entire thing on his phone. As the clown screamed and clutched their big red nose, Sirena demanded Beckett explain why he would do something so pointless. *So unkind.*

He just shrugged. "I thought you could use a laugh."

Sirena clutched her casting hand to her chest to keep from throwing an itchy underwear hex on him. She glared at Beckett and returned to work in the bistro. An odd blend of foolishness and hurt roiled in her gut. Here she thought she was getting along with her coworkers, but apparently, she wasn't *fun* enough for them.

She finished her shift at Night Sky, then went home to get ready for the party of the year.

Fifth event: Sirena embarrassed herself in front of half the Grove.

When *the* Diane Dearworth personally invited the Caraways

to the famous Halloween celebration at the historical society to benefit the Freya Grove Historical Society, Sirena was beyond geeked out to attend. Lucy had plans with Alex, and Callie was working with a high-profile bride. Ursula was handing out candy with Xavier at the shop, so Sirena was left to go alone. She spent weeks piecing her outfit together, sourcing her coastal granddaughter costume from thrift stores and attic finds. Sirena drank two cups of ginger and lemon tea to calm her nerves and listened to her party-prep music as she did her makeup. By the time Sirena arrived at the Dearworths' in her cheerful blue floral dress, floppy bag, and wedge sandals, she was ready to party. The house was decorated with touches of black lace and Gothic decorations. She made small talk with a pixie, ate mini brownies, and awkwardly tried to flirt with a vampire while drinking punch.

Buzzy magic tickled her skin as she danced and swayed to the pop hit playlist.

She was attempting to drop it down low when she knocked into a bookshelf and ended up covered in a bucket of translucent goo. Several guests took out their phones while others cringed at the image of Sirena looking as if she had gotten handsy with a lusty ghost. There was a talk of calling the Ghostbusters, and someone even cued up the classic theme song from the movie. Sirena rushed to the kitchen to find baking soda and vinegar in a vain attempt to save the costume.

But instead, she found Gus Dearworth. Their eyes met.

For an instant, time ceased, and they were suspended in that space together. Her steps halted once she stared up into the richest brown eyes she'd ever seen on a magician. Sirena's brain automatically began comparing them to all the foods she loved to taste and cook with. Melted chocolate. Hazelnuts. No, he was cinnamon, strong and unmistakable.

Behind the beauty of those eyes, there was a shadow of trepidation. He shifted his weight from foot to foot as if he was going to make a choice he didn't feel comfortable with.

Time started again. She blinked and took in the situation before her.

Sixth event: Sirena caught Gus Dearworth wearing a custom-made tuxedo and holding an open velvet box. It held a sparkly piece of jewelry that might have been a ring. She let out a shocked gasp. Was he proposing?! He shoved it into his pocket so quickly that Sirena wondered whether she saw anything in his hand. Out of sight, out of mind.

Gus retreated into his jovial demeanor, flashing her a smile that seemed a little too sharp. What were the odds of her running into Gus Dearworth now, when she looked like a slime monster? They'd seen each other around town over the last few years. Ursula, her cousin, went to school with Diane, his sister, so they knew of each other. They attended the same backyard cookouts and holiday parties but rarely spoke. Tonight, Gus stood before Sirena by the sink, with his thick frame and big shoulders emitting an air of playfulness.

She half expected him to pull a rabbit out of his tux.

He gave her a quick once-over. His smile softened. "You look absolutely frightening."

She grinned at his compliment, noting the hint of concern in his voice.

"Do you need a towel—or the bathroom?" he offered.

"No, I need a hot shower," she said, gesturing to her outfit. "The slime is everywhere."

She shivered as the icy substance trickled down her back and into her underwear. Ugh. Gus eased out of his jacket and wrapped it around her shoulders.

Sirena gently protested this action. "No, Gus. Don't ruin your outfit."

"Hush," he said. "I know a good dry cleaner."

She took the oversized jacket and burrowed herself into it. The spicy scent of cloves and teakwood oil remained in his fabric, easing her nerves. Instantly, she was warm. Gus went over to a cabinet, took out a tea towel, and handed it to her. Their fingertips brushed briefly, sending a light tickle of bright magic over her hand and causing her heart to sprint. She wiped her face with the terry cloth and felt a little less sticky. It wasn't enough, and she would still need to leave.

"Pivot and change your costume," Gus advised.

Sirena gestured to her soaked floral dress. "Who am I supposed to be now?"

"You're a ghost-hunting tourist who got a little too close to the ghost," he said. "Anything can happen tonight."

Sirena snorted. "Anything did happen."

He narrowed his eyes at her. "I can't tempt you into staying?"

"You can try," she said dryly.

He paused for a second, as if weighing his options, and reached into his pants pocket. Sirena eyed him. Magicians were unpredictable. Was he offering her a trick or a treat?

Gus pulled out a coin. "Let's ask fate. Heads, you stay. Tails, you go home."

It was the size of a half-dollar and had a profile of a woman looking off into the distance. The coin sparkled in the overhead light. They shared a look. It was probably better for Sirena to go home, but she saw a quiet longing in his eyes. He didn't want her to leave. For an instant she was tempted to pivot and just stay the night. To see what was building between them. To ask him about that ring he had in his pocket. To learn whether his touch would make her heart race again. Gus was about to toss the coin when two party guests dressed as twins ambled into the room, swaying as one unit.

"There's the birthday boy! We're looking for you to blow out the candles."

"I'm here," he said, that sharp smile resurfacing on his face.

"You are the guest of honor!" the other twin sang.

A feeling of hot guilt washed through her at those words. He had a whole houseful of guests, but he was in here entertaining her. She needed to leave now and stop taking up his time. He glanced at her, his eyes hopeful that she would continue playing this game. Oh, how she hated to let him down. Sirena eased out of the jacket and placed it on the kitchen table.

"Thanks, Gus, for everything, but I'm heading out."

His shoulders lowered and the hope in his eyes dimmed.

He palmed his coin, then nodded. "Get home safe."

They exchanged good nights, and she went out the back kitchen door, giving a final glance over her shoulder. The magician was gone. Her heart ached in his absence.

Once Sirena got home, she undressed and stepped into the shower. She let the water run over her skin. The constant feeling of sticky embarrassment and shame filled her chest and made it hard to think. She stood under the spray until she felt clean. Sirena dried off, changed into her pajamas and robe, and went down to the kitchen. As she stared at the starry wall clock ticking down to midnight, one question kept echoing in her brain.

Why hadn't she made better choices? All the bad decisions Sirena made over the last month had led her to this night of complete failure. Here she stood in the family kitchen alone with an aching hand to match her heart. If Sirena had the power, she'd throw the entire whole month of October in the trash with her slime-covered costume.

The electric kettle clicked off as steam wafted out of the spout.

Sirena went to the tea pantry and studied the rows of brand-new labeled loose teas. She let out a baffled laugh at the new labels taped to the glass jars. Lucy, the family tea witch, must have reorganized the tea closet while Sirena was at work.

Sirena scanned the labels for the words "Sweet Dreamer," her favorite tea, but that container was missing. Add another disappointment to the day. She was about to settle for a nice cup of pure chamomile when she saw the tall jar next to it. The label was written in a delicate script Sirena hadn't seen in years but knew by heart. It was Nana Ruth's spidery handwriting, the same writing that filled the cookbooks and spellbooks Sirena cherished.

She took the jar in her hand, then read the label. "Wish Tea. That's new."

Hmm. Maybe Lucy found an old recipe of Nana's and refilled the jar.

Sirena unscrewed the top and breathed in the strong, distinct aroma.

Goose bumps rose on her skin. As a kitchen witch, she was gifted with the ability to separate the different herbs and ingredients by tasting or smelling a dish. She sniffed deeply, differentiating the scents from each other. Chamomile. Lemon balm. Rosehips. Lavender. There was another herb she couldn't define, but it smelled heavenly. Like baked sunshine on a fall afternoon. Sirena took the jar over to the counter, scooped two spoonfuls of loose tea leaves into the mug, and then poured the water. She drizzled in honey and let the leaves steep for a few minutes.

The water turned a pleasing golden shade. Sirena gently blew on the tea to cool it down and then took a sip. The floral taste of the brew flooded her mouth, and she relished the hotness it delivered. A good cup of tea could make you feel at peace for a precious minute. As Sirena drank, she thought about yesteryear's spells.

When Sirena cast the wish spell that fateful May night, she assumed that her wish would be granted first. It was simple. All she wished was to regain her cooking career that she put on pause when Nana got sick and needed a live-in caregiver. Bittersweet joy fluttered through Sirena as she recalled Nana's last year of life. It was a time of tears and small moments of laughter. On her good days, Nana rattled off rules for kitchen witches from her memory while Sirena wrote them down. They took their afternoon tea in the garden. Nana, in her pink floral housedress, slowly walked on the path, caressing her herbs and plants with an unsteady hand. Nana lamented her regrets on her bad days when it was too difficult for her to get out of bed. Sirena called out of work on those days, not wanting to leave her alone in case she needed anything.

Nana blinked at her, those large brown eyes filled with remorse. Her usually strong voice was wobbly and thin with exhaustion.

"I had so many plans. There wasn't enough time to make them come true. You blink your eyes, and your entire life has passed you by. I was looking at my photo albums the other day and I couldn't believe time went by so fast. If I could do it all over again, I'd do things differently. I'd be braver. I'd have more fun and eat more cake."

Sirena blinked rapidly, trying to keep her tears at bay. *Make a joke. Don't cry. Be fun.*

"What kind of cake?"

Nana gave a small grin. "I think maybe a chocolate harvest cake with rainbow sprinkles. You've got to have sprinkles. Remember that rule. That's rule ninety-nine."

She clutched Sirena's hand in hers and gripped it with the last of her strength. "Promise me, my sweet child, you won't wish away your time. Live your life today, not tomorrow."

Sirena simply nodded, unable to talk through her falling tears. When Nana passed away and joined the ancestors shortly after that conversation, Sirena sought to keep her promise.

She'd made plans to move back to New York and jump right back where she left off once the memorial was over. She bought the train ticket on her phone, had a travel bag in hand, and was literally on her way to the transportation center when she found Lucy sitting at the kitchen table. Her breath caught in her throat at the sight of her big sister. Lucy, still in her black dress, stared vacantly off into space, no light in her eyes. Her face was gaunt, and she was pale, covered in sorrow. *What was the last meal she had?*

Sirena dropped her bag on the table and went to the stove. "Have you eaten?"

Lucy blinked, then cast her eyes downward. "I don't know."

Sirena took out a pan and searched the fridge for cheese, milk, and eggs. She knew how to whip up a quick, tasty omelet that she knew Lucy would love.

Rule one: Kitchen witches always cook for their families.

Lucy glanced at Sirena's travel bag in front of her. "You'll miss your train," she said, her voice small.

"I'll catch the next one," Sirena said. "Do we have any parsley?"

"Check the cabinet."

Four years later, Sirena still hadn't caught the next train, and she didn't know if she would ever leave the Grove. Eventually, she outgrew her old city life the way a child outgrew a beloved sweater, but she still held on to the hope that it might fit her if she just folded her body enough.

It was this desperate hope that would be her undoing.

She pressed her lips together to keep herself from sobbing.

Rule forty-three: Kitchen witches only cry when cutting onions.

Sadness crept into her blood and rooted into her bones. Once upon a time, she delighted in picking fresh herbs, tasting samples, and scribbling down recipes on junk mail envelopes. Now all she cared about was getting the next job and the next gig that would get her to the next day. Her inner fire was quickly dying, and nothing she did stoked the embers in among the ashes. Tonight she didn't feel like cooking anymore. A kitchen witch who didn't want to cook was like a shark that didn't want to swim. It went against her very nature, and she couldn't imagine who she was without her gifts. Getting the head chef job at Lighthouse was supposed to reignite her culinary career. It was her chance to make her wish come true, but she failed.

If only she could hit a Restart button on this entire month.

For the first time in years, Sirena allowed herself to make a request from the universe.

"I wish I had a second chance," she said.

A thrilling tingle of magic strummed through her hands as

the mug's warmth lulled her. A deep feeling of sleepiness entered her body and made everything in the kitchen look fuzzy.

Sirena put the almost empty mug in the sink. She'd clean everything up in the morning.

"You'll start fresh tomorrow," Sirena said. She ran her fingers through her braids and studied the fraying ends once more. She could either reseal them with hot water or take them out after work, but she'd decide in the morning. Everything would look better in the light of day. Sirena took one last look at the kitchen. Hopefully, one day soon she'd feel like she belonged here again. She went upstairs.

Bright red and orange mist bubbled out of the cup from the sink and drifted onto the floor. The mist, fueled by the spoken wish, crept up the wall and seeped into the clock. Two minutes before midnight the clock paused, the hands frozen in place.

After an instant, the hands clicked backward.

Like they say in the Grove, midnight is the best time for magic.

Chapter Two

Is that the smell of burning pumpkins?

Sirena, half awake and confused, jumped up from her bed clad in a ratty athletic T-shirt and black-cat-printed pajamas. Possible situations floated through her tired mind as the burning smell intensified in her room. Did a hungry ghost come over for a treat? Maybe Herbie, one of the neighborhood gnomes, found the Caraway hide-a-key and wanted to cook up a third breakfast.

Sirena yanked her phone from the charger and sprinted out of her bedroom to rescue her griddle. With every hurried step she took downstairs, a murky haze, almost like incense smoke, wafted in the air. Jazzy music and off-key singing filled the air, so her nerves eased a little. Maybe things weren't as dire as she first assumed. Lucy and Callie usually turned on their cooking playlist to signal to Sirena that the kitchen was in safe hands. Hearing Nina Simone croon with her unmistakable voice meant that Lucy was currently working the stove. Lucy probably heard about the Halloween clown prank and decided to make her breakfast before work. Once Sirena hit the bottom stair, she breathed in, trying to figure out what exactly was being cooked—or rather, burned. Sirena, in addition to instilling dishes with magic and emotion, had the uncanny ability to know just from a good whiff what was being made.

She lifted her nose. Brown sugar. Pumpkin puree. Raw magic. Buttermilk.

She reeled back. "Why is Lu making pumpkin pancakes again?"

Sirena loved pumpkins just as much as any other witch, but there was a limit to the gourd madness. Once fall started, Lucy and Callie doubled down on everything pumpkin spiced and pumpkin flavored. Callie even gifted Sirena a body wash set that made her smell like a whole bakery.

When Halloween finally arrived, Sirena had so many pumpkin-flavored muffins, treats, and drinks that she needed a year to recover from the taste. Why was Lucy extending the madness into November? There was mystic trouble brewing in the Caraway kitchen. Sirena walked into the living room and instantly froze.

"What the what?" she said in a horrified whisper. She gripped her phone in her hand.

Fake spiderwebs dripped from every corner and shelf. An orange and white flag banner saying "Keep It Creepy" hung crookedly on the wall. Thick black and orange pillar candles were clustered together on a mirrored chafing dish in the center of the table. Shadow, their ash-gray Chartreux cat, excitedly played with a discarded ball of webbing on the floor. He rolled on his back and meowed gleefully. She jerked back from the huge glittery papier-mâché spider perched on the chair back. Hopefully, it wasn't enchanted with an animated charm to start crawling around the house. The sultry notes of "I Put a Spell on You" played from the pillbox speaker on the mantel, giving the space haunted vibes. Callie, her little sister, tried to hit a note and missed, her voice cracking like a broken mirror. She, with her styled bob, was dressed in an orange and black polka-dot jumpsuit that showed off her curvy figure.

"Hey there, ghoul-friend! Check it out!" she sang.

Sirena blinked rapidly as if trying to make all the living room decorations disappear with just the power of her mind. She blinked several times. Nope. It was all still here. Who was going to clean all this whimsical crap up—again?

Callie stood in the middle of this fancy storm. "Wow. I've stunned you into silence."

Exasperation skittered through Sirena. "Why did you put everything back up?"

They took the decorations down last night before Sirena went to the party, not wanting to come home to clean up a big mess. She was the only witch living in the Caraway house since Lucy lived with Alex and Callie lived in Meadowdale. Therefore, Sirena was the only Caraway left cleaning up the house after holidays. *Not today, spider!*

Sirena reached for the rhinestone spider, but Callie jumped up and waved her away.

Her sister's face furrowed in surprise. "I just finished. Don't take it down. I need photos for my website."

Sirena bit back a sigh and dropped her hands. Of course. Callie made her money event planning for events all over New Jersey and often used their house to show off her decorating skills. Sirena couldn't deny the truth that the living room looked as gorgeous as it did—a month ago.

"You had plenty of time to take photos," Sirena reminded her.

"I'm not an illusionist! Give me a moment," Callie said briskly. "We can take them down before Halloween, but let me have some time with them. They're so pretty!"

Sirena glanced around the living space, not seeing the pumpkins in the corner. Wait. Where were the pumpkins she accidentally kicked? Sirena zeroed in on Callie's words while her still-sleepy brain tried to process what was going on.

Wait. What did she just say? "Did you say 'before Halloween'?"

Callie fist pumped the air. "Yes, I did! We've got thirty-one days to creep it real!"

Sirena scrambled to turn on her phone. The digital display turned on and flashed the month and day. She stared at the date. It was October first. Um. That was suspicious. She flipped the phone over again, noticing the faded sticker-covered case. This one wasn't her new phone—it was the one she had dropped. This was weird. She checked her hand; the ache was gone from her clown misadventure. She took her braids into her hand, letting out a shocked squeak. They were sealed and done up. That thrilling tingle of magic strummed on her skin, just like it had the night before—or in the past? She clicked open her Empty Fridge app and checked her delivery list. The last delivery was made on September 30—it was a new month.

Realization dawned on her. *I got my wish.*

Callie reorganized a handful of pillar candles. "So, what are your plans for today?"

"I worked," Sirena mumbled.

Callie groaned. "You never take a day off. Have fun. Eat. Drink. Be witchy."

Sirena licked her lips, trying to collect herself. "Having fun costs money. I'm on a budget." Those words felt so familiar on her lips. She'd said them before—she knew it in her heart she said them last month.

Callie took her hands off the candles. "Today's the Harvest Festival. That's free if you don't play any games or buy any food."

"Then it's not free," Sirena said. "Besides, how can our town afford so many festivals?"

Callie shrugged. "I thought we had a werewolf millionaire or faery godmother footing the bill for everything. I stopped asking questions years ago. Anyway, you're welcome to join me at the festival. I need fresh pumpkins to complete this whole vibe."

Sirena blinked. "That's right. It's Saturday."

Callie fussed with the faux spiderwebs, extending them out on the corners. The Harvest Festival was held every Saturday in October in the grassy town square and city hall parking lot in the center of Freya Grove. Sirena never found the time to attend the Harvest Festival since she worked Empty Fridge every Saturday, delivering brunch. Her stomach had grumbled in disapproval whenever she caught a hint of the funnel cake and popcorn.

Lucy came out of the kitchen holding a serving dish filled with pumpkin pancakes.

"Morning, peeps!" Lucy sang with a happy trill. She brought the plate over to the living room table and set it down. "Eat up, my loves. I'm sorry I have to reschedule brunch this afternoon."

Sirena studied her big sister. She wore a candy-patterned apron with the words "Trick or Treat" sewn on the front over a swing dress. Her curly Afro was teased out, and a polka-dot bow was pinned in her hair. There was a delightful shimmer to her rich brown skin that made her look like an autumnal princess. Lucy looked lovelier the second time around.

"I loved this outfit," Sirena said, then backpedaled. "I mean, I love it."

"Oh, thanks. I just bought it," Lucy said, doing a little spin. She gave Sirena a quick look. "Are you feeling okay, Si?"

"Yes, I just need to wake up." Sirena bit the inside of her cheek. She'd have to be careful and not give away the fact that she'd cast a time spell. Who knew how long it would last, and she couldn't risk her second chance on an accidental misstep. Callie took a pancake in her hand and ate it like a bagel. Sirena peered down at the pancakes; her stomach hurt at the idea of another month of pumpkin treats. Last time around, Lucy spent her free time and weekends on traveling all over the county looking at wedding venues. Eventually, Lucy and Alex stopped looking at venues because they were all out of their price range and planned on getting married in the backyard this coming spring. But that decision hadn't happened yet. Maybe Sirena could help them find an affordable place this month.

Callie finished her pancake. "Lucy, you can go with me to the festival!"

Lucy gave a small pout. "I wish. I can't go. I'm looking at wedding venues with Alex. I swear, it's all so expensive. I might just get married in the ocean."

"Déjà vu," Sirena muttered.

Lucy faced her. "What's that, Sirena?"

"Nothing. I need a lot of caffeine."

Lucy let out an annoyed grunt. "If I'm not wedding planning, I'm lesson planning or trying to save money. Why did I join the curriculum team this year?! Make a unit plan, they said; you'll have fun, they said. I barely have enough time to work with my seniors because I have so many meetings. Most of the meetings could be emails! If I have one more conversation about rigor, I'm going to quit teaching and sell saltwater taffy on the boardwalk."

"No, Lucy," Callie said. "At least you have the wedding to cheer you up."

Lucy grumbled. "Don't get me started on that stress fest. I can't decide what type of flowers we want. Do you know how many types of roses exist in the world? It's more than five! I've started drinking coffee because I have so much wedding planning to get done after work."

Sirena held back a gasp. Lucy rarely drank coffee because she lived for her cup of tea. She had to be seriously exhausted if she was relying on java rather than her jasmine to help her get through the day.

"I'm this close to eloping," Lucy groaned.

Callie cheered. "Do it, please. I can finally break out my new elopement binder. No one's ever eloped in our family. Let's viva Las Vegas."

"Do you want Mom to hex me into next year?" Lucy demanded with a dry laugh. "I'm not going to be the first witch to do it. We want to take our time. I don't want to rush. Next subject. You're working today, right, Sirena?"

Indecision kept her from answering. She glanced down at her phone in her hand. The Empty Fridge app was still open and waiting for her to accept a delivery request. How many times had she had this same conversation with Lucy and Callie? She clenched her jaw, knowing her answer would be yes—because it never changed. Sirena worked and cooked, because that was all she felt that she was good at doing.

She looked to Lucy. "Maybe. I haven't decided."

Lucy and Callie exchanged surprised looks.

Callie let out a gasp. "Are you...playing hooky today?"

"Maybe," she sighed.

"Sirena Caraway's day off," Lucy quipped. "I like the sound of that."

Callie trilled happily. "There are so many things to do! Zombie walk, Poe's ghost story hour. What about the haunted house? I want to be scared!"

"If I wanted to scare myself, I'll look at my student loans," Lucy said faintly.

Callie rolled her eyes. "Okay, Lu. I hear you. There's the Farmers Square giving out food samples at the festival. That's free. We can get there before they run out of kettle corn!"

The familiar urge to turn Callie down bubbled up in Sirena's mouth, but she said nothing. She claimed that she couldn't take a day off, but—Sirena knew now—taking one day from responsibility might do her some good. It'd motivate her to work a bit harder and give her a chance to relax. It was time to change her fate.

She'll work tonight on Empty Fridge and cover for an extra shift at Night Sky next week.

"Let's go," Sirena said, turning off her phone.

"Seriously? Yes!" Callie clapped her hands and bounced on her heels. "I'm borrowing your infinity scarf!"

She squealed and ran upstairs, singing along with the music. Sirena noticed Lucy was staring carefully at her as if she just turned into a she wolf. Her lips were twisted to the side in disbelief. "Are you sure you're feeling okay?"

Sirena squirmed under her attention. "Fix your face. I'm capable of having fun."

Lucy raised a single brow. "Yeah, but you're always on your grind. What's changed?"

"It is the season of the witch," Sirena said with a chuckle. She had heard that tune played over so many witchy layouts and photos online, but now she reconsidered the trippy song. Maybe this second chance was the best time to be a little strange.

Lucy nodded, seeming to accept this answer. "Well, I'll wrap up the pancakes while you get ready. Reheat them when you get back from the festival."

Sirena kissed her cheek. "Thanks for the food. I'll pick up some maple syrup."

"Buy some kettle corn," Lucy said. "If they have any harvest tea for sale, get me a bag."

Something clicked in Sirena's mind. "Did you restock the tea pantry recently?"

Lucy's brow rose in surprise. "Whoa, that's freaky. I'm restocking it next week. I found something cool I wanted to make."

"Yeah. What did you find?" Sirena knew the answer, but she needed to know exactly where this magic tea came from for her own peace of mind. Time travel wasn't for the faint of heart and she needed to know that she was meant to have this second chance.

Lucy pointed over to the stock of photo albums. "I was looking in Nana's wedding album for inspiration and found a handwritten label *and* recipe for Wish Tea. I mean, she never wrote down her special blends, but she was using it as a bookmark! It was kismet. We're lucky she left this last spell for us."

Sirena's spirit lifted at Lucy's story. Nana had given her one last gift with this wish tea and there was no way in the world she was going to waste it.

Sirena dipped her chin. "You haven't made the tea blend yet?"

"I need golden rosehips to complete it," Lucy said. "I'll let you know when it's done."

24

Sirena hugged Lucy, then went back upstairs to get dressed. As Sirena picked through her cardigan pile, sniffed out a clean shirt, and found her best pair of booty-hugging jeans, she considered her role in their witchy family. Lucy was the stay-at-home academic, Callie was the live-out-loud party girl, and, of course, Sirena was the kitchen witch. Everyone remained in their own zone and didn't step into each other's domains very often. Callie planned birthday parties, but Sirena cooked the menus and ordered the cakes. Lucy might have cooked breakfast for the family once in a while, but Sirena hosted the holiday dinners and large events.

Rule thirteen: Kitchen witches make sure everyone leaves with a plate after a family dinner.

But lately, with everyone else's wishes coming true, their roles transformed and shifted, right before her eyes. Lucy went to scholarly conferences and weekend retreats, coming back with massive binders filled with cool materials. Callie finished her degree and graduated from college last year and had plans to expand her premier event-planning business. But Sirena merely hustled and cooked. In the end, she ended up with nothing tangible in her life that truly belonged to her and no one else. Not this time around. Sirena was getting out of the kitchen and seeing what waited for her at the festival.

Chapter Three

$\mathcal{J}$ ime was never on August "Gus" Dearworth's side. He was overdue by a full week and was born exactly at 12:12 p.m. on Halloween. Of course, his family, the remarkable Dearworth magicians, took his fortuitous birth as a sign that he was destined for spectacular things. As he grew, Gus was always last: he got the last lunch; he caught the late bus and did homework on the way to school; he was the final kid picked for basketball or a science project. While he was in college, Gus set three alarms and reminders for everything. He even asked his sister Diane to call him to make sure that he didn't miss his graduation.

He was constantly on time's bad side, no matter what he did.

When Gus joined the family business of mesmerizing audiences all over the world with their magic act, he was last to perform. As nervous as he was to close the entire show, Gus had decided to give the audience an experience to remember. He rode in on a sleek motorcycle onstage while they played Grandpa Dearworth's favorite song, "Let the Good Times Roll," over the speakers. Gus jumped off, produced two cash cannons from his pockets, and sent dollar bills out into the waiting crowd. The audience went wild before he presented a single illusion. He became Good-Time Gus, because it wasn't a good time until he showed up on the stage or in the club. His jaw-dropping act took him from a sold-out Vegas residency to performing for literal royalty. Bottle service and reserved booths were his MO, and his tight entourage was well known for its party-until-the-sun-comes-up lifestyle. His misadventures were filmed and shared for his family's hit reality television show, *Dealing with the Dearworths*.

But, after a brief yet intense marriage and a long divorce, his party days were long over. He tried to recapture the fun of his former magic act when he fought to get out of bed each morning. Every time Gus went to pull a tiger out from thin air, it felt like he was trying to light a wet match, and he could barely complete his full act.

It was hard to perform magic when you lived with a broken heart.

Gus put his magician act on indefinite hiatus, left the reality show, and moved to Freya Grove. He even sold off his engraved cash cannons and donated the money to charity. He dusted off his history and economics degree from Pennbrooke University and applied to be the official steward of the Freya Grove Historical Society. For the last two and a half years, Gus stayed in the Grove, through seasons and holidays, safekeeping the town's magical legacy and advising young students on their next magic research. His current entourage consisted of Nicolas, a vampire who loved vintage photographs, and Beryl, a gnome who wrote very colorful sea shanties about merfolk.

He built a tight routine to make sure the organization ran smoothly.

Record donations. Unhex spellbooks. Feed the gargoyles on the roof.

Yes, his schedule was a bit boring, but it was safe. He'd had enough enjoyment for two lifetimes, and he wasn't looking to revisit his past. When Gus woke up at dawn before the morning alarm blared, he felt off. He'd had the strangest dream. Vague dreams of his impending Halloween birthday party lingered on the edge of his memory. Blurry faces surrounding him as he stood in front of a cake aglow with candles. Remnants of fresh cinnamon and apple punch remained on his tongue. But the most vivid part of his dream was Sirena, covered in slime and looking like a curvaceous specter. It felt so real that he could still smell her perfume. She smelled fresh and woody, like shredded ginger and lemon slices. Her brown eyes filled with interest, peered up at Gus, and kept him rooted.

For an instant, he didn't know what day it was.

Gus grabbed the phone from the nightstand and checked the date on the screen.

It was October 1.

He dropped the phone and scrubbed a hand over his beard. "Déjà vu."

Man. He really needed to get out of his head. As Gus dressed and got ready for his day out, he tried to shake off this strange feeling. It annoyed him like a price tag dangling off his shirt and tickling his skin. Something was missing, but he didn't know what he was overlooking. He met Diane, his little sister, at the entrance of the Harvest Festival.

Diane's ebony locs were tied in two buns on her head that made her look like a Goth teddy bear. Her dark brown skin was illuminated by the onyx-black sweater, long plaid skirt, and burnt-orange ballet flats she wore.

She checked her phone, then lifted a brow. "You're early. What's up?"

Gus gave her an easy smile, but his gut tightened into a knot. If Diane noticed immediately that he was early, then something strange was going on in town. His sister had the strongest intuition in the Dearworth family and left an area quickly if the vibes were off. *Please*, he begged, *I don't want to start this month off cursed*. Did he get accidentally charmed by a donated item? He hadn't handled anything new recently, but he'd cleanse himself with a balm of dandelions and ginger root when he got home.

"I must have gotten the time wrong," he joked, hiding his concern.

Diane stared at him for a second, then chuckled. "Yeah. You're right. Let's go."

Gus walked with Diane, making a note to pick up ginger root from the Farmers Square.

The Freya Grove Harvest Festival was going all-out for the first weekend, with jugglers, carnival games, and plenty of food options. The scent of fresh hay bales and dirt hit Gus's nostrils as he passed by the makeshift photobooth decorated with scarecrow props and raven puppets. Gus and Diane strolled past the rows of green tables and booths filled with seasonal produce. Vendors called out to customers who wove in between tables, trying to find the best price. Food trucks were lined up in the parking lot, and tables were filled with diners eating their meals from paper bowls and plates. There were wrapped bundles of vivid green herbs and craft tables with knitted and crocheted shawls available for purchase.

Gus stilled when he saw the Weisz Market stand surrounded by tall white coolers filled to the brim with bottles of apple cider in ice. He rubbed his hands together. Anticipation ballooned in his chest, and he smiled deeply. It was on. For Gus, the first taste of apple cider at the Harvest Festival was the best one, and he reveled in it. He didn't indulge in many things during this indefinite hiatus from his magic career, but he loved to grub and feast on only the best food.

Gus paid the capped vendor and took two bottles from the cooler. He handed one to Diane, twisted off the cap, and then drank. The spiced drink went down cold and chilled him all the way to his knees. Instead of the heartfelt feeling of coziness the first taste of apple cider usually gave him, he felt queasy. He took another sip, but his stomach churned. Nothing was wrong with the cider; the problem was with him.

This moment wasn't new. His smile faded, dimmed by confusion.

Diane watched him. "Are you good?"

He lowered his voice. "Something feels off."

Diane took a sip of hers and shrugged. "My bottle tastes fine. Did you get a bad batch?"

Of course, Diane, being the actor in the family, had a voice that carried, and the capped vendor overheard them. A troubled frown flittered over her features.

Gus held up his hand. "No, it's perfect."

The vendor beamed at him. "Thank you. It's an old family recipe."

"It's great. It's me. I'm...probably congested or have some weird taste buds."

Gus heard the words come out of his mouth and winced. *Stop talking*. Could he be any more awkward? The vendor gave Diane a look that said *Is he feeling okay?*

She eased Gus away from the Weisz Market booth. "My sweet, nerdy brother, you need to get out of the house more. That was rough. Maybe you should stick to talking to books."

He bristled a bit at her comment. There hadn't been a haunted book in the library in months, and he worked hard to make sure it stayed that way.

"I don't talk to books," Gus said. "I listen to what they're trying to tell me."

Diane spoke in a low, calm voice. "You're throwing off major woo-woo vibes. You show up early, don't like your cider, and you're...wobbly. What's going on?"

Gus opened and then closed his mouth, unable to explain just yet what he was feeling. He looked around at the Harvest Festival, watching people biting into caramel apples and kids playing tag with their friends. *I've been here before.* An icy tremor of recognition spread over his chest the longer he watched the scene before him. He just *knew* that the carnival games had been moved from the east to the west this year, even though the map said otherwise. It was a last-minute change due to the generators being delivered late. He looked to Diane, who was checking her phone and letting out a small groan at a message on the screen.

"We've been here before," he said.

Diane dropped her phone into her purse. She eyed him. "Yeah. We were here last year and the year before."

"It's different," he insisted. "I had a strange dream."

Diane smiled hopefully. "Please tell me you dreamed of tomorrow's lottery numbers."

Gus scratched his beard. "I dreamed it was Halloween. You threw me a party and invited everyone in town. Ma called me. She asked me to come back on the show, and I said—" He interrupted himself. What did he say to her? His brain drew a blank.

"It felt so real."

Diane leaned back on her heels. "Maybe your subconscious is nervous to celebrate your birthday. It's not every day you turn twenty-eight for the sixth time."

"You could just say I'm turning thirty-three."

"Where's the fun in that?" Diane asked. "Maybe you're feeling excited about this magical age. My hairdresser says that thirty-three is the age of great love and creativity. The universe is going to shine light and wonder into your life."

"Hmm." Gus gave her a nod, but that odd feeling remained.

"So, if it was your birthday, what did you wish for?" she asked. "Tell me about the cake."

What did he wish for? His mind went empty, and he couldn't recall that part of the dream. As if his brain didn't want him to know a truth just yet. "I don't remember."

Diane patted his shoulder. "I get it, brother. Keep your secrets. Speaking of secrets—"

"Great transition. Real smooth," he interjected.

"Did you get Jess's wedding invitation?"

"I did." Gus sipped his apple cider without another word, the tartness of the apple mixed in with the sourness he felt inside. His ex-wife, the world-famous singer Jessalyn "Jess" Clarke, was getting married to Igor, his former magician's apprentice, in Freya Grove this December. His ex was hydrated, blessed, and not looking to talk about him or their short-lived marriage. She wrote an entire album about their relationship. Whenever the song Jess wrote about him, "The Love I Can't Keep," played over an online video, Gus logged off for the rest of the afternoon and took a walk to the beach.

Truthfully, he had never heard the full song and didn't plan on listening to it.

"Not everyone was lucky enough to have their heartbreak be an entire bop," Diane had said after she listened to the entire song.

Jess and Igor had their own new reality show called *Love Magic*. The wedding was airing live on the Telly Channel for their fans. He hoped that no one from his family had pressured Jess to extend an invite to Gus. The Dearworths, with their persuasive skills, could talk a troll out of living near a channel. Seriously, he once watched Auntie Charlene convince a troll that having a beach house would be better than living under a bridge.

Diane pressed her hands together; a scheming look entered her eyes. "Tell me what you are wearing. Would it be too weird if we matched?"

Gus met Diane's expectant stare. "I'm not going."

Diane gave a little frown. "Oh, come on. I don't think that it would be that bad."

Gus cocked his head to the side. "I can already feel the cameras zooming in on me and the sad royalty-free music playing under my entrance into the reception. Why do you want to attend?"

A secret look crossed her face. His stomach tightened.

"Jess asked you to be a bridesmaid," he guessed.

She wrinkled her nose. "What do you think?"

"I think my family likes my ex-wife more than they like me," Gus jested quietly.

He peered at Diane. "You want to say yes, or you've already said yes."

She rocked back and forth. "Jess doesn't have any close family."

Diane always had his back, but she also had a massive heart. Underneath all her Goth clothes and snark, she was a sweet person who loved sending care packages and cards. She'd cared for Jessalyn as a sister and had stayed in contact even after the divorce.

"You don't need my permission. I'm good. Go and have a great time."

"So does that mean you're bringing a date?"

"I'm not going. And I don't date," he said.

Hadn't they talked about this before? Why did he feel like he was repeating himself?

"You don't have one friend who can be your date?"

"I can bring a gnome who loves to sing very raunchy songs about the ocean," he said.

Diane laughed. "Stop playing around. Bro, you've been alone for a long time. I mean, I even bought you an EnChant subscription you barely used."

He gave her a sharp glance that said *Are you kidding me?* "Have you been on EnChant lately? It's horrific. Everyone's there for a hookup. I deleted my account once I got very explicit messages about my wand from a very persistent zombie."

Gus shivered at the thought of his previous DMs. He wanted to pour a vanishing potion in his eyes so he'd forget every terrible photo that he saw online. EnChant was the dating website for the weird, sexy, and supernatural singles of Freya Grove and beyond. The freaks came out at night and logged into the website to find their match.

Diane made a face. "Yikes. I forgot how terrifying internet dating can be. Do you mean you're ready for something serious again?"

"I guess you don't have a wedding date," he teased.

"No, but I might see if Zeke's available. He texted me." Diane weighed him with a serious squint.

"Oh, really." Gus stayed as chill as possible, keeping his voice steady. "How is he?"

Diane kept looking at him. "He's fine. His phone number hasn't changed."

Gus shrugged. His chest burned. "That's good to know."

Zeke, the head of his former entourage and the man he once considered his best friend. Seriously, if it weren't for Zeke, Gus would have stayed trapped in that bank vault for the entire weekend after a vanishing stunt went wrong. When Gus walked away from his career, he left Zeke behind as well, unable to be the fun-loving magician his friend had known for years. He didn't have the heart to explain to Zeke that the fun times were making him miserable. There were times when Google Photos would pull up collages of him and Zeke, acting and laughing like fools. He couldn't bring himself to delete the memories, but rather flicked through them without another thought. Zeke, who had texted and called him the other day. Gus couldn't bring himself to answer, not ready to talk to him just yet.

Put it behind you.

Diane nodded, seemingly ready to move on from the topic. "Does Ma know you were invited to the wedding, too?"

Gus made a *no way* sound. "Does Ma know you're going?"

She sipped her cider and avoided eye contact with him. Even though Diane had left their reality show to study theater and playwriting overseas, she was still a Dearworth. That fact meant that Ma would always find ways to stir up a little drama so that she and her children were the center of attention. To quote Ma, Dearworths deserved to stand on the stage and in the spotlight.

"I'm done with performing," he said.

Diane grunted. "You're a true performer behind that corduroy docent outfit."

Ouch. Tweed and bow ties were cool. Gus pressed a hand to his sweater, which Ms. Alice, his mentor and a society member, had personally knitted for him. It was rainbow tweed, not corduroy, but he wasn't going to correct her mistake.

Diane poked his arm. "You don't play sold-out shows anymore, but you still like being onstage. I mean, who gets a standing ovation at a historians' conference?"

He did. Gus felt his face grow hot. "I wish they hadn't posted that video."

"I'm glad they did," she said. "You did the damn thing, Gus. It was impressive."

Pride filled him from the inside out at her compliment.

He went semi-viral when the Historical Association conference posted his talk about seeking out and preserving the forgotten or sidelined voices of history, especially in the creative arts and entertainment. Gus spoke of the Lincoln Motion Picture Company, which had sought to make films that celebrated the Black experience at the start of the twentieth century; they made five films before they eventually shuttered. Despite their short existence, the company inspired others to create their own enterprises. For Gus, the past had the potential to be an encouragement for those living in the present, and he felt honored to keep that history alive. Due to the video's popularity, he received fan mail, was encouraged to submit grant applications, and built professional relationships with scholars. When Diane saw the video, she had immediately called him up and shouted how proud she was of his nerdy self.

She offered to share it with Ma and Pop Dearworth, but he said it wasn't necessary.

He knew what Ma would say to him if she saw the video.

That's cute, dear, but Dearworths entertain. We don't inform. We're not the internet.

Diane rubbed her forehead. "Ma still doesn't know about the offer."

He bowed his head. The Freya Grove Historical Society Committee, the group who hired him, had offered to extend his position another three years and increase his current salary. It was a generous deal, but Gus couldn't immediately accept it without talking to his manager—Ma.

"My hiatus was supposed to end," he said to the ground.

Diane sighed. "When?"

He lifted his head and winced. "Six months ago. But I can't just pick up and leave."

Empathy shone in her wide eyes. Ma kept emailing Gus about upcoming tour dates, trying to figure out when he could rejoin the act. He immediately responded, saying that he couldn't go until he hired his replacement. He'd promised Ma that he'd leave his job in Freya Grove and rejoin the Dearworths' magic act at the end of the year, in time for the anniversary show.

Gus was caught between his past and his present, trying to balance demands from both sides, and felt like he was failing with both.

"What would Good-Time Gus do?" Diane asked.

"I'm not him anymore," he said, his tone terse.

Diane eyed him, seemingly taken aback by his firm response. Yeah, Good-Time Gus might have been a great showman and magician, but he was a jerk. He took up too much space and didn't relinquish the spotlight to anyone—even his own blood. That version of Gus made careless mistakes and didn't think of the consequences, but thought only of himself and his magic.

Good-Time Gus was everything he disliked about himself— the eager, desperate part of him that demanded people see that he was unforgettable. It was the part of him that he believed was unlovable. His entire body tensed, recalling how thoughtless he was at the height of his fame.

"You look like you're holding a sneeze," Diane said.

No, he was holding back the worst of himself from the world.

She smiled kindly. "You don't have to be him, but tap into that powerful Good-Time Gus energy. Take chances. Get messy."

"Now you're just quoting Ms. Frizzle," he said.

"Make magic!" Diane shouted gleefully. "You need to...have fun."

"I'm fine," he answered thickly. *I've had enough fun. I want peace.*

For Gus, fun wasn't a blessing, but rather a burden on him. He couldn't remember exactly when people stopped laughing with him and instead started laughing at him. The audiences who once gasped at his magical act started giggling and cringing at his powers. Something ugly and painful twisted within him at that moment and he couldn't bring himself to even pull a dove out of his top hat. Instead of being seen as fun, he turned into a fool.

Diane tapped Gus's half-filled cider bottle. She took it from him and held it up to the sun like an enchantress who had finished brewing a perfect batch. "Pretend you're drinking a mystic potion. Behold the bewitching tonic that tastes of fall apples and spice. It has the amazing power to remove the stick from one's—"

Gus cleared his throat. He held up a warning hand. "Hey. Chill."

She batted her eyes innocently. "Heart. I was going to say heart."

Diane wiggled her fingers over his bottle. She raised her voice to a dramatic, attention-grabbing boom. "And with this juice, I'll open his eyes and make him full of delightful impulses."

The liquid glistened under the midmorning sun. A few guests applauded her performance, and she took a stage bow. Diane handed it back to him with a wink.

Gus chuckled at her Shakespeare improvisation, knowing that her favorite play to preform and quote had been *A Midsummer Night's Dream* since she attended Freya Grove High School. Of course, Diane used any reason to remind him that she was the trained actor of the family. Not only did she play the character Puck for an international audience, but she was well versed in countless plays and dramatic works. He'd seen her play a heartbreaking Rose from August Wilson's *Fences* to a haughty Queenie in a local production of *Wild Party*. His sister was truly a chameleon when she performed—literally embodying any role required of her as an actress.

"Once a theater kid, always a theater kid," he said warmly.

Diane nodded. "Speaking of theater, I've got to head out early. Work calls."

"Today's your day off," Gus said, gesturing to the food trucks. They hadn't had a single pumpkin treat.

She let out a tired groan. "It was, but the playhouse is about to become a house of horror."

"Oh, that's not good," he said.

Diane worked as an artistic associate and director of community outreach at the Freya Grove Playhouse. She was always being called to keep her boss from calling the gnomes to dismantle the place.

Diane rubbed her forehead once again. "Our playwright keeps threatening to bewitch all the actors on opening night," she explained. "They keep forgetting their lines, but he keeps tweaking the pages every other day. I've been asked to step in and mediate at an emergency meeting. If I don't go, someone will be turned into a frog or a fish."

"I can give you a ride," he offered.

Diane smiled. "Thanks, I'm good. It's a lovely day for a walk." She opened her arms. "Bring it in."

Gus scooped Diane into a big hug and squeezed. He let her go and pressed a kiss to the top of her head. "Text me when you get in."

"I will." Diane waved and left him standing in the middle of the Harvest Festival.

Gus looked at the bottle in his hand, noticing that the amber liquid had a silvery shimmer. Hmm. The coloring was probably the cinnamon or allspice that Weisz Market added to the cider. Diane's words echoed in his mind. *Open his eyes, and make him full of delightful impulses.*

His thoughts worked overtime. He couldn't recall the last time he was impulsive.

You ordered from that new goblin fusion restaurant last week. That was impulsive, right?

No, it wasn't. He used to look up a map, snap his fingers, and appear in a new country with nothing but his passport in his pocket. Gus had transferred the appetite he had for making tigers disappear into presenting documents and telling stories about the history of Freya Grove, his adopted hometown. People dreamed of being the wife or girlfriend of a world-famous magician, and he had the DM screenshots to prove it. No one thirsted over the local historian and conservator of magical items and ephemera in a quirky Jersey Shore town.

What did he have to offer a future partner other than an antique house filled with artifacts and a barely healed-over heart?

His phone buzzed quickly. Gus checked the incoming messages, reading as he scrolled through the requests for assistance from Quentin Jacobsen, one of the festival organizers. Quentin was a mover and shaker around town and could throw together a world-class festival with catering from a big-box store and dollar-store decorations. He was always referring people to rent out the historical society for special events and gatherings, which helped bring in much-needed funds that Gus used to serve the community. Gus was thankful for him looking out for the society and was ready to return the favor.

> Good morning, Dearworth. Are you at the Fest? I need your expertise.

Gus responded.

> Yes. I'm here. How can I help?

Two texts lit up his phone.

Thanks! Check out the balloon pop game for me.

We've heard from guests the booth might have a
distraction charm.

Quentin followed up with a few more texts explaining the
situation further. Apparently, the carnival games were being
magically rigged to keep people from winning and enjoying
themselves. Balloons were unpoppable. Darts landed in the
grass. Steady hands were suddenly unsteady when trying to hit a
target. His blood simmered with annoyance, hating that magic
was being used to harm people in any way. Attendees deserved a
chance to win and have fun.

Gus looked down at the apple cider in his other hand. He
twisted off the bottle cap and gulped down the remainder of the
drink. The earthy blend of sweet and tart touched his lips and
went down smooth. A fizzy energy zipped through his brain, hit
his heart, and reached all the way down to the soles of his feet.
He tossed the empty bottle into the trash. A new sense of pleasure was roused within him with every step he took toward the
games.

It was time to be a little impulsive.

Chapter Four

Leaves fluttered around Sirena like dizzy fireflies from the nearly bare trees. The mixture of cinnamon sugar blended in with fresh cut grass and buttered popcorn. She brought her hand up to her mouth to stifle her giddy laughter. This second chance was real, and it was hers for the making. *Would it be too much if I twirled right here?* No. She'd save the twirling for later when she figured out what she was going to do this time around. Callie went off to buy her pumpkins in the Farmers Square, while Sirena scanned the food and game booths, twisting her braids in her fingers. She had a taste for something, but she didn't know what would satisfy her appetite. Last time around, she turned down attending the weekly Harvest Festival with her sisters to pick up an extra shift at Night Sky Bistro. Now she had the entire day to just chill out and relax. Sirena lingered by a carnival booth as she realized a sad truth.

She hadn't taken a day off in almost two years. How did she have fun again?

A carnival barker with clipped brown hair, dressed in a screen-printed crop top and a pair of worn overalls, called out to Sirena from his balloon-pop booth.

Stuffed animals dangled above guests to tempt luck and win a prize.

"Hey there, pretty lady! Step right up! Let your man win you something nice."

Sirena grumbled. Did she really want to explain to a random stranger that she was living a very single life? A teasing yet persistent look entered the barker's eyes. This man was determined to make some money from her.

"Oh, who will step up and win this pretty lady a prize?!" he bellowed.

The festival attendees swiveled to watch the amusing exchange.

"I'm good," she said, raising her voice.

"Come on, now. You're pretty for a big girl. You're telling me *you* can't get a date?" he mocked.

Sirena froze. Oh no he didn't. Watch out. She was going to toss this man into the dunk tank. She tensed up and tightened her fists once she heard the false disbelief in the word "you." Yes, how could anyone date a woman like her? Stars forbid that she'd attract any attention and take up any space. Sirena had been a big girl ever since she was a little girl, which meant for some people they could comment freely about her size without feeling an ounce of shame. Anger sprinted through her bloodstream as she recalled all the careless words strangers and sometimes so-called friends would say to her.

You have such a pretty face.

A man would have so much fun with a thick chick like you.

Of course you can cook well. You look like you enjoy a good meal. Look at you.

Yes. Look at her.

That's why Sirena wore the brightest clothes and didn't shrink away from comments or judgments about her body. She showed off her full cleavage and rounded curves without shame. Sirena stared at this carnival worker, not willing to hide from his gaze. His eyes assessed her as if he was sizing her up and figuring out the best approach to weaken her defenses.

No. She was going to make sure he'd remember her.

Sirena opened her mouth to shut him down when Gus Dearworth appeared by her side.

He stood close enough that a person might assume that they were on a date, but far enough that he wasn't crowding her.

"Hey, chef," he said smoothly. "Sorry I'm late."

He offered her a comforting smile. The tension eased away from her body, and she felt relief.

She unclenched her fists and managed to give him a small, guarded smile. "Hey."

Sirena became acutely conscious of his physique. He was taller than her by a few inches, and his body had some weight to it, but there was a sense of athletic grace about him. Gus could easily be at home on a football field as well as in a lecture hall. His medium-brown skin had a glow, as if he carried a personal spotlight. He, with his curly dark hair and clipped beard, was of course handsome, but there was something else about him that drew her attention. Sirena studied his outfit and held back an amused chuckle. Gus was dressed like a stuffy history professor or a museum docent on vacation, wearing a sweater-vest over a button-down shirt and corduroy pants.

He was wearing rainbow tweed. Did he just come from an academic conference?

She had to admit that the fabric looked good on him. His cologne wafted around her head. Her kitchen witch super-nose was on high alert. She sighed softly. Today he smelled like a brand-new book—dried ink, fresh paper, and the crispness of a fall apple.

Sirena faced the booth. *Stop sniffing the magician.*

"I see we have a champion for the lady," the barker said with a hint of dare.

"Yes," Gus said. "I love a challenge."

She lowered her voice so only he could hear. "You don't have to do this—it's a hustle." In all her years in the Grove, Sirena hadn't seen anyone win a prize better than a cheap key chain at the balloon pop. She suspected that there was a confusion enchantment hidden in the booth, making hands and eyes unsteady so that players would lose the game.

"Watch me," he said, giving her a self-confident wink. Gus placed his money down and picked up the five darts the barker gave him. The barker scooped up the cash and pointed to the board, where the half-inflated balloons were taped up in a square pattern.

"Hit three balloons and win a small prize, hit four balloons and get a medium prize, and hit five and you get your choice of prize—including the jumbo."

Gus moved closer to the throw line and squared up to the booth.

Sirena clapped loudly, trying to encourage him. He aimed, threw the dart, and missed the balloon. She whooped. He was probably anxious. Gus tried again and missed his mark. A crowd was starting to gather to watch the unfolding scene. Sirena's face burned. No matter what, she wasn't leaving his side. There was a good chance she might have to buy him a "you tried your best" ice cream after this adventure.

The barker let out a mock sigh of regret. "Nerves getting to you?"

Gus frowned, then gestured to Sirena with his chin. He lowered his eyes and toed the dirt with his shoes, trying his best to look uneasy.

"I'm sorry. I must be distracted. It's our first date."

He made his eyes wide and big, trying his best to look like a besotted teenager. Sirena bit back a smile. Give this man a Daytime Emmy, because he was acting his behind off.

The barker glanced from Sirena to Gus.

He scratched his slender chin. "You know what? I'll give you two darts for free since it's your special night. Now you're back to five. Do your best."

The barker rolled his tongue in his mouth, as if tasting all the money he could make off a seemingly lovestruck Gus. Sirena, worried and annoyed, placed a light hand on his forearm. If she had to, she was ready to drag him away from the booth and buy him a double scoop of cookie dough ice cream. She'd had enough of hustlers in her life, and she didn't want him to lose any more money to this rigged game.

Gus peered at her. He reached over and squeezed her hand. "I've got this."

Her skin tingled from his touch. The pulse of his natural magic felt like touching a warm bowl, inviting and familiar. There was a thread of confidence in his voice that eased her worry. For a second, his words and touch made her feel safe. She let her hand fall away.

Gus scooped up the darts. All the tension left his body. He stepped back, giving his body enough room to move. The darts in his hands sparkled with an energetic red glow.

Oh. Things just got real.

"It helps to look at what you want to win," the barker suggested with a hint of smugness.

"You're right. I should focus on what I want," Gus said.

He turned toward Sirena, palmed the darts in his hand, and released them one by one. A deliberate, suggestive smile grew on Gus's face as his darts found their mark, each successful hit sending a resounding *pop* into the air. He didn't even bother to peek at the balloon board. Everything within her lit up like an electric carnival game, and Sirena became instantly aware of what was happening. An expression of self-satisfied delight glimmered in his lovely eyes.

This performance was only for her and her alone. He wanted to thrill her.

What did everyone say around town? A Dearworth magician will leave you speechless.

She forced herself to talk. "How did you do that?"

"Magic," he said, with a hint of triumph.

Oh. My. She was enthralled by what she saw, a magician standing in his power and not standing down. He had that spark about him, the intensity that made everyone around him pay attention. The gathering crowd watched Gus Dearworth with impressed grins and ogling stares. *He was born to be a performer. It's in his blood.*

No one would scare Gus with a clown. No one would try to prank him.

No one would forget his name. *I want that spark.*

Sirena tore her eyes away from Gus, unable to take the power of his stare. The barker glared at Gus with a begrudging look of respect before directing his attention toward Sirena.

"Pick your prize," he grumbled. "You can have anything you want, pretty lady."

Sirena bit the inside of her cheek and flicked a quick glance at Gus. *I want him.*

Nope. He wasn't up for grabs—at least not yet. This time was her second chance to change her fate. She couldn't let herself get caught up in his charms until she figured out how she was going to use this entire redo. She'd heard the low-key rumors about Gus Dearworth, the magician who stole the hearts and panties of countless Grove creatures and folks.

Sirena's panties wouldn't be stolen, thank you very much.

She searched the collection of plush prizes swinging in the booth. A small phoenix with red, gold, and crimson feathers dangled off a hook. She perked up. What did the family spell-book say about phoenixes? The bird, a symbol of rebirth, could live for over five hundred years before setting itself on fire. But it was reborn from the ashes to start its next life. Okay, she didn't believe in signs, but she knew how to recognize them—how could she not see that this gift was meant to be? She'd given her previous wish to the fire, but she could start again. She could allow herself to wish again.

Sirena pointed to the plushie. The barker furrowed his brow, as if expecting her to pick the biggest prize he had. "You sure?"

She nodded. The barker delivered the prize to her waiting hands.

Gus stood close to Sirena, his attention squarely on the barker.

"I hope everyone had as much fun as I did," he said, hitting each word empathically, as if trying to convey a hidden meaning. Sirena glanced back and forth between the two men, picking up major mess-around-and-find-out energy coming from Gus.

The barker's eyes widened a fraction, but he gave a blunt nod. "You and your lady have a good time."

Gus dropped twenty dollars into the barker's hand, then guided Sirena away from the booth. Together, Sirena walked in step with Gus, not wanting to break the moment between him. What were the odds that she would run into Gus Dearworth today of all days. Sirena saw Gus around the Grove, but they kept a friendly distance from each other. She had no reason to hang out at the historical society and Gus didn't seem interested in culinary things.

She peeked at him, realizing that Gus was looking at her with a curious stare.

"What's its name?" Gus glanced at the plushie.

"Her name's Ember," she said.

"Why not Spark?" he joked. "Or Ash?"

"She's my phoenix, so I get to name her." Sirena played with one of Ember's wings, making it flap in Gus's direction. He smiled and inclined his head in her direction.

"Thanks for helping me out back there," she said.

"You helped me out. I needed a reason to approach the booth. You were the right person at the right time."

Ah. Sirena felt something was off between Gus and the barker. Her stomach knotted. Was he using her to hustle a stranger? She didn't like being used by anyone for their own game.

She tucked Ember into her tote bag, then faced Gus. "Do you make it a habit to hustle carnivals, Mr. Dearworth?"

He lifted a single brow.

"No, chef. I make it a habit to test out prize booths that don't follow festival rules," Gus corrected. "We've got several complaints about that booth today. No charms, no spells. That's the rule. There's nothing wrong with having a challenge, but we got to give people a chance to win. I figured I'd gently remind him our festival is about fun."

Sirena bobbed her head, hearing his words. "You're literally the fun patrol."

"I like rules," he said.

"I get it. You didn't use any charms or spells back there?" she inquired.

"No, that trick was all me." His voice was a whisper that roamed over her skin. "I have moves you couldn't even imagine."

Oh, Dearworth, you don't know my imagination.

"I can imagine what amazing things you're capable of doing," Sirena admitted.

Something dangerous flashed over his face, as if she had opened a secret door and unleashed a powerful being from a hidden place. Like a sleeping giant crawling out of a cave and waking up to see the world.

"Have dinner with me." His voice was almost unrecognizable.

She hesitated. "I don't know if that's a good idea."

"Why? I'm harmless," he said.

Sirena scoffed. "I'm not."

An easy smile played on the corners of his mouth.

"Well, I'm pretty good at bad decisions," Sirena said.

"Okay," Gus said. "Then let fate decide."

He reached into his pocket and pulled out a half-dollar coin. Déjà vu. She examined it. Surprise skittered through her once she saw the face. This one was different from the one on Halloween night; this one had a profile of a woman with two faces.

"Heads, you have lunch with me now," he offered. "Tails, you give me your phone number so I can call you later."

"Tell me where we're having lunch. I might not be dressed for it."

When a witch went on a date with a magician, she had to bring the sparkle.

"Trust me. You're dressed perfectly." Gus let his eyes roam over her body. She grew heated underneath her cardigan and fought the urge to fan her face.

"Will you take me to Mimi's Diner?"

Mimi's had the best diner food in town, and Sirena loved going there for their hashbrowns.

"If you want." He tossed the coin in the air. Sirena watched as it flipped.

Gus reached up, caught it, and brought it to the back of his hand.

"Call it." He covered the coin and met her eyes. Her heart squeezed.

"Heads," she whispered a little breathlessly.

Flirting with Gus Dearworth was fine; it was enjoyable, like a grilled cheese sandwich for lunch. But going out with and liking was a whole different and treacherous matter. A man like him, with his effortless magic and charm, would make her forget all her promises and goals.

Sirena reached out and covered the coin with her hand. "Wait."

She glanced down at their intertwined hands. Cherry-red sparks, like a surge of high voltage, lit up their fingers. Anticipation darted over her skin, and Sirena's mind skipped a little from his contact. Sirena forced herself to look at Gus. He stood there by the cotton candy machine, and the air around him filled with spun sugar. The man was a whole treat she couldn't enjoy just yet. She'd just gotten a second chance; she didn't want to waste it until she had a plan for her life. Also, she couldn't forget about seeing Gus on Halloween holding that ring box. He didn't seem the type to flirt when his heart belonged to another woman, but someone else was out there waiting and wishing for him.

Gus stared at her, waiting for a response.

"I have plans," she said. "I can't go with you."

Yet, her heart added. A cold sense of disappointment went through her body.

A realization came to her. She was always giving up what gave her fun and joy for the sake of work. But maybe this time around, she'd reconsider letting more joy into her life. Something kind sparkled in his eyes.

He slipped the coin into her palm. "I get it. No worries. Keep it for next time."

His full mouth curved up into a clever smile. Gus gave her a deep stage bow, spun on his heel, and walked away. She watched him stroll off through the crowd until he disappeared, leaving her alone with her thoughts. Sirena studied the coin in her hand and gasped.

He'd given her his magician's piece, the one used for bets and challenges. It was a two-headed coin. It was the tool that you used when you wanted to bend fate your way. She pressed it into her palm, and the remaining Dearworth magic in the coin prickled her skin. Her disappointment morphed into pure astonishment. When Sirena and her family had gathered in their living room to make their wishes, she'd hesitated as she thought about what she wanted.

She had written down two wishes but debated about which one to give to the fire and complete the spell. Sirena eventually wrote down the right wish, the one that didn't appeal to her heart but to her head. But two years later, she couldn't help but wonder, had she picked the wrong one?

Chapter Five

The Freya Grove Historical Society house was three and half stories of brick and mysticism and located on the corner of Emory and Third. The Queen Anne–style house boasted a high five-story circular tower on the east side of the house that looked out toward the ocean and a wraparound porch. More than once, Gus had been told that he basically lived in a Gothic dreamhouse. He, always the historian, liked to believe that he lived in a castle by the sea filled with spells and books. Despite his best efforts, he couldn't rid the romance from his soul.

Gus parked in front of the house, immediately noticing an older person pacing in front of the glass door. He got out of the car and walked up the stairs, a mixture of expectation and anxiety building within him. Once he got closer and saw the designer animal print with the matching purse and charm necklace, Gus blinked. It was his ma, Ms. Anais Dearworth, who waited on the porch, dressed in her usual animal-print sweater, dress pants, and high-heeled boots.

"Surprise, darling," she cooed. Ma opened her arms and gave him a tight hug. Her perfume, the familiar scent of blooming jasmine and orchids, kicked up his nerves a fraction.

"I thought you were in Las Vegas," he said. He hugged her back, then let her go.

Ma lifted a perfectly plucked brow. "I told Diane I was in Vegas, but I was really in Atlantic City. You know how I love a good misdirection."

Her metallic makeup made her golden-brown skin pop. Her dyed ash-blond hair clustered in short curls around her slender face. Ma loved to be dressed in the color gold, claiming that she wanted to look like a walking award. She might have been barely five feet, but she carried herself with the confidence of a six-nine basketball player.

Gus kissed her cheek and then invited her into the historical society building.

Ma's eyes swept over the foyer and waiting room.

She gave him a stiff grin. "Well, it's clean."

"It's not a luxurious hotel room, but it has history," he said.

"Hmm. Are you still renovating?"

He paused at her polite tone. If the place didn't have room service or an indoor pool, Ma didn't want to stay there for long. The lady magician only stayed in four-star hotels or rented out vacation houses.

Gus pointed to the hallway. "We've finished with the exhibition area, and we've expanded the library on the second floor. I'm hoping to offer classes and lectures about local history."

Ma gave another grin. This one seemed tighter. "Ah, yes. I forgot about your hobby."

Gus held back his usual response. *Ma, it's not a hobby. It's a job.* The last thing he wanted to do was sound like a whiny child. Ma loved to label his current career as a local historian and speaker as a fun little hobby, as if he hadn't worked hard or taken countless hours of training just to stand here in this position. To Ma, his steward job was a break from his real life.

It was a distraction.

She reached up and picked a piece of lint from his vest.

"Diane texted me you went to the festival. Did you have a nice time?"

"It was fine," he said easily.

Ma rolled her eyes. "Just fine. You're being nice. I bet it was boring. Did you have fun?"

Gus pressed his mouth into a thin line. Oh, he had fun. He drank that apple cider and temporarily lost his damn mind. He reverted right back into Good-Time Gus. He'd seen Sirena being heckled by that carnival barker, and something protective snapped within him.

Gus wanted to shut that guy down and shut him up. He looked at Sirena and saw the relief that shimmered in those eyes of hers when he stood by her side. The barker had some nerve, commenting about her or anyone else's size. Gus wanted to win her every single prize in that booth but restrained himself to putting the barker in his place. His show of magic must have worked because Quentin texted Gus an update before he left the festival. The balloon pop ceased to have any more complaints for the rest of the afternoon. Even now, as he stood next to Ma, his palm itched with his lingering enchanted energy.

It truly felt delightful to use his magic to save the day and impress the witch. Gus shoved that thought out of his brain. Fun time was over. Now it was time to get back to serious matters.

Gus decided to redirect the conversation toward a topic Ma would love to talk about for hours.

"How's the show?" he asked.

Ma clapped her hands together. "It's going wonderfully. The producers are finalizing our anniversary show in January. We're going to London and performing at the Savoy Theater for a limited-time engagement. Your father's trying to find his passport. He's so proud."

"I bet he is." The patriarch of the Dearworth family, Peter Dearworth, who performed through constant discrimination and open theft of his magical acts, would have a great time. Gus was looking forward to seeing Ma and Pop taking pictures in front of Big Ben and the London Eye.

Ma beamed. "Can you believe it? The Dearworth name on the marquee in the West End."

"Diane's performed on the West End," Gus reminded her lightly.

Ma playfully tapped his arm. "Yes, I know that, but she wasn't doing *magic*. She was acting! I do have to say the spotlight loved her."

Gus nodded in agreement. Diane had stolen the show and received a standing ovation with her memorable turn as the scheming fae Puck. The energy from the crowd had been so electric that Gus's skin hummed all the way to the airport. There was nothing like the energy you get from an attentive audience.

Ma's copper-shaded eyes grew sharp as she assessed him.

"Tell me you don't miss it," Ma challenged. "Tell me you don't miss that feeling."

Gus stilled. Ma wasn't wrong. He thought back to the balloon-pop game and Sirena. Exhilaration flowed through his bloodstream at the recent memory. He could still hear how her breath hitched and see the blush on her cheeks when he performed just for her. Only her. Gus relished watching those divine brown eyes of hers widen with amazement. Sirena had been the best audience. She was so responsive, leaning forward so she could see more of his magic. His body burned under her attention. He hadn't dazzled her with historical facts and population data, but with his natural magic.

"I can't tell you that," he said.

A light of triumph lit up her eyes. Ma loved being right the same way seagulls loved stealing food from humans. "You've still got the hunger. I can see it. You know what would help?"

"I know," Gus said reluctantly.

Ma studied him. He knew the answer. "The hunger" was what Ma called that desire to perform for audiences. The only way he knew how to keep that hunger at bay was to get up onstage and shine. That's why Gus had given the speech at the conference, to feed that desire and to find a new path away from his past. He needed to find something to feed his soul and leave him satisfied.

Ma caught his eye with a sharp look. "Have you found your replacement yet?" she inquired.

Gus forced himself to look at her, not backing down from her fierce glare. "I'm making progress."

He had invited a few prospects from the local college to come and interview for the steward position. Still, he wouldn't be able to hand over the society until the new year. The position was a two-year commitment in Freya Grove, and that requirement often made people turn down the offer.

"So, you think you'll be done with your . . . progress by December?" she ventured, her voice tinged with impatience. Her voice dropped to a dramatic whisper. "If you can't find anyone, just lock up the house and time the lights to come on at random. I'm sure no one will notice you're gone."

Gus bristled. "Someone will notice."

Ma wiggled her fingers in the air. "Use a little charm to bewitch the house while you're gone. It's harmless fun."

There was a long, brittle silence between them. Good-Time Gus would have emailed his resignation letter to the committee and handed the keys to Diane before he left town. He would've done exactly what Ma suggested, because that's what he did. But he didn't want to be that man anymore. He couldn't just lock up the society and abandon his responsibilities.

The society held not only the history of Freya Grove, but also countless magic artifacts that could cause trouble if they fell into the wrong hands. He needed a replacement who would protect the magic from any harm or negligence. He was done being careless with precious things and he was going to be a better man.

"I can't hand the keys over to just anyone," he said finally.

"Yes, who will mind the antiques?" she quipped tersely.

Gus paused. Huh. Ma's comments were sharper than usual today.

"I know you didn't come over here to remind me of my life choices," he said.

Ma checked her nails, trying her best to look casual. "You've heard about Jess?"

"Yes. Di told me."

"She's getting married. You know, she invited me."

"Oh. That's kind of her."

Ma gave him a withering glare. "There's nothing nice about this invite. Did Jess hire a chaos gremlin as a wedding planner or is there another motive behind this niceness?"

Gus shrugged. Who was inviting all the Dearworths to the wedding?

Ma continued talking, her tone doubtful. "I'm sure she's just putting on a show. Watch the brokenhearted songstress find true love after fleeing a loveless marriage to a Dearworth magician."

He stared at the wall, his chest churning with hot frustration. *It wasn't a loveless marriage for me.* Of course, if he showed any emotion to Ma, she'd assume that he was still in love with Jess. Yeah, no.

"I had to call in a lot of favors to take care of that video."

Gus glanced at the wall clock. It took Ma less than twenty minutes for her to mention the video. He flinched inwardly, a feeling of humiliation coating his skin like soap residue. Yes, reality show cameras and microphones picked up everything. They picked up the painful moment when Gus told his wife that he loved her and she said nothing. The video was only up for a day before Ma sent a cease-and-desist letter to get it taken down. He watched his heart get broken repeatedly for twenty-four hours.

Love could break your soul if you let it.

Ma pressed her hands together. "You should attend the wedding. Show the world that you've moved on."

"You want the *cameras* to see that I've moved on," he said.

"Have you?" Ma shot back.

"I have moved on," he said.

She raised her painted brows to her hairline. "Then why haven't I met anyone?"

Because I haven't met anyone who wants to be with this version of Gus.

Truthfully, there hadn't been anyone worth bringing home, and it was his fault. His previous reputation as a fun-loving magician had undermined his goal to settle down for real.

His dates wanted to be with Good-Time Gus, who popped

bottles until dawn and turned ice cubes into faux diamonds with a spell. However, when regular Take a Melatonin Gummy Before Bed Gus showed up to the date instead, he was lucky if he got a good-night text. He'd come to the Grove to escape from his past, but he was now bound by it.

"I like being alone," he said.

Ma scoffed. "Nonsense. What about your cat?" Gus furrowed his brow.

Ma pointed toward the bookshelf in the waiting room. "I know I'm not imagining it."

Cinder, the black cat in question, lay supine by the bell jar of seashells, scanning the room for anything that interested her. She blinked lazily and didn't move, even under the glare of Ma. Oh right. Sometimes, he forgot he was now a cat dad. Gus pressed two fingers into his left eyelid, then dropped his hand. "Cinder's not technically mine."

"You just left your door open, and a cat just walked in?" Ma glowered.

"My neighbor decided he wasn't a cat person, so...he put her out on the street," he said.

Ma's mouth dropped open to her chest. She was a major animal lover and often donated money to the local shelter. She struggled for words, but eventually found three. "What a chump."

"You're not wrong," he added.

It was nice having Cinder slinking around the front stairs and in his top-floor apartment. Visitors found her a welcome addition to the building, and the groundskeeper, Mr. Mac, always had a pocket of treats for the curious black cat.

Ma snapped her fingers, her nails glittering in the overhead light. "See! You have a cat."

"Okay."

She took out her phone from her purse. "That's proof that you don't want to be alone. If you can love a cat, then you can love again. You can live again. Let me set you up on a date."

A stony knot formed in his stomach. This well-meaning offer was a step too far and he didn't even want to imagine the poor, clueless woman Ma would set him up with for the wedding.

"Ma," he said firmly. "I'll find a date."

Maybe he could ask Beryl if she had a sister who was single and enjoyed weddings.

Ma pursed her lips at him, then let out a sharp breath. "Okay. I'll say one more thing, and then I'm done."

She fiddled with her phone, tapping a few buttons; then she faced Gus. Her eyes grew dewy, and she gave him a look that made his chest feel like it would burst. It was the same upset look that she gave him when he told her that he was going on hiatus and leaving the stage.

"I find it hard to believe that you'll stay here, watching the world go by. I remember how you used to be and . . . I worry about you finding your way back." Gus opened his mouth to protest, but Ma shushed him. "Take a moment when you're cataloging dusty top hats and stale books to consider what you're doing with your life and if it's worth your time. Think about the people you've left behind, wondering if you're coming back. Think of your friends and fans who keep asking about you."

He remained silent. Fans found recordings of his performances online and emailed him, thanking him for bringing magic and fun into their lives for a moment.

"What do you think I do here?" he asked, frustration bleeding into his voice.

She gave him a guarded glance. "I don't know, but I know it's not what you're meant to do. You are a Dearworth. You belong on the stage performing *magic*."

The walls trembled as Ma's voice broke on the last word. Cinder stirred from her place and hopped down to the floor. He was a Dearworth magician until the last stars burned out in the sky. Her face fell, and she took a second to compose herself. A twinge of regret went through his chest. *Come on. Tell her who you are.* Gus was tempted to sit her down and show her the video on his phone.

To show her what he made of his new life in the Grove. To show who he was now.

He stopped himself. It seemed Ma wasn't interested in listening to anything unless it had to do with Gus rejoining the Dearworth act. Since he stopped performing for large audiences, Ma was always worried that his underused powers would diminish over time. No, he couldn't tame a tiger anymore, but he could convince the seagulls not to steal food from tourists.

Gus learned in the Grove that small acts of magic were just as important as the grand performances; both brought joy to those folks who needed to feel wonder.

Her phone beeped a warning chime. "That's my ride; it's a minute away. I'm going to surprise Diane. We're going out for dinner. I'll be back after Halloween. Hopefully you'll have an answer for me about ending this hiatus."

He couldn't keep avoiding the issue. *Stand up and tell her.*

"Ma, I'm not rejoining the show." His voice was steady.

She stared at him for a beat, then smiled tightly, betraying nothing of her displeasure. Her tone was soft but held a hidden edge when she said, "Give it time."

Those three words held so much meaning, but Gus knew from her tone that Ma meant one thing: *Don't do anything you will regret.*

She said those exact words when it came to getting married to Jess, and he hadn't listened to her then. Apprehension, like slick oil, oozed through him. Ma blew him a kiss, then walked out the front door and down the stairs. Gus stood in the doorway and watched Ma climb into the sleek black car and depart. He felt Cinder wind herself around his legs and didn't move.

Since he made his first tricycle disappear from the backyard at four years old, Gus leaned into that idea of being unpredictable. He lived by the words of the first Dearworth magician in the family: *If they're going to stare at you, you might as well give them a show.*

So, he gave them a show. He leaned into his persona Good-Time Gus and gave the audience an enchanting time. He had been the hype man for years on end, flirting with glamorous women and hanging out with A-list celebrities.

When Gus accidentally conjured a hundred rabbits in a casino lobby to the horror of the guests, Ma had insisted that he finally settle down. Ma Dearworth, with her unmatched skills and illusions, wasn't to be fooled with, so Gus went about trying to "settle down." But he'd been Good-Time Gus for so long, he struggled to turn off that persona when he went on dates.

Gus met Jess, an up-and-coming singer, at a family barbecue, and they immediately clicked. Jess, draped in paisley print and with flowers in her hair, had a mesmerizing voice like a siren and thought he was fun. They were struggling to take their careers to the next level and were aware that people loved the idea of a showmance—a fake romance. Even though he and Jess weren't in passionate love, they were in serious like. Back then, he thought that feeling was enough for them to have a marriage of convenience.

For Gus, like was safer than love, and it didn't have the power to break his heart.

They got married in a tiny wedding chapel on a weekday and became the hit couple of his family's reality show. The audience adored their love story, and ratings soared to record numbers. Ma was excited that he finally got his act together, and made plans to add Jess to their tour. Everything was going great; they had brand collaborations and sponsorship deals and were looking to become the next big lifestyle brand. Then, one day, while Gus was wondering what flowers to bring home to his wife, a wave of terror washed over him.

He didn't just like his wife; he was in love with her.

Gus decided he was going to put on a show and dazzle her with his newly realized love.

He made them a candlelit dinner and told her the whole truth, while presenting a dozen bouquets of red roses. She visibly paled, stood up, and left their shared apartment. Two weeks after Gus admitted his true feelings to Jess, she served him with divorce papers. The video came out and slowed their proceedings to a crawl.

"I should've known better than to marry a good time," she had said gently at their divorce hearing. "I should've left when I had a chance."

She had sounded regretful, as if she wished she hadn't agreed to be his wife.

After the divorce, Gus continued performing, but the act grew stale and became exhausting. Gus needed to find a new role.

Currently, he relished his job as the historical society steward, but there was that desire to play, to dazzle, that remained embedded in him. The hunger was getting worse, and it seemed nothing he did would satisfy its need. *Give it time.* How much time would it take for him to become the man—carefree, unbothered, and blessed—he wished to be?

Chapter Six

As Sirena and Callie returned to the Caraway house, clutching their bags filled with their many purchases, one thing was clear: this year's Harvest Festival lived up to the hype, with the rides, games, and food trucks. They'd returned from the festival talking about their plans to go back next Saturday and check out the hot apple cider truck.

"I'm glad we went together." Callie gave Sirena a big smile. "I had fun."

"So did I." This day was pure nostalgia, with Sirena and Callie taking goofy pictures with a painted scarecrow and sharing a plate of sweet potato fries. Of course, she couldn't forget Gus. She still had his coin. Its weight pulled down her cardigan pocket.

Callie lingered as if she wanted to add something.

"What's up, sis?" Sirena said.

Callie stared at her. "I don't want to bring down the mood, but I know things have been hard for you."

Sirena clutched her tote bag to her chest, steadying herself for whatever Callie was going to say. Ah, of course. She was going to bring up the hard time. Last spring, Sirena finally found an investor looking for bold ideas and passionate chefs. Helena Kingsley, with her mermaid-beautiful hair, flawless skin, and designer clothes, spoke of how she had the perfect vision for Sirena's restaurant. They picked out paint samples and made a whole concept board.

Helena even gifted her with a gold necklace.

For a while, Sirena believed that her wish was coming true and gave so much of herself in pursuit of that belief. She gave in to hope. In the end, Helena had not only taken Sirena's money but had also stolen her idea book filled with her restaurant concepts.

Helena had disappeared with her hopes and dreams like a thief into the night. Everything was fake about Helena Kingsley; even the necklace was made of fool's gold. Once Sirena confessed her financial situation to her family, everyone reacted differently, from Lucy's fury to Ursula's empathy to Alex's support. Sirena heard nothing from Callie, who always had a sense of divining the future. The absence of her voice had added to Sirena's uncertainty about herself, but she knew her sister was probably waiting for the best time to speak to her.

A strange, faintly eager look flashed in Callie's eyes. "I have a good feeling. Things are going to get better."

Sirena stood frozen once she heard those words. They stared at each other across the living room. Callie's eyes clung to hers, gauging her reaction. Had her little sister detected the time spell, or was Sirena looking for someone to talk about her next steps?

Callie blinked and the look vanished. She lifted the heavier of the two bags. "These pumpkins aren't going to bedazzle themselves. I'm in the kitchen if you need me."

Sirena stood there for a moment, letting Callie's words comfort her. Things were going to get better if she made better choices. If she fought against fate. It was research time. She went upstairs to her bedroom and settled with a large bag of kettle corn, a note-pad, and a pen on her bed. She checked her phone one last time for any deliveries from Empty Fridge, then put it on silent. Sirena cued up *Groundhog Day*, the only time loop movie she could find on streaming. As Phil the weatherman kept repeating the same day and romancing his producer, Rita, Sirena scribbled down a few notes about her situation.

> *You are both in a time loop.*
> *He's repeating a day; you're repeating the whole month.*
> *Phil had many, many times to fix things.*
> <u>*You have one chance [as far as you know].*</u>

Sirena underlined the last line. If she was going to change her fate, then she had to make the best choices and stick to them. She laughed at Phil's antics and repeated the iconic lines. When it came to the diner scene, where Phil pointed out everything he noticed about Rita, Sirena grew uncomfortable. She paused the movie once Phil finished his speech to his love interest. Had she ever known or loved a man so intimately that she knew his childhood fears, his dreams, and his plans? She racked her brain but couldn't come up with a name.

Hmm. Had she ever been in love? Like, true end-of-the-storybook, happily-ever-after love?

Sirena mentally stopped herself from going down that rabbit hole. She had to focus on one issue at a time. Callie popped into her room.

"Si, have you seen the glitter? I ran out of rhinestones!"

Sirena flipped over the notepad to hide her list. "Check the craft drawer."

Callie approached the bed. "Oooh, movie night! What are we watching? I love a good scary movie." She watched the movie playing on the laptop for a beat. Her mouth twitched with humor. "Are you watching *Groundhog Day* in October?"

"Uh, I was in the mood for a fantasy romantic comedy," she said.

"Okay. Why?"

Sirena's other hand paused over the bag of kettle corn as she considered Callie's inquiry. If she told Callie about the time loop, then she'd have to explain why she was in the loop in the first place, and she wasn't ready to have that talk.

From what she could tell, Callie and Lucy had a great October the first time around, and Sirena didn't want her brand-new wish to mess up their perfect lives. Her gut twisted in guilt about casting another wish spell without telling her witchy family, but she had to walk this path alone.

"I was in a fun mood," she said.

Callie gave her an amused glance. "I'll leave you alone. Enjoy your movie."

She walked out, singing to herself. Sirena let out a sigh of relief and closed the movie window. She'd have to be a little more discreet with her time-loop investigation.

Maybe there was a note about time loops in the Caraway spellbook.

No one would question a kitchen witch looking at a spellbook. Sirena went downstairs and over to the bookshelf on the far wall. She took out a thick tome, which had a brown leather cover, two ribbon markers, and a symbol embossed on the front. Her fingers traced the cover's etched symbol, and it glowed under her attention. She smiled fondly and recalled Nana's stories about the casters and conjurers who came before them. *Each heart represents our ancestors Lucinda Mae and Jacob's four children—Jacob Junior, George, Daniel, and Lula, who were born free and blessed. They were her four heartbeats. She taught them her magic, they taught their children the magic, until it was passed down to us. Remember, my love, you are made of magic.*

She brought the book over to the living room table. Carefully, she eased the spellbook open and searched through the pages, until she finally located the tea-stained page. It had a drawing of an hourglass that was never empty and filled with sand.

Neat writing outlined the rules behind time loops. Sirena scanned the page.

She read the words out loud to make sure she wasn't missing anything.

Most time loops last the span of twenty-four hours; some loops can repeat an entire year. One can break or interrupt the loop by fulfilling the promise, wish, or purpose of the loop. Take care to learn from the past, or be bound to repeat it.

Uh, okay. Sirena became lost in thought, biting her thumbnail. If she failed, would she be trapped to repeat October forever? Magic was unpredictable and didn't always play by the rules. Cold alarm went through her body, threatening to steal her breath. Sirena might have liked pumpkin spice, but she liked drinking it once a year, not for an entire lifetime. She noticed a final line at the bottom of the page written in Nana's distinct script.

Don't wish away your time; carefully time your wishes.

She read that line over twice; the alarm morphed into a glow of hope. This loop was about making the most of the time she'd been gifted. She wasn't going to spend this second chance grinding and hustling herself in the wrong direction. When was the last time she called off work and just let go? Sirena thought about everything she loved about this season. Walking around in an oversized cozy sweatshirt and leggings, listening to the leaves crunch under her boots. Eating a jumbo chocolate bar and drinking out of a pumpkin-decorated tumbler on the porch. Watching the ghosts and gnomes frolic in the Grove. Maybe, just maybe, she'd catch the eye of a handsome creature who wanted to spend the night together and keep away the dark.

It was time. Change those six events and change her fate.

First she had to leave Empty Fridge. Sirena pulled her phone from her pocket and held down her finger on the Empty Fridge app. A little menu popped up, and she clicked on the "Delete App" option. The logo vanished from the screen. Her stomach jumped in nervousness.

No Empty Fridge job, no rolled ankle, and no broken phone. She had a little money to help float her for the next few weeks, and she was going to focus on herself.

She was on hiatus from her life. What was she going to do this time around?

Open my heart to good things. Reclaim my kitchen magic. Have fun again.

Lately, she hadn't felt like she was living up to her kitchen witch legacy. Nana had personally trained her to pick up the wooden spoon and even gifted her a notebook covered with woodland creatures. Nana taught her the kitchen witch rules, which she devotedly followed to this day. Sirena hadn't picked up her spatula in a while, feeling bored whenever she thought about taking out her stock pot. She used to have fun stirring up a bubbling soup or creating a new dish with whatever she found in the pantry. That sense of dismay began to build within her, clouding her eyes with impending tears.

No. She mentally pushed that feeling down and wiped her eyes.

Sirena scanned down to Nana's words.

"Time your wishes," she said. Her voice had a new strength to it that she hadn't heard in weeks. This time around, Sirena was going to come up with brand-new recipes and protect herself.

If Sirena had any chance at landing that Lighthouse job, then she needed to get her spark back and cook her behind off. She didn't want to bother Lucy or Callie with her magically inclined problems, but she needed someone she could trust. Sirena looked over at Ember poking out of her tote bag on the couch. The plushie's button eyes seemed to twinkle, reminding her of the cute magician who won her. A sudden thought jumped up from the back of Sirena's mind.

What if you asked Gus to help you have fun?

She and Gus had a lot in common—they were both from magic-rooted families, were both water signs, and were relatively successful in their careers. Well, she used to be successful, while Gus, according to the Dearworth family's website, was taking an extended hiatus from his performance career. Rumor had it that the Dearworths hid in plain sight, pretending their stage magic was fake when it was completely real. Sirena used to watch his family's reality hit show, *Dealing with the Dearworths*, whenever she couldn't sleep at night. There was something comforting about watching the dysfunctional, lovable family of magicians who entertained, loved, and feuded in Las Vegas. The Dearworths were no strangers to magical drama—but they were more glamorous. They were more outlandish. They were freaking fun.

The Caraways were no strangers to drama, either, but according to Nana, instead of hiding their skeletons, the witches invited them to tea and fed them coffee cake. She saw no point in keeping secrets from anyone or feeling shame for their beliefs.

People were going to dislike them whether they danced under the full moon or didn't, so they might as well dance freely. A sting of frustration went through her as she tried to remember the last time she danced in the moonlight. Sirena couldn't remember, and this thought didn't just make her uncomfortable. It made her furious. She wanted to reclaim her sense of fun.

It was decided. She was going to ask Gus to help her get her magic mojo back, or at least get her creative, fun juices flowing. Besides, what was the worst that could happen? Her overactive mind answered with a quickness that left her thunderstruck. *Well, you could accidentally trip and fall and make sweaty love to Gus, then cook him scrambled eggs.*

She froze, momentarily stunned by her carnal thoughts. Huh. The worst thing she could think about sounded a little too appealing. Whatever. The man once had pet tigers. Sirena didn't like when pigeons got too close to her.

She was probably too boring for someone as exciting as Gus.

No matter what, she was going to need a safe place to hold her thoughts, to-do lists, and goals while she was on this wild trip. Sirena went back up to her bedroom. She searched her bookshelf, looking through half-filled journals, sticky-note-covered cookbooks, and recipe cards. Wistfulness lifted her spirits with every old note and paper she unearthed, connecting the pieces of her discarded dreams together into a big pile. Eventually Sirena found the softcover notebook with the drawing of a fox dancing in a woody area. It was Nana's last present to Sirena, and she'd been saving it for a special moment, yearning to fill it with her plans to return to New York. Years passed, and the notebook remained blank. She hesitated to open the gift, torn by conflicting emotions.

Sirena laughed. "You just traveled through time. That's kind of special."

She plucked a pen from her desk and opened to the *This Book Belongs to* inner page.

Doubt whispered in her head. *You could fall on your face. You could do all this work and still fail.* She pushed through those doubts and wrote her name in the blank space. If Sirena was going to fall, then she was going to have fun on the way down to the ground.

Chapter Seven

The gargoyles finally returned to their perch. Bay leaves were placed in the windowsill. Spellbooks were safely locked away in the special collections room. It was just another Monday at the Freya Grove Historical Society. Gus poured Cinder's food into her bowl and was about to dig into his overnight oats when he heard his phone buzz on the kitchen counter. He picked it up and saw a long text from an unknown number on his phone: Hi, Gus. Good morning. I got your number from Diane. Do you have plans for breakfast?

Who was texting him this early? Nicolas was asleep and Beryl was probably working on making her third breakfast. Another text popped in. This is Sirena BTW. ☺

His heartbeat kicked up. He'd been thinking about her ever since they had a little fun at Harvest Festival on Saturday. A third text was an image of Ember, propped up on a dresser, looking like an eagle perched on a ledge. He laughed out loud.

Gus responded without missing a beat. I'm free. Meet me at Mimi's at 9.

She replied, See you then. I have a business proposal for you.

Gus stared at the text for a long moment. Hmm. Interesting. What kind of proposal did she have in mind? Even though he wasn't as famous as he used to be, townsfolk would sometimes pick his brain about a financial opportunity. Maybe Sirena wanted to talk about investing in a pop-up restaurant, or a tasting menu. The trickster side of him, the one that delighted in making her gasp, whispered, *I wonder what treats she has planned for you.*

He had had Sirena's cooking only once and craved another taste. His rational side took over and told him to calm down. Sirena was inviting him to breakfast, not cooking for him at all.

He was about to leave out the back door through the kitchen, but he stopped. Gus heard a loud *thump* on the front porch. Did he forget a scheduled delivery? He went through the house to the front door and opened it. A delivery driver walked down the stairs talking to someone on her wireless device.

"Have a good day!" she yelled over her shoulder.

He glanced down at the thick package. Okay. He wasn't expecting anything from Diane or Ma, but he was always receiving random donations from strangers. Gus scooped up the package and brought it into the living room. It was lucky that he hadn't left for the diner yet. Lately, porch trolls had been scooping up packages, hoping to get a finder's fee for locating the "missing" parcel. He got his spare wand from the front desk and waved it over the package. The wand glowed white, then turned green, signaling that the package was safe to open. As a magician, he was always on guard for surprise hexes that might be attached to older items. Ever since Gus had a terrible experience with an enchanted puppet, he always made sure to do a magical check on all packages.

He pocketed his wand and slit the box open to reveal two Bubble-Wrapped items. There was an envelope addressed to him taped to the larger item. Gus opened it and read the enclosed letter. The handwriting was straightforward and a little shaky.

Dear Mr. Dearworth,

I found these items. I didn't know what to do with them, but I saw your video. What you said about protecting the past got to me. I sent you what I found. You seem like the best man for the job.

Best,
A Friend of the Grove

Gus sent a silent word of thanks to that anonymous donor for this gift. Most times, when people were cleaning out attics and basements, they didn't have the time to look through everything and just tossed it all. He couldn't begin to imagine the countless treasures that had been lost because of negligence, but at least he could preserve whatever remained here. Nothing felt off about these items, so he picked up the larger bundle and unwrapped it. It was a leather-bound journal that seemed to be a cookbook. He brought it to the table to examine it further without stressing the binding.

Gus leaned forward, taking in the handwritten notes about measurements and watercolor sketches of local herbs and extensive marginalia. A low sound of interest escaped his lips. He took a few photos with his phone and typed a message to himself, then looked up a few things in the historical society records.

The second item was a wooden spoon carved with symbols and etchings. He'd have to check in with his contact in the History

Department at Meadowdale College to examine the item. Cinder meowed at him.

Gus looked up from the pages and saw the clock. It was ten after nine. His chest jumped.

"Oh, damn." He gently returned the book to the box and put it up on the donation shelf. It was just like him to lose track of time.

As Gus left the house, he hoped that Sirena would still be there waiting for him.

Spells, potions, and home fries were being traded at Mimi's Diner at any given time. Gus walked into Mimi's and surveyed the scene before him. The eatery, located in downtown Freya Grove, was designed with classic blue and white tile and chrome edges. Navy blue swivel stools lined the mosaic-tiled counter, sea-glass blue and green stained glass lamps gave the place a nostalgic feel. The walls were painted in shades of blue and white to invoke the feeling of the seaside inside the restaurant. The case next to the cashier held a selection of apple cider donuts, pumpkin spice muffins, and cookies shaped like leaves. Gus noticed Sirena sitting in a booth by the window. She scribbled a note into the open notebook before her on the table. Her nimble fingers danced over her phone as she looked something up. He approached the booth, his heart pounding as if he were meeting a date for a study session. Diane was right. He was super nerdy.

Sirena looked up and quickly closed her book with a snap. Her face brightened.

She slid out of the booth and stood to greet him, giving him a brief hug. "Thanks for meeting me, Gus."

His body hummed at the press of her body against his chest. He leaned back and gave her a once-over. Her fuzzy apple-red sweater popped against her gorgeous brown skin and was fitted to her ample bust and body. A long pendant, an egg-shaped red stone, dangled from her neck. Black jeggings encased her shapely thighs and made her legs long and thick. Gus peeked down at her feet and grinned. The striped socks she wore under her buckled shoes gave her the perfect witchy touch. He brought his attention up to her face. Sirena was smiling and dazzling. Her braids were swept up away from her face into a side bun that was pinned up with a felt apple fascinator. Sunlight streamed from the window onto her and made her sparkle like a ruby.

He checked his mouth to make sure he wasn't drooling.

"You look nice," he said, sliding into the booth on the opposite side from her.

Sirena joined him. "Thanks. I figured I'd try to match what you might wear."

Gus did an outfit check. He wore his usual rainbow tweed sweater, red jacket, and khakis, the unofficial outfit he wore at this time of the year. Based on the colors present in both their outfits, they could definitely match. What were the chances?

He fiddled with the salt and pepper shakers. "Sorry I'm late. I got caught up with work."

Sirena checked her phone on the table and smiled. "It's okay. I should've planned better and called you earlier. But I'll get straight to the point. I know you're busy. I hope I didn't interrupt breakfast with Diane or your girlfriend."

"Diane's at work and I was having breakfast with my cat," he said.

She perked up. "I didn't know you had a cat."

"Cinder's all right. My sister thinks I'm going to become a cat daddy—whatever that means."

Sirena nodded. "Listen, it happens. You tell yourself you're buying one toy and then you end up purchasing a cat-friendly birthday outfit at two a.m."

Gus chuckled. Cinder would probably crawl under the house if he tried to put anything on her.

"You mentioned a business proposal," he reminded her gently.

Was she looking for an investor for a restaurant? Maybe that's what she was writing about when he arrived. He had a decent amount of money in savings that he could lend her, depending on her pitch.

Sirena straightened and folded her hands over her notebook. "I'm making a few changes in my life, and I need your help. Let's talk about fun," she said. A cheerful sparkle entered her eyes.

Gus forced a smile once he heard this word. Of all the things in the world, why did she want to talk about fun? Aside from his outburst at the Harvest Festival, he didn't have real excitement anymore. Back when he was Good-Time Gus, he was the foolish one who partied until dawn with Vegas showgirls while eating lobster burgers and fries covered in edible gold dust.

Now his idea of fun was finding a new podcast to stream and having two pumpkin spice donuts with his coffee.

"I don't know if I'm the right guy," he said.

"No, you're the best person for the job," she responded. "Hear me out."

He leaned in over the table, interested in what else she had to say.

She played with her pendant necklace. "There's an it factor that some people have. You have it. You have this fun spark about you."

His forced smile morphed into a real one. *She thinks you have a spark.*

"I've saw it at the festival and when I've watched your show."

Satisfaction jolted through him. "You've watched *Dealing with the Dearworths*." Why did he like the idea that she'd seen his act?

She blushed and dropped her necklace. "I might have watched it once—or twice. Anyway, I want you to show me how to get that spark, that fire."

He rubbed the back of his neck. Hmm. He had to be missing some information, because Sirena Caraway was one of the most talented witches in town. Gus had watched her cook before, and the graceful way she worked her grill reminded him of a conductor guiding an orchestra of flavor rather than sound. If he had a spark of talent, then she had a whole firework shed of talent. Gus opened his mouth to ask for more details, but Mimi, the owner and head waitress, came over to them, cradling two glasses of water. She wore a paper hat over her steel-gray hair with her blue and white diner uniform and name tag.

"Welcome, folks, to Mimi's. Good morning," Mimi chirped. "Sorry for the wait. We're short-staffed today."

She placed the glasses on the table with a practiced ease.

"Our special menus are on the table. I'll give you time to decide what y'all want."

Mimi went off to tend to another table, leaving them alone to make their selection. Sirena plucked the menus from between the napkins and ketchup.

He furrowed his brow. "You don't need my help. I've seen you cook."

She picked at the peeling edge of her menu with a grimace. "You've seen me flip burgers and cut fries."

"It was the best burger I've ever eaten," he said without hesitation. Sirena slid a menu over to him and met his eyes.

The memory of that last July replayed in his brain. Gus had taken a rare day off to visit Freya Grove Beach and decided to have lunch at the Shore Shack, the open-air boardwalk eatery. The shaded area was being run by Sirena, one waitress, and a single cashier. He watched from a counter seat as Sirena, dressed in a T-shirt dress and sneakers, effortlessly cooked up food for waiting customers. Despite the restless crowd, she never lost her cool and made sure that everyone's order was cooked to satisfaction. She served up hot plates while singing aloud the R & B hits on the streaming radio station, getting a few tanned surfers to back her up on a silly rendition of "We Belong Together." The first bite of his burger was fresh and tasted so intense, as if he had bitten into the sun itself. Even now, his mouth watered at the memory.

She didn't need a spark when she had her own fire.

The memory of summer faded away. He mentally returned to the booth.

Sirena's eyes swept over him admiringly. "See, that's what I mean. You're charming and nice. I'm grumpy and sharp. I haven't been fun in a long time. I'd like to hire you to give me lessons in fun."

Gus blinked. This offer was appealing. Too good to be true.

To spend time with Sirena, who he nursed a little crush on, and get to know her better.

She lowered her voice. "Money's a little tight right now for me, but we can talk."

"Make me an offer," he said, his voice coming off a little too zealous.

Sirena dropped her menu. "I'll reorganize your kitchen or come up with a fun menu for you. I can help you shop the weekly circular and help you budget your meals. If you have any recipes you want to cook, I'm your chef."

Gus took out his phone. "Actually, you might be the witch I need."

He told her about the package he received that morning. Gus opened his photo gallery to show Sirena the picture he took of the cookbook and recipe cards.

"Apparently, the journal belonged to a local cook named Juliette Saybrooke."

Sirena's attention remained on the photo. "Keep going."

She took the phone from him. Her fingers brushed against his palm, briefly tickling him with a stroke of bubbly magic. Wild. He'd never felt a magic like hers before—it was like touching a birthday sparkler with his hand. It was—for lack of a better word—delightful. Gus cleared his throat and pulled back. Get back to business. Sirena rubbed her fingers together as she studied the images.

"I did some light research. She lived in Freya Grove at the turn of the century and opened a small restaurant called the Glass Slipper in 1910. I couldn't find too much about her other than that she wrote down a lot about cooking folklore and charms."

She scrolled through the photo album. "Ms. Juliette wasn't

just a cook; she was a kitchen witch." Sirena pinched the screen to enlarge the photo. "Check out the marginalia."

Gus moved to sit next to her on her side of the booth to get a better view. He accidentally brushed up against her arm. The bubbly magic shocked him, and he jerked away. Gus noticed Sirena shiver a little at their contact, but she didn't say anything.

Sirena gestured to the phone with her chin. "There are some kitchen witches who like to use certain energies of the moon or sun in their craft. She notes cooking in time with the phases of the moon."

"What about your craft?" he asked.

Sirena clicked her teeth. "I tend to go with emotions and vibes. I'm the crier in my family. I feel things deeply and it shows in my food. Rainy and cold days call for soup, sunny days for sandwiches and garden salads. Grilled cheese tends to be my comfort food."

"I like tomato soup," he said.

"I'll keep that in mind," Sirena murmured warmly. "Did the book come with anything else? Maybe a bowl or a spoon?"

"Yes," he said. "It came with a wooden spoon."

"There's a good chance that Juliette might have carved the spoon herself or had it made for her conjuring work."

Sirena swiped to another page in the gallery, pinched to enlarge it, and gasped. She smiled. "There's a recipe for stone soup!"

She let out a little excited laugh. Despite himself, he smiled at the cute sound. Was it possible to catch a case of excitement from another person?

Gus shrugged. "Is that a good thing?"

"It's a great thing," she said sagely. "Nana Ruth made stone soup when we were little. Unfortunately, she never wrote down the recipe. She taught it to me once, but I can never get it right. I've never seen a recipe like Nana's, but from what I remember, this version is close."

"Your nana didn't write it down," Gus said carefully, trying to comprehend her reasoning. As a magician, he wrote everything down, much to his ma's annoyance. She used to fuss at him about writing down the key to their illusions. *How can you keep our secrets if you write them all down?!* Of course, those books were firmly locked away in a bank vault. Gus wanted to have a record of every Dearworth illusion and charm to be shared with the next generation. Gus reluctantly moved back to his side of the booth, not wanting to crowd Sirena.

She wrinkled her brow. "Kitchen witches can be protective of our work, especially when it comes to magic potions. Whatever you write down to keep, be prepared to lose it. The wrong potion used in the wrong way could spell disaster."

"Like a love potion?" he suggested.

"Why does everyone immediately use that potion as an example?" she muttered.

"People want to fall in love."

Their eyes connected; an unreadable emotion appeared in hers. "Love potions are a myth. You can't magically make someone fall in love with you, despite the stories you've heard. You can tempt and tease desire and passion—but from what I've seen, real love can't be conjured. There aren't any magical shortcuts when it comes to love."

"What about aphrodisiacs?" he asked.

She twisted her lips to the side, then spoke. "I mean, they work well in a pinch. Aphrodisiacs have been around since ancient times."

Sirena held up her hand, listing the items on her fingers. "Chocolate-covered strawberries, pomegranate juice, and clover honey can get you in the mood and kick up your desire. But they don't make your heart race or take your breath away. From what I've heard, love can do that."

What makes your heart race? "You've made your share of love potions."

Sirena chuckled. "I have thought about it, but I chickened out. I guess it isn't in the cards."

"Maybe it wasn't the right time," he said. *Or the right man.*

Sirena stared at him with her vivid eyes, pinning him to where he sat. The odd feeling that bothered him yesterday came roaring back. Had he stared into those eyes of hers before—in his dreams? No. He pushed that feeling away. Here he was, seeing something that probably wasn't there.

She played with her place setting. "So, what are your next steps? If Ms. Juliette was a kitchen witch who wrote down everything she made, then this journal is...priceless."

He dipped his head in agreement. "I'll ensure that the journal wasn't stolen or taken from a family member."

She frowned. "It could've been stolen?"

His expression grew tight with anger.

"It happens. People think that they can make a quick dollar selling a rare book they've stolen. Someone might panic and try to pass on the book by trying to donate it."

Sirena let out a seemingly concerned groan. "Do you think that's the reason you were sent this cookbook?"

Gus paused. "My gut tells me no, but I have to check."

Since Gus took over as a steward at the historical society, he lived by his personal motto: *Everything in its right place.* He spent his own money and hired a local private investigator to follow up with any anonymous donations that he received. Gus wanted to do right by the anonymous gift and make sure the Saybrooke journal was cared for by the society.

"I'll do my best to track the provenance, the record of ownership, of the book," he said.

"How long does it take to find the record?"

He bobbed his head to the side. "It depends. The process can take a few days or few weeks to get answers, but it'll work out. Many times, people are happy to have the item returned or will donate it to the society for safekeeping. I record and document the items until I've concluded my search."

A look of awe crossed over her face. "I didn't know our historical society stored magical items like this journal."

He set his shoulders as an idea took form. Maybe he had a proposal for her. "The society has plenty of other culinary notes and items that need TLC. We have a whole bookshelf filled with donated cookbooks. I've been looking for a contemporary expert to help me make sense of everything, but . . . I've been busy."

Busy trying to find your replacement, he privately grumbled.

"I like hearing about cool stuff like this. I wish you had called me," she said regretfully.

Gus stared at the water glass, hating to hear the regret in her voice. "You seemed busy. I didn't want to bother you with something so . . ." His voice trailed off into silence and he lowered his chin. Recognizable words people said about him and his preservation work popped into his head. *Boring. Useless. Mundane.* Gus snapped his head up and focused on the curious gleam in

Sirena's eye. She didn't find him mundane, but she saw the spark he thought he lost years ago.

He was still the steward of the society, and he could do what he wanted. Invite her in.

"If you're interested in the consulting job, it's yours," he said. "You can make your own hours. I'm flexible. You can start this afternoon, if you'd like."

Shock drove Sirena's head back against the booth. "No. I'm hiring you to help me. How are you paying me to help you?"

Gus winked. "I'm just that good, chef."

She let out a big laugh. "I haven't cooked in a professional kitchen in a long time. I'm hardly a chef. I appreciate the job offer," she said.

"So, do you accept?"

She paused, then gave him a curt nod. "I accept, but I need help with my fun problem. Can that issue be part of our deal?"

He stilled. He understood the fun trap. How many times had he been called on to "get the party started" or act the fool to ease the tension? He wasn't going to lead her down the primrose path of easy gratification. Fun times ended quickly, and all you were left with were remorse and an empty life. Sirena Caraway didn't need his help learning how to have fun, because he'd seen glimpses of fun in her and could list them for her.

Last summer he could've spent the entire day at the Shore Shack just basking in her lively sunshine energy. Their brief time they'd spent at the Harvest Festival had been the most amusing time he'd spent with another person in weeks. Right now, in this booth, he was having fun talking to her about love potions and kitchen witch journals. There was no need to put on airs or illusions with her. He could just be still. Whoever had the nerve to think that she wasn't fun deserved to be trapped in a room with week-old fish and wet socks. He didn't want to take advantage of her. It didn't feel right teaching her about a power she already had but probably didn't recognize.

"We can talk about it later," he said.

Her voice was silky but laced with iron. "Do you want to have fun with me, August?"

Whoa. His pulse quickened at the question. Something hot and fiery pounded through his bloodstream. She'd never said his first name before—ever. It was always "Gus" if she was feeling friendly or "Mr. Dearworth" if she was annoyed with him. Not many people called him by his full name—they automatically shortened his name or assumed that he preferred his nickname. But the way she said his name with a hint of huskiness and exasperation zinged through his chest. Gus swallowed deeply, keeping his desire in check.

He liked the way he felt when she was around.

Did he want to have fun? Absolutely. But he wasn't going to be Good-Time Gus.

He was going to be better than the careless man he used to be.

"Yes, I do," he said carefully. "But we need to establish ground rules."

Her eyes tightened; then, after a second, she nodded. "Okay."

Gus stroked his beard. "I decide when and where we have fun. I won't push you. We're not doing anything dangerous or unethical. You tell me when to stop."

"I won't tell you to stop," she said roughly.

A wave of heat washed over him when she said those words. He could imagine her whispering those words while he leaned in to capture her mouth with his. Maybe there was a little magic in his apple cider because he was feeling strange. Gus scooped up his glass of water and guzzled it until it was empty. He slid the glass to the edge, hoping for a refill.

She pursed her full lips at him. "I'll tell you 'play' if I'm game and 'pause' if it's too much."

His jaw twitched as the heat wave became a whole ocean and threatened to overwhelm him. He was going to need to drink the whole damn pitcher to quell this feeling. The trickster he'd kept in check for so long was finally going to come out, and there was a witch who was going to play with him. He'd help her have fun, but with rules in place.

Yes, but rules were meant to be bent and broken.

He nodded. "Sounds good. You don't have to pay me a dime. I'm yours." Gus was surprised at how chill he sounded, despite the anticipation rushing through his bloodstream. He could do this job.

Sirena gave him a side-eye. "Just to be clear, Dearworth, this is a business deal."

"Yes, chef," he murmured.

She waved him off. "I'm treating you this morning, so put your wallet away."

"We'll see." He'd use a sleight-of-hand trick to get the check paid before she could get out her debit card.

She lifted her chin. "Are you always this stubborn?"

"I was going to ask you the same thing," he mused.

Mimi returned to their table, holding up her order pad. "Are you ready to order?"

Sirena glanced at the menu, then gave Mimi a sweet grin. "I'll have the cinnamon roll. I have a taste for something soft and sweet."

He mentally slapped a hand over his mouth. *Don't flirt with her. This job is business, not pleasure.*

Mimi scribbled something down on her order pad, then looked at Gus. "Let me guess. You'll have Belgian waffles with sliced strawberries, two pats of butter, syrup on the side, with turkey bacon and orange juice."

Was Ms. Mimi going to tell him the color of his boxers next? He felt his face flush with humiliation.

Gus forced an amused tone into his voice. "Am I that boring?"

Was he getting too stale and predictable?

Mimi winked at him; her grin softened. "No, hon. You're just a creature of habit. There's nothing wrong with that. My Henry, bless him, has made his coffee the same way since we were newlyweds. Thirty-five years, and he's always had his coffee with cream and two sugars, no more, no less."

There was comfort in the predictable routine, but also there was the possibility of losing that taste for adventure. Did Gus want that? If Sirena was going to have a little fun, he could join her just a little. He had rules and he had his head on straight. It would be fine.

"Maybe it's time for a change." He closed his eyes and randomly pointed to something on the menu. Gus opened them and read out what food his finger landed on. Mimi nodded with approval, scribbled it down, then left their table. Gus peered at Sirena, who stared at him over the privacy of their booth. There was a mixture of glee and interest in her stare. His heart tumbled and flipped in his chest as if it had been placed inside a warm dryer.

"I see you, August," she said.

"I see you too, Sirena," he responded.

Chapter Eight

The Freya Grove Historical Society was bigger on the inside and held more items than Sirena could imagine. Nana had taught her all about the types of houses that were built around the Grove, but she had a special fondness for this house. Whenever they drove or walked past the historical society, Nana told her that it held all the stories and mysteries of the Grove. Sirena thought it was charmingly Gothic. Her *Beetlejuice-* and red-lace-loving heart felt giddy whenever she drove past during her previous Empty Fridge deliveries. It didn't really give off wild party vibes, more like midnight séance gathering space. Sirena quickly adapted to her new second-chance schedule. She'd spent her mornings working at Night Sky, took her lunch, then headed over to the historical society to start her shift as a culinary consultant, as Gus had titled her.

"Can I be a magician's assistant instead?" she had joked.

Gus only smiled at her question and told her that she'd be stationed in the library.

Cherrywood bookshelves lining the walls were stuffed with large and oversized tomes filled with decades of Grove lore and fables. A spiral staircase wound up to a second level, where even more shelves were located. Deep-red couches were arranged so patrons could comfortably sit and read for hours when the building was open. Sirena stood in the room and breathed in the scent of crisp paper and cracked leather spines. She felt like Belle in that classic scene where the Beast gifted her his entire library.

She looked at Gus. "Can I spend my birthday here?"

His dark eyes flashed with glee. "If you'd like," he said in a low voice.

He brought her over to the three shelves. Gus wasn't lying about the number of culinary and cooking materials that the society possessed, or about needing a culinary eye to help decipher the information. There were a lot of archive rules Sirena had to follow before she could even touch a single item: *Wash and dry your hands before you handle the documents. Keep the workspace clean. Make sure the documents have minimal exposure to light.*

There were a dozen more rules that the society insisted on following, but she kept herself aware of how she was treating the documents. So far, she'd been working at the society for five afternoons, and she had barely managed to get through one small box and make a dent in the second box. One day Sirena was reading a pixie's shopping list, and the next day she was trying to make sense of a gnome's recipe for beer mash. Each scrap of paper she held possessed a bit of worn magic that felt like warm dust underneath her fingers.

Something dormant within her kindled when she was reading these notes and faded recipes and saw how passionate previous Grove residents were about cooking. Sirena grabbed a yellow legal pad and got a pencil, scribbling down everything that piqued her interest. She copied down a few herbs and food items that she could pick up at the Farmers Square.

Rule twenty-six: Make a shopping list before you go to the store. Check it twice.

Her phone beeped, and she checked the message.

She grinned once she saw the email's subject line on her screen: **Interview for head chef at Lighthouse.** It was about time. Sirena sat back in her seat, dropping the pencil on the table. She already knew what was in the email, but this time around she didn't feel the sense of self-assuredness that she once had. The doubt that she had managed to outrun these last few days crept back in the more she stared at the email invitation. She needed a great—no, a *spellbinding*—dish to help her land this interview and get the job for good. *Can I trust my magic not to mess up this time around?*

She winced, unable to confidently answer that question yet.

Sirena needed to get that creative spark in check. Once she got that feeling back, it would allow her to cook any dish she wanted. She went to the first box on the shelf and found a yellowed recipe that she couldn't get out of her brain. Shore croquettes. Did Auntie Niesha cook this dish a long time ago?

She snapped a picture of it on her phone, then returned the paper to its proper place.

Getting a job at Lighthouse would help get her back on track and back to what she used to be: the best kitchen witch the Garden State could offer.

The door opened, and a steady footfall echoed on the hardwood floor.

Sirena turned to see Gus strolling in. "It's closing time."

A sudden warmth surged through her body the longer she stared at Gus. Why did he have to wear the tweed blazer with the tailored pants today? There was something enjoyable about it; maybe it was the thread of color about this outfit that made her smile. Most of the time, Gus was super serious when it came to his job, but there were moments when she saw the humorous side of him appear. His full, thick beard gave him a mysterious aura, as if he'd just walked out of his potion-making room to check in with her.

His handsome face lit up with an inquiring expression. "Do you see anything you like?"

Yes, I do. Sirena forced herself to look away from Gus. "Um, yes. I'm interested in the Saybrooke journal."

Whenever she walked past the book waiting on the shelf, she felt a jolt of energy. Of course, Sirena couldn't touch the journal until Gus finished researching the item's provenance.

He made a low sound of agreement. "I have an update. My investigator just sent me her final report. She did an extensive search about Juliette Saybrooke. Apparently, she didn't have any children and has no living family. She lived a very interesting life."

Sirena leaned against the table. "How so?"

"She knew Madame Zora and even cooked for her and her family on a regular basis."

Wow. Sirena's brow rose to her hairline. Madame Zora, the world-famous psychic, was one of the most famous people who ever left the Grove. Everyone in the Grove claimed that they were related to Madame Zora, but her true descendants were unknown.

An eager smile crossed Gus's face. "I'll continue to search for any relatives, but I think we can officially call it."

He spoke in his serious voice, which reminded Sirena of a head librarian at an enchanted circulation desk. "I can officially declare that the Saybrooke journal is part of the permanent collection of the historical society."

Sirena let out a yell of delight and clapped her hands. She jumped up and down and did a little shimmy dance at this news. When was the last time she'd been excited to read a journal that wasn't her sister's? Her heart lifted. She'd been dreaming of this moment for the last week.

Gus watched her, seemingly dazed by her shimmy, then cleared his throat.

"You can come over tomorrow to look at it," he offered.

Oh no. Her shoulders dropped. Tomorrow was Saturday, and she was going to the Harvest Festival with Callie. "I have plans." Sirena groaned. She really wanted to look at the journal as soon as possible.

"The journal will be here on Monday."

Sirena started gathering her notebook and her items. "I'll be here early. I'll bring my lunch from Night Sky."

"You've got the bug," he said kindly.

Sirena peered at him. "Is that a magician thing?"

"It's a family thing. Grandpa Gus used to say that whenever you got fascinated with a topic, you got bitten by the curiosity bug."

"You're named after your grandpa," she said.

He gave a short nod.

Sirena grinned, happy to add another piece to the Gus puzzle. "I have gotten the bug for all this. History. I mean, who knew that a kitchen witch like me would go completely batty over old papers? It makes no sense."

"It does make sense. The herbs and foods you cook with are a direct reflection of the history and heritage you're a product of. I mean, your last name means so much in magic."

Sirena laughed. "Trust me, Nana Ruth schooled us about our family history."

"Was the name always Caraway?" he inquired.

"It's the name we claimed," Sirena said confidently. "Caraway seeds are used in protection charms, and it's believed that whoever carries them will remain safe. So, Lucinda and Jacob took the name for themselves and gave it to their children. They wanted to keep us protected."

One corner of his mouth lifted. "I like that. Once you read the Saybrooke journal, you'll see yourself in those pages."

The warmth in her body went up a notch. "You know how to make a witch feel special."

"Well, you are special." His words were as cool and clear as an evening breeze.

She peered at him for a long second, her interest in him blooming in her chest. His dark eyes were gentle but heavy with exhaustion.

"How are you still standing? You must be tired."

"I'll sleep when the work is done," he said.

Her brow creased with worry.

The Freya Grove Historical Society was a hive of constant activity. The work never seemed to get done, but Gus never complained or faltered.

Mondays he held open hours for local college and high school students to come in and ask questions about local history and examine items from the collection. He gave hour-long tours to people who were interested in having anniversary parties or wedding receptions in the library. On Wednesdays he hosted a genealogy workshop for older adults who wanted to create a family tree as a gift. She overheard booming laughter from the meeting room as Gus told his pun-filled jokes and charmed visitors. On Thursdays, he opened the society to caregivers and stay-at-home parents to have a safe place to meet and connect. Sirena heard Gus join in with the toddlers when they started singing the alphabet song, his voice kind yet strong. She had to keep from melting in a puddle of admiration. Seeing people charged Gus up, and he seemed to bask in the light of their attention. Even though she'd been there for only five days, she'd seen many sides to Gus.

She liked all of them. This man was captivating, like a faceted crystal in the sun—refracting light from other sources and catching her attention with how brilliant he shined.

She yearned to gain a fraction of the light he held.

"You really love what you do here," she said.

Gus cleared his throat. "It's a job."

No. It was more than that, but she didn't push him to change his answer. Instead, she gave him a knowing smile. Would she ever love cooking or magic again as much as he loved this place and its history? When the time came to answer that question, she hoped she had an answer that wouldn't break her spirit.

Sirena gathered her coat and purse from the library's desk. They left the library together, walked down the stairs, and stood in the foyer of the historical society.

Her stomach grumbled.

"Dinner or dessert?" he asked.

She considered the two options. Which one was more fun? "Dessert."

He gave her a curt nod. "Sprinkles and Scoops, the dessert place on Main, is debuting their fall favors tonight. I thought it would be fun to try them all—or try a few favorites."

She blinked rapidly at his offer. He hadn't forgotten about the fun lessons. As if reading the stunned look on her face, he smirked. "I wanted to make sure our first lesson fit your personality."

"Have you been taking notes about me?" she joked.

Gus stroked his beard as he considered her comment. Was his beard soft or rough? She rubbed her palms, itching to touch his face and quell her curiousity. Her eyes dipped down to his mouth, which seemed to be always on the edge of a laugh. He, with his dry words and style, reminded her of a well-dressed rogue who watched over the world but didn't interact with it. A rogue who would be ready to jump into action when he was called to cause a disruption.

"A magician never reveals his secrets, but a historian examines the records, takes detailed notes, and considers the next step," he said.

Gus waved his fingers. The front door opened before them, and the evening sounds of passing cars and faint televisions were heard. He offered his arm to her. Sirena took it without another word, and then they walked out the door. Her crush on him felt new yet familiar—like a song she hadn't heard in a long time but felt brand-new every time she heard it.

Whenever Gus had appeared on-screen during *Dealing with the Dearworths*, Sirena had stopped what she was doing—cooking, cleaning, or brewing—and watched him do his magical act. He walked with a powerful swagger, a magician on a mission to thrill the world, one audience member at a time. She had watched the episode "Like a Phoenix" on repeat just to see Gus practice his breathtaking fire illusion and step into his power. No matter how many times she saw that moment when he took a single match and turned it into a soaring phoenix, Sirena was spellbound. He even got nominated for an Emmy for that episode. She was smitten with Gus in the fun way you had a crush on an internet celebrity. It was harmless.

But now, when he looked at her with his roguish smile, filled with mischief, her crush on Gus was renewed like a library book.

Sirena watched him for a long beat, not knowing whether to be charmed or on guard. From what she knew about magicians, they learned their magic just like a person learned a musical instrument. The more a magician performed their craft, the better they became at using it. *What wonders could he do with the snap of his fingers?*

She was afraid and a little thrilled to find out the extent of his charms.

Chapter Nine

Sprinkles and Scoops, the ice cream parlor, was the newest business in the Grove and the best place to get dessert. The neon-pink sign against the flowered wallpaper by the entrance said "You deserve an extra scoop." There was a chalkboard menu on the wall that listed the new fall flavors and prices. Customers stood in a line, buzzing about which flavors they wanted to try over the whir of the blender. The sugary scent of waffle cones being pressed and cooked filled the air and tickled Sirena's nose. She tapped her fingers together as she surveyed the flavors behind the glass. The titles were attached to the tubs: Pumpkin pie. Butter pecan. Caramel apple. Candy brownie. Harvest cake.

Sirena turned to Gus, who stood at her side. "I want them all."

He dipped his head. "Good. I'll get us the sample platter of them all." A playful, almost hopeful gleam entered his eyes. "I hope we don't cause too much trouble."

"A little trouble can be a good thing," she said enthusiastically.

Gus gave her a sly wink, as if they were planning an ice cream heist. How did he make the simplest things feel like an adventure?

Sirena got a table in the corner while Gus got and paid for their order.

She glanced around the ice cream shop, giving smiles to the

other customers, who happily gobbled down their treats. Wow. That pixie who was practically swimming into his waffle cone seemed to be enjoying his caramel apple ice cream a lot. She wiggled in her seat, ready to have a taste of their treats. Ten minutes later, Gus joined her at their table, holding a tray of five cups, each filled with a different flavor. He produced a spoon from his pocket for Sirena. Her fingers brushed against his, and she felt how soft they were. She quickly yanked the spoon from Gus, trying to keep her mind from going off into dreamland.

"Tell me who told you that you weren't fun," Gus said as he settled into his seat. "Give me their address. I want to talk to them about a few things."

The gruff note of protectiveness in his voice made her grin.

Sirena dug her spoon into the caramel apple scoop. "Thanks for the offer but no one told me anything. I figured I need to change things."

"I'm curious why you started with fun," he said. Gus scooped up some candy brownie and ate a bite. He visibly brightened. "That's nice."

She tasted her ice cream, sliding the generous amount into her mouth. *Ooh.* That was the good stuff. It was rich and creamy, with hints of cider and a ribbon of caramel. Sirena did a little dance. Gus nodded; a smile played on his lips. "It's good, huh?"

Sirena groaned in satisfaction.

There was a faint glint of enjoyment in his eyes. As if he liked seeing her have pleasure.

"I don't have a lot of time to make some changes in my life," she admitted.

If the spellbook was right, if she didn't achieve her goal, she'd repeat the entire month.

Gus tilted his head to the side. "Are you going somewhere?"

Not if I can help it. Sirena scooped another flavor of ice cream into her mouth to keep herself from telling him everything. Well, since he was helping her, she could tell him something—at least enough to calm his concerns.

She finished her bite. "I have a cooking interview that can't be moved. Lately, my cooking has been boring."

"How? Are you forgetting the salt and pepper?"

Sirena swirled her spoon between her fingers, fighting against the rising pain of a brain freeze. "No, but it tastes bland. It doesn't even taste good or bad—it tastes floppy. Imagine eating dry cardboard on top of wet carboard. That's how my food tastes now."

Gus gave her a sympathetic glance. "I'm sorry."

She batted the pain down and forced a calm grin onto her face. "I figured that if I jump-start my creative brain, then maybe my cooking will get better."

His eyes glowed with a quiet mischief. "When's the last time you played a game?" he asked.

"Hmm." Sirena pondered his question. "I think I completed a crossword puzzle in July."

"Ah. There it is. Whenever I get stuck trying to figure out an issue with work, I stop working and go play a game. Your creative brain is looking to play, and you've been hustling and grinding instead."

Gus jabbed his spoon in the air to punctuate his point.

I don't get paid to play. Sirena held back her knee-jerk response and stared at Gus.

He was helping her, and she didn't have to snap at him just because he was right. When Sirena let herself play around with an old dish in the kitchen, she often came up with new and exciting meals. He *was* right. Somewhere over the last year she forgot that the best magic came from a heart that embraced fun and joy.

Gus watched her with a sly smirk. "You know I'm right."

"You might have a point," she admitted begrudgingly. "I'm busy, Gus."

He held up his spoon. "An hour of play will let your brain rest and think of new ideas."

It was time. If she was going to change her fate, then she needed to commit to her plan. Sirena couldn't be hesitant or shy with her request. *Ask him if he wants to play.*

Having fun could be innocent, but playing around could be daring. A pleasant shudder heated her body, making her sweater feel itchy and tight. Her heart hammered against her ribs as her imagination went running wild. She could see Gus showing up at her doorstep, holding two tickets and a weekend bag. He'd whisk her away somewhere no one knew their names or their histories, somewhere they could watch the stars come out and bathe in the moonlight. They'd trade confessions and kisses in the dark and learn the contours of their bodies.

The question fell from her lips before she could stop it.

"So, will you play with me?"

Sirena held her breath waiting for him to respond. *Please. Say it.*

"I thought you'd never ask," he said in a rumbly voice. "Yes, I'll play with you." Why did he have to say it like that? Like he was licking the ice cream off her spoon—unhurriedly. Like he was kissing her while lowering her down onto a feather-soft bed. Sweet basil. Sirena gripped her spoon so hard, she was worried it would snap in her hand.

"What game are we playing?" she said, forcing herself to stay cool.

She hoped Gus said a paper-and-pen game like tic-tac-toe or MASH.

"Be impulsive," he said. "Go with the flow, and when the time is right, the right game will come up tonight. You can't always plan your fun."

"Says you," Sirena grumbled.

He gave her an interested look. "What have you been conjuring up in the kitchen?"

She drew a blank. Sirena gritted her teeth, unable to come up with a single new dish. Her skin grew clammy at that truth.

"Eh, does a peanut butter and jelly sandwich count as conjuring?"

She hadn't been cooking anything big lately, feeling burned out on cooking.

His lips puckered in thoughtfulness. "Of course. Who doesn't love a classic PB and J? I enjoy a late-night snack when the mood strikes. Besides, I'm terrible at cooking."

"You're just out of practice," she said.

Gus made a face. "I don't think I can handle the heat in the kitchen."

"You can handle it. Cooking can be fun when you do it with a friend."

"We're friends now," he said.

Sirena felt her face flush. "I mean, I'm working in your library and feeding your cat treats. You've made my holiday card list."

"Are you offering to let me in your kitchen?" he asked with a rasp of interest.

She laughed, trying to mask the jolt of pleasure that went

through her when he asked that simple question. Lately, she didn't let anyone in; it was just better to take care of her space by herself. Lucy and Callie offered to cook, but Sirena politely declined their help. Nana had picked her to carry on her legacy and she wasn't going to let her down. *Rule nine: A kitchen witch is solely responsible for keeping their space and magic safe.*

Letting Gus into her kitchen didn't feel like a safe move; it felt thrilling and hot—like biting into a handful of ghost peppers.

"I'll put you on the waiting list," she teased.

Gus took another bite of ice cream.

"Tell me about your society work," he said.

"I want to make sure the recipes are scanned and digitized. They're too valuable to Freya Grove history to let them stay on a shelf. I found an interesting dish in the library."

Gus dropped his spoon on the tray. "I agree. Show me what you found."

Sirena picked up her phone and opened it to her picture gallery.

She leaned over the table and showed Gus the recipe page. "I was thinking about making it and seeing how it tasted."

Gus scanned the recipe, running his tongue over his lips in thought. "Hmm. This dish sounds good. Save me a plate when you make it."

Sirena hesitated when she heard something odd in his voice. What was that—longing? When was the last time he had a meal that left him feeling satisfied? That urge to feed him hijacked her brain. The words popped out of her mouth before she could take them back.

"I can cook it at your house."

The historical society had a full, very lived-in kitchen. She'd eaten her afternoon snacks in there once, not wanting to risk spilling anything on the documents.

"I don't know if our kitchen is up your standards. The sink is older than me," he warned.

"Let's try." Where did this untested confidence come from? She decided to stop before she committed to cooking him a whole turkey. Sirena stuffed her mouth with another spoonful of caramel apple.

Gus merely smiled, and they ate their ice cream scoops in peace. An eager glint materialized in his eyes. Oh. He appeared too appealing when he had that glint in his eyes. Like a swash-buckler ready to woo his lady into a high-seas adventure or a starry-eyed night of romance in his private cabin. Sirena tried to rid her brain of that fantasy and failed. She could see him sauntering over to her bed wearing a loose jacket, baggy trousers, and a sash that would sit right on his solid body. How he would sweep her up into his arms and, with those skilled hands of his, rid her of her nightgown and leave her bare naked for his pleasure. She groaned and took another bite of caramel apple ice cream. She experienced two fantasies in one night. If she had a third one, she'd probably overheat like a car with the AC turned on high.

She fanned herself with her spoon. *Do not fantasize about him—too much.*

Gus shot her a concerned look. "Is everything okay?"

Sirena gave him a thumbs-up. She really needed to stop staying up late and watching old-school pirate films on the Telly app.

As she ate, the feeling of doubt grew in her brain, overpowering her confidence. Who was she to cook a nearly hundred-year-old recipe for a magician?! Gus had probably had meals made by world-class chefs from all over the world when he was performing. Yeah, he said all those nice things in the diner, but he hadn't had her cooking recently. She couldn't scramble eggs without making them taste rubbery. Sirena kept rethinking her offer as they emptied their ice cream bowls. She wanted to impress him, to see his eyes light up in wonder when he tasted her food. *It's not even your recipe.* She thought about the Lighthouse interview and the wince of disgust on the manager's face when she tasted Sirena's meal. She'd hate to see that disgust on his face.

She frowned. How was she going to explain to him that she couldn't cook for him? Gus must have seen the look on her face, because he spoke.

"Don't worry," he said. "I'll reimburse you for anything you buy or cook for me—for the society. Save the receipts."

"You already pay me too much." Sirena bit the inside of her cheek. She could practically feel Callie at her side, hissing at her. *Hush up and take the money.*

Gus leaned over the table. "Like my grandpa said, when you know your worth, kid, make sure to add tax. I'm paying for your experience and knowledge."

"I hope I'm worth it," she said. The hourly salary was very generous and easily replaced the money she made with Empty Fridge. Sirena didn't have to worry about having her deliveries stolen by hungry porch trolls or soggy paper bags costing her a high tip.

"I'm not paying you enough," he responded. "You deserve double."

Sirena laughed, stunned. "You always seem to have the right words. How do you do that?"

They paused and then said at the same time, "Magic."

"Jinx," Sirena said automatically. A flash of red sparks popped around Gus's mouth. This was it—the perfect game at the right time. She and her sisters used to make a game of jinx last for days—or until Nana threatened to put crushed black pepper into their morning tea to get them to talk.

Gus squeaked, unable to get a word out of his lips.

Sirena waved her hand. "This is impulsive, right?!"

Gus grumbled in what sounded like agreement. Good. Ready to play. He rolled his hand, gesturing for her to set down the rules of this game of jinx.

"You can only speak when you buy me...uh...a root beer," she said quickly.

He shrugged as if it was no big deal. Sirena snapped her fingers in defeat as she remembered where she was. Scoops and Sprinkles always had bottles of root beer and cola for an impromptu ice cream float. Her shoulders slumped, and she sighed. Well, it was fun for the five seconds that the game lasted.

Gus went over to the drink fridge, glanced around the shelves, and turned back to her. He slashed his hand over his neck and frowned. Sirena got up and stood next to him and searched the drink case.

She held back a grin. "Oh no. It looks like they're out. No talking until you buy me a root beer."

Gus sighed, then folded his arms over his broad chest. He gave her a raised brow as if to say *You must be having so much fun right now.*

The game wasn't over yet and the night was just beginning.

"I'm having a great time," she said. And she actually meant it.

Gus never knew that he could make anyone so happy by not speaking. Grandpa once told Gus he was blessed with the gift of gab, so playing a game of jinx was challenging for him. He could've easily ended the game back at Sprinkles and Scoops when he spied a random root beer in the back of the fridge. He could've ended it by opening the Empty Fridge app and having an entire six-pack of root beer delivered to their table. But it became apparent to him that the longer he played this game with Sirena, the more she seemed to relax. Gus saw the glow of amusement light up her face, and he didn't want to take it away. He snagged a peppermint from the bowl on the counter and popped it into his mouth after they cleaned up their table. They left the ice cream shop and strolled down Main Street, watching ghouls and people parade on the sidewalk. He breathed in the crisp scent of decaying leaves mixed with the heady sea air and natural magic. They walked by pumpkins glowing on porches and four-foot-high skeletons on front lawns. There was nothing like autumn in Freya Grove. The Grove was alive tonight.

Gus waited for Sirena outside Lee's Bodega.

She exited the shop almost as quickly as she went in, holding up her hands. "This store doesn't have a single can, either. Is everyone making root beer floats tonight?!"

Gus shrugged carelessly. It wasn't a big deal. He crushed the peppermint in his mouth and let the pieces linger on his tongue.

"I didn't mean to pick the one soda they don't have in town," she said. "I bet you probably want to go home."

He swung his head in a no. How long had it been since he truly let himself toss out his schedule and go with the flow? His Friday nights usually consisted of him eating dinner alone in his study, answering emails, and completing the week's paperwork. The combination of eating delicious ice cream and talking about playing with Sirena left him hyped up. The trickster within had been ready to whisk her away right then, but Gus kept himself in check. He had this burst of buzzy energy and he wanted to burn it off.

"Where do you want to go?" she asked.

Gus extended his hand to her. For tonight, he'd settle for taking her to his favorite place in the Grove. She took it and interlaced her fingers with his. Her hand fit in his neatly and his skin warmed. It was as if he held a small flame in his palm, and he savored her touch. They went down away from the stores, through the town square, and toward the boardwalk. She yanked his hand and halted when they walked by a curio storefront window. The display consisted of snow globes of different sizes mounted on a rising platform.

She focused on a medium-sized globe directly in front of her. "How lovely."

Gus noticed the glass globe in question. The castle by the sea inside the globe was impressively crafted. The undisturbed glitter rested on its towers and shimmered under the store lights.

"Nana used to say I was her magpie. I liked collecting sparkly things when I was little."

Sirena watched the snow globe carefully. It was as if she was committing the item to her memory. He noticed the price tag and filed it away for a future shopping trip. Society guests and members had nothing but praise for his new culinary consultant, who put out water and snacks in the afternoon. Gus wished to give her a tangible thank-you when her time came to close at the society. The budget allowed Sirena to work for a limited amount of time and then she would have to leave. Unhappiness thrummed through him at the thought of her walking out the front door and not returning.

She studied it for a few more seconds, then looked at Gus. "We can go now."

He slowly eased her away from the storefront. Their footsteps echoed on the planks as they walked in tandem. It was dark enough that you couldn't see the waves roll in, but you could hear the roll and crash of them on the beach. Seagulls wheeled overhead, and the wind filled the silence between them. They walked down until they reached the illuminated carousel.

The Freya Grove carousel, protected by glass walls, was held in an elaborate copper rotunda on the waterfront. It had three rows of different animal figures and creatures that children and adults could ride during open hours. Wonder, light and refreshing, like an evening rain coated his skin. No matter how many times he saw the carousel, he was always engrossed by this ride. They walked close enough to make out the prancing unicorns and bears suspended in motion. According to local lore, the designer was a gifted magician who created this amusement that took riders on a journey through a coastal fairyland. In his dreams he could hear the gleeful laughter and feel the joy this place brought so many riders.

Yearning wrung his heart out and left it dry. Could he ever make anything so beautiful?

He watched Sirena, standing rapt in the glow of the carousel. The wind gently kicked up the loose braids around her face. Her skin appeared to shimmer as if her full cheeks had been kissed with glitter. By the water and in the evening light, she looked ethereal, like a water sprite come to visit the land.

Gus had noticed Sirena with her rounded lush body and big smile around the Grove, leaving a job or headed to another. It never seemed to be the right time to ask Sirena out or to see if she was interested in him. He often saw her in Night Sky Bistro, giving out so-called baking mistakes to people who couldn't afford a sandwich or were having a rough day.

Gus noticed that her attention had left the carousel. Instead, she stared at the fancy maritime restaurant that looked out over the ocean. The fancy place was called the Lighthouse and he thought that the food was a bit too fussy for his tastes. Her eyes went glassy, and the teasing light that was there faded. She paled as if she'd seen a terrifying phantom.

Gus took a step forward, but Sirena held a hand to keep him at bay. He halted.

She licked her lips and squared her shoulders. "Um, I have to be honest. I don't know if I can cook for you. I mean, I can prep the ingredients, put everything together, and make it look good. I don't know if it'll...taste good."

He wrinkled his brow. A growl of frustration left Sirena's throat.

"I'm probably not making sense, but I'm going to try. Just listen, please."

He nodded, genuinely concerned. She drew in a breath, as if she was trying to summon up courage to tell him an unpleasant truth. His stomach twisted a bit. Was she hiding from him?

The words *Are you okay? I can help* lingered on his lips, but he remained true to the game.

Her words came out in a furious tumble.

"I can cook, but I can't conjure. I used to have so much fun whenever I made anything, Gus. I mean, I used to smile when I made peanut butter and cinnamon toast for my sisters. I was happy because I was able to make them happy with my magic. I felt that exciting spark when I just touched the stove or read over a recipe, but now...I can't easily feel it anymore. I have to work hard to find it. It's hiding, or it's gone. I was born to do this, to be a kitchen witch. I was chosen. Like my nana and her mother. I barely feel that magic, and that's not...okay. I don't know who I am without it, and I want the spark back."

The fury transformed into misery as she stopped talking. Sirena wiped away the tears that rolled down her cheeks, but they kept coming. Her lips trembled, and she let out shuddering cries that racked her whole body. A mixture of empathy and protectiveness stirred within him. Gus watched her cry for an instant, then brought her into the safety of his arms. He held her close, supporting her against his chest. She could rant and rave if she needed to, but he'd take whatever she needed to let out. Her body shook even more, but he held on. Why couldn't he make her hurt disappear as easily as he could make doves vanish into thin air? He wasn't letting her go, even if the tide came in, swallowed them up, and pulled them out to sea. They stayed together for a long time, remaining in the glow of the carousel lights. Sirena stepped back from his arms. Her tears had subsided, but they still fell down her cheeks and underneath her chin. She looked up at him under the twinkle lights above.

"Who am I without that magic?" she said, and her voice broke.

Her question slipped inside his chest and struck his heart like a throwing knife. Gus had asked himself the same question when he walked away from his career and his family's legacy act. Years later, he'd been able to answer it, but it took time to see himself outside of his last name and the demands that he be only Good-Time Gus. He had to find a new mirror, a new place to see who he could be away from his family's gaze. The Grove, this mystic, wonderful town by the sea, showed him the person he once dreamed of being.

Someone who was steadfast and thoughtful.

He could be the mirror to show Sirena how wonderful she was. Even though she'd been coming to the historical society for barely a week, she had made herself invaluable. When she took a break from going through documents, Sirena went out and bought treats for visiting students who needed a quick bite. She made iced tea for the older adults who came in to find clues about their families and raptly listened to their stories. She entertained the toddlers with silly dances and wacky games while the parents got a chance to take a break. Gus waited in the lobby every afternoon to personally greet her, every fiber of him rejoicing at the sight of her on the porch. Cinder followed Sirena wherever she went and meowed after her whenever she left the society. He watched her give pieces of herself without any expectations that she'd get anything back.

No one would ever take her place.

Sirena deserved to have a tangible reminder that she was more than the magic she held. He reached into his shirt pocket and took out his notepad and pencil. Gus slowly wrote a note for Sirena, ripped it off the pad, and handed it to her. He dropped the pad back into his pocket.

She swallowed hard, lifted her chin, and met his gaze.

Sirena took the note and read it for a long moment. She gasped, pressing a hand to her chest. The tears didn't fall anymore but glistened in those lovely eyes. All that was on the paper were two words, but they were the best ones he knew that captured what he believed about Sirena.

You're irreplaceable.

He took her face into his hands, studying her deliberately, as if she were a valuable artifact that had been placed in his path. People searched their entire lives for something as beautiful as the woman in his arms. They dug up the earth and combed entire oceans just to have something as precious as Sirena. His blood hammered wildly as he leaned down into her space.

He hesitated, waiting for her to invite him to close the space between them.

She watched him for a second, then gave him a single nod.

He softly brushed his lips over hers. She let out a soft moan and he deepened their kiss.

A hot ache grew in his throat. She tasted of tart apples and sweet cream, of fresh sugar and unspoken enchantments. Her kisses were kindling, generating heat, and sending a part of his soul on fire. He felt her hands moving underneath his jacket, and she pressed herself firmly against his body. It still wasn't close enough. Gus allowed his hands to explore the softness of her cheeks and the delicate lines of her shoulders. He held back, wanting to comfort her but not take advantage of her tender heart. He kept kissing Sirena, greedily wanting to devour every inch of her until there was nothing left but embers. The time for words had passed.

Sparks, as small as fireflies, floated from their intertwined bodies and drifted into the carousel's mechanics. Those sparks, as playful as air sprites, went into the lights and gears. The carousel whirred to life, and the sound of calliope music filled the air. Gus held Sirena as they watched the ride move and glide, powered by the magic they'd made together.

Chapter Ten

The pale blue light of the morning filled Sirena's bedroom, giving the space a sleepy lo-fi screensaver vibe. Giddiness shot through her body, making it impossible for her to go back to sleep. Sirena woke up holding the slip of paper Gus had given her. She read the words again, half scared that they would disappear if she stared at them too long. But the words remained and sent her heart into full-mouse-squeal, kick-up-your-heels, and hug-a-fluffy-pillow mode. She hadn't dreamed in months, but last night her imagination made up for lost time. In her dreams, she had stayed with Gus by the carousel. They caressed and kissed each other until dawn on the boardwalk, beyond the need for words. In reality, Gus had kissed her for a little while longer, then took her home before midnight.

Gus never broke the game of jinx. His curly, thick beard tickled her skin, and the taste of him—sugar and crushed peppermint— made her lips buzz with excitement. He kissed her senseless by the boardwalk and never spoke a single word. His hands were deft and careful, roaming all over her face and shoulders but never falling below and exploring her body. Sirena touched her cheek, mimicking Gus's fingers as he gently caressed her. The rogue was a gentleman. The rest of her body yearned to experience that thoughtful touch, but she went home. Even though she knew it was the right decision to end the night, a pin of frustration jabbed at her skin.

Kissing Gus was not part of the plan. Liking Gus was not part of the plan. But talking to him about her lost magic and her desire to reclaim her spark had lifted her spirits.

His kiss had filled her with a strange delight, an anticipation that she'd never felt before after she kissed a guy.

But this wasn't a guy she kissed randomly; it was Gus Dearworth, the magician who peered at her as if she were a precious gem he found on the beach. She'd asked him to play with her and he said yes. Their game of jinx ended with them kissing. What excitement would their next game bring? The giddiness went up a notch and was now full-blown excitement.

Sirena threw off her covers. She might as well get up now and start the day. Sirena got out of bed, found her notebook in her purse, and tucked the paper into its pages. She hadn't expected for things to move this quickly with Gus, but it had happened.

Liking Gus had the potential to be distractingly addictive, almost as much as any sugary treat left you yearning for more. She'd never been so charged with a single kiss like that first one; the electricity between them had powered a whole carousel.

Her stomach twisted in dismay. She had to keep it casual and fun between her and Gus. The month would be over in a blink, and then she'd be worse off than when she started—but this time around she'd possibly have a crushed heart. Sirena didn't have time for anything as serious as possibly falling for Gus. Even though her lips still prickled from the delightful magic of their kiss, she couldn't let herself give in to this spell.

Besides, why would a magician who could play with fire date a kitchen witch who couldn't handle her own stove?

If she was going to figure out her next steps, then she was going to need some caffeine. Sirena went downstairs and into the kitchen. Lucy stood by the coffee maker in a gray and purple hoodie and fitted jeans. Her hair was tucked up under a crocheted beanie, almost making her look like one of the teenagers that she taught in her class.

"Good morning, Si!" she said sweetly. "You're up early."

"I couldn't sleep much."

Lucy pouted. "Oh, did you have a bad dream?"

"No," Sirena said, groggy and annoyed. Her dreams were good, too good.

"Okay. Is there something on your mind?"

Sirena answered with a groan. She wasn't ready to share the news that she was jonesing for a certain rainbow tweed magician who left her spellbound. Lucy would get super invested in this news, due to her romantic, loving heart, and might invite Gus over for dinner. No. It was too soon for Gus to be invited into the lovely chaos that was the Caraway family.

"I'm good, Lu."

Lucy shook her head and poured herself a cup of coffee.

"Well, coffee's on. Breakfast is in the fridge. I finished cleaning up the tea pantry last night. I think we're good for the next year." Lucy made a *pew-pew* party horn sound. "I'm killing it today."

Sirena groaned. "Please, have mercy. Some of us aren't this perky in the morning."

"How's work at the historical society?" Lucy asked.

Sirena gave her a look. Lucy rolled her eyes kindly. "You put me down as a reference, and Gus called me to confirm a few details. He takes his job very seriously."

He also takes kissing seriously.

Sirena fought the urge to ask Lucy what he had confirmed about her résumé. He was probably wondering how she, an award-nominated chef, ended up slinging burgers in her hometown. She didn't want to tell him the whole story, not wanting to risk seeing pity in his eyes.

"How do you like it?" Lucy said.

Sirena considered the past week. It was surprisingly enjoyable hunting through faded papers and finding recipes from fae, trolls, and other magical creatures who once called the Grove home. Even though they were long gone, their recipes and stories remained. It took her so long to go through the papers because she stopped every ten minutes to write down a piece of lore or fact that she wanted to remember.

"It's fun," she finally said. "I'm really enjoying learning more about the Grove."

Lucy leveled her with a shocked stare. "You, the Caraway who slept through history class, thinks looking at old papers is *fun*?"

Sirena scoffed. "Hey, I was working late at the Neptune Nook junior year, and I had first-period history. That's not my fault."

"I must be in an alternate universe, because I never thought you'd say that."

Sirena shrugged. "Why not?"

Lucy seemed to grow sheepish, as if she were a nervous student being forced to introduce herself. "It's so silly, but I always thought books and history things were my zone. I wish I could've joined you in the kitchen more, but I didn't want to get in your way. Nana told me you had it handled, so I left you alone. Now you're talking about *my* history stuff, and I want to completely geek out with you."

A smile crept onto Sirena's face. She'd never heard Lucy talk about being in her own zone. It was comforting to know her big sister felt the same way she did.

"You've cooked in the kitchen before," Sirena said.

"Yeah, but not with you," Lucy pointed out.

Sirena raised a brow at her words. It was true. Nana Ruth had insisted that as a kitchen witch, she couldn't relinquish her stove or invite everyone into her space. *Rule fourteen: You always stay in control of your fire.* Yes, Sirena was in control, but she was also alone in her craft.

"Well, maybe it's time for a change," Sirena said.

Lucy raised her cup. "I'm down for it."

She yanked out a mug from the cabinet, poured herself a huge cup, and returned the pot to the carafe. *Sweet caffeine, feed me.* Maybe today was the time for getting out of her magic zone even more. Sirena took a huge sip, gagged, and promptly spat it back out into the mug. It tasted as though someone doused her coffee with the striped treat of her childhood nightmares. Her senses were attacked with the nauseatingly sweet taste that she hated since she first went trick-or-treating.

"Candy corn?!" Sirena coughed. She dumped the brew in the sink.

Lucy sighed. "Gwen said everyone can't stop drinking it at the bistro."

Sirena noticed that Lucy held the cup but hadn't taken a sip yet.

"Those people are under an evil spell. That was—*blech*. Please stick to brewing tea."

"Whatever. Alex likes my coffee and my tea."

A blissful look crossed Lucy's face as she thought about her mer-husband to be. A whiny question popped in Sirena's brain: *Who likes your tea now? Maybe Gus would like your...tea.* Sirena pushed it away. Pesky hormones weren't going to get in the way of her wish. She wasn't sure she wanted to make Gus a slice of toast after her confession by the carousel.

"So, are you headed to see another venue with Alex?"

Lucy groaned. "Don't remind me. I don't know where we're getting married."

She took a sip of coffee, spat it back out, and said, "Nope. That was just...nope."

Sirena waved her arms around the house. "Get married here."

Lucy poured the coffee into the sink and dropped the mug in there with a clatter.

"Where are we going to put the merfolk? It's not big enough for all our guests, and we have two bathrooms that need serious work. We need a venue big enough for the ceremony and reception. Most places are booked up years in advance. What place is available now?"

"What about the historical society?" Sirena offered. Last week Gus had given a tour of the place to an adorable fae couple who were looking to host an engagement party.

Lucy stared at Sirena in sheer disbelief. "There's no way it's available. That place is gorgeous."

Sirena clapped her hands excitedly. "It's perfect. It has a full kitchen, there are five bathrooms, and there's room for at least a hundred and fifty people."

Lucy took out her phone from her sweatshirt pocket. Her fingers flew over the keyboard. "I'm emailing Gus right now. Maybe we can get a spot for next year."

Sirena crossed her fingers on both hands.

"I'll follow up with Gus when I see him on Monday," Sirena said. She'd clip a few basil leaves from the windowsill garden and put them in Lucy's purse for good luck.

Lucy perked up, phone still in her hand. "I'll call Alex and talk to him about the location. I have a good feeling about this, Si! I think you might have saved my weekend. This news deserves a trip to the bookstore."

"I'm going to the Farmers Square," Sirena said. "I need to pick up a few things."

"Is Callie going with you?"

Sirena frowned. "No, I'm shopping alone. Callie had an emergency meeting with her client."

Lucy winced. "Yeah. I overheard Callie talking to her the other day. I'm going to give her grace because wedding planning is hard, but no one talks to our little sister that way."

The familiar urge to soothe and help Callie rose within Sirena. She couldn't take away Callie's stressful work, but she could give her a warm cup of chamomile tea or make her favorite kitchen-sink cookies. Sirena hadn't traveled back through time just to repeat her mistakes. Changing your habits took courage, and she was doing her best to be brave. Even though she was terrified to cook or bake for another person, she had to try.

"I'll treat Callie to something nice when she gets home," Sirena said.

"When you're done food shopping, do you want to join me at Rain or Shine?" Lucy asked.

Rain or Shine Bookstore was the local indie bookstore and event space that was owned by their friend Poe. Lucy had helped design and decorate the place with her HGTV level of design talent. Lucy hadn't invited her to go to the bookstore in a long time.

Sirena's throat swelled with emotion. "Lu, are you asking me to geek out with you?"

"Absolutely," Lucy said with a grin. "I think it's time to try something new."

Lucy kissed her goodbye and then left Sirena in the kitchen. Sirena looked from the roll of cinnamon raisin bagels on the counter to the fruit bowl on top of the fridge. Her stomach grumbled loudly. Indecision kept her from making a choice, so she remained by the sink.

What do you want?

Sirena glanced behind the fruit bowl and noticed the bag of peanut butter granola cereal. Perfect choice. She went into the fridge to get the milk for her bowl and thought about her next moves as she assembled her breakfast.

She wanted to cook an amazing meal for Lighthouse but hadn't decided on a final dish. Sirena wanted to have fun and play around with Gus, but she didn't want to lead him on and make him think that they were serious. She'd never been so vulnerable before with any man about her feelings and powers, but Gus wasn't any man.

He was sheer magic.

She sighed roughly. Gus deserved a partner who was sure about him, and she wasn't sure she could give anything more than friendship right now. The most successful relationship Sirena had ever had was with the ten-piece cookware set she bought in college, which she still used when it was soup-making weather. Love was not on the menu for her anytime soon.

Forget that love had never been available for her to order.

She'd talk to him on Monday about their situation, but for now she had to decide whether she wanted to wear jeans or leggings. The choices never seemed to end.

The twang of a local band singing a Top 40 hit song echoed over the Farmers Square of the Harvest Festival. Booths were filled with bundles of carrots, bags of sweet potatoes, and plastic crates filled with tomatoes. Hay bales were arranged nearby for people to sit on and eat their food. Gus cradled his hot apple cider, the rich aroma of the cinnamon stick tickling his nose and calming his nerves. It would be a miracle if he finished his drink before it got cold.

Diane was in full artistic mode and looking for a few items for the upcoming story hour at the playhouse. When Di got into this mode, she zeroed in on one thing and would obsess over it for hours. She had called him this morning at the last minute, asking him to help her stay on track to get the fairy-tale props for Tuesday's story.

He glanced down at the massive pumpkin near his boots and sighed. "It doesn't take this long to pick out a single pumpkin," he said.

"I need the perfect one!" she yelled.

So far they had bought delicious red apples and green magic beans, and, of course, they were looking for the enchanted gourd. Gus looked to Diane in her black sweaterdress and sneakers, her arms gesturing to the pumpkin pile around them.

He should talk to her about something else to keep her from freaking out about the story props.

"How's the bridesmaid gig going?" he asked.

A shadow crossed her face. "It's fine. No one wants to wear the dress, but I had to remind them we're supposed to be there for the bride. Red is a good color! Chiffon is fine! We're going to pop in the photos! I'll look like a cute tomato for a few hours just to make her happy."

"I hope the bridal party's acting right," he said slowly.

Gus tried to remain cool, but he was concerned about whether Diane was taking on too much responsibility between wedding duties and playhouse work. He was ready to step in and help in any way she needed, whether to pay for her bridesmaid expenses or help her fix the puppet theater.

Diane gave him a side-eye. "Don't worry, bro. I've got this. What I don't have is a pumpkin that a faery godmother would love!"

"It's going to be okay. You'll find the right one." He hoped his voice was soothing.

She hunched toward the ground to get a better look at her selection. Determination glinted in her wide eyes. "I need the best one. Listen, this is *the* pumpkin for our story hour! I don't see a pumpkin fit for Cinderella. She wouldn't ride any of these gourds to Atlantic City, let alone the ball!"

Nope. He failed to soothe her. "You've told me several times."

Diane shot him a pleading look. "The babies need to believe that gourd is magical! It must be flawless. It needs to look pretty, like it fell out of a storybook! I want these kids to get so excited about our stories that they'll want to read them all at the library."

She'd be here all day if he didn't assist her. This item was the last one she needed before they could go and get lunch at Mimi's.

"Okay." Gus put down his apple cider cup on the booth's edge and repeated her qualifications. Magic. Flawless. Storybook pretty. He surveyed the collection around him, and his attention fell on a pumpkin to his left. Not too big, not too small, and round enough that one could imagine it transforming into a shimmering carriage. Bingo. Job done.

He picked it up and held it out to her. "Does this look magical enough?"

Diane inspected it and then glanced over his shoulder.

Her brow lifted. "Speaking of magical..." she sang.

Gus turned around. Surprise zinged in his chest once he saw Sirena. She stood a foot away in front of a pile of carrots, cradling a shopping basket in the crook of her arm. Her braids were loose around her lovely face. She wore a beige shirt underneath her burnt-orange jacket, and dark denim jeans. Gus studied how the jeans molded to her round, apple-shaped behind and showed off her zaftig body. Sirena put the dirt-flecked carrots in her basket, then looked in his direction.

"Hey." Her brown eyes seemed to dance with disbelief.

Gus clutched the pumpkin to his side. His mouth went dry. "Hey."

He didn't break eye contact with Sirena. The last time they'd seen each other, they...were kissing. A lot. Intensely. Time slowed to a crawl. The sound dropped out, and all he could hear was his heart beating frantically. Everything moved at half speed, but his blood was racing in triple time. Sirena blinked and everything went back to normal. She came over to him and stood close by. Close enough that he could tuck a braid behind her ear. Close enough for a kiss.

Her voice was quiet. "What are you doing here?"

"I was picking out a storybook-pretty pumpkin," he blurted out.

Sirena beamed at him. "That sounds sweet. I'm food shopping. Obviously."

Diane took the pumpkin out of his arm but Gus didn't move an inch. Sirena waved to Diane, who wordlessly slipped away to the cashier, leaving them alone by the pumpkin patch.

"What's for dinner?"

She frowned a little at her basket. "I don't know. I'm grabbing up whatever calls to me. I was thinking about making a carrot and apple soup."

"That sounds good."

"They have a sale on tomatoes, but I'm not sure I can eat all that soup myself."

"If you need help eating it, feel free to call me."

Sirena readjusted her shopping basket. It swung and knocked into Gus's drink, spilling it on the ground. *Aw, man.* He literally had had only a sip of his cider.

She winced. "I'm so sorry. Let me make it up to you."

He nodded. "Sure. I'd like that."

"Let me go pay for my stuff. I'll be right back."

Sirena went over to the cashier's table and stood in line with the other customers. Gus looked at Diane, who cradled her pumpkin to her side, a sold sticker taped to it. "So, what was that awkward attempt at talking?" Diane asked dramatically. "Are you two...dating?"

Gus frowned lightly. He didn't date. "We were just saying hello."

"Sure. Saying hello is what y'all call it nowadays."

"Don't start with me."

Diane gasped. "You should ask her to go to the wedding."

"I don't know if I'm going yet," he said. "I haven't decided."

He looked back at Sirena. An elderly man with a cane approached her and pointed to her basket. She spoke animatedly as she gestured to the items, as if she was talking to him about her dinner plans. Gus watched how her face lit up when she spoke about cooking and making meals. Who couldn't see that she had a spark?

He turned to Diane, who watched him with a grin.

"I'm headed out," she said.

His heart dipped. "You don't have to go." Gus was dropping the ball when it came to spending time with his little sister.

"I'd rather not be a third wheel." Diane cocked her head to the side. "Besides, it's about time you got all twitterpated."

He reeled back at her suggestion. The last time he'd seen that word, *twitterpated*, was in a sixty-year-old love letter from a soldier writing to his love. If Diane was breaking out that old-school word, then she saw something he couldn't or wouldn't name. She was implying that he wasn't merely crushing on her but that he was smitten. Sprung. Heartsick.

He didn't do that—fall in love instantly—anymore.

"It's nothing," he insisted.

"He doth protest—greatly." Diane gave him a wave and went off.

Gus waved back, then found Sirena, who was done checking out but still talking to the elderly gentleman, who was holding out a pen and small pad. She took the items from him and wrote a few short notes. It looked like she was writing down a shopping list for him. That was so sweet of her. Okay. So. It wasn't nothing. It was a crush. Crushes went away, right? But the longer Gus watched

Sirena scribble down a note and hand it over to the gentleman, the more he knew it was more than a crush. These feelings he had for Sirena weren't a simple crush; it was something more. Something exciting.

Something close to being twitterpated. He shut down that thought immediately. All this talk of fairy tales, faery godmothers, and princesses was feeding his overactive imagination, and he needed to keep his head on straight.

Sirena returned to Gus, holding her tote bag over her shoulder. She looked around, confused. "What happened to Diane and your pumpkin?"

Chapter Eleven

Gus explained Diane's sudden departure, then took Sirena over to the Weisz Market booth. She purchased not only his hot apple cider but also a cold cider for herself. They walked around the festival until they found a seating area surrounded by hay bales, pumpkins, and flowerpots. Gus sat down on a bale of hay. He gently patted the space next to him. Sirena eased herself down onto the seat, brushing up against Gus. Instead of the usual buzzing, his body hummed, which was a bit more pleasant. Maybe the kiss had helped him adjust to her magic.

"I'm impressed with Diane's work at the playhouse," Sirena said. "I used to love story hour when I was little."

Gus scratched his chin. "Let me guess. You probably love *Cinderella*."

"I don't. I'm all about the witch in *Hansel and Gretel*," she said.

Well, that was unexpected. He didn't think that she'd be a fan of the story of two kids who had to outlast a witch who wanted to have them for an evening snack. From what he had noticed, Sirena enjoyed working with the little ones who came in for Caregiver Corner on Thursday.

Sirena let out an impressed whistle. "Can you imagine the

potbelly stove that witch must have had? I'd love to have a kitchen like that."

Laughter welled up inside him. "You know there's more to that fairy tale."

She shook her head. "Yes, I'm aware, but in my story, the witch gives the house to the kids."

Gus laughed softly. "Okay. Keep going."

Sirena propped her hand on her chin. A flash of amusement entered her eyes. "The witch goes off to live in a cottage. She'll open a bakery and sell tea cakes to the villagers." She played with her bottle's label. Her voice grew soft, dreamy. "Or maybe she'll find a castle by the sea where she can live in peace."

She stared off into space, as if her mind was playing out the story for her. "That's a happily-ever-after I could get behind."

"I like how your story ends," he said.

Sirena sipped from her bottle. "I might write it down."

Gus drank his apple cider, letting the heated drink warm him up in the cool air. Flashes of last night flickered in his mind like a photo gallery. The confession. The note. The kisses. Since they were alone now, he figured it was a good time to talk about it.

"How are you feeling?"

Sirena sighed. "I'm better, thanks. I appreciate you listening to me vent last night."

"It was my pleasure."

"I never did get my root beer," she joked.

Gus winced. "Check the fridge when you come in on Monday. I might have bought a case or two for you."

Sirena smiled, and his heart nearly doubled in size. "Gus, you're going to spoil me."

"A deal's a deal," he said.

After Gus had dropped Sirena off at home, he'd driven over to the J. J. Newberry superstore in Meadowdale and bought her two large cases of organic root beer. He left them in the fridge to chill so they would be nice and cold for her. One kiss, and he was already running around trying to impress her. Maybe he could invite her to Jess's wedding and see where things went between them. *Stop. Slow down*, his head warned. *Act rational.*

Her smile faded a bit. Discomfort entered her eyes. "Last night was...nice, but I have a lot going on with me. I want to focus on my career, my magic, and my upcoming interview."

His face furrowed. "Okay."

"I don't want anything serious now. I only want to have—" Sirena cut herself off, as if trying not to hurt him with her next words.

"Fun," he supplied. His heart contracted a tiny bit. That was the deal he agreed to, but for an instant he forgot and got caught up in the moment.

She let out a big sigh of what sounded like relief. "Yes. Is that okay? I still want to have fun with you, but can we stay friends? If it's too much, we can call it off."

The man Gus used to be years ago would've loved this arrangement. No real commitment. No promises. But now he was done being a good time. He sought to be someone's forever. But he understood that she didn't want to lead him on and make him believe that there could be more between them.

"Consider it a simple kiss between friends," he said.

She blushed. There's nothing simple about the kiss he gave her last night, and he knew it.

"So, when can I expect this great dinner?"

Sirena's brow popped up to her hairline. "You still want me to cook for you? Even after everything I said last night, you're still game?"

"I'd be a fool not to try your food," he said. "I'm in if you're in."

"Thanks, Gus. I just remembered something about that carrot recipe." Sirena put down her bottle and took out a notebook and pen from her tote. "If I don't write it down, I'll forget it."

After jotting her note, she said, "I've got to prep and get a few more herbs, but I'll be ready by Friday. Are you free Friday night?"

He wanted Sirena to feel comfortable in her own space when she cooked. "I'm free. I'll come to your house."

"No, I'll meet you at the society." Sirena gasped and slapped her notebook as if she just remembered something else. "You know my sister Lucy?"

Gus nodded slowly. He and Lucy'd had a nice conversation about teaching with primary sources after Gus had asked about Sirena's qualifications.

"You've got a gem with Sirena," Lucy had said. "She's the smartest chef and witch you'll ever meet. Treat her right."

Gus had promised that he'd take care of Sirena, and he was a man of his word.

Sirena rubbed her hands together. "Well, Lucy's getting married, and she's looking for a location for the wedding and ceremony. I need to know more about renting out the society."

Gus went into steward mode and started reciting details. "Yes, members can rent out the first two floors and the library for events. Guests are responsible for cleaning and any damages, but the space is available on a first come, first served basis. All we need is a deposit to hold your date."

Sirena cheered. "Great. Check your email, and she'll fill you in on the details."

"I try not to check my emails on the weekend, but I'll take a look when I get home."

"Gus, you're my personal hero right now."

"We have some availability in December," he said.

Sirena grimaced. "I don't know if she's looking to get married that soon, but I'll let her know."

Sirena jotted down another note to herself in the pages, then closed it.

Gus glanced at the cover.

It was an illustrated painting of a woodland fox dancing in a forest. "You like foxes."

She touched the cover with her fingertips. "I've always liked them. I even did a report on them in third grade. I practiced for days, repeating my facts. Red foxes are omnivorous, have large ears that help them track prey, and dig dens in sand."

Gus studied her. "Red foxes are also monogamous," he added. "They seek their mate in the fall to keep them warm in the winter. Yeah, I know way too much about local animals."

She gave him an impressed glance. "I like it. You're telling me foxes have a cuffing season."

"Yes, but it lasts the rest of their lives," he said.

Cuffing season, from October to February, was the prime time when single folks looking to cuddle up during the colder months pursued a short-term situationship. Unfortunately, one effect of this season was that those who got cuffed up often got wifed up in the spring.

"It makes sense that humans do the same thing when the weather turns cold," Sirena admitted.

Sirena dropped her notebook in her shopper tote. Gus used to love to cuff up a cutie who was looking to get through the holiday season without commitments. Sirena wasn't wrong. It was natural to want someone to wait out the dark nights and spend the holidays with. Gus noticed that many of his friends were getting engaged or married during this time. Countless friends on social media started the new year with joyful engagement posts and sparkling rings. His thoughts flirted with the idea of being cuffed up to anyone. No, not anyone. Sirena. Would she throw a fuzzy blanket over them on the couch? Or would she want to get cozy by a roaring fireplace? Friends could get cozy.

"Who doesn't want to get nice and cozy with a warm body?"

He noticed a blush in her cheeks that made her look rosy.

"Tell me something I don't know," she said.

"I like cozy things," he said suddenly.

He was a big man who enjoyed the few moments of comfort he allowed himself. Good food. Good drink. Good company. Sirena sipped from her cider, trying to hide a smile behind her bottle. Gus merely stared, dazed once more by her beauty. It was impossible. Sirena trying to hide her smile was like trying to hide the moon with your hand. It was futile, to try to hide such natural beauty. "What else don't I know about you?" she asked.

"I collect coins. It's a hobby I shared with my grandpa."

"I assumed you'd collect something less—" Her face furrowed as she seemed to search for the correct word.

"Boring?" he offered.

She gave him a small grin. "No, I'd thought you'd collect something sillier. I was expecting you to collect magic potions, or baby dragons."

Gus sputtered, unable to hide his bewilderment. "Baby dragons?! Come on, now. I barely remember to feed Cinder. I couldn't imagine how to care for a dragon."

"I'm sure you have a book that can help you," she teased. "You're a Dearworth."

Gus bristled a little bit at her words. They did have a book in the library about dragon care, but he wasn't going to admit that out loud. His bewilderment increased once he heard those recognizable words. He knew what those words meant to his family, but what could they mean to someone as talented as Sirena?

She must have noticed the confusion play on his face because she spoke up. "When I say 'You're a Dearworth,' I mean you are extraordinary."

The air rushed out of his lungs. He couldn't respond even if he wanted to, but he just wanted to hear her talk. "People like you because you remind them of good times. People say to me, 'You're a Caraway; of course you have that homebound magic, of course you have a big heart.' They find comfort in the spells we cast and the magic we perform."

Gus sat there, taking in her words. He continued to get fan messages and emails from new magicians who wanted to talk about his craft. The guilt Gus felt for leaving his career and his fans eased a fraction as he considered what she told him.

Sirena took out the magician's piece from her purse. "I'm sure you want this back."

She held it out to him. He waved her off. "Keep it. I like knowing it's safe with you."

Sirena held it, then tucked it in her pocket. "How useful is a two-headed coin?"

"There are some things you don't leave up to fate," he said. That day by the balloon pop, Gus wanted to bend fate to his will and wanted to spend time with Sirena. Fate had been kind to him and now she was becoming a close friend of his. He was lucky to have Sirena in his life.

"You can start a coin collection if you want," he said.

Sirena snorted. "I'm terrible at collecting valuable things."

Gus gave her a sideways glance. He noticed the way she followed the rules, caring for the documents with the skill of a trained archivist. She didn't seem like the type of person who was careless with objects or people.

Sirena peered at him. "I told you I used to collect snow globes. I mean, my collection was only two globes, but they were mine. They weren't anything too special, but they captured special life moments."

He leaned closer to her. "Tell me about them."

Sirena sighed, and her eyes lit up. "Oh, one had a cityscape of New York, and another had a figure of the Statue of Liberty. I bought them when I moved to New York. I lived in a four-story walk-up and could only afford hot buttered rolls, but I was cooking in a real kitchen. I made it, you know. People came from around the world to taste my food. They asked for my menu."

"I hear you," he said. "I felt the same way when I became a headliner. My name was first on the marquee and people were coming to see my magic. I took a dozen pictures of that sign."

The light in her eyes dimmed. "Mama told me Nana was sick and needed a caregiver. I was in between jobs; I was feeling burned out and tapped out creatively. I volunteered to come home and help take care of Nana Ruth. My globes broke when I was packing up to move back to the Grove. I took it as a sign that I wasn't meant to keep anything pretty."

She finished her drink, then tossed the bottle into the nearby recycling bin. He wanted to lift up her spirit and see the light return to her.

"Let's play a game," he offered.

"Okay, but let's make it short. I've got a date with a bookstore."

Oh. His gut twisted into something ugly that he didn't like. Was he jealous?

"Lucy invited me to check out some new books," she added. "I don't want to be late."

He had no reason to be jealous, because—*knucklehead*—she wasn't his girlfriend.

"Let's play I Spy," she said.

He let out a laugh. "I haven't played that game in years."

"You know the rules?"

"Let me guess. Pick an object that everyone can see and give a clue with the letter, color, or an adjective that describes the object. If the other person can't guess, they can ask for a hint until they get it, but they lose a turn."

She gave him a thumbs-up. "You got it. Let's go for a few rounds."

The Harvest Festival was the perfect place to play the game since the space had dozens if not over a hundred things to spy.

Gus decided to go easy on her for now. "I spy with my eye something...orange."

Sirena pointed to the pile of pumpkins next to them. Gus shrugged. "Eh, there are a lot of orange things around here, but you're right."

"I spy...something blue," she said.

Oh. Gus glanced around the Farmers Square, scanning the booths for anything blue. His eyes landed on the Loops with Love booth filled with knitted and crochet hats, scarves, and beanies. The vendor, who had curly silver hair down to her shoulders, which popped against her pretty black skin, and wore a knitted sweater, gave them a friendly wave.

He waved back. "It's the blue knit caps for sale."

Sirena narrowed her eyes and smiled. "You got it, but I thought that was crochet. Anyway, I think that color would look good on you. It'll bring out your eyes."

Gus felt his cheeks glow under the compliment. He'd never had anyone talk about his eyes, but he'd take it. When he was performing, he wore every shade of the rainbow—every sequin and beaded outfit known on earth, just to stand out onstage. Now he was more drawn to tweeds and plaids that helped him blend into the background.

"I'll leave my merfolk to rock the blues and greens. Also, I have a weird time with hats. I let my hair grow out for the winter and it catches on any hats without a lining."

Sirena studied his hair closely. "I wish I had your curls."

"Thanks," he said.

"Your turn."

He was ready to turn up the heat. "I spy something…brown."

Sirena brightened. "Okay, now we're talking."

She scanned the booths, clicking her tongue in thought. A few minutes passed, and she made an annoyed sound. "Ahh—you win. Give me a letter!"

"Okay, it starts with a B."

She pointed with her chin to the Madame Mystic booth a few feet away. "It's a broom."

"You got it," he said.

Sirena blew out a breath. "I should've known. Witch. Broom. Don't tell anyone, but I like to use a power mop, too."

"Your secret is safe with me."

"I lose a turn. You go again."

Gus looked at Sirena. "I spy something beautiful," he said thoughtfully.

Her brown eyes swept over the booths and stands. Her brow furrowed in confusion as she continued to search for the item in question.

Sirena tapped her chin. "Where?"

Gus noticed something different about Sirena each time they met. She ran to his office to show him an old troll dip recipe or a sheet of pressed flowers, doing her usual excitement shimmy dance.

How she had fun with her braids, arranging them into different creative updos and styles every time he saw her. She loved wearing shades of red, from deep scarlet to bright cherry. How she made little gasps whenever she found a note or a picture that interested her. She was always concerned about him and the people she cared for.

Sirena fed his soul in small, gentle ways.

He stared at her, so she wasn't mistaken about who he was talking about.

Realization sparked in her eyes. She blushed, her cheeks turning a lovely pink.

Sirena took Gus by the arm. *What was another kiss between friends?* She looked at him, her stare unwavering. "I spy something enchanting," she said quietly.

Sirena hesitated, but then she moved in and kissed his cheek. Her lips felt soft and tender, like a stray leaf against his face. He held her for a quick, tight hug. Bliss strummed in his chest at their contact. He had waited so long to find a soul that moved in harmony with his and now he knew that he connected with hers.

Chapter Twelve

The Caraways strolled through the massive book aisles of the Rain or Shine Bookstore, scanning the tote bags and checking out the racks filled with bookish apparel. Cotton cobwebs decorated shoulder-high bookshelves, end displays, and tall shelves along the walls, which were filled with bestselling and local books. Ursula read the message on the large tote bag: " 'Readers are never alone. They always have books.' "

Lucy chuckled. "I like that."

Sirena eyed a sweatshirt that said "Read More Romance" with a couple embracing in a passionate kiss in front of a castle backdrop. Her lips still burned from their contact with Gus's cheek, and his sweet words played in her brain. Talking to him had conjured up her imagination and inspired her to revisit the curio shop to get that pretty snow globe after she left the Farmers Square. The shop owner informed her, to her disappointment, the globe had been purchased that morning. Next time, she'd get lucky and find another snow globe that spoke to her imagination.

Callie approached a bookseller. "Excuse me, where can I find your wedding planning guides?"

The bookseller, whose name tag read "Edwina," gestured over

to the bookshelf on the left wall. "Try the self-help and relationships section."

They went over to that area. Sirena read a book spine. *Friend, Lover, or Bedfellow? Label Your Relationship.*

The universe was speaking to her heart. Callie's annoyed grumble caught Sirena's attention.

Their baby sister needed her help. "Is there something you want to tell us, Callie?"

Callie spoke over her shoulder. "I need help with my client Gigi. She changed her mind again at our emergency meeting. She wants a tropical-themed wedding, but she doesn't like pineapple, mango, colorful flowers, or bright patterns."

Sirena made a stunned sound. "Does she know what tropical means?"

Callie squawked in fury. "Don't start. I'm already dealing with that new Enchanted Events emailing my clients and offering steep discounts. Those decorating elves are getting on my last nerve."

Ursula checked her phone. "Hey, y'all. I can't stay too long. We're running a full-moon sale. I've got to double-check whether we have enough candles. Xavier says we've got plenty, but I don't want to risk running out."

"How's that fae of yours?" Lucy asked.

Ursula's eyes crinkled and took on a faraway look. "He's great. He's taking a woodworking class. He's learning how to make a spice rack and next month he'll make us a bookshelf."

"Ugh, I'm totally not jealous and I'm happy for you," Sirena said teasingly. Seriously, she was a little jealous, but she knew what Ursula went through to get her fae prince. It was nice to see her cousin get her literal happily-ever-after.

Ursula gave Sirena a big hug. "You're next," she sang. "You're going to find your prince."

Sirena bit her tongue. Ursula lived the soft-princess life, but Sirena leaned into the witch-in-the-dark-woods life. She wasn't above eating mushroom melts and foraging for herbs in the community garden. Sirena didn't vibe with the fairy tales that had royalty and happy endings but liked the ones with charms and dangerous magic. She might not find her prince, but she'd settle for a rogue who would whisk her away on his horse.

Would she ever find that storybook type of love?

Callie's voice interrupted Sirena's thoughts. "Pause the prince talk, fam! Start looking for wedding advice books. I'm one bad cake tasting away from losing this client and I can't afford to lose this job."

Poe came over to the shelf with a wide smile on their face. They were dressed in a button-down shirt covered in bats and light blue jeans. "Hey, Caraways."

Everyone returned Poe's greeting.

"How's business?" Sirena asked.

Their face took on a light of pride. "Business is good. We're starting up our book club in January. Sales are strong, and we've been given an award from the Independent Bookstore Society."

"That's great," Sirena said.

"We've been talking about opening a second location in Meadowdale to serve the college students, but..." Poe winced. "Rent's not cheap."

"I'm sure you can get a small business grant to help out with expenses," Ursula said. "The chamber of commerce might be able to hook you up with resources. Email me."

Poe nodded. "Thanks, Sula. I'd appreciate that."

"Poe, are these all the books you have on relationships?" Callie asked, her words tinged with exasperation. "I don't see the book I need, which came out this week."

Poe grimaced. "I'll double-check the back stock, but these are all the books we have in-store. It is cuffing season, and these books have been flying off the shelves."

The words "cuffing season" kicked off an image of Gus sitting next to her in the Farmers Square. His cologne, spicy and rich, like leather-bound books, loitered in her senses. His beard was oiled and neatly clipped. His voice echoed in her mind. *They seek their mate in the fall to keep them warm in the winter.* There was something so appealing about the word "mate"; she felt a sense of restlessness about being uncuffed.

Callie glared at the shelf. "I don't have time to drive to the Seaview Square Mall to get this freaking book. I'm meeting with Gigi and Dorian, the groom, tomorrow night."

"Why don't you just ask her what's going on?" Lucy asked.

Callie's mouth twisted upward. "I did. She said she hired me to be her planner, not to pretend to be her friend. I can't force Gigi to tell me what's going on with her."

"You could give her a special tea to loosen her up," Ursula said.

Sirena turned to her. "You're not talking about dosing her with a truth potion."

Ursula's jaw dropped a fraction. "No, cuz. I'm talking about making a special calming blend. One part each of chamomile, rosehips, and lemon balm. Shake, combine, and serve two table-spoons per cup. Planning a wedding is *super* hectic. You can't be too bossy, or you'll be called a monster. If you don't make decisions, you'll be seen as a flake or uninterested. Gigi needs someone to help her make decisions. Give her a big cup of tea and listen."

Callie peered at Ursula, impressed. "Are you sure you don't want to come work with me?"

"Thanks, but I'm happy where I am. I'll leave the planning to you."

Poe jumped into the conversation. "I have a plan. I'm getting married by a Prince impersonator."

Lucy perked up. "Oh, are you engaged?"

Poe shook their head. "I'm single all the way, but I'm prepared. You never know when a billionaire might need you to fake a sham marriage to claim his inheritance. One bed, one stormy night, and *bam*—you've got your happily-ever-after."

Poe's declaration sent the Caraways into a fit of bubbly laughter. Theo, their business partner, came from the back room, carrying a box. He placed it on the display table and glanced around at their smirking and giggling faces. "Do I even want to know?"

"We're talking about marrying desperate billionaires," Poe said. "Do you know any?"

"No, but I do know a few cash-strapped graduate students who have big feelings about the Gothic." Theo, dressed in a B horror movie T-shirt and jeans, took out a box cutter from his back pocket and cut open the box.

He pulled out some hardcovers and placed them on the table in a neat stack. "Sounds like Poe's been reading romance again."

"Again? I never stopped." Poe shot a cunning look at Theo. He held back a grin as he said, "Who's getting hitched?"

Lucy pointed to herself. A flash of surprise went over Theo's face, but he schooled it back into place. "I thought you and Alex were already married."

Lucy gave an uncomfortable look. "No, we're still just engaged."

"Sorry, my fault. Y'all have that whole 'we've been together for, like, ten years' energy."

Sirena moved closer to Lucy, who had tensed at Theo's well-meaning words. How many times had Lucy heard the same sentence repeatedly over the last year and a half?

"That special energy just means that you're probably soul-mates," Ursula said confidently. "There's a chance you've known each other across decades or even centuries. I bet you were married to Alex back in the Byzantine Empire with the blessings of the emperor."

Lucy sighed. "Thanks for the support, Sula. I'm trying to get married in this lifetime."

Sirena raised a single brow at Ursula. "You believe in soul-mates."

All these years, she hadn't heard her cousin express any belief in the soul connection idea. She thought she knew everything about Ursula, but this information was a little surprising.

"I live above a psychic shop with my boyfriend who's a fae prince who talks to plants. I'm a whole crystal witch. Of course I believe in soulmates. Don't you?"

Good question. Her mind struggled to answer it. She knew magic existed because she'd been practicing it since she had hair barrettes. Sirena had heard the legend of the Caraway soul click, but she thought it was just a family fairy tale. She'd had flings and romances, but she'd never felt her soul connect with any of her lovers or boyfriends. Maybe her soul was meant to be alone, like that single sock in her dresser without its mate.

Lucy took out her phone and checked the screen. She growled. "Mom's texting about invitations. We don't even have a location! We're this close to throwing up balloons in the backyard. I emailed Gus, but I haven't heard from him yet."

A flash of guilt went through Sirena when she heard Lucy's words. She'd been so busy daydreaming and thinking about Gus that she had forgotten to update Lucy about the rental conversation.

Theo shared a private look with Poe, who gave a small nod of support.

He faced Lucy. "I know we're not fancy, but you can get married in the store."

Poe grunted in agreement. "Yes, you can. You did such a fabulous job designing Rain or Shine, the least we can do is offer our space. It would be our honor to have it here."

A sense of warm gratitude filled Sirena at their selfless offer. No wonder the bookstore was so successful; the owners welcomed people into their space wholeheartedly.

Lucy let out a slow breath. "Thank you so much, but we can't fit everyone in here. Mama Dwyer wants to invite fifty merfolk to the ceremony alone."

Theo nodded. "I get it."

"But we do need wedding favors, and I'd love to buy all my guests gifts from your store," Lucy said. "Can y'all help me select a few budget-friendly options?"

Theo clapped his hands. "Leave it to me. I've got you."

Poe coughed. "No, we've got you."

Poe and Theo went to the other side of the store, where the bookish merch and items were neatly arranged.

"Why don't we ask Whitney to host the wedding?" Ursula

suggested. "She loves to plan." Whitney was Xavier's faery god-mother, who lived in a Gilded Age mansion on the edge of the Grove. Sirena had only seen pictures, but the house, with its wide rooms and crown molding, looked like a glamorous *Architectural Digest* video.

Lucy frowned. "We'd have to decorate the whole space. Parking would be an issue."

Ursula winced. "Oh, right. I don't even want to know how many flowers you'll need."

"Do you know how much a wedding costs in New Jersey?" Lucy asked.

"I remember," Ursula muttered. She gave a number that made Sirena's eyes water. That was a lot of money, like down-payment-on-a-house money.

Ursula gave Lucy a quick hug. "I'm going to repeat my advice to you. Make a cup of tea, get your favorite snack, and talk to Alex about what you want and what you can afford."

Ursula kissed her cousins and left them in the self-help aisle. Callie's phone went off loudly in the store. The ringtone sounded like a warning klaxon.

"It's Gigi." Callie took the phone call outside. Lucy and Sirena were the only ones left in the aisle.

Lucy spoke in a hushed voice. "I spoke to Alex after breakfast. Don't say anything, but we're pushing back the wedding."

Sirena's heart ached. "Oh, sis. For how long?"

Lucy continued, her voice on the edge of irritation. "We're thinking of pushing it back another six or nine months. We've hit a few money bumps, but we're fine. I mean, most couples are engaged for a year or more, so it's not unusual. We'll get back on track."

"I thought you were saving up," Sirena said.

"There's barely anything in our wedding fund. I got only partial salary when I was on leave. Alex is waiting on a few large payments from his freelance jobs, but these companies take their time to pay him. We own the house, but there are still unexpected costs."

"I can imagine." The century-old Caraway house was filled with love and familial magic, but the roof and rain gutters needed constant, expensive care. Sirena had dipped into savings to cover house repairs and sudden issues, and she was aware that Lucy and Alex had similar house troubles. The repair van seemed to be constantly parked outside their home.

Lucy fiddled with her engagement ring, twisting it around her finger with her thumb.

"One of the gnomes, Half-Pint, heard the septic tank acting up, so we had to get that fixed. Then we found the pipes were rotting. Do you know how much copper pipes cost?! Oh, I wish I could wiggle my nose and *bam*, make everything perfect, but I'm not that powerful."

Lucy shot Sirena a pained look that hurt her down to her bones. Her wonderful big sister had gotten everything that she wished for, but it seemed that she was struggling to find balance. Sirena was going to help Lucy, come hawthorn or hurricane water.

Sirena nudged her shoulder. "Listen. I ran into Gus, and the historical society is available to be rented out in December, but you have to book it now."

Lucy's eyes bugged out. "Today's October eighth."

"Trust me, I know the date." Sirena only had twenty-three

days to fix her life, but she could at least do what she could to help Lucy.

"You want me to plan a whole wedding in less than ninety days?" Lucy said these words in a horrified tone as if Sirena suggested that Lucy feed the gnomes right before a full moon. No one fed the gnomes during that crazy lunar time unless they wanted their house painted lime green and their lawn ornaments arranged in erotic positions.

Sirena tented her hands together. "It can be done. What's your budget?"

Lucy rocked back and forth. "Hopes and dreams is our current price range. Seriously, we have enough money for a nice vacation but not enough for a big wedding."

"Make it a Freya Grove elopement!" Sirena insisted.

"That's not what an elopement is!" Lucy hissed. "You can't just change the meaning of words whenever you want. If we're eloping, then we'd have tickets to Las Vegas and a honeymoon suite. You can't plan to elope; it's spontaneous! It's romantic!"

Callie popped up from behind a bookshelf. "Did I hear the word 'elope'?"

"Shh," Lucy hissed. She waved her sisters toward the front door and took them outside the bookstore. "Our sister is trying to convince me to plan a December wedding."

Callie glanced up at the sky briefly, then faced Lucy. "We can make it happen. I'll make it happen for you, but you've got to let Alex know what you're thinking."

"Call him," Sirena said. "Now."

Something in Sirena's voice must have gotten to Lucy, because she gave her an alarmed stare. Lucy pulled out her phone and dialed Alex's number. Callie and Sirena moved away to give Lucy some privacy. There was a hushed conversation, but after a few minutes, Lucy hung up the phone.

"So, what did he say?"

Lucy appeared spellbound, as if she'd been hit with a faery godmother's wand.

"It looks like you're getting a new binder, Cal! We're getting married in December!"

Sirena let out a grateful squeal and hugged Lucy tightly. The wedding countdown was on.

It was official.

Sirena was obsessed with everything about the Saybrooke journal. The cover, the table of contents, and even the drawings gave her pause and made her trill with glee. She'd been reading so long in the library chair that her butt was getting numb. The journal was smaller than their family spellbook, and the pages were covered in different spills, bits of flowers, and pasted-in items.

It was stuffed with a lifetime of knowledge about kitchen witchery, from making burnt food poppets to sauces that elevated dishes. Sirena stopped on the page titled "Sauces, Dips, and Blends," checking out the possible combinations. Ooh, there was a recipe that used clover honey. A meal of shore croquettes with that honey sauce would absolutely impress the Lighthouse hiring manager. Sirena took out her notebook from her tote. She wrote down the list of ingredients, making a note: *Add some spice to give the sauce some oomph, black pepper, or peppercorn.* Her words seemed to sparkle and glow. Hope buoyed her spirits.

Ever since Nana passed away, Sirena felt isolated in her craft, since she was the only practicing kitchen witch in the family. The rules helped guide her within her family, but Sirena yearned for more information to help reignite her spark. Reading Ms. Saybrooke's recipes gave Sirena a deep sense of connection with a fellow kitchen witch that crossed over time. There were special recipes in this journal that she had only heard about from Nana Ruth. A mixture of grief and anger churned through Sirena the more she read the cookbook. Her talent, generosity, and passion about keeping a hearth and cooking were etched on each page. If Juliette Saybrooke were born a hundred years later and had had half the chances Sirena did, the Food Network might be plugging her next cookbook. She deserved more than what the world would allow her to achieve when she was alive.

The library door creaked opened, and Gus leaned inside. "It's closing time."

She made a face. "What? I literally just got here."

Gus stepped into the library and stood next to her table. "You've been here six hours."

She glanced down at her phone and pressed the screen. Yikes, it was seven o'clock. She wasn't done yet. There was so much left to look at in the journal, and she was still finalizing her demo meal. Sirena had received an email from Lighthouse informing her that she'd have access to their staple pantry. It was nice to know she wouldn't have to bring salt and pepper, but she was responsible for bringing her other food and supplies.

"Have you ever thought about writing a cookbook?" he asked.

Sirena reeled back. "No. Why?"

Gus eyed her. "Why not? You've got a whole stack of notebooks and recipes in the society that you can use. They've all fallen into the public domain, so you can amend and adapt them if you're interested."

"Magic Meals in Thirty Minutes," she quipped. It did sound appealing, but that wasn't why she was reluctant. No shade to cooks and chefs who published cookbooks, but she wasn't ready for that step. Sirena wanted to see if she still possessed the talent to run and rule a professional, award-winning kitchen. She was destined to get her perfect job this time around.

The perfect job would keep her in the Grove and keep her close to her family.

Everything was going to work out as long as she followed her plan.

"Thanks, but I'm going to stay focused on the interview," she said.

Gus was quiet, but Sirena noticed that his mouth had tightened, as if he was holding back a response. He did that a lot, holding his tongue whenever he wanted to add more to the conversation. As if he didn't want to offend her.

"Say it, Gus. I can take it," she said.

He regarded her with a discreet glance. "You have the talent it takes to write a cookbook. Keep your options open."

"I'll do that. Thanks." She touched the journal with a light hand. "I wish I could take this book home."

That wish wasn't to be granted, because if Shadow accidentally peed on or damaged the journal, Sirena would probably change her name and leave the Grove. She'd already been so careless with her recipes; she didn't dare be careless with someone else's life work.

Gus suddenly had a funny expression on his face. Was there something else he wanted to tell her?

"Well, you could stay the night," he offered.

"Are you inviting me to sleep over?" she asked playfully.

Gus blinked deliberately, as if his brain shut down and then turned back on. "Um...what...um...I mean is—"

Sirena stood up. "I'm joking. I've never seen a magician short-circuit before."

Gus drew in a breath, then let it out slowly. "I open the library for college students to come study at night during midterms and finals. I keep a sleeping bag just in case anyone wants to camp out here. Most times they end up staying up and studying."

Sirena eyed the stiff-looking fainting couch in the corner. Her back was already aching just at the idea of sleeping on that pretty but uncomfortable furniture. "I see."

"I *do* have an extra room upstairs," he said.

Hold up. "You live upstairs."

He nodded. "The historical society steward position includes living accommodations and a living stipend."

Sirena tossed up her hands. She motioned to the library walls filled with priceless books.

"Okay. Who pays for this place? I mean, this house must cost, like, a million dollars, and the society always hosts the Founders' Day Festival every year. Does the society have a secret money tree somewhere, or a werewolf billionaire, or what?"

Gus narrowed his eyes at her. "Yes and no."

"There's really a werewolf billionaire?!" Sirena's jaw dropped. Callie was right.

There was a trace of authority in his voice as he spoke. "The Grove was founded by Chance Bridlewood, a business tycoon and one of the richest men of the Gilded Age. He earned his fortune through lucky investments. He was the son of vaudeville performers and didn't forget his roots. During a visit to the Jersey Shore, he bought five thousand acres where vaudeville entertainers could live. Magical beings heard about the Grove and settled down here. The Grove has been a place where magic has thrived for the last century. No one here is afraid of what goes bump in the night because we're the ones who revel in the dark."

His voice dropped to a husky whisper. He spoke with such confidence that Sirena found it hard to breathe. Desire gripped her throat. Was it just her or did he get hotter when he talked about history and magic?

She gave her head a tiny shake. *Chill out, lady.*

"I didn't hear anything about a money tree or a werewolf," she said lightly.

He gave her a patient look. "I'm getting there. Chance and his wife, Hester, didn't have any children, so he bequeathed his entire fortune to the citizens of the Grove. In his will, he wrote that he wanted his fortune to be a tree that could provide shade for those who needed rest. The historical society was founded and continues to use the money to celebrate Chance's vision of fun, magic, and amusement. It was part of the original charter that the steward would live in the society building. The top floor is a fully furnished apartment that is maintained by the steward."

Sirena quickly packed up her bag and slung it over her shoulder.

"Why are we here when there's a couch we could be sitting on? Can we go up there?"

"If you'd like," he said.

She followed Gus to a hidden stairwell that brought them

into the apartment. *Hello, comfort.* The apartment had a spacious living area, a standard kitchenette, and a full bathroom. There were two bedrooms, one large and one small, toward the back of the building. The walls were decorated with framed posters of old movies and one sheets from classic films. A luxe plum couch was positioned in front of a television and stereo system.

Sirena pointed to the stairway. "Do you ever go to the turret?"

Gus said, "I go there all the time. It's accessible through the door in the corner. You can see the entire neighborhood and all the way to the ocean."

"It must be quite the view," she said.

"If you're feeling up to it, I'll take you up there later," he proposed. "It's a nice place to watch the moonrise. You can stay if you like."

She let herself imagine that they'd climb up into the turret with hot apple ciders and watch the stars come out. Sirena let that brief fantasy disappear from her mind. She was here for business, not cuddles and cider. Besides, she'd asked him if they could stay friends, and she didn't want to cross that line with him. *Get your mind right.*

"Thanks for the offer to stay. I don't have anything to sleep in."

Gus gave a short nod. "I got you."

He went into his bedroom and came back holding a long nightshirt covered in dancing hardback books. He handed it to her. She held back a squee. The pattern was so adorable, and the nightshirt smelled of cologne and Gus. There was a good chance he wouldn't be getting the nightshirt back when she left.

As comfortable as the shirt felt, she still needed to check the size. She, like many Caraway women, was generously shaped with hips, legs, and plenty of body. To paraphrase a certain song, she was thicker than a Snickers ice cream bar on a summer day.

Sirena checked the tag and made a frustrated sound. Her stomach dipped. It was too small, but she might be able to make it work—if she didn't sit down or drink anything. She didn't want to risk having an accident and end up flashing her panties to Gus. Nope. No.

"I don't think it'll fit," she said.

His touch was firm as he gently took the nightshirt from her. "Let me check the size."

Gus held it up and shook it three times, and in a blink the fabric expanded. He handed it back to her. She held the new nightgown to her chest, a trace of his magic still lingering on the fabric.

"Now it's perfect," he said, peering at her for a moment. Sirena held the nightgown against her body, as if trying to shield herself from those burning eyes.

"Feel free to keep that shirt," he said.

She murmured a thank-you to him.

Gus pointed Sirena to an open door on the far wall. "You can change in the bathroom when you're ready. Make yourself at home."

Gus was inviting her to stay in his space. She wanted to do something for him and felt brave enough to attempt a grilled cheese sandwich. "Have you eaten yet?"

He made a *nah* face. "Let's order out. I know you want to get back to reading the journal. I'll be in my study finishing up my work. Let's keep it chill."

"Okay," she said. She could do this. Friends stayed over at friends' houses all the time. It wasn't a big deal.

"Let me know if there's anything else that you want or need."

Her eyes flashed to his lips. *I know what I want.* Everything pulsed at the idea of kissing him again. She took a mental step back, reminding herself of what was at stake. *You don't have time to mess around with Gus. Land the job, get your life right, then ask him out.*

Do everything in the right order.

Chapter Thirteen

Gus was a whole fool if he thought he could be chill with Sirena. He thought he could be fine with her staying over at his apartment and examining the Saybrooke journal. So what that they kissed at the boardwalk and almost kissed again at the Harvest Festival? It was fine. They were friends. He was going to be as cool as an iced tea on a hot spring day when it came to Sirena.

They ordered pizza from Rapunzel's, half pepperoni and half veggie, and watched a silly but scary television episode of *The Twilight Zone.* True to his word, Gus returned to his study once they finished eating dinner and wrote the quarterly newsletter for the historical society. His mind kept drifting to the idea of Sirena sitting on his couch. Drinking his tea. Watching reruns on his TV. He was so distracted by the thought of her, it took him an hour to write a single page. It wasn't until the grandfather clock chimed that Gus realized he'd worked until midnight. He expected to come back to a darkened apartment, like he'd done countless times before. But instead, Gus found the living room light on and Sirena slumbering on the couch. She held the journal against her chest, her eyes shut and her body curled protectively over the book. Awe settled deep in his heart as he watched her slumber. Her braids fell over her face, and her body rose and fell in a steady rhythm. All his chill flew out the window when he realized the truth.

She'd tried to stay up and wait for him to come back.

Affection welled in his chest. She'd left the light on for him.

He eased the book from her hands and placed it on the table, then pulled out a blanket from the closet and draped it over her.

"Dream sweet dreams," he whispered softly. Her mouth twitched upward as if she heard him in her sleep, and she settled deeper into the couch.

Hours later, Gus was still awake and feeling absolutely foolish.

How had he missed Sirena Caraway all this time? Before the Harvest Festival, they had only politely spoken to each other. Her head was always tucked down in her phone or in serious thought, disregarding the ghouls and creatures living around her. She was on her grind, working or manning the Shore Shack on the boardwalk, flipping burgers and delivering crispy fries to visitors. But something had changed within him, and his eyes were finally noticing the witch he'd known for years.

Gus shut his eyes and forced himself to get some sleep. May the cooking gods be with him. He was going to wake up early and make her breakfast.

Gus got up early, but Sirena was already up, reading the journal while scribbling down notes. They exchanged morning greetings and he retreated into the kitchenette with his phone clutched in his hand. Hopefully, Gus had enough food in his apartment to make a decent meal for Sirena. Despite his best efforts, Gus had failed to buy her the snow globe, but he could at least attempt to make scrambled eggs.

Of course, he couldn't make scrambled anything because his milk was expired.

He opened the search engine on his phone. *Save me from myself, internet.*

After a quick search, Gus found a sausage, egg, and cheese sandwich recipe blog post on his phone. He scrolled down past the cute but long story the blogger wrote about why they loved this certain sandwich.

"Is that a tablespoon or a teaspoon of sage?" he muttered, his thumb moving over the screen.

Eventually he found the complete recipe, read over the ingredients, and began gathering them on his tiny kitchen counter. He was going to pull this breakfast off. *You've got this.*

Sirena's voice called out from the living room, but her voice was muffled.

"Say that again, Si," he said.

She repeated herself, louder this time. "Have you ever eaten pomegranate seeds?"

Gus thought for a second, then responded, "No, but I'm open to trying them."

She answered him with an interested grunt. He stood in the kitchen doorway. Sirena sat on the couch with the journal and her notebook on her lap. Her braids were swept up into a messy bun, and her face was furrowed in thought.

"I'm making a quick sausage, egg, and cheese sandwich. How does that sound?"

Sirena looked up from the journal. "That sounds great."

"Salt and pepper with a dash of mayo, everything on it." He mimicked the common response that he heard whenever he ordered his sandwich from Lee's Bodega.

She smiled. "No mayo for me, please. Thank you."

Gus gave a thumbs-up and went back into the kitchen. He put the frozen sausage patties on a plate and popped them into the microwave. While the microwave hummed to life, he parted the English muffins and put them in the toaster. His skin tingled as he moved about the kitchen assembling the parts of the sandwich. The space filled with the aroma of pungent spices and heated bread. Gus cracked the eggs and fried them in a pan, waiting for the edges to get crispy.

He heard the squeak of the couch springs, then shot a glance over to Sirena standing in the kitchenette's doorway. He yanked his attention back to the sizzling pan.

Gus didn't want to accidentally burn the food because he was too busy gawking at her. That nightgown graced her curves and fell to her ankles.

She breathed in and sighed. "It smells good."

Gus pulled out a chair at the table, quickly returning over to the stove. He placed a few slices of cheese on the eggs, turned off the burner, then put on the lid. The chair creaked as she sat down.

He faced her. "You were up late."

Sirena nodded. "I was reading about stitching a dream pillow, and then I was knocked out. How did you sleep?"

His brain answered. *Terribly. I couldn't stop thinking of you.* "I slept great," he lied. "How about you?"

Sirena looked down at her lap.

"I had a strange dream."

"You can tell me if you want," he said.

"Eh—I dreamed that I was cooking at the Shore Shack, but I was butt naked. I wasn't wearing an apron. I was getting a full-body tan."

Hmm. "What were you cooking?"

She looked up at him through her lashes. "I was grilling foot-long hot dogs on a flat top. I broke, like, all the sanitary codes."

Great. Just great. Now Gus had another image of Sirena in his head that would keep him up at night.

He watched a slight frown play on her lips. "Something's on your mind."

"I know I'm stressed out about work when I dream about cooking naked," she said.

"How many times have you had this dream?" he asked, trying not to burst into flames.

He wanted to know the answer, but then he didn't want to know the answer. Friends talked about their odd dreams.

"I've had this dream several times but never about a former job," she said. "I've got a menu, I've finished my shopping, but something's missing. It's too early for me to have stress dreams about this interview."

"You shouldn't stress out too much."

"Tell that to my brain," she teased.

Gus put on his magician's cap and thought about her dream critically.

"I'm not a dream expert, but maybe your intuition is trying to help you discover what you're missing. You dreamed about cooking at the Shore Shack. Tell me about your favorite day there."

Sirena huffed. "My favorite day was the day I got fired."

Gus blinked and waited. He had to hear this story.

"It was the last weekend of the summer. A half an hour after we opened the shack, the freezer broke down and threatened to spoil all our food. Our manager was freaking out and scared to call the owner. We couldn't get in contact with the owner, so I made the decision to cook everything. I made every type of burger I could think of that day. I made an upside-down burger with onion rings and pickles."

"What about a fried egg and black bean burger?" Gus chuckled.

"It was on the menu," she said.

Her voice went soft as she lost herself to the memory. "We turned up the radio and had a dance party on the boardwalk. Customers paid what they wished, and we sold out every single item. I got interviewed for the *Freya Grove Press* and we managed to make a lot of money. It was a fun time." Sirena let out a rough breath. "I wish the story ended there."

"I hope the owner got down and kissed your feet," he said.

She shook her head. "No, he screamed at me. He said there was a reason I was just a loser cook and he was a successful business owner. I was told I wasn't special, and I was replaceable."

Anger tightened his gut.

"He fired me," Sirena said. Her smile turned dangerously sharp. "The joke was on him. All that press and attention brought in customers who wanted to try my food. He begged me to come back, and I asked him why he would need help from a loser cook."

Gus nodded; a sense of satisfaction filled his chest.

"Tell me you turned him down."

Sirena shrugged. "I needed the check. I worked the rest of the summer; then I moved over to Night Sky. Gwen needed help, so I offered to work for her."

"Why don't I remember this party happening?" he asked.

"You were probably busy at a history conference," Sirena said. "We didn't really know each other well back then."

Gus took her in. His plaid blanket was wrapped around her shoulders, and Cinder wound around her bare feet. His heart drank her in, and his chest lightened at the sight of her. She reminded him of a domestic goddess, soft and warm and looking at home in his apartment.

"You're getting your spark back. I can see it when you talk about cooking."

She lowered her head. "I really want this job."

"You've got this, Chef Caraway," he said, without a doubt.

The microwave beeped. Gus took out the warmed sausage platter and assembled two sandwiches, making sure to put the right amount of salt and pepper on them, and placed each one on a separate plate. He brought them over to the table and presented the meal to her with a small flourish. "Ta-da."

She rubbed her hands together. "It looks great. Thank you for this."

"Hopefully it tastes good," he said.

Sirena picked up her sandwich and took a bite. As she chewed, a muted, seemingly pleased sound came out of her mouth. Gus didn't eat, but rather waited for her to finish tasting. "I know it's not as good as your cooking, but I think I can throw down a little."

Sirena tasted it purposefully, as if trying to figure out the ingredients. "What's in this?"

He had done his best to stick to the recipe. "I don't think I added anything extra. We've got ketchup and hot sauce if you want it."

She took another bite and swallowed. "It's perfect. I can taste salt and pepper in the egg. There's sage and brown sugar in the sausage, but there's something else. It's subtle, but it's there."

Sudden realization lit her face. "I got it! You put your foot into this. My compliments to the cook."

Sirena finished the sandwich with a flourish. He hadn't put his foot into it, but his heart and a bit of his soul. If she was able to taste it, then he had to be careful to hide his feelings for her. She hadn't asked for his heart, but he was literally serving it to her on a platter. Maybe he added too much emotion. Next time he'd know better.

He wanted there to be a next time with Sirena.

"I've got a surprise for you!" Ma sang.

Dread pooled in his gut. Gus eased into the leather chair in his study, wanting to be comfortable for what Ma had in store for him. Ma was on speakerphone, chatting about the impending trip to London and what illusions she was performing, when she interrupted herself.

"What's the surprise?"

"I found you a wedding date," she said.

Gus sat up in his chair. "I said I'd take care of it."

"You were taking too long!" Ma groaned.

"I haven't said I'm going," he said.

Ma let out an outraged squawk.

"You have to go! It'll look strange if Diane and Zeke go but you don't attend."

Gus felt like yanking his beard out hair by hair.

"How will it look? You'll look bitter, or hung up on your ex," Ma pressed him further.

Okay. So, Zeke, who was once his close friend, was going to the wedding, but Gus wasn't. It would look weird, but he'd spent so much time concerned about what other people thought about him that he was exhausted. *Who cares what anyone else thinks about you?*

He took a second to answer that question. Everyone would care about him not being there. Jess and Igor had their reality show, which would be filming at the wedding and capturing the guests. Millions of people would rewatch this wedding episode and notice that he wasn't there. The rumor mill would take off, and the celebrity bloggers would get online and speculate about why *he* wasn't there. Attention would be taken away from Jess and Igor's wedding. Gus didn't want that to happen to either of them. His resolve folded like a piece of paper. He'd already taken so much time and focus from Jess in the past; he didn't want to take more time from her and her future.

"I don't need a date," he ground out. "I can find my own."

A cheer echoed over the speakerphone. "Oh! So, you're going now."

His head pounded. He didn't miss the note of smug happiness in Ma's voice. Gus picked up his phone and opened the internet browser. He searched for Jess and Igor's wedding site and found the RSVP tab. Before Gus could think, he quickly entered his name and clicked off that he was bringing a plus-one.

"In for a penny, in for a pound," he muttered.

"Oh, you'll have so much fun! You won't regret it, Gus," Ma insisted.

Too late. Gus pressed enter and officially submitted his response. He was now an underling of fate.

Ma continued talking on about wearing matching colors or chipping in for a large wedding gift. Gus half-listened to her debating whether to wear maroon or ruby. He was going to buy Jess and Igor the second biggest item on their wedding registry. Screw it. Gus was going to buy them two items and monogrammed towels.

"Remember to play to the cameras," she reminded him.

Gus grumbled noncommittally. Ma said goodbye and ended the conversation.

Who was going to be his plus-one? He recalled what Diane had said earlier: *You don't have one friend who could be your date?*

His brain conjured up an image of Sirena, shimmying and shaking her generous hips in time with the music. How good would it feel to sway with her in his arms? To watch her lip sync to the pop songs and cackle with his sister about a private joke? To see how freaking sexy she'd look dressed in crimson red. *Sirena's your friend. A friend you kissed and can't stop dreaming about—and wanting.*

Gus pressed his hands to his forehead, an impending headache building behind his eyes. There were going to be cameras everywhere at the wedding, picking up his every action and every mistake. He was completely screwed. He wouldn't be able to hide his feelings for Sirena. Distress snaked through his chest and slowed his breath. He was going right back into the manufactured world he'd left years ago. It was the filming of *Dealing with the Dearworths* that pushed his relationship with his family to the breaking point. His extended family were reality TV royalty, with their dramatic and funny antics. They played off their real spells as mere stage illusions and tricks, much to the entertainment of their fans.

Whenever he went to cast a small spell, Ma stopped Gus and gestured to the film crew, who were switching out their batteries.

"Save it for them," she'd whisper to him out the side of her mouth.

He made sure to play it up once the cameras were on. During the divorce proceedings, Gus couldn't pull a rabbit out of a hat or saw a lovely assistant in half. The thrill was gone. Ma gently encouraged him to work through the heartbreak to become a better performer. Gus stopped playing to the camera and became "boring." He dressed in gray tones, gave one-word answers, and read thick nonfiction books that could double as door stops.

He was too tired to pretend that he was happy and having fun. Once, when they were alone, after a completely dull filming session, Ma spun on him.

"You weren't giving us anything," she shouted. "I could hear people turning off their screens. You're not getting any screen time because you're just so...so...*boring*."

"Is that such a bad thing?" he asked.

She dismissed his question with a flick of her hand. "Dearworths can't be boring. My son isn't boring. I need you to be magical," Ma pleaded. "They're going to cut you out of the show."

Ma had been concerned that his cousin Walt would be given his storylines. Gus wanted to become the son she needed for the show, but he couldn't maintain that illusion. He didn't want to work; he wanted to sit down and rest for once. Gus listened as Ma spoke about how the producers wanted to see something truly exciting, or they would stop filming him.

Gus sat there silent, unable to think of a single spell. It was time for him to go.

He managed to reply through stiff lips. "I don't want to put on a show."

Her face fell. "I don't believe you."

Gus asked to be written off the show. The producers, ready for a big season finale storyline, agreed to his request. Throughout his final episode, Ma kept repeating to him and anyone who would listen: "This is just a hiatus. You'll be back."

A tiny part of him wanted to come back to the stage. To show those trolls, both real and online, that he was still talented and amazing. But the more Gus settled into his life in Freya Grove, the less he thought about going back to his magic career ever. He could still astonish, but in a different way, a way that made strangers and students want to learn about the past. Gus didn't want to deal with the edits, the hot mic packs pressed on his back, and being unable to speak freely without his words being turned into a Frankenbite.

But he'd go to Jess's wedding to keep his absence from being a distraction.

He owed her that much after their marriage. Gus, broken-hearted and drained by fame and magic, retreated to Freya Grove once his divorce was finalized. With Ms. Alice's support and invitation, he landed the job of society steward and moved into the Freya Grove Historical Society.

Now that Jess and Igor were getting married in his hometown, he was being asked to put on a show again. Be the heartbroken ex. Be the understanding son. Be the fun-time guy. Be anyone but himself. No amount of magic or illusions would change the fact he didn't want to rejoin the act permanently. Gus wanted to learn how to unlock the parts of his heart that he'd long shut up and abandoned.

A ring chimed in the air, breaking into his thoughts. Someone was at the back kitchen door. Did he miss another delivery time? Gus left his study, walked through the house, and went to answer the door.

"Happy Friday!" Sirena stood on the stair landing, then walked into the kitchen. She wore a cherry-red dress that wrapped around her lush body and showed off her plentiful bust. How did she look like a strawberry treat? His eyes dipped down momentarily to admire her smooth cleavage. *Stop. It.* He snapped his attention back to her face. His ribs expanded at the sight of her ruby lips. Why did they look so kissable?

Arms. Look at her arms. Her shoulders held two overflowing totes of groceries.

She thrust a full bag at him. "I hope you're ready to eat."

He took the bag, racking his brain. *It's Friday.* It was *that* Friday. Gus let out an annoyed grunt. He had a whole calendar on his phone, and he needed to use it.

Sirena stopped, hesitancy flashing in her eyes. "You forgot."

He reached out and touched her shoulder with her free hand. "No, I didn't forget. I just…lost track of time. I still have a few things to finish before I can join you."

Gus placed the groceries on the counter. He needed to respond to his next steward applicant and finish an in-process grant application before Monday.

"That's fine. Keep working. I'll cook," she said.

"Clock in, so I can get you paid." Her time was valuable.

Sirena tilted her head to the side. "Gus, please. Tonight's my treat."

Gus put his hands in his pockets and paced the floor a little. He stood by the table, watching her make herself at home. Sirena emptied the bags as she spoke to him, filling the counter with various herbs, poultry, and broccoli florets. She dropped a squeeze bottle of honey on the table. "Besides, I should be paying you. My cooking magic's been so wacky, you're doing me a favor by being my taster. Be honest."

"You're giving me jester's privilege," he said.

Sirena gave him a curious look. "You're talking about the guy with the funny hat who entertained the king?"

They were always in sync when it came to random topics.

Gus leaned against the wall next to the stove. "Yes, I am. The jester's privilege was a right. He could talk freely to royalty without being harmed. He could tell the queen if her wig was crooked with a joke and not get tossed into the river."

Sirena lifted a brow. "Are you calling me a queen?"

If the crown fits. Gus held back from speaking the truth. He needed to keep his cool when it came to Sirena. "I promise to be honest, my lady."

"Thank you." Sirena took out her phone and her fox journal from a bag and put them on the counter. The cover and a few pages of the journal were warped, as though she had spilled water on it. Maybe he could replace it for her. She snapped the book open to a page with notes and scribbles.

"I hope you're feeling adventurous," she said.

"How adventurous are we talking? Like, are we eating fried jellyfish?"

Sirena connected her phone to the charger that was plugged in to the wall. "I'm combining the shore croquettes recipe from the society library with a honey sauce I found in the Saybrooke journal."

"Oh, I'm getting a Caraway original," he said. He licked his lips at the idea of the honey sauce. Gus knew he was going to lick his plate clean tonight.

"It's more of an homage," she corrected. "I need you to fall head over heels for this dish."

He looked at her. "I'm sure I'll love it."

She met Gus's gaze; an optimistic light entered her eyes, transforming them from their usual umber into a pretty mocha shade. His breath caught in his throat. Looking at Sirena reminded Gus of late evenings studying in coffeehouses, cupping his hands around a hot drink, and letting the liquid warm him up from the inside out. Looking at her made him feel like he was a student discovering the world and learning the depths of his heart.

She blinked and wrinkled her brow. "Don't let me distract you. I know you have work to do."

Sirena gave him a smile before pulling out a knife from the drawer. She worked on chopping the broccoli, gently easing Gus out of her mental space. He stood there momentarily, deciding whether to just bring his laptop downstairs. Gus hesitated. That idea was a little too homey, too personal. She'd already stayed the night, and her perfume lingered on his couch. Now she was in the society's kitchen, conjuring and brewing, her magic touching everything. He stared at her back, noticing the creamy skin of her neck. What if he walked up to her and placed his lips right at the crook of her neck? Would she sigh or let out a sweet, needy moan? A fresh hunger, like a vengeful zombie, crawled up within him and hissed in his head.

It hissed the one thing that would satisfy him. *Her.* The hunger demanded *her.*

That one word forced him to flee from the kitchen and into the protection of his study.

Chapter Fourteen

irena glanced around the kitchen. Her eyes drifted over the wooden cupboards, which appeared so old and well loved that she knew that they must be original to the house. The countertop was lined with culinary knickknacks, like a rotund witch-shaped cookie jar and vintage tins labeled with cooking ingredients. There were brand-new chrome appliances, like a dishwasher and fridge, mixed with older but still working items.

Let me tap into whatever witchy power remains in this place.

Sirena picked up a tasting spoon and studied the honey sauce. It was starting to thicken, and she wanted to make sure that she got the taste right. The journal said that if the sauce tasted like fresh nectar and dripped slowly from the spoon, then it was ready to be served.

"Please be amazing," she whispered. *Please let him love it.*

She dipped a tasting spoon, brought it up to her lips, and sampled it. The sweetness hit the back of her mouth and tingled over her tongue. Oh, that was good, but it needed a little something more. She put in an extra dash of apple cider vinegar, stirred it with the wooden spoon, then tasted it again with a fresh utensil. Flawless.

Sirena grunted with gratification and bounced her shoulders, dropping the spoon in the sink. She did the damn thing with this meal. The chicken croquettes were almost done in the air fryer, and the glaze would go perfectly on top of it. The pumpkin cake was cooling on the counter. She had a little nibble from the side, and hid the dent with a layer of royal icing. She turned down the sauce and checked on the broccoli, which was looking nice and bright.

A blast of heat rolled over her body, weakening her knees. Sirena waved at her face as sweat gathered in different places. It was hot in here. She turned off the burners.

Gus was going to devour this sauce. Her heart fluttered in her chest at the idea of Gus eating her meal. *This isn't a date. You're cooking for your friend.*

He leaned into the kitchen. "Are we ready to eat? I can smell the food from the office."

She waved him away playfully. "I'll tell you when it's ready."

He gave her an impish grin that stoked the heat inside her. "Yes, chef. You're in charge."

Whoa. Sirena felt a sizzle of searing heat from her heart down to her core.

How could she take charge? In her mind, she'd carefully strip off her dress right here, drop it to the floor, and stand before him, bare naked. She'd let him drink her in. The sizzle turned into a powerful flame the longer she thought about it. Would he be a gentleman and turn away? Or would he stay and be with her with that mischief-making smile? She'd seen flashes of that trickster rogue, but she hadn't seen him in full force. Would he fall to his knees? Would she beg him to kiss her where she ached to be licked? Sirena groaned.

Gus stepped into the kitchen. He stepped closer. "You look a little flushed."

He pressed his hand to her forehead.

Even though his hands were cool, she felt like she was burning up. "You're warm."

You're hot, her juvenile brain whined. Sirena took a step back from Gus. If he got any closer, she'd be compelled to kiss him— or worse, beg him to bend her over the table.

Sirena undid her apron and threw it over a chair. "I'm fine. I just got a little overheated." She fanned herself. Air. Had the room suddenly run out of air?

Gus pointed to the stove. "Can I have a little taste?"

Sirena paused and closed her eyes. *Yes*, her body hissed. Think of unsexy things. Tomatoes. Fruit. Forbidden. Apples. Bite. Gus. Her hands balled into tight fists. Another rush of arousal went through her, and she was filled with the sudden urge to grind up against Gus until she—

Sirena pivoted from Gus and willed herself to calm down.

"Set up the dining room table for me. Thank you," she said in a quick rush.

She didn't wait for a response as she rushed to the bathroom down the hallway and locked the door. Her brain went over the last hour. *What did I eat? There was something in the sauce—or maybe I did something wrong to the dish. What did I use?*

She kept adding things to the sauce—a touch of ginger, a sprinkle of rosehips and pepper. Finished with a dash of apple cider vinegar—

Oh no. The pieces locked into place.

Sirena had made a passion brew. It was used to stimulate the blood. She was so busy worrying about whether the sauce was going to be good, she made it impossible to resist. Her hands gripped the sink as she felt that fire fill her up from the tips of her toes to the top of her head. How could she have messed up this dinner so badly? She'd have to toss out the sauce and start over again. Or maybe she could just serve him the chicken bare.

You'd like to give him something else bare: you naked on a plate.

Sirena shoved that horny thought down, but it kept bopping up like a balloon. Everything pulsed and ached to be touched, and she ached to touch another willing body. *Right. Freaking. Now.* Okay. New plan. Show Gus how to assemble the plate, then take your witchy butt home. She'd have to swing by the store and buy a value pack of batteries to power her *personal* massager, but that was still better than the alternative.

What was the alternative? Her imagination answered with vivid examples.

Dropping to her knees, yanking Gus's pants down to his ankles, and taking him into her hand. Taking him into her mouth. Stroking him until he begged for release with her. *Oh.* She faced her reflection in the mounted oval mirror over the sink, pointing a finger at her nose.

"Whatever you do, don't kiss him," she growled. "Don't even touch him."

Her reflection appeared to smirk and say *Good luck with that.* Sirena turned on the tap and splashed water on her cheeks and neck. She dried off, opened the door, and returned to the kitchen. It was empty. He was gone. Maybe Gus got a phone call. She looked at the stove. The pot was gone, too. Panic skittered over the back of her neck. Did he throw it out? There was a loud noise, like a distressed moan, in the dining room, so she went there. Gus stood in front of the table, licking the honey sauce from the wooden spoon she had discarded.

He clutched the pot by its handle.

"August!" she cried.

He dropped the pot to the floor without a second thought. It clattered. She jumped.

Sirena looked at Gus, her sauce dripping from his lips and onto his beard. Drops of honey landed on his button-down shirt and on his hand. The thick honey sauce made him look sticky and edible. Craving, as deep and strong as the pull of the ocean, drove her forward against her better judgment. She stood a foot away from him, fighting against the emotion that threatened to pull her under.

A mischievous, eager gleam entered his eyes.

"I couldn't help it. I had to have a taste." His voice was rough and desperate.

She glanced down at the pot at his feet. It had been scraped clean.

Did he really eat it all? *Maybe it spilled out*, her brain hoped stupidly.

Sirena met his eager stare. "How...much did you have?"

"Not enough. Is there more?" Gus dropped the spoon on the table and drew his thumb into his mouth to clean it with his tongue. She let out a strangled gasp imagining that tongue lapping her up. He sounded hungry. Ravenous. No, he was yearning to feed his soul.

The craving deepened as her body ordered her to act.

Feed him anything you can find. Gingerbread. Apples. Hearts.

Her brain countered with a last-ditch attempt at reason. Wait, tell him the truth. He's got to know so he can make a choice. Even if he doesn't choose you, tell him so he knows. She forced her mouth to work, pushing out the words, fighting against the magic that threatened to take control of her.

"Listen. There's something wrong with the sauce."

Sirena explained to Gus, as clearly as she could, what happened and how she might have messed up their dinner. Her breath quickened; her cheeks flushed in shame at the realization that she accidentally put him under a passion spell. Some kitchen witch she was. She couldn't properly make a simple glaze without hurting someone she really cared for. His eyes suddenly darkened with— She glanced away before she could see his disappointment. Once Sirena finished talking, she moved to leave the dining room, but he held out his hand to block her path.

"Stay," he whispered. "Please."

An unwelcome blush crept over her body. She wasn't strong enough to resist him, and if she stayed, then everything would change between them.

"If I stay, then—" She halted. "I won't be able to stop."

"I know," he said. His gaze turned from hopeful to wonderfully greedy.

She gave a quick nod, placed her hands around his neck, and pulled him down to her. It was settled. Sirena wasn't going to just kiss him. She was going to lick him dry. Sirena brushed her lips against his, an urgent kiss. It was fiery and brief. She ran her tongue over his lips, taking the sauce into her mouth. He tasted like hot honey and peppercorn, of passionate magic and barely restrained lust. Blood rushed in her ears, sending her body into a tizzy. He ran his hand up the length of her body; his fingers skimmed her arms, her stomach, and settled on her chest. All fires started with a spark, and this moment was the spark that would start the fire between them.

Chapter Fifteen

The spark within him in that instant turned dangerous; it turned greedy.

More. He wanted more. He stopped for a second, then plunged forward, capturing her mouth with his. A gasp escaped her lips, and he deepened the kiss. Finally. Liquid fire trickled through his body and set every inch of him ablaze. His hands roamed down from her face to her neck. He ran his hands over her body, committing her shape to his memory. This instant was every midnight kiss and desperate caress wrapped up in one moment. Sound dropped out, and all that he could hear was them breathing and gasping for air in between their wild, frantic kisses.

Her scent—of warm hearths and bonfires—stirred all his base desires.

He pinned her lightly against the dining room table. She smelled smoky and inviting, like a stone hearth filled with fire. Gus wanted to lay himself before her light. Their bodies were pressed together. He watched the play of emotions—desire, uncertainty, and anticipation—on her lovely features. His heartbeat picked up. He'd seen that same look on countless audience members' faces, but never on a woman he was about to kiss.

His heart flipped backward. He slipped his hands up her arms, feeling the heat of her body underneath the thin fabric of her dress. Gods of fire, how was she so blazing hot? Gus lowered his mouth and captured her lips in another kiss. She let out a low gasp. He ran his tongue over her full bottom lip, tasting the pumpkin and sugar of the icing of the cake she had made.

He licked her again, drawing her lip between his teeth and giving her a playful bite.

That move elicited a deeper gasp from Sirena. All he wanted to do the rest of the night was take her breath away. This kiss was needier, greedier than the one they had shared outside at the beach. The trickster in him rejoiced. She probably loved denying herself pleasure at first but then fully giving in when no one was looking. He surveyed her body.

Her dress crept up her thick thighs as she leaned back on the dining room table. Her braids had come undone from their high bun and framed her face. Her skin was flushed with heat and desire. Gus ran his hands down her back and cupped her butt. She let out a squeak that turned into a full squeal when he lifted her onto the table. She held on to him as he nestled into her space. He leaned down and pressed a kiss to her bare shoulder, and she shouted in pleasure. Every atom in his body burned. How was she softer than he could ever fantasize?

Gus gently tugged the dress down to her waist so that her bra was visible. Her breath came out in sharp pants. Nothing would rush him from taking his fill. He ran his thumb up and down the long line of her cleavage. The cups of her bra were bountiful and generous, like someone had overpoured a glass of champagne to the edge. He was going to get drunk on her.

Gus ran his tongue over his bottom lip. He eased the lacy cup of her bra aside, freeing her breast, and lowered his head to taste her. His tongue swirled and explored her skin, causing her to press against him. Sirena bucked against his mouth as he nipped and then swirled his tongue around her budding nipple. She moaned, and blood rushed through every inch of him.

That sound made Gus want to fall to his knees and taste her all over.

Sirena matched his passion, grinding her body against his as if trying to ignite a spark. She was flint, as fiery and precious as an agate or quartz. He was steel, hard and stout.

His touch created a delicious friction that set his senses on fire. Whatever energy she gave him, he would gratefully take and respond in kind.

Large sparks, crimson-red starbursts, popped from her skin everywhere he caressed.

Her breath hitched higher as he continued to lick and suck tenderly. Her fingers clutched his neck and shoulders, as if trying to pull him underneath her skin. She was so responsive that he grew harder at the mere thought of having her underneath him. Forget that—he wanted her in charge and on top. Wanted her rolling those hips and taking every inch of him inside of her on every flat surface they could find. The room seemed to dissolve away around them.

Her voice came out in a raspy whisper. "Gus, where are we going?"

Where are we going? There was a hint of expectation in her question that pulled him out of his fog of lust. Wait—where were they going? Gus braced his hands on either side of Sirena on the table. The room solidified. He took a few deep breaths and assessed the situation. "Uh..."

It's not too late. He promised they'd stay just friends. He could fight this enchantment.

Gus paused, trying to figure out what was going on.

He lowered his head to gain some clarity in this heated moment. He'd been in the kitchen, playfully sneaking a taste of her food, and then...the magic took hold when he licked the spoon. In a flash, every secret dream related to Sirena came true in vivid color. Time seemed to slip away from him, and he couldn't pull his thoughts together coherently. He was in control if he didn't look at Sirena. If he looked at her, his last shred of focus would be gone. Everything was moving so fast, and his rational side fought for an inch of control, barking orders at him.

You're under a spell. Think smart. Be rational.

"Gus?"

He closed his eyes and clutched the table. *Be smart before you hurt her.*

He felt her lift his head and affectionately stroke his beard, gently running her fingers up and cupping the sides of his face. It was nice to have her hands on him. His resolve weakened for an instant, but that was enough time for him to let go. He opened his eyes.

"Gus, where are we going?" Sirena repeated.

She took his hand and held it to her chest. He could feel her heart fluttering like a hummingbird trying to break free from a cage. His hand lingered too long, and he could feel the deep pulse of her magic. For a magician like him, his hands were his tools. He drank in magic through his fingertips. He felt her natural power through his palms. Everything whirred at the simple contact. Parts of him that hadn't been used in years whirred to life.

She felt so good. Too good to deny. Gus was gone.

He pulled her from the table and held her flush against him. "We're going to my bed."

Gus snapped his fingers, and they disappeared together upstairs into his bedroom.

Gus and Sirena slipped down into a vague space where time flowed like fine sand through cupped hands. As they discarded their clothes and tumbled naked into his sheets, minutes held the same weight as hours and fled by without them noticing. Gus kissed her all over, whispering promises and fidelity to her, only her. He licked the swell of her breasts and traced every curve and dip of her body with his fingertips. She ran her hands over his broad chest and soft stomach, learning the geography of his scars. He gasped in sweet agony as she took him into his hands and stroked the length of him. His pleasure stretched on for what felt like hours. Gus came with a strangled shout that might have rattled the stone gargoyles off the roof. The moon fell and the sun rose. When they finally returned from that space, they collapsed in each other's arms, sweaty and hungry. Gus brought the food she had made to bed, and they fed each other every bite, wrapping themselves in bedsheets. They studied each other's blemishes and hurts and gave each other more pleasure. The sun set, and the moon rose, and they found themselves in the company of starlight.

They fell back into the space where time had no power over them and they could indulge in every fantasy. Gus snapped his fingers, and red rose petals fell from the ceiling like rain. He watched as the petals touched her skin and kissed them away from her body. Sirena eased her legs open, and he bent his head between her thighs, feasting on her desire. She arched against him as if trying to give him better access to the hidden parts of her heart. He moved gracefully over her body, donned protection, and slid inside her. They devoured each other greedily, like fire being fed kindling, and burned bright in the darkness of the bedroom.

The fire between them did not burn out.

Chapter Sixteen

Gus had been hungover on alcohol, but he'd never been hungover on passion—until now. He pinched his nose, then pressed his hand to his head. Every inch of his skin ached, even the space between his toes. The bedroom smelled of stale roses and sweat. The grumble and hiss of the garbage truck outside startled him awake. A sleepy moan next to him interrupted his thoughts. He glanced over to see Sirena, lying next to him, sleeping, her braids fanned out on the pillow. Her breathing was easy and deep. The sunshine made her skin glow with an otherworldly light that filled him with wonder. How did one wake up a sleeping sprite? He leaned in close, brushing a kiss to her cheek. She stirred and her eyes opened. They looked a little dazed from sleep, but there appeared to be a deep shine of satisfaction.

I did that. She stretched her back and squeaked. "Morning."

"Morning. How'd you sleep?"

She gave him with a coy smile. "I barely slept. What a night. How about you?"

"It was great." Gus lay back on the pillow, letting his fingers lazily intertwine with her braids, recalling how her hair fanned over his body when she pleasured him.

Sirena brought his hand into hers. She gave his palm a quick peck. "I was thinking about a repeat."

His hunger was strong, but his body needed a lot of food.

Gus nodded. "Well, let's talk about breakfast first. I'm jonesing for carbs."

Sirena sat up and glanced around the bedroom. She ran a hand through her braids, then climbed out of bed. The flash of her flesh ignited a small burst of fire in his gut. Gus watched as she dressed, adorning herself in that red dress. She turned to the mirror, smoothing her hands over the wrinkles. The wrinkles he caused when he yanked the dress over her head and tossed it to the floor. Oh yeah. He was that guy.

Gus watched her. "I hate to see you get dressed. Then again, I get to undress you later."

"Good point," she said over her shoulder.

"I could undress you now," he offered. He'd eat later. He needed Sirena naked.

"Later," she pressed. "I need a breakfast platter and two gallons of iced tea."

Gus got out of bed and dressed in a T-shirt and jeans—his weekend knock-around clothes. Sirena gave him a heated once-over that made him pause. "Wear more jeans. Please."

Noted. He was going to add jeans into his rotation. They descended from the apartment to the kitchen, where the sink was filled with dirty dishes. He swung his head to look around the room and winced. What was that smell? The pungent scent of left-out food hung in the air. How did it get so nasty overnight?

Sirena wrinkled her nose. "I should've cleaned up better."

"It's fine," he said. "I'll take care of it."

"Kitchen witches don't leave messes," she said grumpily. Her phone dinged.

He watched as Sirena sauntered over to her charging phone lying on the counter and opened the screen. "Who's texting me?" Sirena studied her phone for a moment, and a sharp gasp left her mouth. She paled. "Um . . . Gus, what day is it?"

"Saturday. Yesterday was Friday, so today is Saturday," Gus said carefully.

She yanked her phone from the charger and thrust it at him. Her voice shook with barely controlled distress. "Why does my phone say it's Tuesday?"

Gus took her phone and glared at the lock screen. *Tuesday, October 18* was the date that hovered over a snapshot picture of Sirena and her sisters posing in front of a Ferris wheel.

Blood drained from his face. "I—"

"We've been gone for three days," she said anxiously.

He hated hearing the anxiety in her voice, but he was going to figure it out. It would be okay. There had to be an answer in one of the books in the library. *Lighten the mood. Make a joke. Don't freak out that you might have accidentally time traveled with Sirena with your magic.*

"We probably slipped and fell into a wormhole," he said.

She stiffened, and her eyes turned furious. "Don't joke. Please don't. My family must be freaking out, and my boss—Gwen probably fired me because I didn't show up to work this weekend! This is my fault. I don't have time. I should've left when I had a chance."

Gus reeled back as if she'd tossed a fistful of glitter in his face.

He rubbed his chest to ease the ache of her sharp words. Jess had said those same words when she left him. *Sirena's not Jess.* But this time the words weren't filled with embarrassment; it sounded like desperation. And it sounded as if she couldn't afford to stay here a moment longer.

"I'll call you." Sirena grabbed her purse from the table, shot him a glance, and rushed out the front door. She hustled like a witch who had left her cauldron burning on the stove. Gus went to the sink. He needed to clean up these dishes and then clean up the mess he made with his magic.

Bloom On Flower Shop was the place to be this Friday evening, with their free drinks and discounted flowers. Shoppers cradled their flower selections in one hand while sipping peach mimosas. Tall glass coolers were filled with fresh flower arrangements of dahlias, sweet peas, and crabapples. Earthy and floral scents filled the wide space and gave it a cozy feeling. The owner chatted with customers, and the rustle of tissue paper and the snipping of stems added to the shop's bustling noise.

"What's the cheapest flower here?" Lucy asked, eyeing the massive bucket of carnations.

"No." Ursula eased Lucy away from the blooms. "We're going to ask for what's in season and take pictures."

"Don't worry about the cost," Sirena said. "I'm buying your flowers, so don't worry about it."

Ursula gave Sirena a concerned look. "Um, are you sure, Si? Flowers can get pricey."

"It's the least I can do," Sirena said, reaching out and touching a flower petal on a table. *Rule seventeen: Kitchen witches stay in contact with their families.*

For the last three days, Sirena had been groveling for forgiveness after going dark when she was with Gus. Callie was happy Sirena was okay, and Ursula had called Diane, who updated the family on Sirena's whereabouts. Lucy, however, had been eerily quiet. Even now in the flower shop, Lucy hadn't looked at Sirena much and kept her eyes on the potted plants.

"You can tell us what really happened," Lucy said.

Sirena let out a breath. "We've gone over this. I don't know what happened."

"Let's go over it again," Lucy demanded. Her voice was hard and unrelenting. Sirena glanced around the flower shop. The other customers were toward the front of the store, making their purchases, so they at least had some privacy to talk.

"I made Gus dinner, we fell under a spell, and we were together for three days."

Lucy pointed a finger at her. "Ah! You didn't mention a spell. Did you cast it, did he cast it on you?"

Sirena huffed. "I tried something new."

Lucy folded her arms. "Ever since you started hanging around the society, you've been...acting different. Quitting jobs. Trying new dishes."

"I hope you didn't give him a come-hither potion," Ursula said with an embarrassed frown. "I tried one back in high school and I ended up with three dates for homecoming. It was a crazy night."

Lucy and Sirena gave Ursula a look that said *Not the right time*, then faced each other.

"I tried a new recipe," Sirena admitted.

Lucy eyed her skeptically. "Did you find it on Pinterest?"

"No, it was in an old journal written by a kitchen witch like me. It was legit. I thought I could trust it."

"Well, apparently you couldn't," Lucy said sharply.

Sirena threw up her hands. There was so much magic and mayhem that she couldn't even be sure who did what. She could've influenced Gus with her magic, or vice versa. Sirena searched their family spellbook twice but couldn't find an answer for why she and Gus evaporated into a sexy zone for three days.

Lucy cleared her throat. Her voice was soft but firm. "I'm not mad that it happened. I'm worried that it might happen again, but next time you won't come back, or we can't help you. We were so freaked out when you didn't answer our calls or our texts. I mean, I was going to start opening portals to alternate universes to find you!"

Guilt crawled its way up from inside and nearly stole Sirena's breath.

"I know you're grown, but I'm your big sister. It's my job to take care of you."

"I'm sorry," Sirena said.

Lucy came over and held her close to her side. She squeezed her shoulder tightly. "I know. You don't have to buy me guilt flowers. Promise me you'll be careful with Gus and whatever magic you're cooking up with him."

"I will. Let me buy you at least one bouquet," Sirena said. Lucy and Alex's cottage always looked nice when they had fresh flowers on the mantel.

"Deal," Lucy said. Sirena smacked a kiss on her forehead, then looked at Ursula.

"When we couldn't find you, I called Diane, and she told us

you were safe but unreachable," Ursula said carefully. "I asked her if you slipped into another universe, and she said probably not."

Sirena tilted her head. This was new information. "Diane knows what happened to us?"

Ursula lifted a shoulder. "I don't know, but she could sense Gus's magic. She managed to locate you and Gus but said she couldn't get to you. We scried for you, but the crystal just kept spinning on the map as if you were here, but not here."

Sirena blinked, and a flash of where she and Gus had been snapped into her brain. The bedroom had a clock with no arms on the wall, showing time but not keeping it. They were in the space between, the time between the past and the present. She and Gus were in a place where no one could reach them and they could be alone. Awareness smacked her on the forehead.

"Have you ever woken up, and you didn't know what time it was?" Sirena asked.

Lucy groaned. "You just described every morning before my alarm goes off."

Sirena nodded. "Or have you fallen asleep at eleven, then you blink your eyes and suddenly it's time to go to work at seven? You feel like you've been in bed for, like, five minutes."

Ursula eyed her. "Um, yes. I think everyone has felt that way. What's your point, Si?"

"I was there with him, in that same space."

Lucy wrinkled her brow. "That's a real place that physically exists?"

"We were there," Sirena insisted. "That precious time where you feel like you could stay suspended forever. Five hours feels like five minutes. Time is experienced rather than measured and

I . . . I . . ." She halted, unable to let the words leave her mouth. *I let time slip away with Gus. I could have stayed there with him and let time forget about us.*

Understanding entered Lucy's face. "I feel that way when I wake up next to Alex."

Hope fluttered in her chest. "You do?"

"I wish I could stretch out those last minutes in bed so I can cuddle up with him."

Ursula made a sound of sympathy. "Will you slip away into that space when . . . you know, you talk to Gus or touch him?"

"I don't know. We haven't spoken since I left on Tuesday."

This past week, Sirena had managed to avoid Gus by coming in the back door and leaving before he left his office. They hadn't talked about anything, because she didn't talk to Gus, scared that she might accidentally slip away with him again.

Sirena pressed her hands to her mouth, trying to compose herself next to the balloon rack. Her second chance to make things right was slipping away. The Lighthouse interview was next Friday, and she hadn't finalized her menu. She had to work extra shifts at Night Sky to make up for her missing hours on the schedule. It didn't help that every time she closed her eyes, she dreamed of Gus, being with Gus, and, oh right, touching Gus.

Fun time was over for Sirena. There was too much magic and mayhem brewing between them. She'd find a way to have fun without Gus, but she couldn't risk being with him.

She'd send an email Monday morning explaining her situation and why she couldn't work with him anymore. He was rational. They were friends. He'd understand. Right? Sirena would return to making deliveries for Empty Fridge, and she'd get her rhythm back. She wasn't moving backward; she was assessing her situation from a familiar position.

"I'll email Gus and say that we can't work together anymore," she said.

Lucy made a face. "Be professional. You should tell him in person."

One searing look from Gus might weaken the little control she had over her heart.

Sirena winced. "I'd rather have a clean break."

Lucy stared at her for a beat. "Okay, clean break it is. I'll cancel my booking with the society. We'll get married at the bookstore."

"No," Sirena cried. She wasn't going to be the reason for Lucy having to scramble to find a new venue. The e-save the dates had already gone out, and she wasn't going to make Lucy's life harder. "Keep the booking. I'll figure it out—or I'll call him on Monday."

Ursula stepped between them. "We need a witchy day to relax. Callie won four tickets to the Harvest Maze for tomorrow. Why don't we eat some caramel apples and get lost with a scarecrow?"

"That sounds like a good time," Lucy said. "The Four Musketeers in the Harvest Maze."

"It's going to be a fun time," Ursula said.

"Yay," Sirena said weakly.

Focus on the interview. Protect your magic. Get your head right. Everything between her heart and stomach fluttered like spinning leaves falling from trees, leaving her feeling bare. No. If being intimate with Gus was going to make her lose time, then she couldn't be with him. Forget the fun lessons; she needed to protect herself and her family from whatever was happening with her. If she wasn't careful, she was going to end up right back in his arms, where she couldn't stay. If she was willing to lose three days with Gus, what would she lose to him next? If she was willing to give him three days, then she might be tempted to give him the rest of her days and nights.

Chapter Seventeen

D o I add two drops of patchouli, or sandalwood?"

Gus held the black stone pendant and ring in his hand, studying the magician's handbook.

He didn't always consult the book, but he was thankful to find an extra copy in the special collection. He now stood at his desk in his study, trying to figure out how to charm a few pieces of jewelry. Gus studied the table of contents. "Wood Types for Making Wands." "Instructions for a Safe-Travels Talisman." "What to Do When You Bend Time." He flipped to the page and ran his hands over it, studying the book's marginalia and added notes.

As he reread the entry, his gut twisted.

Time bending is a rare event where a magician slips out of their current time and moves through the time and space continuum. This bending occurs whenever a magician reaches a high level of emotion or interacts with a powerful source of magic. Should this bend occur, eating a meal of root vegetables or wearing obsidian, tourmaline, quartz, or black agate will keep you grounded. To aid with grounding, add two drops of sandalwood to the stones mentioned and rub it in counterclockwise. In addition, repeated interactions with the magic source and balancing your emotions might halt the time bends.

Well at least he had an answer. Gus quickly carried out the instructions and slipped on the necklace. The floor felt sturdy under his shoes. He held on to the ring. *Please let this work.*

Now he had to see if the items worked for Sirena.

Maybe he could swing by Sirena's house this afternoon and talk to her. He could explain to her what happened and how he could hopefully keep it from happening again. Gus had spent the last week catching up on all the work he neglected when he was in his... How should he term it?... Time sex bubble.

It was mid-October, and everything in his life seemed so messy. He had missed the grant application deadline, he had nearly a dozen unanswered emails, and Ma had left him six voicemails. His applicant accepted another job in the Midwest because Gus hadn't responded in time. His brain demanded, *How could you lose three days?* Falling off the face of the earth, ignoring calls, and being thoughtless was something Good-Time Gus would do, but he wasn't that man anymore. Gus wasn't going to be that guy.

However, this time Gus had been completely caught up in the pull of Sirena and all her magic. No, it was the magic they made together. Most of those three days were a blur, but there would be a moment when he'd be drinking his coffee and suddenly he'd get a flash of Sirena trailing a path of kisses on his stomach. Or he'd check his email and feel the ghost of her hands caressing his skin and squeezing his thighs. His knees would weaken, and he would have to pause whatever he was doing. They had talked in the dark, trading secrets and giggling about private jokes.

His body and brain were a mess over the time bend, but his heart felt complete.

As if it found its missing piece and could function again.

Gus had last seen Sirena on Tuesday, braids tousled in his hands and her face bare and beautiful. She was a lovely sight even as she rushed from his house. It was now Saturday, and they had only exchanged texts and updates about her consultancy work with the historical society. She'd sign in, immediately go to the library, and stay there until it was closing time. They hadn't had any fun lessons or even a conversation about what happened. They'd gone backward in their friendship and might as well have been strangers.

He couldn't allow himself to bend time, but he wanted to see Sirena again. Wanted to be with Sirena. He missed talking to her about cooking and historical ephemera. There was a chance that they could slip out of time again should they fall into bed again. So, he made enchanted jewelry to keep them rooted.

Diane walked into the study, waving her phone in the air. "Good morning! When are you seeing Sirena Caraway again?"

Gus snapped his head up from the book.

"You're dating her, right?" Diane put the phone in his face, showing him an image of Sirena reaching over and kissing him right before him in living color. The photo was blurry, and thankfully they were draped in bedsheets, surrounded by plates of food, but they were kissing. Confusion darted on his skin. When did they take that picture?

She lowered the phone. "You're not denying it. I need details."

Gus schooled his face into a chill mask. *Be cool. Be cool.* "We're not dating. We're just . . . figuring things out. It's not serious."

Diane leveled a stare at him. "You don't bend time for anyone."

There was a note of triumph in her voice that reminded him of their ma. Gus went silent. He just stared at Diane. His sister knew. His brain was in tumult trying to understand how he was able to bend time with Sirena. It had never happened with Jess or any of his other dates.

"You didn't answer my texts," Diane said. "The only way you wouldn't answer me for days was if you couldn't text. Cell service is terrible when you fall into time."

He forced himself to speak. "You've bent before."

Diane dipped her head. "My first performance. I was so terrified. I ended up slipping back into a previous performance from last year. Once I worked out my feelings, I snapped back into the right place and crushed the role."

Gus let her words sink in.

"But I have never bent with another person," she said cautiously.

"I . . . I just got a little worked up," he said firmly.

She narrowed her eyes with a doubtful squint. "You can't bend forward into time; you can only bend back. You can find lost time and forgotten memories when you bend."

Something clicked once he heard the word "memories." His brain repeated his motto: *Everything in its right place.* There had been instances in the bubble when not only had their bodies sparked, but also their souls. It felt kismet. Gus looked down at the handbook. A thought came to him, and he searched the book until he found the page he wanted. "Signs You've Found Your Kindred."

Gus swallowed. He read the entry. It wasn't possible. It couldn't be true. This entire page could have been written about their friendship. The signs were clear and adding up: the feeling that he had known Sirena a long time, the feeling that he could talk to her about anything, the way they moved in sync when they worked together at the society. How they moved in tandem in bed. The words stuck in his mouth like a big bite of pizza. No, she couldn't be his kindred. It was too soon.

"I think this might be it, Gus," Diane said.

"I've only known her three weeks," he countered.

Even as Gus said those words, his heart sped up as if it was trying to talk to him. As if it knew a secret it wanted to yell. He couldn't listen. A kindred, a magician's soul match, didn't always lead to love. You could match with a person's soul and not be with them romantically. He sat down at his desk.

Diane glanced at the page over his shoulder. "What are you thinking?"

He shrugged at her question, unable to come up with a timely answer.

Gus, for the first time in a while, wasn't thinking; he was feeling first. He knew something was familiar about Sirena. He felt like he'd known her for longer than he had. The time bend revealed memories of lifetimes and moments from yesteryear. He mistook the memories he had as dreams, but now he knew that he'd known. Meeting your kindred was different from loving your kindred. He was already halfway in love with Sirena before he knew that she matched his soul. Did she feel the same way, and could he trust his heart? He'd been painfully wrong before, and he didn't want to be wrong about Sirena.

Diane reached out and patted Gus's arm. "I hope Sirena can

be a person you can call on, no matter what happens. You can never have too much magic in your life."

He gave her a half smile. Once again, Diane was one of his favorite people on the planet.

Her phone rang, so she retrieved it from her pocket and answered it. "Hey, what's up?" she said cheerfully. There was a long pause and the friendliness in her voice instantly morphed into concern. "Oh no. That's not good. I don't know much about mazes, but Gus might be able to help. Yeah, he's here. I'll ask him."

Diane covered the phone with her hand. "It's Zeke. He's at the Grove Gardens. Apparently, a few people got lost in the Harvest Maze, and they need volunteers to guide them out."

Gus eyed Diane, as thoughts turned in his mind about the Harvest Maze. The fire department could break through the hay bales and get the people out. It's not like the walls were made of stone. What type of maze was it that you could enter but not leave?

A sickening feeling went through him, and his stomach turned uneasy.

"It's a Merlin maze, isn't it," he said.

Diane asked Zeke, then nodded in confirmation. Gus scrubbed a hand over his face and flipped through the book. He let out an unsteady sigh as he found the entry he was looking for.

"How to Escape from a Merlin Maze." Gus read over the page as Diane spoke to Zeke over the phone about the situation. Merlin mazes were extremely difficult to escape, since every person who walked through it influenced the pathway with their emotions. No two people walked the same maze. People who were in a positive mood solved the maze within fifteen minutes, but those who might feel conflicted about their feelings would have a tougher time with the maze. The more frustrated a person became on the path, the more it shifted and changed. Due to the magic imbued into the maze by the builders, the path changed from minute to minute.

The walls could change from hay to garden hedges to stone.

Getting into the maze would be easy, but getting out of it could be difficult.

Gus had been stuck in a Merlin maze only once before, when he was a teenager, and he'd hated every second of it. He'd forgo bringing his wand, due to the unpredictable nature of the maze builder's magic. Hopefully his performance cloak still held enough protection that he could step in and help those who needed it without his emotions infusing the maze. He could only imagine how panicked those people were and how their emotions were feeding the maze's energy. Gus took off the necklace, got the ring, and slipped them into his pocket. He hoped to see Sirena after he helped get those innocent people out of the maze. Time was not on his side.

"'Go to a harvest maze,' they said. 'It will be fun,' they said," Sirena murmured.

It was getting dark, and she still hadn't gotten out of the maze despite walking around what she was sure was the perimeter of the maze at least twenty-seven times. She had hay stuck in her hair and dirt all over her cute wrap dress, and she hadn't eaten anything since she'd had breakfast at Mimi's. If she got out of this maze before the moon came out, she'd eat all the pumpkin pancakes in the state of New Jersey.

A low, gurgling croak went through the air, causing Sirena to look around.

She spotted the large black bird—a raven—sitting on top of the wall.

"Oh no," Sirena said. She wagged her head in disbelief.

Why was the universe throwing her signs? Of course, she just had to see a raven. She recalled what Nana used to tell her and her sisters when they went on evening strolls: *When you see a raven, take care. You're going to reach a crossroads, and you'll have to make a choice.* Sirena reeled away from the cawing raven and went in the opposite direction. *Nope. No thank you. Do not want to deal with that magic.*

How did she get into this mess?

Lucy, Callie, and Ursula had walked out of the maze just a few steps ahead of her. Those precious steps gave the maze just enough time to shift and change, blocking off the exit and forcing Sirena to find another way out. The last time she saw her family, they were reaching their hands out to her, but the wall closed and cut her off from them. Sirena had banged and kicked at the hay, but nothing changed. Panic nipped at her legs like a kitten trying to get a ball of yarn. Sirena tried to push her way out, but the hay pushed back like a rubbery wall.

She walked around for a while, but then she heard her phone ring. Sirena answered.

Lucy came on the line and kept trying to give her directions to escape the maze.

She yelled out from the phone's speaker. "Walk toward my voice!"

Sirena quieted, trying to hear Lucy's voice, but all she heard were the ambient sounds of fall playing overhead. She'd been listening to the crunching of fall leaves and birdsong for three hours. There was another caw from behind her, but Sirena didn't turn around.

That raven needed to go somewhere else and leave her alone. Whoever created this terraforming maze must have tapped into the unpredictable magic of autumn, or they just loved making terrible mazes. Sirena fought against tossing her phone into the hay.

"I can't hear you. The maze won't let me get any help."

She had to figure out her path on her own.

Diane's voice came on the line. "Hey, Si. Describe what you see around you."

She jolted at the sound of her voice. Why was Diane here? Were things so bad that they had to call a magician to help?

"I see hay! Lots of hay!" Sirena grumbled. She leaned against the wall, then glanced down at the ground. Her heart jumped once she saw a symbol etched on the ground.

"Wait! I can see a compass rose. I'm standing near the ruby rose."

Once she gave those details, there was a clamoring of voices over the line.

"Help's coming. Hold on, lady," Diane said.

Sirena went over to the compass rose, which was etched with the eight principal winds. Her phone beeped a warning. She glanced at the screen, noticing the battery life was down to 5 percent. Why hadn't she charged her phone before she left the house? Oh, that's right. She didn't want to be tempted to call Gus, so she left her phone in her purse.

"I'm almost out of power," she said.

Lucy's voice came back on the line. "Save your battery. Help's on the way. Love you."

"Love you too." Sirena ended the phone call.

She turned on battery-save mode and tucked the phone into her crossbody purse. Okay, so she was lost. Okay, she was super lost. She woke up this morning, got dressed, and had been determined to have a great time. Sirena was going to fix her spark, nail her Lighthouse interview, and get her life together. She changed her clothes twice in anticipation of taking cute pictures with a scarecrow. It was all planned out. Everything was working out fine, but then the Harvest Maze interrupted her life.

She was supposed to change her fate and land her dream job.

But she couldn't get that job if she couldn't get out of this freaking place!

Sirena flopped down next to the compass rose with her whole body. She was torn between wanting to leave and wanting to stay where she was. That tiny voice of intuition she'd been ignoring for a long time spoke from her soul. *You don't know what will happen. You don't know if landing the job will get you out of this loop. You don't know if you can stay in the Grove.* Sirena let out a cry of frustration and tossed her hands up to the darkening sky, reminding her of yet another day she wasted.

"Forget it. I live here now. This maze is my home!"

The air above her head sparkled with orange and red bubbles as she heard his voice.

"You can do better than this," he drawled.

Sirena sat up. Gus stood off to the side, dressed in his usual dapper sweater-vest but with a performing cape draped over his shoulders.

"What about a bungalow on Ocean Ave?" he quipped.

A relieved cry tore from her throat. She jumped up and launched herself into his arms, gripping him tightly. His hands rubbed her back as she held on to him and nestled in closer.

His familiar scent of books and heat eased her frayed nerves. Sirena didn't know how cold she was until she was in his arms.

"I've got you," he said tenderly. They lingered in the embrace before she pulled away.

Sirena studied his face. His bright eyes were rimmed with fatigue. How long had he been out here? Distress filled her.

"When was the last time you ate?" she demanded.

Gus grinned at her. "I'm fine."

"Is everyone else out?" she asked.

Sirena had overheard other guests in the maze and tried to find them. The magic kept them separated and divided. Over time, she stopped hearing other people and assumed she was the only one left.

He cupped her cheek. "We managed to get everyone else, but you've been the trickiest to find." His touch was careful, as if he was afraid to scare her with his next words. "It's been shifting every few minutes, so it's been difficult to track your exact location. You're the last one."

"Every time I think about leaving, the wall shifts," she said.

He wrinkled his nose. "I figured. Merlin mazes tend to tap into hidden feelings."

She stepped away from Gus, suddenly becoming aware of their

closeness and his heat. This was not a sweet encounter between them; this was Magic Gone Wild.

Sirena rolled her eyes at the wall. "I thought the town got rid of them after what happened to those high schoolers after junior prom."

He bit out his words: "Apparently, someone didn't get the message."

She took a deep breath. Gus was here. He was a whole magician and could do cool stuff.

"So, let's snap your fingers and leave. Presto, chango, let's go."

Unease filled her when she noticed the caution in his face. "It's not that easy. You only get out of the maze when you balance out your emotions." Gus paused. "It helps to talk."

Sirena blinked. He wanted to *talk*. Why would anything be easy for her?

I'm the reason I'm trapped here. The walls transformed from hay bales into lush green hedges and grew a full extra foot, almost blocking out the fading sun. She pressed her hands to her cheeks, letting out a tense laugh. Talk about what she was feeling? Talk to him, the magician she was falling for? Sirena yanked that thought out of her head and threw it out like an old receipt.

"Do you have, like, fourteen hours?" she asked.

"I have all the time you need."

"It's not your problem." *I'm not your problem*, she added quietly.

Gus took a protective step toward Sirena. "Well, I'm making it my problem." He waggled his eyebrows at her. "I've never spent a night in a Merlin maze."

214

Sirena stepped back. "I'm not asking you to stay. I'll get out on my own."

Gus raised a brow. "How's that working out for you?" he said, his tone joking yet firm.

Frustration splintered over her skin. She'd done the whole damsel-in-distress act before, but it hadn't worked out. She fed herself. She saved herself.

"Thanks for checking in on me," Sirena said with as much confidence as she could muster. "Leave me a bottle of water and snacks. I'll be out of this maze by sunset—or midnight."

Gus's mouth opened, closed, then opened again. "You'd rather stay here than talk to me."

"Stubbornness runs in my family," she said.

"I promised Lucy I'd take care of you," Gus said.

Sirena froze. It wasn't that easy. She wasn't used to relying on anyone—even her family.

Sirena didn't want to rely on him and get used to him being there, because when they ended—everything good ended in her life—she'd miss him. She'd miss his humor and his light. Her heart couldn't get used to his light, because she had to learn how to live without it if he left.

She had her spark to reignite and to protect.

"Ask me." Gus took a step forward. "Ask me anything."

He was close enough that she could see all the exquisite shades of brown that made up his eyes. She saw sheer vulnerability and trust in his face. Her heart leapt so high, she felt as if it could clear the high walls. *Goddess, why did you have to bring him into my life now? Why couldn't you have saved him for the right time?*

She licked her lips. "Why don't you perform anymore?"

Gus peered at Sirena. "I gave it everything I had. The well was dry. There's nothing left for me onstage. If I go back now, then my audience won't be getting the best of me."

He paused, then stared at Sirena. "Why don't you cook professionally anymore?"

She shrugged. "Pick a reason. My ideas were stolen by an investor. I lost my spark. I don't have the energy to boil an egg. I can't stand to cook for myself anymore."

"You cooked for me," he said. A swift shadow of desire crossed over his face.

A realization entered her brain. That night was the first time in months that she hadn't second-guessed or rethought her additions. It just came naturally to her. She was acting out of affection for Gus. Out of a desire to feed someone she cared about. Sirena studied the maze. The walls of the maze seemed to shrink a little. Her eyes darted to Gus. He must have noticed it, too, because his shoulders lifted in hope.

"Why didn't you go back to New York?"

Sirena peered at him. "My family needed me to stay. Why are you still here in the Grove?"

"I'm here until I can find my replacement. I might be leaving in the new year."

Her heart pinwheeled. He was leaving the Grove. Why hadn't he mentioned it before now?

"Come on, Sirena. Ask me what you really want to know."

Sirena played with the strap of her purse. *Why do you call to my soul?*

"I can't think of anything else," she said.

"Don't be shy. I won't bite unless you ask me. Again."

Her breath hitched in her lungs. She asked the question that haunted her days.

"What really happened between us?"

A quiet laugh rippled out of his mouth. Sirena eyed him. Well, that reaction was unexpected. A magician like Gus could manipulate the elements effortlessly, like a child played with glitter and glue sticks, so his answer would probably be something magnificent. But instead, he laughed. She watched as Gus laughed for a long moment, then let it fade out until he was silent. A tense smile played on his lips. Even though he said nothing else, she knew the answer. Somehow, she just knew what he wanted to say but couldn't bring himself to speak out loud.

I forgot about time when I held you in my arms.

Gus leaned in close enough that she could smell the base notes of his cologne: fresh ink on parchment paper and pressed oil. He smelled of old grimoires and…something appealing. Peeled apples covered in sprinkled cinnamon. She bit the inside of her cheek to keep from sighing.

Her heart ached. Oh. The walls of the maze grew fuller, blocking out the light.

"Sirena." There was a soft plea in his voice. He anchored her gaze to his, willing her to talk. The walls seemed to close in on them, growing thicker. Hopefully, he'd accept her response, and they could figure out another way to get out of the maze.

She shrank back from his gaze. "I can't."

Sirena wasn't going to let herself get caught up in his magic, his swashbuckler smiles, or his affection. She'd already lost three days—she didn't have to lose her heart. If she lost him in the maze, then maybe he'd give up and leave her alone. He deserved more than to waste time with her. Sirena took a step away from him, moving toward the bend behind her. Gus looked her over, and a predatory glint entered his eyes, as if he were a hungry lion who'd spied a lost zebra by a water hole. She slipped off her shoes, knowing that she could run faster if she was barefoot.

His eyes flicked down, noticing the action.

"If you run, I'll catch you." His words weren't an empty threat. It was a promise.

An odd feeling of anticipation went through her. She'd never played a game of tag as an adult, but there was a first time for everything. *Let's go.*

Chapter Eighteen

Sirena took off in a sprint, digging her toes into the dirt, pushing herself forward.

Her heart pounded as she took off down the path. She forgot what it meant to run fast enough that she felt as if she were flying. For a few seconds, her feet lifted off the ground and she was floating. It had been a long time since she had run, always pushing off her evening runs to pick up more deliveries. Lucy invited her to work out with her after school, but Sirena usually declined. There was always another hustle or job that needed her time. As she kept running, it felt good to move and feel the blood rush through her body. Her arms pumped back and forth, the wind was whipping, her braids were falling from her updo, and her dress kicked up around her thighs. Every inch of her was free and in control. The atoms within her hummed the closer Gus got.

The late-afternoon wind whipped around her, chilling her skin. She could feel him one step behind her, his fingers brushing against her back as he reached out for her. Her skin warmed under his touch. Sirena pushed herself until she managed to escape his grasp. She heard his irritated yet amused laugh behind her. Sirena noticed that she was running toward a junction, where a passage branched off in two separate directions. Left. Right. *You can lose him here.*

She quietly battled within herself. *Do you want to get lost with him or without him?*

Sirena knew instantly.

The answer was clear. Sirena glanced back to see how close Gus was, then stopped and waited for him. Elm and elder tree. She gulped through a dry throat; the sight of Gus running toward her, his cloak thrashing behind his powerful body, made her thirsty. This spellbinding magician wasn't just a tall drink of water; he was an entire gallon.

The longer she looked at Gus, the more she felt foolish for running away. From denying herself the pleasure of his company. He was on her in three seconds. Gus scooped her up, pressing their bodies together, his arms wrapped around her and lifting her.

They fit together. Effortlessly.

"I caught you," he said, out of breath, his eyes shimmering with magic.

"You did," she said, drawing in a breath. She wrapped her arms around his neck, leaned down, and captured his lips with hers. Gus returned the kiss. Their bodies pulsated with natural energy, a crackle of electricity, like a lightning strike, that reverberated between them.

She slid down the length of him, her feet finally touching the ground.

Sirena broke off the kiss, slightly breathless. "What's your plan? To tickle me?"

He flicked a lazy glance over her from head to toe, sending a sizzle of heat up her spine. "I wasn't thinking about tickling you." Hunger glistened in his eyes.

"Ask me something," she requested.

"What now?" His voice filled with raw need.

She moved in close, brushing her mouth with his. "Touch me," she insisted.

Gus didn't hesitate. He took off his cloak and placed it on the ground. Sirena twisted off her purse and lay down on the cloak. It seemed to stretch out big, like the size of a fitted sheet. She ran her hand over the red satin fabric; it felt smooth and luxurious under her palm. Gus lowered himself down next to Sirena, his eyes eager to hold her. Sirena yanked Gus into her arms. Her mouth found the space where his pulse throbbed, and she licked the salt off his skin. She shuddered. The taste of him reminded her of the sea salt dragged from the ocean, raw and elemental. A splinter of fear went through Sirena, but she willed herself to stay calm. She could do this. She could keep from slipping away with him. Stay grounded.

Gus let out a guttural moan that hit her right in her core.

Sirena nipped until she felt him reach for her and yank at her dress in desperate fistfuls. He captured her mouth in a rough kiss; his beard lightly scratched her. She whispered words of magic and enticement against him. *Kiss me. Thrill me. Tease me.* Her eyes shuttered closed. She breathed in; the woodsy scent of his beard oil made her think of campfires and dark forests. She whimpered as he deepened the kiss, his hand roaming slowly over her stomach and chest.

The ground seemed to slip away from them—as if it were made of quicksand. Suddenly, her body dipped as if she were on a descending elevator, and she was slipping away.

Away from the Grove. Away from her family and friends. Away from time.

I want to stay. The raven's call forced Sirena to snap her eyes open. She slammed her hand on the ground, making it become solid again. They were back in the maze.

"I—" Sirena licked her lips. She met his eyes. "I don't want to slip away."

Gus pinned her with his stare. "I won't let you."

He shifted around and then produced a ring from his pocket. The air in her lungs suspended for an instant. She studied the item; it sparkled as if it had been hand carved from a meteorite.

"May what fall from the stars keep us bound to earth," he chanted.

He slipped the ring on her finger, then kissed it. Comfort swathed her like a fluffy blanket. Any lingering fear eased away and was replaced with a sense of protection. Whoa. She touched the ground and felt the coarse dirt between her fingers. Sirena pressed a hand to Gus's chest, his form solid and his heart beating rapidly under his shirt. Everything felt safe and unshakable.

Sirena looked at Gus. "You made this charm."

Only her family used their magic to help her, but Gus had made this small thing for her peace of mind. He used his magic not to dazzle, but to comfort.

He merely nodded and took out a pendant dangling from a long chain. Her fingers wrapped around the silver centerpiece; her thumb ran over the smooth stone oval. Gus bowed his head. Wordlessly, she slipped the pendant around his neck and lowered it against his chest.

She looked between the ring and the oval pendant, noticing

that they were made from the same element. Surprise fluttered through Sirena. They matched. They were mates.

The question *why* played on her lips, but her brain cautioned her not to ask. Instead, Sirena kissed him, letting her eyes shutter closed once more. She felt him grasp and squeeze her body, sending ripples of delight through her. His breath came out in eager pants. Sirena breathed in the crisp leaves and felt his body's heat under her palm. She wanted to drag him into her dreams, where she could keep him close. This moment was theirs alone, and she didn't want life to interrupt it. But life waited outside these maze walls.

"Someone might walk in," she sighed.

"No," he said, his voice coming out strangled. "Look what you've done."

Sirena glanced around them. Whoa. The maze walls had receded, revealing a private orchard. The leaves remaining on the trees were golden yellow, and the ground outside the cloak was matted with fallen leaves among the rocks. A gust of wind came through and rustled the branches, causing the air to fill with the musky-sweet smell of fall. She recognized this place. It was the part of her that once loved Octobers and Novembers, where it was forever autumn, the perfect temperature for hoodies and steaming cups of tea. This illusion was the part of her that wished for apple orchards, ghost stories, and handmade brooms. The setting sun cast shadows over their entangled bodies.

Sirena pressed herself against Gus, feeling his other hand yank at the tie of her dress.

It eased open. He pulled and opened the dress, unwrapping her like a piece of candy. The cool air brushed her skin, and she was left in her underwear. Sirena propped herself on her elbows and arched her back, giving him a full view of her black lace bra and panties. This time was different from before. They weren't under a passion brew spell now, and there was nothing but the fire they'd been slowly burning between them. She didn't want the fire to go out.

Gus looked her over in a slow scan; his brown eyes darkened as he held her gaze.

Silently, she called upon the strength and beauty of all the fashion pages she saw online.

"On the air, the earth, and the fire..." Gus took a strained breath, then continued. "You're gorgeous."

His fingers slid up the length of her thigh until he reached the apex between her legs.

She gasped. He ground his hand against her barely covered flesh, creating a delicious sensation. Gus touched her under the fabric, slipping his fingers against her. His movements became steadier and more intense. The fire inside her flared and licked her from within. Every inch of her body pulsated in need. She grew damp quickly; the rhythmic movement of his hand sent a growing surge of bliss through her body. Delicious shivers filled Sirena as she muttered words of encouragement.

Right there. Keep going. Please. Please. Faster. Don't stop.

She sucked her lower lip between her teeth, trying to hold back a scream. From lowered lids, she met his eyes; greed glittered in their depths as he toyed with her. Gus didn't let up; he continued his deliberate motions, and she felt herself moving closer to the edge. He shot her a penetrating stare as she rolled her hips and rode against him. His words came out low and desperate as her desire grew to a feverish crescendo.

"Come for me. Now."

A scream tore from her throat, and she pressed her mouth against his shoulder. He sent her spiraling into euphoria. She rode out her release, and she held on to Gus, not wanting to let him go. Their hidden world fell away, and she let out another cry of relief.

Who chased and then hooked up with their witch crush in the middle of a Merlin maze?

Who did that? Apparently, Gus Dearworth did. He'd never been this wild and reckless in the Grove, but she'd teased it out of him. As their hidden world disappeared, Gus rolled away from Sirena, taking several deep breaths. He was so hard and ready that he fought to keep from busting out of his pants and sinking into her. He glanced at Sirena. She was laid out on his cape, her red and black dress pushed up to reveal her thick, dimpled thighs, the scent of her arousal lingering in the air. Her eyes were closed, her head thrown back as she rode out her orgasm. His body could still feel the graze of her lips on his neck as she had teased him with her tongue and teeth. He still felt her hips rocking against him as he stroked her. How her sweet warmth tightened around his fingers as he teased and pleasured her over the edge. Sirena's scent filled his brain and called on him to keep going. A bird call—it sounded like a raven—played overhead. His blood raced. To hear a raven's call signaled an impending change. Yes, he wasn't the same magician who walked into the maze.

Being around her made him feel alive—like a half-powered

machine suddenly whirring to life after being unplugged for years. He wished it were as simple as just being charmed by Sirena. Gus was starting to fall for her, and that truth was absolutely frightening. He was thinking about reaching for a future he didn't know if he was brave enough to hold on to or attempt to try again. Could he name her his kindred and declare to the universe that her soul matched his?

You have to try, his head encouraged.

His phone beeped, reminding him of the world outside. Sirena's eyes snapped open, unfocused with need. She'd been sated but not satisfied. His phone beeped twice more. Gus let out an annoyed growl and checked his text messages.

All the texts were from Diane.

Y'all okay?

If you're not out in 2 min, I'm coming in with a magical chainsaw.

You've got sixty seconds. Zeke and I are coming in!

Sirena watched him in anticipation. Gus showed her the texts. Irritation flickered in her eyes at their game being interrupted. "Pause."

Gus texted Diane. No need for the chainsaw. We're leaving now.

He helped her fix her dress. She brushed the lingering hay and leaves from her body. Gus stood and extended his hand to her. Sirena took his hand, and he helped her stand up. He kissed her slowly and deeply, pressed his lips to her cheeks and chin.

The sweet aroma of fallen leaves and Sirena remained in his nostrils. He picked up his cloak, brushed off the dirt, then draped it over her shoulders. Sirena pulled it closer around her body. "I'm ready."

His chest lifted. *She looks good in my cloak.*

Sirena took him by the crook of his arm and strolled over to the nearest maze wall. It slid out of the path. They stepped out into the gardens, not meeting the curious looks being tossed their way. Zeke gave Gus a thumbs-up. Gus mouthed a *thank you* to him and he gave him a small salute in return. He'd have to make good with Zeke and finally talk to him about his ghosting act.

The chief and the members of the Freya Grove fire department leaned tiredly against the truck. It appeared from their exhausted postures that everyone was relieved that this maze nonsense was over. The fire truck and other emergency vehicles were in the parking lot down the path. The paramedics checked them out for injuries and issues, then allowed them to rejoin Sirena's sisters, who were waiting by the benches.

Callie ran over to Sirena and hugged her tightly. "I'll let Ursula know you're safe. She had to leave. There's a crystal problem at the shop and they needed her help."

Lucy fussed over Sirena, brushing the few remaining strands of hay from her braids.

Diane peppered them with questions. "What took you so long?"

Sirena shot a searing look at Gus. Lust pounded through his bloodstream when their eyes connected. He licked his lips, remembering how it felt to shower her face with kisses. Gus answered her question the best he could without embarrassing himself or Sirena.

"We got lost again," he said warmly.

Satisfied, Diane gestured to the parking lot and held up her keys. "I'm starting the car. It's cold out here, and we've got to warm y'all up."

Diane left them to continue to be fussed over by the Caraway sisters.

"You must be hungry," Lucy said.

Sirena spoke up. "I'm starving. I'm taking Gus out for dinner."

"It's late. You're never getting a table now."

"You can't go out covered in dirt and hay," Callie said, aghast. "You look like a wood nymph. A cute wood nymph, but still— you can't go out looking like this." She slid a glance over to Gus. "Both of you look like you've been in the wilderness."

Gus squeezed Sirena's hand; the image of their private orchard vivid in his mind.

"Why don't you cook for him at the house?" Lucy said.

"Um—" Sirena winced. "I don't know what we have to cook in the house."

Callie jumped in. "It's the least we could do for Gus. You'll just whip food together."

Gus glanced around at the Caraway sisters, briefly taken aback by the request. Didn't they know she was having issues with her powers? He noticed that Lucy stared at Sirena with her face bright with silent expectation. A low whine slipped from Sirena's mouth and panic entered her eyes. She looked at Gus, her eyes silently telling him the truth. *They don't know.*

He stepped in. "I'm fine with ordering a pizza. I'm just happy Sirena's safe and out of the maze. Let's take a night off."

The sisters took this comment in, then nodded in agreement.

"Rapunzel's does have the scary pie special," Callie suggested.

"I like the way you think, Mr. Dearworth." Lucy pointed to the parking lot. "Let's ride."

Their group tiredly walked away from the maze.

Sirena's brown eyes shone with gratitude.

Gus gave her a discreet nod. Sirena pulled him close, wrapping her arm around his waist. She leaned into his side and whispered; her breath brushed against his ear. "Wild looks good on you, Dearworth."

Desire slid down his spine. Wild. He liked being a little wild.

Chapter Nineteen

As Gus stood in front of the Caraway hallway mirror, he thought, *I've never borrowed a merman's clothes before.* He didn't really wear blues, greens, and grays—the colors weren't his favorite—but he had to admit that the cool shades were growing on him the longer he wore them. Lucy and Callie had shooed Sirena upstairs to take a bath, while Alex took one look at Gus and immediately offered him a T-shirt and sweatpants. He had hung his cloak up on the porch after cleaning it outside, then called Diane to let her know that he was staying with Sirena.

"Have some fun. I'll take care of Cinder," she said.

"Thanks, sis." Gus ended the call and went back inside the house. Alex stood nearby in the living room.

"Thanks for the clothes."

Alex gave him a thumbs-up. His glittery scales on his brow and chin sparkled in the overhead light, hinting at his aquatic heritage. "No problem. It's the least I can do after you helped my family."

Gus paused, noting the clear love and fondness for the Caraways in his words.

When they had arrived at the house, Alex had fawned over Lucy with kisses and tender shoulder squeezes. The merman kept a close eye on Sirena and Callie, pouring them water and offering to order the food while they cleaned up. Callie gave him a huge bear hug before she left to pick up the pizza from Rapunzel's Pizzeria. Gus, who, as a magician, made a habit of studying body language, picked up on the little actions people did. From the outside looking in at the Caraways, it was clear to Gus that Alex was already part of the family.

"I'm glad I could help," Gus said. "It was a long day for everyone."

"Why make an enchanted maze? I didn't think October could get any weirder in the Grove," Alex said. He shook his head in utter disbelief. "I thought the year we had haunted apple trees was the worst! We were dodging apples for weeks!"

"The maker probably got a little too extreme with his vision," Gus suggested. "It's like *Jurassic Park*. They were too busy thinking they could but they didn't ask if they *should* make a magical maze."

Alex shivered in horror. "Please don't say that idea too loud. Our town is wacky enough that *Jurassic Park: Jersey Shore* could happen here. I don't want to wake up to see raptors jumping my lawn. I have gnomes and a future wife to take care of."

Gus let out a booming laugh. Alex, with his sense of humor, reminded him a lot of his friend Zeke. A swift rush of regret went through him at the idea of avoiding his friend's texts.

He'd catch up with him soon. A soft footfall from the kitchen caused Gus to turn his head. The laughter dried up in his throat at the sight of Sirena.

He did a double take. *Hello there, enchanting one.*

She wore a fluffy robe that made her look like a tuft of blue raspberry cotton candy. Gus ran his tongue along his bottom lip, thinking about how she had tasted in the maze. She was fresh faced, her braids wrapped up into a side ponytail, her hands tucked into the robe's pockets. All thoughts dropped from his head the longer he stared at her, delighting in her beauty. Sirena dipped her chin, her cheeks still rosy from the bath.

She pressed a hand to her chest, and he saw the ring. His ring. Something selfish flared within him. *She's still wearing my ring.*

Her skin took on a charming glow, as if she were covered in candlelight. She appeared to him like a flame. Uncertainty tiptoed into his brain as he pondered one question.

Could he possess enough magic to play with fire again?

She fidgeted under his attention. "What's so funny?"

"I forgot," Gus said. He peered at Alex, who glanced from Gus to Sirena, a knowing grin on his face like a big brother watching his little brother trying to flirt. Was he that obviously sprung on her?

She took a breath, then faced Alex. "Lucy called. She needs you at the house. The gnomes are asking about their lilac wine."

"Ah, it seems we have a drink emergency," Alex said.

He clapped a friendly hand to Gus's shoulder, then walked out the front door, closing it behind him.

She tucked her hands into the robe's pockets.

Her gaze fell on him. "I knew blue would look good on you."

Gus pressed a hand to his chest; his heart sped up under her rapt attention. "Thanks, but I think I'll leave the aquatic colors to Alex. I like to blend in."

He itched for the rainbow tweed, brown, and beige colors that he wore every day.

Sirena leveled an easy stare on him. "August, you can do many things, but you don't blend in. You stand out."

He stayed quiet, letting her compliment settle into his skin. Sirena went into the living room and stood by the bookshelf. She pulled a leather-bound book into her hands and flipped through the pages carefully. He joined her, letting his gaze roam over her lush form. For him, there was nothing more alluring than a woman with a book in her hand. Gus rubbed his fingertips together to keep from brushing her skin or yanking open the robe to touch her again. Being around her brought out that side of him, the playful side of him that he was starting to miss.

"I bet you're wearing something cute under that robe," Gus said.

Sirena returned the book to the shelf, then faced him. "I'm afraid not. Just an old sleep shirt and shorts that have seen better days. I don't want to accidentally flash anyone."

"What about if you want to purposefully flash me?" he joked.

Sirena placed a hand to his chest. His skin tingled beneath her fingertips below the fabric.

"Under all those history geek clothes beats the heart of a rogue," she said.

Hmm, he was only a rogue. "I'd thought I'd achieve rake or scoundrel status at least."

A teasing tone entered her voice. "You'd have to compromise me in a gazebo first."

"Is that a request?" he rasped. He could find a gazebo; he had a guy who could help him get one delivered within twenty-four hours.

Sirena merely smirked. "I had a lovely time in the maze," she said. "I was worried that we'd . . . slip away."

He touched her ringed finger. "We won't have to worry about it happening again as long as we're wearing our charms. Your ring and my pendant keep us grounded no matter what we do or where we are."

Sirena let her hand run up and touch his pendant. Her thumb stroked the oval as she studied it. "So, you know what happened to us."

Her eyes lifted and she watched him with a guarded squint.

This conversation was overdue. "I was planning to come over and talk to you. Magicians can sometimes bend certain elements and states with our will when we're in a high state of emotion. We slipped into a time bubble due to our connection."

"So, we have to wear these charms for the rest of our lives?" Sirena asked. "If we want to touch each other or be together?"

Oh, that was a good question. "Probably. Maybe. I'll check the spell, but the charms are a temporary solution to our problem."

"So, it can happen again if we don't wear these charms."

"Yes," he said faintly.

Sirena dropped her hand away from his stone, letting it fall against his chest. It hit him like a wrecking ball. "I can't afford to lose any more time."

She stepped away from Gus. The air chilled between them.

Oh. Something close to dissatisfaction coiled through him like a satin ribbon.

She shut her eyes, then opened them. Regret flashed in her gaze. "I'm sorry. That came out wrong. I made a wish. I wanted a second chance to fix my life and the universe delivered. I thought I could have a little fun this time around, but everything's getting too complicated. My days are literally numbered, and I can't afford to waste time on anything other than my magic."

"Tell me everything," he said.

Gus listened as Sirena explained the magic of wish tea and the start of the time loop. Her lip trembled as she told him about the unlucky October that had been swallowed by time. He knew he'd felt something was different weeks ago, but he'd dismissed it as déjà vu.

When Sirena finished her story, she pinned Gus with a stare. "I should've told you sooner, but...I didn't know how to tell you."

"Why haven't you told your sisters?"

"Kitchen witches clean up their messes," she said primly. "My sisters have their own problems. I don't need to bother them with mine. Do you remember anything about last October?"

He didn't move. "I remember my birthday party vaguely. I know you were there."

Sirena bowed her head. "We barely talked. I was so embarrassed about my life, and all I wanted was a do-over."

An image of himself standing in front of a birthday cake covered in candles flickered in his brain. "I made a wish that night too," Gus blurted out.

Her eyes widened a fraction. "I know it's rude to ask what you wished for, but—do you know what you asked for?"

Gus shook his head apologetically. "I hope I wished for something good," he said.

Gus watched the play of emotions on her face. Now that he knew that this time was his second chance, he was going to make the most of it. He was going to reconnect with Zeke, recommit to the man he was becoming, and he was going to figure out whether Sirena was truly his kindred.

"Is there anything else you want to tell me?" she asked.

He opened his mouth to tell her about their soul connection, but he held back. After everything that happened in the maze, he didn't want to overwhelm her with more talk of magic and fate.

Instead, he pivoted. "I'll help you prep for your interview at Lighthouse."

Her eyes grew watery. "You still want to help me?"

She said the last word with disbelief as if she'd fed him a plate of gnome party leftovers. He'd take everything she'd feed him if it got Sirena the job of her dreams.

"I do," Gus said.

"You've done so much. I feel bad that I can't do more for you," she said.

You're enough. His soul wouldn't stop speaking to him. "I'd like for you to keep coming to the society and working on preserving the recipes."

"What about the...passion spell and the...everything sexy between us?"

Their time together meant so much, more than he could admit.

"What's a little passion spell between friends?" he joked.

"We're still friends?" she asked, and he noticed the hint of vulnerability in her voice.

He nodded. "Yes, we are."

"What about our fun lessons?"

"I don't think you need my help anymore. You played tag in a Merlin maze. You're a fun expert now. I think you can teach *me* a lesson or two," he said.

"I like the sound of that," she said.

"I'm sure we'll get this passion out of our systems—eventually," he said. Gus almost believed the lie he just told himself.

Sirena regarded him with a speculative glance. "Sure."

Secretly, he didn't want to get rid of whatever he had for her. The fire he carried for Sirena wasn't being extinguished, but rather he was feeding it the longer he stayed around her.

"I should probably head out." He didn't move but lingered. It would be the smart move to leave, to go back home and recenter.

Sirena glanced at the bookshelf. "Wait. I had an art book I wanted to show you."

Gus scanned the cracked spines of the books. He'd help find her book and then he was taking his behind home. "What does it look like?"

"It's wide and has a red binding," she said.

He explored until he found a book on the third shelf and yanked it out. The book bounced and fell open to a random page on the floor. Sirena inhaled sharply and reeled back.

Gus peered at the page. What was so shocking?

A woodcut depicted a stocky woman lying in a wooded area while an eager satyr did very pleasing things to her. With his mouth. His hands.

The picture was so vivid he could practically hear their moans of shared pleasure.

He blinked as the images on the page moved and shifted before his eyes. What terrible and freaky magic was at work? The satyr was biting his lip as he guided himself inside his willing companion. The woman, in turn, spread herself and stared wantonly at her partner.

Gus glanced away to rein in his growing lust. They hadn't finished with what they started in the maze. He pulsed with desire and fought the urge to run home to take care of himself. A wave of hunger swept over him, causing him to breathe heavier. Rougher. Gus looked at Sirena. Her hand was pressed to her throat, her lips parted as she watched the picture. Her dark eyes widened in shock and interest. After a strained instant, he scooped up the book and snapped it closed.

Gus dropped the book on a nearby shelf. His body throbbed, aware of her closeness. Of her scent. Of her softness. "That wasn't the book I wanted to show you," she sighed.

He opened his mouth to apologize, but she interrupted him.

"I wouldn't leave my bed with that book."

His imagination took that sentence and ran with it down the block. He could see her in bed wearing nothing but a T-shirt. Sirena would probably run her hands over her dips and valleys, tossing her head back and closing her eyes to shut out the world. How would she sound while she stroked herself? Would she pant in desperation, or would she softly moan as she climaxed? Would she wish that he was there to watch her?

He let out a choked response. "Really?"

Her eyes grew heavy with need. "Really."

The remaining lust in his blood sent his heart pounding. Gus couldn't ignore the ache that was growing from the inside out. How could any creature, human or otherwise, keep away from her? How had he stayed away from her for days? Resentment tightened in his chest.

He'd wasted so much time waiting, denying his one simple desire.

I want to take your breath away. Gus moved toward her. "Pause or play?" he asked.

Sirena watched with an interested eye. "Play," she whispered and leaned forward into his space. "Let's go have some fun."

Over his magic career, Gus had found himself in various places and situations and had never broken out into a sweat. He'd snuck into a royal's living room to return a book he borrowed. He even managed to hang out at the Metropolitan Museum of Art after hours to check out the Temple of Dendur. But walking into Sirena's bedroom this chilly October night, he practically felt the beads of sweat roll down his face. The word "cozy" wished it was as comfortable as this room was. The queen-sized bed was pushed up against the wall, covered in a plush red comforter and pillows. It was the type of bed that you'd dream about sinking into at the end of a long day. Inviting. Beckoning. A place made for comfort.

The dresser was lined with jar candles, index cards covered with recipes, and hair care products. Ember, the prize Gus had won for Sirena, was perched there, looking regal. He liked having a piece of him in her space. The desk and chair combo held opened cookbooks, half-burned incense sticks and ashes, and a row of fragrant perfume bottles. His attention fell on the stack of spiral notebooks on the edge of the desk.

Gus pointed to the stack. "Spells?" he teased.

Sirena gave the notebooks an open smile. "No, they're goals."

She reached over and pressed a finger to his lips.

Sirena mouthed the words *Don't make a sound*. Hot teeth of desire bit into his backbone.

They were playing the quiet game. He wanted to be the first to make her break, to hear her moan and end the silence. She shrugged off her robe and tossed it on the back of her chair. Gus yanked off his shirt and dropped it on the floor. Her attention followed the item, then snapped up to his chest.

Her gaze turned fiery. Game on. Sirena tossed off her night-shirt and stood in her shorts and sporty bra. Her breasts strained against the cups. Anticipation inched through his veins. He yearned to stroke her with his tongue and feel her writhe with pleasure.

She went over to her dresser and pulled out a box of condoms, then tossed them on the bed. He took a small step toward Sirena. Gus stripped naked, not wanting anything to get in between them. For too long, he had hidden behind his pretty words and illusions. Sirena approached Gus and stood before him. She traced the upright triangle, the alchemy symbol for fire, on his chest tenderly. He sighed at her feather-soft touch. Sirena took care with him, the same way he watched her handle onion-skin papers and fragile documents. Her fingers sparked pops of magic that tickled his skin. He gave her a wicked smile, felt himself harden and pulsate.

His mouth swooped down to capture hers, kissing her with reckless abandon.

One thought replayed in his mind as he tasted her lips: *Next time*.

Next time they'd be gentle and caring. Next time they'd caress and stroke each other tenderly. But now they were greedy and driven by one single goal: to burn together.

She pushed back from Gus and undid her sporty bra, freeing herself and showing off more skin. He stared down at her, his eyes taking her in. *You are lovely and uniquely made.*

She undressed quickly and closed the distance between them. Gus caressed her broad curves, his hands unhurriedly exploring the lines of her body. She bit back a moan as he lowered his hands down her belly and touched her. He felt the slickness there and nearly came undone as he carefully explored. He looked at Sirena. She breathed heavily between parted lips, her eyes heavy with want. Gus bit the skin of her neck and drew lazy circles with his tongue.

Sirena released a stifled breath and yanked away from his hand.

Damn. Gus had almost gotten her to break. She wagged her finger at him in warning, then climbed into the bed while he stood at the edge. He watched the swing of her round ass twitching as she got comfortable. She lay on her pillows, her body prone and laid out like a goddess in waiting. Gus loitered at the edge of the bed. The thought of Sirena begging him to take her, whispering his name like an enchantment, made him impatient. Needy. He reached down and stroked himself. Wanting to feel her naked underneath him. Teasing her with what she could have if she invited him in. Sirena eyed him back and raised a saucy brow; the evidence of his arousal was clear and impressive to her.

Gus gestured downward. She gave him a ready nod. *Yes. Please. Now.*

He joined her in bed, his pendant swinging against his bare chest. A few well-placed kisses would send her over the edge. He moved between her thighs, eased them open, and pressed his lips right there. No. Not there. Right. There. Sirena arched her back and pressed herself against his mouth. A shock of pleasure and heat blasted behind his eyes the moment they connected.

He tasted her again, using his tongue and his lips to savor her. Sirena gasped and her breathing grew tense. Still, she didn't say a word. Oh, she was stubborn. Gus wasn't going to stop until he heard her say his name. Resolve stormed through his bones. Gus nipped the inside of her thigh and continued his mission, stroking his lips against her core. He felt her hands gently tug at his hair. The tugging encouraged him to keep going. Gus plundered her further, coaxing out more sweet gasps, but no words. The heat increased twofold, as if he were standing in the middle of a kiln and the air was ablaze. Her breath hitched higher and higher. It wasn't enough.

I want to hear you moan.

He added his fingers to stroke her from within, to add a little friction to the slickness of her. A tiny moan escaped her lips. He felt her tighten around him. Good. She was close. So close.

"August, please," she begged.

Gus peeked up from between her legs, feeling joyfully smug at the sound of her voice. *She said my name.* He continued stroking, and moments later she shouted in blissful release. He watched as the pleasure crashed down upon her in waves, her body shuddering with aftershocks.

"Do you know how sexy you look right now?" he said, panting.

She shook her head languidly, seemingly unable to form sentences. Gus could spend the rest of his life finding ways to make her speechless. The smugness changed into another deeper emotion—one that threatened to steal his sanity. No. This is about diversion. Fun. It can't be about anything else.

"I need you inside of me," she said.

Sirena pushed Gus onto his back. She grabbed a condom and unwrapped it. *Keep it fun.* She took the length of him in her hand, stroking him until he was hard and throbbing. He opened his mouth, and for a horrific second he thought he was going to say something heartbreakingly romantic. Something that would break his soul.

I belong to you. All I am, all I have is yours.

She quieted him with a searing kiss. He returned the kiss, being gentle and tender. His heart stirred, and she broke off the kiss. *Now.* No—he needed her yesterday. Sirena sheathed Gus, then straddled him, lowering herself inch by inch until hip met hip and flesh met flesh. He hissed out a breath once they were fully joined. *Finally.* As their bodies intertwined, Gus reveled in everything about Sirena. Her braids fell around her face like a curtain. Her scent, herbaceous and delightful, was so potent, all he could think about was staying buried within her for days.

She rode him hard, using him to pleasure herself.

Gus knew right then what it truly meant to burn, as they found their private rhythm. The moment when gasoline was fed oxygen and the chemical caught fire. The fire he fought to control tore through him, burning every thought he had. All that remained was the base instinct that fueled his actions: *Possess her. Charm her. Dazzle her.*

He was burning so quickly, with every thrust and stroke, he felt his body threaten to combust. Gus trembled. There would be nothing left of him but embers.

"Sirena, I—" Gus rasped underneath her; his hands went to her soft hips and dug in. He wanted to hold back for Sirena, to let her find her release once more. His eyes didn't leave hers, which grew hazy with ecstasy. She changed up her motions, eliciting a shocked groan from him as she slowed to a playful bounce. She rode him, rolling her hips around and around. Seconds later, he came, his breath escaping from his mouth in shuddering groans.

She pressed kisses to his mouth, chin, and cheek and brushed her lips against his tattoo.

"You," he sighed.

Sirena feigned innocence, blinking. "Me what? What did I do?"

"I had plans for you," Gus said. Plans that included getting her on all fours and entering her from the back. Plans that included positioning a mirror in front of her bed and watching himself enter her.

"We'll make the time for those plans," she said. "Next time."

Sirena swung her legs and freed Gus from underneath her body. She picked her robe up off the floor but decided to stay naked. Gus merely watched her while he cleaned himself up. He was naked in a witch's bedroom. His body still craved her hands, her mouth . . . her everything. There was no way that he was going back to his original state. Being with Sirena had changed him at his fundamental core. His troubles would still be there in the morning, but for now he wanted to stay here in this bed.

He met her stare. She ran her tongue over her lips in eagerness.

"You keep looking at me like that—" He broke off. Gus leapt up and went over to Sirena. He held her face in his hands and kissed her until she was boneless. She pressed against him, skin to skin, and they crashed back into the bed. Apparently, "next time" was now.

Chapter Twenty

*C*an you live a lifetime in a single week? Gus was going to try to do it by spending as much time as possible with Sirena. She brought him lunches every day when she finished work at Night Sky, still in her work outfit, her T-shirt and jeans smelling of fresh bread and rosemary.

"I need you to be honest," she had said, handing him a paper bag while he was in his office. "Jester's privilege!"

Monday, he was given grilled cheese and homemade tomato soup that made him yearn for rainy days and cartoon reruns.

"It was a plate of pure coziness," he said.

Sirena shook her head, seemingly unsatisfied with his praise.

"Thank you, but I need you to want to hire me!" she said. She clapped her hands. "Back to the kitchen!"

On Tuesday, he ate a mushroom and Swiss sandwich with sliced turkey breast that made him feel nostalgic. With every bite, Gus felt like he was back home eating leftovers after watching football with his cousins.

"It was perfection," he said.

Sirena narrowed her eyes at his empty plate. "I can do better. I'm not done yet."

"When am I going to cook for you?" he asked. Sirena answered him with a sly grin.

On Wednesday, she handed him a domed tray. "Get ready to have your mind rocked."

Gus lifted the dome to find a steaming plate of chicken and dumplings. His mouth watered. The rich scent of parsley, butter, and garlic wafted up from the plate of tender chicken and pillowy dumplings. Grandma Amelia made this dish whenever they came over to visit her home.

Gus sat down at his desk with the meal and immediately took a single bite. His eyes rolled into the back of his head. Food shouldn't taste this good, but it did, and it was divine.

Showstopping. Amazing. Wonderful.

Sirena stood in the doorway, her hands pressed together. "So?"

"When can you start?" he said, shoving another forkful into his mouth. "You're hired."

She did a little celebration dance, waving her hands like a jellyfish on summer vacation.

As Gus watched her, his spirits kicked up. He'd spent every night with Sirena after their eventful frolic following the Harvest Maze, finding many ways to pleasure her and make her laugh. One time he couldn't wait until work was over, so he ended up lifting her onto his desk and having her for an afternoon snack. She seemed comfortable with their friends-with-benefits arrangement, and he didn't want to ask for more until she was ready. For real, he wasn't quite ready to believe that Sirena was truly his kindred, even though he knew it in his soul. His brain needed to catch up with what truth his heart already recognized.

Now she had invited him over to her house for dinner, her official Lighthouse demo meal. Gus sat in the living room, checking on his phone. He got an email from Jess's wedding planner. They needed the name of his plus-one. *Oh.* He'd completely forgotten to find a date for the wedding. He frowned. Sirena came out of the kitchen, wearing an apron over her sweater and jeans. Her hair was wrapped up in a messy bun, and there were flour smudges on her cheek.

Why did she have to look so cute?

She clasped her hands together absentmindedly. "Is everything okay?"

He gripped his phone. "Maybe."

Sirena peered at him. "Can I help?"

If only. He was still feeling a little hesitant about even attending the wedding. Gus needed to get in touch with someone who knew the whole story. He didn't want to burden Sirena with his problems before her important interview. If Sirena had the courage to push herself to achieve her best, then he could push himself to be a better man.

It was time he called Zeke. "I have to make a call."

Sirena gestured to the porch. "It's all yours. Dinner should be done soon."

He kissed her forehead. Gus watched with a troubled brow as Sirena walked back into the kitchen, her shoulders slumped, muttering about roux sauce. Lately, she'd been distracted and looking off into space when it came to her cooking and her menu talk. When he asked her about it, she said she was fine and shooed him away. *Make this call, then check on her immediately.*

Gus walked out the front door and sat down on the porch stairs. He scrolled through his contacts until he found Zeke. Nervousness swept over him as he pressed the button. It rang for a few seconds before Zeke picked up.

His familiar voice, deep and a little snarky, came on the line. "What's good, Dearworth? I was starting to think you were avoiding me."

"I . . . was," Gus said.

Zeke barked out a laugh. "Damn, you weren't even going to lie."

"You would've called me out," Gus reminded.

"You're right," Zeke said. Suddenly, there was a roar of a crowd and the cheering of people in the background. "Hold on, Gus."

Gus heard Zeke move and shuffle around over the phone. He overheard the noisy conversation and then heard the shutting of a door. It was quieter wherever Zeke had moved to.

"I can call back if you're busy."

"Nah, some of the guys recorded the Rutgers game and they're watching on my big screen. You wanted to talk."

Gus could always trust Zeke to be real with him. Good old Zeke. He didn't have time for fools or thieves and always had a good sense about people.

"I heard you're going to Jess's wedding," Gus said.

A jagged sigh was heard over the line. "Yeah. I figured you'd reach out to me about that soon. You didn't hear it from me but no one from her side is coming. They all declined to go, including her parents. They think that she's making a mistake marrying Igor."

Gus flinched at this news. "Damn, that's rough."

His jaw tightened as he sat with this new information. From what he heard from Diane and saw in clips his ma liked to "accidentally" send him, Igor loved Jess, and she seemed truly happy.

"She's torn up about it," Zeke said plainly. "Jess asked me to send out invitations to people who'd show up for her, so I sent one to you and the family. I wanted to give you a heads-up, but I underestimated my postman."

"That's why you called me," Gus figured. He hadn't had the courage to listen to the message, but watching Sirena facing her fears encouraged him to do better with his relationships. "I made a fool of myself when I was with her."

"Eh. Who isn't a fool when they're in love?" Zeke inquired.

"I didn't like who I was with her," he said.

"But you've changed," he said confidently. Gus tried to cut in, but Zeke spoke over him. "Trust me, you have. Good-Time Gus wouldn't have gone to a history conference without bringing, like, a dozen doves or dollar bills to toss out at people."

"You saw the video."

"Diane forwarded me the link. I read the comments. People are impressed with your new path," Zeke said, a hint of pride in his voice.

Gus stirred uneasily on the stair. "I thought everyone only liked Good-Time Gus."

Zeke gave a little cough. "It was cool when we were younger to get into bars and skip to the head of the line, but it didn't feel like it was fun for you. Sorry for just blurting that out. I'm still getting a handle on my powers."

Gus peered at the phone, blinking slowly. "Um...what powers?"

"I would've said something to you earlier, but there never seemed to be a good time. Apparently, I'm an empath."

Gus sat back on his elbows.

Zeke filled the silence. "Yeah. It was a bit of a shock to me, too. I took one of those LegacyAndMe tests, and well...apparently,

I've got some magic in the blood. We've had some interesting talks at our family reunion."

"We host genealogy classes at the society," Gus said.

Zeke grunted. "Bet. I'd like to hang out with Nerdy Gus. Talk about history and stuff."

Gus laughed. "If you're free next week, swing by my birthday party."

"I'll try to come by. I think it should work with my shift at the firehouse. I'll text Di for the day and time."

An alarm pierced the air, followed by a startled scream. Gus ended the call with Zeke and sprinted back into the house. A smoky haze was coming from the kitchen. Terror seized his system, but Gus went forward to find his Sirena.

Chapter Twenty-One

How did the chicken catch on fire?!

Sirena looked away for what felt like a second to her phone, and suddenly the alarm was going off and Shadow was howling. Smoke was billowing from the pan, and the chicken looked like a charred brick. Panic jolted through her veins. Sirena snapped off the burner and dropped the smoking pan into the sink. She backed away from the stove, not trusting herself to do anything else but stand there. The pan hissed and sizzled, and she watched the smoke snake up to the ceiling.

Gus raced into the kitchen, his forehead wrinkled.

"Are you okay?" he said, his voice laced with concern.

She nodded woodenly. A painful stab of regret went through her body. *I scared him.* Gus went over to the windows and opened them to let the smoke out. Sirena seemed to watch him from a distance as he turned on the exhaust fan over the stove. The whir jerked her back into herself. The Lighthouse interview was tomorrow, and she couldn't cook a piece of chicken? That familiar mixture of failure and doubt stole the breath from her lungs.

A whine escaped her mouth, but nothing else came out. Gus reached out for Sirena, but she reeled away from him, feeling lightheaded. Her lungs screamed for air, but no matter what she did she couldn't get enough of it.

He met her eyes; his gaze didn't waver from hers. "It's going to be okay. We're going to figure it out."

No, it wasn't okay. Nothing she did mattered. Despair pressed on her chest, and her inner voice mocked her. *You went back in time just to fail. You wasted his time just to fail.*

She was giving it her all, but she couldn't keep herself from failing. Sirena tried to force words out from her mouth, but nothing came out but gasps. Nana gave her so many rules, but there wasn't a rule for how to come back from failure. Gus took her hands. *Focus on his touch*, her brain demanded. His hands were smooth and warm. She squeezed them and held on tight.

He brought her over to the kitchen table and sat down with her. Gus took a big, exaggerated inhale and let it out with an exhale. She took a half breath; her body shuddered. Her chest loosened up a little. He repeated the actions, and somehow her brain was able to process what he was doing. *Inhale. Exhale. Repeat.* She followed his example, gulped down steadying breaths. Cool air rushed into her lungs. *Inhale. Exhale. Repeat.* Gus kept going, and with each breath, she regained her calmness. Her thoughts slowed down.

"Tell me what's going on," he said.

Sirena just blinked. She was too tired to cry. "My interview is tomorrow, and I can't get the recipe right. I've messed up twice and it's too late to change anything and I've got to reschedule."

"Wait," Gus pleaded gently. She didn't deserve his tenderness.

"I can't get the recipe right!" she shouted. "I've messed up twice and it's too late to change anything and I...I have to reschedule. I've done—we've done—too much work just for me to screw up again."

Sirena swallowed hard. "I can't slow down. There's not enough time. I keep making silly mistakes. Salt instead of sugar. Flour instead of baking soda. Hot rather than cold."

"Let's slow down and figure out what we can do," he said. "You cooked all this wonderful food at the society. Why can't you replicate that same experience here?" He squeezed her hands. "Talk it out."

She looked away from Gus and focused on the stove. "I remember the day Nana Ruth got that fancy new stove. She was so happy, she turned on the radio and danced. She applied to cooking school, but her parents told her that it wasn't a real career and refused to pay for it. Nana picked another career, but she always wished she did things differently."

His eyes took on a kind glint. "I hear you."

Sirena took a calming breath. "She was my biggest supporter. My career is everything Nana Ruth and my aunties ever wanted and hoped for themselves. I've been biding my time and waiting until I could get a shot at Lighthouse, and finally, I have a chance to make good. Nana Ruth picked *me*, over my sisters, over my cousin, to be the one to carry her magic. I messed up. I lost all my recipes to a scammer. What kind of witch am I if I can't protect my magic? I don't deserve to touch her stove."

She faced Gus.

He spoke, his voice a ruthless whisper. "Let them have those papers."

"Excuse me?" Her nerves tensed immediately. The kindness drained from his eyes, and what remained was a polite coldness that stole her voice. Gus wasn't going to hold his tongue. Sirena stilled and waited for him to continue.

"Let that thief try to duplicate what you already possess, a natural talent and magic for conjuring meals. They get those papers, but they don't get to have you. I know what it's like to carry on a magical legacy and have the responsibility. Plenty of people stole my illusions, but they couldn't steal my talent. Let me remind you in case you forgot. My bewitching dear, you are a Caraway. With the power you possess, you take the most ordinary items and make them into extraordinary meals. Some chefs fill bellies. You fill up souls."

Sirena listened, his words a balm to the wounds she'd inflicted on herself.

Gus brought her hand to his lips and kissed it. He ran his thumb over her knuckles, making sure to touch the ring. She never took it off. "Do you remember what I told you you are?"

Sirena recalled the words he'd written down for her by the carousel. "I remember."

You're irreplaceable.

She'd gotten so busy planning out the menu and tinkering with recipes that she hadn't looked at the paper again.

"It's not enough to know it," he said. "You have to believe it."

She looked down at her lap. It was hard to forgive herself for being so careless. "But—"

He tucked his hand under her chin and lifted her head. "Believe."

That single word vibrated in her soul. She looked into his eyes, and she allowed herself to let the words take root. Sirena leaned away from Gus's touch and truly thought about what she had to do to get herself to believe in her magic.

What makes you so irreplaceable? She thought about everything she'd achieved and everything she'd done in her life. Sirena showed up and showed out at events for her family, friends, and community. She was the keeper of the hearth and left fresh lavender and sage at the family altar. She invoked the ancestors with every recipe that was handed down to her from Nana.

Doubt hissed in her ear. *What would Nana say about your big mistake?*

Sirena couldn't bring herself to respond, and the doubt chuckled in nasty glee.

Immediately, she heard a small, slivery voice from within her heart. She gasped as the voice spoke to her, strong and filled with compassion.

My sweet child, I'd say, in this family we forgive each other. When we make mistakes, we move forward with love and support. We get back up when we fall.

Sirena wiped away a stray tear as Nana's voice faded away, taking the doubt along with it. Everything felt weary, but she wasn't going to quit on herself anymore. Sirena had the rules and could find her way. She went to stand up and claim her stove, but Gus eased her back into her seat.

"Sit down and rest for a moment," he said. "I'm going to make you a cup of tea, and we're going to figure this out."

That evening, Sirena invited him into her kitchen.

Over three cups of tea, Sirena told Gus about the first meal she ever made. She was five years old when Nana Ruth had told her the story of stone soup. For days, Sirena begged Nana to help her cook that magical soup for her and her sisters. Sirena picked the perfect stone from the garden. It was smooth and gray, the size of her small palm. She washed it off in the sink. Nana dropped it into the pot. She added the chopped vegetables, stock, and seasonings and stirred the mixture. Nana let Sirena sprinkle in the salt, pepper, and fresh oregano from the garden.

Sirena jumped up from the table and got out her notebook from the counter before she finished the story. An intense desire to write down everything she remembered fueled her fingers as she scribbled on the pages. She filled several pages with everything she recalled about the soup and sketched out the ingredients in the margins. By the time Sirena was finished writing the story and recipe, her fingertips were covered in ink. She turned to Gus at the table and showed him her hands, and her heart sang in appreciation.

Sirena: Good morning. Happy birthday!

Gus: Good morning. Thank you. ♥ Have you heard from Lighthouse about an offer?

Sirena: Not yet. No news is good news. But the manager did email me to say how much she loved the stone soup and sandwich combo. 🎂 😉 I think she wanted the recipe.

Gus: That's nice. They can have the recipe WHEN they hire you. 📖 You're too talented to be ignored. ☆

Sirena: You're so sweet. This is why I love you.

Gus: [no response]

Sirena: I'll see you at the party tonight.

Chapter Twenty-Two

Sirena stood in the middle of Night Sky, holding her phone and staring at her last text. *Did you just tell Gus you* love *him?* Sirena studied the ghostly and ghoulish decorations around the bistro to keep herself from freaking out. The black-and-orange pom-pom garland hung over the treat counter. Vintage postcards were taped up against the wall. She noticed a smiling magician on one of the postcards and groaned. Now she was officially freaking out.

You just told Gus you loved him—on his birthday—on Halloween.

Sirena dropped her phone in her apron, her face feeling numb.

Where the heck did that come from? She shook her head, trying to understand why she just told her fine-as-hell magician friend and sometime hookup that she loved him. Her hand yanked at her Night Sky shirt, which was suddenly feeling too tight.

"Hey, Si," Beckett said. "Can you take out the trash for me? I'm busy."

She rubbed her sweaty palms on her jeans, trying to dry them. "Um, sure."

You're taking out the trash and you love Gus.

It had just popped out. She'd been so charmed by his words and his confidence that she'd get the job that she just texted it. Her heart hijacked her thumbs and she texted him that?! Sirena walked through the kitchen, scooped up the trash, and went out the back door. The sour aroma of trash hit her nose, but she pushed through because she—oh, that's right—had told Gus she *loved* him.

He hadn't responded. Yet. She lifted the trash can lid.

A clown wearing a rainbow wig and rubber teeth popped out at her.

"Trick or treat!" it cackled.

Damn it, she forgot about the stupid clown! *Don't punch the clown. Run away.* Sirena dropped the trash at her feet and tried to pivot away, but her leg caught the edge of the can. She twisted and fell awkwardly on her wrist. A blast of searing pain shot up her arm.

Sirena yelled out, then cradled her hand to her chest. *No.* Not her wrist.

The clown jumped out of the trash. "Oh, man. Y'all come out! I think she's really hurt."

A two-man camera crew ran out from their hiding spots. Beckett popped out from behind the trash can, holding his phone. "Yo, Si. Are you okay?"

Sirena ignored him and focused on her wrist. She tried to flex it, but it hurt too much to move. She hissed. *No, please. I'm so close to getting what I need.* There was a commotion and a flurry of activity. Gwen, her boss, rushed outside and approached Sirena. Fury shone in her eyes as she surveyed the situation, then looked at Beckett.

"Someone starts talking, or I'm firing someone today," she barked.

While Gwen went toe-to-toe with a cameraman for filming her without permission, Sirena dully sat on the ground. Defeat squeezed her sides. She was so freaking close to changing her fate, but it wasn't possible. If her wrist was broken, she'd struggle to keep up with the demands of running a professional kitchen. It wouldn't be impossible, but it would be hard as hell to cook the way she wanted while she was healing. Sirena noticed that Beckett didn't look in her direction.

"I need to go to the hospital," Sirena said loudly. "Please."

Gwen dropped down to her knees. "Okay. Who can I call to meet you there?"

Call Gus, a part of her requested. No. It was his birthday. She'd explain to him later what happened, but she'd handle this emergency on her own. He wasn't her boyfriend; he was just a guy she really, really liked. Not loved. It was too soon for love, or that's what she had to tell herself.

"Can you call Callie for me?" she said eventually.

The local emergency room was packed because apparently it was the season for pumpkin-carving accidents, tripping over scary lawn decorations, and random troll fights. Sirena sat between a masked superhero with a bandaged hand and a flannel-clad homeowner with an elevated knee. Callie sat with her until her name was called. The doctor clucked at Sirena about avoiding clowns. According to the X-ray, her wrist was indeed broken and would heal in six to twelve weeks.

She was given a half cast and a prescription for pain medicine. By the time Sirena was on her way home from the pharmacy with her filled prescription and discounted candy, the sky was quickly darkening. The orange streetlights were flickering on, giving the Grove an eerie autumn glow. She rolled down the window with the automatic button, letting the cool breeze flow through the car. As Callie drove them home, Sirena watched the trick-or-treaters skipping from house to house, swinging their candy bags, weighed down with loot. She held the discharge papers in her uninjured hand, thanking her lucky stars that she had managed to get health insurance through her job at Night Sky Bistro.

Sirena rested in the passenger seat. "I'm sorry you have to babysit me on Halloween."

Callie made a face. "Don't worry about it. I'm just glad that you're okay."

Callie's phone vibrated on the dashboard. She clicked her tongue but didn't answer it.

Sirena pointed to the phone. "Who's calling you now?"

The phone vibrated again; Callie didn't answer it. She checked the screen quickly and sighed. "That would be Gigi. I didn't want to take the call in the ER. I sent her a text explaining what happened, but I don't think she got it. I'll call her when we get home."

Sirena's stomach twisted. "I'm ruining your Halloween."

Callie shook her head. "Eh, I woke up on the wrong side of the broom this morning. I thought if I had all the decorations, the frills, and the food, I'd get in the scary mood."

"Let me guess. It didn't work?"

A look of exhaustion passed over Callie's pretty features. "I was trying to hype myself up, but I've been getting requests for me to plan Christmas parties! Like, can't a witch get a break? I'm trying to get my bride down the aisle. Gigi might go with Enchanted Events if I don't step up my game."

Sirena tilted her head and watched her little sister. Callie was busting her behind trying to get her event planning business off the ground, but she still found time to take care of her.

"I'll celebrate Halloween tomorrow in November," Callie said, giving her a sad smile.

That's right. The spell would probably send her right back to the start of October.

Sirena clutched her medicine bag in her fingers. "I don't want to get in the way of your hustle. You can still go meet her for dinner. It's only six o'clock."

Her eyes went to the time on the dashboard. Gus's party was in full swing by now. She had texted him what happened at the bistro, and he'd asked if there was anything he could do for her. She downplayed her injury, not wanting to spoil his evening. A twinge went through her heart that felt a little like regret.

Callie shrugged. "I'll get in contact with Gigi when we get home. The doctor said that you need to be observed for any pain. We've got to make sure you're okay for the next day or so...Get ready to listen to Studio Ghibli soundtracks."

"We can watch horror films," Sirena offered.

Callie stuck out her tongue. "Nah. Let's watch *Hocus Pocus*. You know you've always had a crush on the zombie. I'll order pizza bones from Rapunzel's."

"We'll have a great time," Sirena said.

Callie pulled up and parked in front of the house. Sirena

glanced across the street, where Lucy and Alex's cottage was illuminated with jack-o'-lanterns and bales of hay. A steady thumping of music came from their home, and guests were coming in and out of the party.

"Someone wants to win the Best Block Decoration," she said.

Sirena and Callie exited the car. Callie took her by the shoulder and led her up the stairs. Her legs were a little wobbly from having to lie down in a makeshift bed in the ER. They paused when they noticed the tuxedoed man sitting on the top step of their porch.

"Who ordered the magician?" Callie joked.

Gus straightened and stood as they approached, holding a bouquet of white and orange daisies. "Good evening."

His eyes roamed over Sirena in a protective way. He lingered briefly on her hurt arm, then met her stare. "I wanted to see if you're okay."

Callie let out a small "Aw."

Gus presented her with the bouquet. Sirena fidgeted uncomfortably under his attention. She wasn't used to being babied over by anyone outside of her family.

Sirena took the flowers, cradling them in the crook of her arm with her medicine. "I'm fine, for the most part. Doctor says I have six weeks in the half cast, then I can switch to a soft cast for the next six weeks."

"I wish you had called me," he said.

Her heart fluttered a bit, but her head pounded. She should have checked in with him earlier, but she didn't know how to face him after . . . she texted him what she texted.

Callie's phone went off, interrupting their moment. She glanced at her screen and winced. "Sorry, Si. Gus. Excuse me."

Callie turned away from Gus and Sirena, giving them some privacy.

"It's your birthday. You should be out having a good time."

He graced her with a buccaneer smile, sly and cunning, as if he just found a treasure chest. "I'm right where I need to be."

Gus lowered his voice. "I'm not leaving without you. I won't be able to sleep knowing you're in pain. Come home with me. I'll keep you in my bed and feed you birthday cake."

"Or you can come upstairs with me, and we can watch some movies," she said.

Gus took a step forward. "You sure I can't tempt you?"

"You can try," she said automatically. His eyes grew tender. There was a hint of longing in his eyes. Did he want to talk about the text? Sirena opened her mouth to ask, but an angry screech from Callie pierced the air.

She spoke in a quick, frantic rush. "Si! I've got to go. Gigi called."

"Is everything okay?"

"Gigi's bridesmaid hid her wedding dress somewhere under the boardwalk. I've got to keep Gigi from turning her bridesmaid into a cat! But I don't feel comfortable leaving you alone," Callie said hesitantly.

Gus jumped in. "I'll keep her company, if that's okay with Sirena."

Guilt reverberated through Sirena's chest at his offer. "It's your birthday."

"I'm right where I want to be," he repeated. Gus placed a hand on her shoulder, steadying her to his side. Sirena let herself lean on him. The guilt faded and was replaced with another sweeter and better emotion.

"Thank you, Gus! I'll be back soon." Callie blew Sirena a kiss and waved. She ran down the stairs and jumped into her car.

Gus reached over and brushed a loose braid from her face. Her skin fizzled under his gentle, careful touch. "I guess you're coming home with me."

Chapter Twenty-Three

☾

Party guests lingered on the porch of the historical society, muffled music could be heard from outside, and a line of lit pumpkins tied with black ribbons around the stems decorated the front lawn. Gus dropped Sirena in the front and went to park the car behind the house. Sparkly magic and mayhem oozed from the roof. She walked inside and moved toward the sound of guests chatting over funky, bouncy music.

Burning candles with fragrance notes of hot cinnamon sticks and fresh grated clove hovered overhead. She joined the guests standing around the massive living room, the chairs and sofas artfully arranged in circles. Winding her way around the party, she narrowly avoided a group of dapperly dressed gnomes slamming back half-filled beer steins. Sleek elves, jovial water sprites, fae, and witches adorned in various costumes were cradling snacks and drinks in their hands and paws. She reviewed the bubbling cauldron in the hearth, filled to the brim with an oozing green brew.

It couldn't be denied. The Dearworths knew how to throw a party.

Glass bowls of red delicious apples were placed on various tabletops, along with glass jars of roasted chestnuts, wrapped candies, and popcorn balls. She found Gus. He faced Sirena and a rogu-ish grin crossed his face, as if he was imagining something devi-ous. Like snapping his fingers and making her clothes disappear. Fissures of excitement went through Sirena, turning her knees to jelly. *Girl, stand up. You don't need to break your other wrist.*

Diane hugged her and gave her a quick makeover in the bath-room. She painted her face with gold and glitter makeup, swear-ing that Sirena needed to sparkle a little for tonight. When Diane presented a sparkly Sirena to a waiting Gus, he pressed his hand to his heart and swooned.

Gus introduced Sirena to his friend Zeke, who kissed her free hand like a knight in waiting. He was tall and lanky and barely filled out his armor.

He gave her a critical, assessing squint. "What are you dressed as?"

"I'm an overworked, underpaid witch with a broken wrist," she said without missing a beat.

Gus held back a laugh. Zeke looked taken aback for an instant.

His eyes, a shade of raw honey, shined. "I like you."

There was a blast of music from the speakers in the corner of the living room that had been turned into a makeshift dance space. Cheers went up from the crowd at the first recognizable notes of the song. Guests started slinking to the music and grooving. Sirena listened for a moment, then smiled. The smooth falsetto of the singer echoed through the air along with the deep bassline and steady guitar.

She bopped her body to the music. "I haven't heard this song in a minute."

Gus rubbed the back of his neck. "Same here."

They stood there awkwardly, like two sheepish kids at a middle school dance. Zeke stood there between them like a chaperone, giving them encouraging looks.

After about ten seconds, Sirena took Gus by the hand and led him out onto the floor.

They needed to dance out these emotions. "Let's go, Dearworth."

He twirled her once, eliciting a giggle from Sirena and pulled her into his space. They danced jubilantly as the playlist rolled on. Gus brushed the dirt off his shoulder. Sirena gestured her unhurt hand like the single lady that she truly was. They rocked back and forth, losing themselves to the music. There was a brief pause before the next song, letting them catch their breath. Sirena studied Gus. His skin had a sheen of sweat on it, making him shine in the low lights. She yearned to kiss him clean.

Another song played. It was slower, sultrier than the previous ones. Sirena stopped once she heard the full blast of the singer's honey butter voice. This tune absolutely wasn't a Halloween song; this was a grab-your-lover-and-make-them-perspire-until-the-morning-light song.

It was a grind-up-against-a-willing-dance-partner jam.

Gus held out his arms. Sirena stepped into them, folding herself into the heat of his body. She took in the lyrics. The singer crooned about missing her estranged love and yearning for them. Sirena nestled herself against him and pressed her ear to his chest. His heart pounded out a steady rhythm that made her feel as if nothing in the world could harm her. She burrowed closer, wrapping her hands around his waist, his scent enveloping her and making her feel secure. His arms tightened and held her to him, and she did the same. She pinched her eyes shut, and for a second, all Sirena wanted was to make a bed here in his arms, so she could fall asleep listening to his heartbeat. Whoa. Her eyes snapped open, dazed by that thought. A flash from behind Sirena pulled her out of the bubble and forced her to glance around. Why wasn't anyone else dancing? They were the only ones on the dance floor, while everyone else stood off to the side, watching them.

Sirena lowered her voice. "Everyone's looking at us."

She felt his lips move against her forehead. "Are they? I didn't notice."

His voice came out grumbly and sincere. Gus pressed a quick kiss to her temple.

Diane's high voice called out above the music. "It's time for cake! Where's Gus?"

He leaned in to steal a kiss, but Sirena pressed a finger to his lips. Gus playfully nipped at it, then stepped back.

"Pause," she whispered.

He pressed one last kiss to her hand. Yes, they'd hit pause for now, but eventually they would pick up where they left off. How could she be so spellbound over a man she barely knew? Sirena, Zeke, and the other guests all squeezed into the dining room. Gus and Diane stood at the head of the table, in front of the three-tier cake adorned with a large candle. "It's cake time."

Sirena let out an exhale. Zeke slid next to her, playfully bumping her with his shoulder.

He spoke under his breath. "I thought we were never going to get any cake. The night's almost over."

That's right. Her stomach dipped like she was riding in a descending elevator. Tonight was the last night of the time loop, and it looked as though she hadn't made good with her second chance. Hopelessness clawed at her throat, rendering her speechless. Sirena's heart pounded against her ribs. *No!* This night was when everything went wrong and...She wasn't that same witch.

This time would not be stolen from her.

Her wrist was broken, she hadn't heard anything from Lighthouse about the job offer, and she hadn't done anything meaningful with the society notebook. Sirena felt lost. Yet, as lost as she felt, there was a sense of hope that she hadn't felt that previous night in the kitchen. Every day could be her second chance to find the satisfaction that she yearned for with every breath. She wanted...satisfaction. In her career. In her life. In her spirit.

Sirena glanced over at Gus, and the fire within her body flared. It became crystal clear. She didn't need or want the month to repeat.

Diane clapped her hands, breaking into Sirena's thoughts. "Let's light this candle. Everyone, let's sing."

She led the crowd in singing "Happy Birthday," and the guests became joyous and raucous. Zeke was one of the loudest singers, using his baritone voice to carry the low notes. Gus ducked his head down and bit his lip, as if embarrassed by all the attention.

Sirena wanted to take him by the hand and lift his head up. As if he heard her, his head snapped up, and he found her in the crowd. She blinked. Were her eyes playing tricks on her? She could see Gus older, just as handsome, being sung to over a cake with many candles, his face covered in smile lines, his curly hair a lovely shade of gray. Sirena blinked again and he was youthful.

"Make a wish!" Diane sang. Gus's and Sirena's eyes met over the flame. There were moments in life that Sirena would never forget: the first spell she cast, the first time a dish stole her breath, and this moment. It wasn't love at first sight, but rather a faint recognition that she felt down to her soul. *There you are. Where have you been all this time?* The candle on the cake bloomed like a sparkler. The room filled with candlelight and enchantment. Everywhere. All at once. Guests clapped and gasped at the display.

Zeke let out a low, impressed whistle. "What a show."

She held Gus's stare. Sirena had seen Gus around town and spoken to him plenty of times, but in the candlelight tonight she truly saw him. She saw the glimmer of innate magic that shone in his face. He didn't move as the flame settled down into a flicker. Diane leaned in and whispered a few words in Gus's ear. He refocused his attention on the glowing candle. The spell was broken between them. He took in a deep breath and blew out the candle.

Did he make a wish? Sirena wondered.

Suddenly, the entire space was plunged into darkness. A collective gasp of shock erupted from the crowd, and cell phone lights turned on. Zeke grumbled, and a key chain flashlight turned on, illuminating the darkened room. Diane clapped her hands.

The lights flipped on, but the magician had vanished.

Chapter Twenty-Four

Gus did what he did best when he panicked. He vanished into thin air.

Well, he pulled the usual teleportation act his uncle Jon had taught him when he wanted to win at hide-and-seek. He reappeared in the library on the second floor, far away from his guests. The faint sounds of music and conversation only irritated his already frayed nerves.

Diane's words, right before he blew out his candle, had rattled him to his core.

Don't be afraid to wish. Immediately, he remembered everything. The slime. The coin flip. The ring box. He remembered that missing birthday and the desperate wish he made the first time he blew out the candle.

I wish I knew what I was missing.

He knew what he was missing, and it was his kindred. It was Sirena.

The library door creaked open. Gus hid behind the bookshelf. Sirena walked in. His heart punched against his ribs as if trying to escape and be with her. He wanted Sirena. Nothing else would appease his hunger. Nothing but his kindred would do.

He could barely breathe when he spied her in her wrinkled

Night Sky clothes, her hand in a half cast and her braids in a ponytail. Sirena was here. For him. He took her in from where he hid. She held a plate with a slice of birthday cake. She came to feed him. Gus moved from behind the bookshelf and met her by one of the large tables.

"Hello, you," she crooned.

She offered him the plate with her unscathed hand. "I've never seen anyone run from cake," she said. "I saved you the first slice. It's good luck."

Gus took it from her, their fingers brushing.

Her touch shocked his senses as if he brushed up against a heated touchstone.

Gus cleared his throat as she pulled back. "Did you get a taste?"

She raised her chin. "I might have had a bite. You disappeared. Are you feeling all right?"

Gus gave a forced smile, trying to hide his inner turmoil. "I'm not used to being the center of attention."

Sirena let out a little laugh of surprise. "You've performed for royalty and celebrities all over the world. I'm sure you can deal with a few people singing to you."

"You were singing to me," he pointed out. Gus could deal with many people singing to him, but the fact that it was Sirena singing to him gave him pause. It gave him joy.

Sirena winced. "You heard that, huh? I wish I had a pretty voice, like Lucy and Ursula. I can hum, but that's it."

"It's perfect."

She turned serious. "Tonight's the night when I cast the second-chance spell. It repeats tonight. I asked for a second chance, and I don't know if I've done enough with my time."

"You have," he said.

She breathed in shallow, quick gasps. "Even if I get the job, I broke my wrist. I need time to heal—Lighthouse might move on from me."

"It'll work out," he insisted. Gus had to believe that it would work out.

A cold knot formed in his stomach. He had to be honest with her in case she was sent back in time. In case he lost her. "What happened the last birthday we met? You said we talked briefly, but you didn't give me the details."

She thought for a second. "Oh, I found you with a ring box in the kitchen."

Gus reached into his suit pocket and took out a ring box. He opened it and placed it on the library table. "Was it this one?"

The anxious look on her face told her everything he needed to know.

"It's my grandma Amelia's engagement ring. This tuxedo belonged to my grandpa Gus. He never performed without this ring on him. Magicians tend to be very superstitious. That night, I was looking at the ring and wondering whether I would ever love again. If I'd ever use my heart. Then you walked into the kitchen covered in ghost slime, and I said you looked absolutely frightening."

Sirena let out a ragged breath. Her eyes widened. "You remember that Halloween."

Gus only nodded, not wanting to waste any more time on the past. He glanced at the clock on the wall. Midnight was approaching. He was running out of time.

"You texted that you love me today."

The instant Gus saw those words on his phone, he'd practically sprinted over to Night Sky Bistro. He wanted to tell her in person that he loved her, too, wanted to scoop her into his arms and shower her with kisses. Gus was running so fast to get there, he had accidentally knocked over his neighbor's faery garden village. He stopped to clean up his mess and it took him an embarrassingly long time to rearrange all the teacup houses. Once Gus had arrived at the bistro, Gwen told him that Sirena had left because of a personal emergency. Concern had slithered in his belly when he heard this news. Gus had sent Sirena a text, but she didn't respond to him immediately. He'd thought about calling Lucy and Callie to find out if everything was okay with their family, but he hesitated to call.

Who was he to Sirena? He'd danced around their status for weeks, not wanting to formally declare their connection. Thwarted in his love mission, Gus had gone back to the historical society and helped Diane decorate the space for his birthday. He'd gone out and bought the prettiest flowers he could find at the flower shop once he got the text from Sirena about her injury. If Callie hadn't been there on the porch, he would've held her in his arms and done anything to ease her pain.

Those three words she'd texted were everything he wanted to hear but was scared to hear from her. He'd loved before and he'd been terribly wrong. He didn't want to be wrong with her.

Gus returned his attention to the moment. He noticed that Sirena had clenched her hand into a fist.

Regret clouded her beautiful eyes, and she stepped forward. "It was an accident. Forget it, please."

"I can't," he said raggedly. "I can't."

He didn't want to forget; he wanted to remember everything. He wanted to experience it all, her wacky dances, her laughs, and her magic, but as her boyfriend. As her kindred.

Sirena reached up and covered his mouth with her fingers, keeping his words at bay. "It's too soon. We've only known each other a month."

Nerves made his heart thrash, but he willed himself to calm down. Gus took her hand away and held it against his chest. Her ring sparkled in the overhead light, almost signaling to him to tell her everything. It was time.

"That's not exactly true," he said.

Sirena rolled her eyes a little. "Okay, so our families know each other, but this thing between us is new."

He gave her hand a light squeeze. "We haven't spent only a month together; we've been together for centuries, but it still isn't enough time for me."

"We haven't? It isn't?" Her voice was low and halting.

Gus continued talking, hoping to make her understand what it meant to be kindred.

"We've been together before, but our bodies forgot, our souls forgot, but when we intertwined…It clicked for me. You kept me warm by bonfires on the open plains. We tracked the stars and kept records of the seasons in gilded books. We promenaded by gaslight and watched the world become modern. We've lived this story before but in different eras. In different places. We've known each other across lifetimes and oceans."

The color drained from her face. "You're telling me we're *soulmates*."

He licked his lips, taking a beat. "Magicians call us kindred. Our souls have met before."

She narrowed her eyes. "Wait. Does that mean we're destined for each other?"

He lowered his head, hearing the disbelief in her voice. "It depends. We might connect for a day, a month, or a lifetime. Being kindred doesn't guarantee true love. So, you texted you loved me and I...wanted to tell you."

If Gus could do it over again, he'd text her *I love you too* and rent a limo to pick her up and take her out on the town.

"I know it was unexpected," she muttered with a laugh.

Gus raked a hand through his beard. "I didn't want to tell you, but I needed you to know if—"

"If time resets," she finished. His heart dropped, but he had to try again.

"You texted me you loved me. Tell me I'm not too late."

Doubt flashed across her face. "Well, I'll be honest. You've told me so much tonight that my head's a mess. Are we pawns for the gods, or have I chosen you freely? Is what we have magic or love?"

Gus didn't know the answer to her question, so he said nothing.

Despair burned in his gut. *Why can't we have both?*

"I don't know what to do," she said. "We might not have tomorrow."

Gus breathed steadily. He knew in his soul that no matter how many times they might redo this month, he'd always find his way back to Sirena.

"Let's have tonight," he offered. She gave him a steady nod.

Gus led her upstairs to his apartment. All he wanted to do for his birthday was to fall asleep with her. If tonight was going to be their last night together, then they deserved candlelight. He snapped his fingers. The entire apartment, from the bookshelves to the kitchenette, was aglow with enchanted candles of every size and width. The flickering of charmed candlelight crept against the walls; the light grew in the room, burning bright. Scented candle wax and flame filled the air, giving the space a dreamy vibe. They undressed and held each other in his bed. One by one, the flames snuffed out until Gus and Sirena were left alone in the bliss of the darkness.

When midnight came, Gus kissed her good night and tucked her against his side.

He drifted off to sleep. A final thought fluttered in his mind as he descended into his dreams.

Even if this month repeats, I'm ready to spend a lifetime of Octobers with her.

November

Dried rosemary by a doorway helps drive away
thieves and keep a home safe.

Chapter Twenty-Five

I don't want to leave this bed.

Gus stared up at the ceiling, the morning light illuminating his bedroom. When he woke up, Sirena wasn't in his bed, and her clothes were gone. He held back a sob. Grief swept through him. It was done. The spell must have failed.

He looked over at his nightstand and snatched up his phone to see what time it was.

His phone was out of battery. Great. Who knew how many calls he had missed? Had Sirena called?

At least he had been able to spend another perfect night with Sirena before the reboot. She hadn't heard anything about the interview. He didn't know what the day held, but he wanted to see her again. Maybe he'd meet her at the Harvest Festival. Maybe this time around, they'd go to the pumpkin patch or the zombie stroll. This time around, he would romance her the right way. Gus pressed his nose to the pillow, trying hard to get a hint of her perfume.

He just wanted to hold on to a little bit of their magic.

She was his kindred, and he was hers. They'd find their way back to each other.

He had to believe in them.

A soft groan from the bedroom doorway startled him from his thoughts. Gus snapped his head up from the bed. Surprise lit up within him like a broken Atlantic City slot machine. There was a half-naked witch in his apartment. He sat up in bed and took in Sirena's sumptuous form. With a bedsheet wrapped around her body like a toga, she appeared like a wrinkled goddess.

Her brown skin sparkled in the morning light.

There were remnants of glitter on her eyelids, giving her an otherworldly glow.

"You're here!" He leapt from the bed and pulled on his boxers. Gus stood before her, drinking her in. He pinched his stomach. Ouch. Nope. He wasn't dreaming, and if he was, it was a beautiful dream of Sirena in the morning light. They held each other for a long moment.

He kissed her forehead, nuzzling her skin with his beard and lips.

Her voice was sleepy. "I'm here. What now?"

Gus stiffened. Right. Things were much more complicated in the light of day.

Sirena stole a look at him.

"I didn't want to say last night, but I…I have a hard time believing in the idea of soulmates and kindred because…" She took a breath. "I've never really been in love."

Gus blinked rapidly, trying to collect his thoughts.

"You've never been in love? Ever?"

"I'm talking about storybook, happily-ever-after, buy-you-the-soap-and-cologne-set-for-the-holiday true love. I've never experienced that with any man."

He regarded her quizzically, trying not to be shocked by this confession.

Sirena pointed at him, a helpless look on her face. "See, that look! You're staring at me like I just turned into the Mothman's sister! Like I'm a big old freak. I've seen that look on every one of my boyfriend's faces when I told them."

"Does that make me your boyfriend?" he said lightly.

Sirena stared at Gus. "Why would you want to be with me? I'm a hot mess."

"A beautiful hot mess," he joked kindly.

Sirena let out a dry laugh. "Thank you. We can talk about labels and names later, but I'd like to take it slow between us."

"How slow are we talking? Like a sloth crawling up a branch slow?"

Sirena wrinkled her nose. "We can go faster than that. I'm thinking, like, a leisurely pace. Like a sea star living their best life."

He grinned. "That sounds good to me."

They could take this relationship slow for as long as she wanted. A wiggle of doubt nestled inside his chest, and a mocking voice spoke in his head: *You're not a sea star; you're a marlin who likes to go super fast. Like sixty-seven-miles-per-hour fast when it comes to love.* Gus willed that voice away. *It's fine. It is going to be fine.*

Her forehead furrowed. "We go out on dates and hang out, but there's no pressure to spend the night. I'm not seeing anyone else, but... if you find some other woman you're interested in, you can see her."

He met her eyes. "There is no one else." There would never be anyone else for him, but he wasn't going to tell her that fact right now. He was taking it slow.

Sirena blinked. "So, would you feel comfortable being my date to Lucy's wedding?"

"Would you do me the honor of being *my* wedding date for Jess's wedding?"

"It would be my pleasure," she said.

"Okay, so what do you want right now?" he asked.

"I want scrambled eggs."

Gus kissed her brow. "Then I'll make them for you."

Sirena clutched the sheet to her chest. He went to his closet and pulled out a few shirts and a pair of sweatpants. He handed her a distressed Freya Grove Gladiators T-shirt, which she slipped on, giving him a flash of her naked body. Want flared within him. *Focus, Dearworth. She knows that she's your kindred. Now you have to figure out how to convince her to believe in the idea of being a kindred.* He went into the kitchenette and checked the fridge, groaning when he checked the carton.

"We don't have eggs."

He turned to the doorway. Sirena stood there looking deliciously rumpled. Gus itched to pull her into his arms and tumble back into the sheets with her. All he wanted to do was lose himself in her and forget that today was the tomorrow that he had feared.

Sirena reached for her purse. "I'll go get some."

"No, you rest. I'll get the eggs," Gus said.

He kissed her quickly on the cheek, stepping back before he could scoop her up into his arms again. How many times was he going to kiss her? Luther Vandross didn't lie. A thousand kisses with her would never be too much for him. He'd charm her when she had a full stomach. He grabbed his phone from the bedroom and flashed a shy grin as he went downstairs. Last night and all the nights they'd spent together had been wonderful, if not disorienting. The loop was over. His legs were shaky and wobbly with excitement. It felt like he'd just gotten off an out-of-control roller coaster and was trying to get his balance after being on a ride for so long. He whistled a sea shanty that Beryl had recorded as he walked out the back door off the kitchen. His car, a beat-up green Grand Am, was parked in the back parking lot away from the front door. He got in the driver's seat, plugged his phone into his car charger, and turned it on.

It vibrated, then buzzed with unread messages. That wasn't a good sign.

As Gus flicked past his lock screen and read a text, a sense of dread filled him.

"Oh no." Hurricane Anais was about to make landfall.

He switched the car off and went back to the house.

Sirena's arm throbbed uncomfortably, and she was sleepy and hungry, but she felt deliriously happy. The time loop was done. She walked gingerly down the stairs, trying to avoid the squeaky steps and not make too much noise. Sirena relished the homespun academia vibe this place gave her every time she visited the society. You could find turn-of-the-century photos of Freya Grove alongside crocheted blankets and handmade kitchen poppets around every corner. It was no wonder Gus loved this space, and she didn't want him to hand it over to anyone.

Her heart squealed in a low, happy whine. *Gus.* She spent her Halloween night with Gus.

He had peppered her with so many kisses this morning and been so tender with her last night. She wanted him to stay here and—maybe she could stay here with him. Was she asking him to extend his stewardship and stay in the Grove? Her heart raced at that idea, but her brain told her to stay under the speed limit. She was going to take things slow and not pressure him to make any big decisions.

Her current life and possible future were existing in the same space, and it felt overwhelming. She didn't want to think about it. All she wanted was scrambled eggs, whole wheat toast, and honey vanilla tea. Once she had food in her stomach, she was going to talk to Gus and learn more about this kindred idea.

Gus seemed so sure about their past, but she was unsure of their future.

She cared for him greatly, but she hadn't felt the click, that telltale click that every Caraway witch felt when they met their soulmate.

Her phone beeped with a waiting message, but she decided to ignore it for now. Eventually, Sirena made her way to the society kitchen and opened the fridge, looking to see what was there. A clacking of heels came from down the hallway. It was probably Diane coming back to look for something she had left behind, rocking those high stilettos that she wore last night. But then the hair stood up on the back of her neck, and Sirena felt her skin tingle. The air grew heavy and dark, as if a raincloud hovered in the sky.

An amused cackle filled the kitchen. "So, you're the fabulous witch my son likes."

Sirena turned, immediately recognizing the voice from the reruns she watched. Anais Dearworth. The older woman was on point and perfect with everything about her. Nails, done. Hair, done. Outfit, flawless. Even the shoes were fabulous. She was meeting *the* lady magician in a borrowed sweatshirt, sweatpants, and bare feet.

Anais blinked slowly, her long lashes showing off her hazel eyes. "Are you or are you not my son's new girlfriend? That's what my daughter told me."

Did she temporarily forget her name? "Um . . . I'm Sirena."

Anais gave her an amused smirk, then extended her hand to Sirena. "It's nice to meet you. I'm pretty sure you know who I am."

Sirena shook her waiting hand. Um, yeah. Half the internet knew who she was. She'd watched Anais Dearworth read countless fools down for filth on her highly rated talent competition, *Star Avenue.* She could be kind and inspiring, then turn on a dime, putting the biggest star's ego in its place.

Gus joined them in the kitchen.

He was breathing heavily, smoothing his hand on his shirt. "Mom! You're here."

She threw open her arms and hugged him. "August, love! I texted you to let you know I was coming over! Diane is parking the car out front."

Gus stepped back and rubbed his face. "My phone died, and I just connected it to the charger. I literally just got your message." He glanced from his mother to Sirena, a troubled look in his eyes. Her stomach dropped. "You've met Sirena."

"Don't worry. I borrowed Di's key and let myself in. Yes, I've met your girlfriend, Sirena."

Gus and Sirena traded a look.

"It's not like that," he said.

"Then what is it like?" Mrs. Dearworth drawled. "A month ago, you said you weren't dating anyone, and now you have a whole girlfriend. I saw pictures from last night. Slow dancing? Kisses? It seems like something to me. Are you together?"

She shifted her designer bag to the crook her arm and tilted her head to the side, as if daring him to refute her statement. Gus opened and then closed his mouth.

Sirena bit the inside of her cheek, trying to come up with an explanation. Well. She had literally just asked Gus to take things slow and now his mom was asking if they were a couple. She'd let Gus closer to her than any man had gotten in a long time, and she liked having him close.

Were they together?

"We are," she said simply.

Anais clicked her tongue dismissively. "Okay. You young folks don't want to put labels on things, so I'll leave you alone—for now. I'm ravenous. I'll order something tasty on Empty Fridge. If it wasn't for that app, I'd have to forage for mushrooms in the backyard and grow pizza in my garden."

Gus grinned. "Mom, I can cook."

Anais gave him a side-eye. "Excuse me, son. When did you learn how to cook? The last time you were near a stove, you couldn't boil water."

"You don't know what I've learned in the Grove," Gus said.

"I have an idea of what you been studying," she muttered.

Sirena froze in place when Anais raised a plucked brow and looked her over. She forced herself to keep from making any sudden movements. *Can she see into my brain?*

Anais waved her hand. "Cook for us next time, sweetheart. Besides, I want to get to know your...new friend. Maybe you can take pity on my son and be his wedding date."

Sirena grinned. "No need. He already asked me to be his date."

"Wow," Anais said. "My son actually listened to me! I don't know what spell you cast on him, but keep it up."

Gus groaned, but there was a twinkle of mischief in his eyes. He was still her rogue.

Anais looped her arm around Sirena and yanked her to her side. She forced herself to relax. *The lady magician is standing right next to me.* She was suddenly enfolded in a cloud of eau de parfum that smelled of sweet honey and primroses. They walked out of the kitchen into the living room. Diane strolled in through the front door, giving Sirena a dumbfounded look.

Anais laughed. "Let's talk about blueberry muffins."

Chapter Twenty-Six

"Cheers, witches!" Callie whooped. "Our girl's getting married for real!"

Sirena held her flute filled with sparkling apple cider against her sisters' and cousin's matching glasses. They sat together in the private back booth in Mimi's Diner behind the gauzy curtain. Their table was covered with two platters filled with delicious finger foods, two bottles of apple cider, and, of course, wedding planning materials. One entire half of the table was scattered with wedding binders, papers, and a folded mood board that Callie kept shooing Lucy away from seeing just yet. Ursula kept fidgeting with her elbow-length gloves, which seemed super out of place with her long-sleeve T-shirt, open sweater, and jeggings.

Sirena clinked her glass with theirs, but her mind was elsewhere.

A week had passed since Sirena had brunch with Gus, Diane, and Ms. Anais Dearworth. It was a nice meal, but Sirena had felt guilty for not cooking for Gus and his family. She knew she was born to be in the kitchen, but her confidence was shaken by so many unknown factors.

She still didn't know if she had gotten the job at Lighthouse. Her wrist was healing but it itched so much under the half cast.

Due to her injury, Sirena had been moved out of the kitchen and worked the register at Night Sky. Beckett avoided her for the most part and was on permanent trash duty. She recorded her cookbook ideas and notes on her phone during her break. Sirena had thought she was doing great with her cooking spark and attempted to make breakfast this morning. When she tried to boil an egg, it exploded.

A sudden commotion pulled Sirena out of her memory. Ursula cried out as her still-full glass nearly slipped out of her hands due to the silky fabric of her gloves.

Callie pulled the binders out of harm's way. "Take off those weird gloves!"

Ursula held the glass to her chest and lifted her chin. "My opera gloves are cool!"

"If you spill a drop on my binders, I'm billing you for supplies."

"No, it completes my outfit," Ursula drawled.

"When was the last time you went to the opera?!" Callie yelled.

Lucy shot Sirena a look that said *Please say something.* It was time for the maid of honor to step in and get everyone to act right.

Sirena said, "Focus up, witches! Let's get this wedding party together."

Callie and Ursula murmured apologies.

Sirena raised her chin. "Callie, show us what you've got."

Callie opened the folded board to reveal pictures, fabric swatches, and a color palette. They all let out impressed gasps. "We're going to give you glamour, sparkle, and a whole lot of love! The theme of your New Year's Eve wedding will be 'Midnight Kisses, Champagne Wishes'!" Callie spoke with an animated flourish. "Our bride will be draped in confetti and shimmer to ring in the new year with her new hubby. Bridesmaids will be dressed in the color of fresh champagne, bright and fizzy. The groom and groomsmen will wear bow ties with a hint of shine. Decorations will be starlight and star themed."

"Whoa. I'm loving this entire board," Lucy said in awe. "Callie, I knew you were good, but you're freaking ah-mazing."

Sirena and Ursula echoed Lucy's compliments.

A proud blush covered Callie's cheeks. "Thanks, sis. I'm just happy you're hiring me instead of my competitor. I swear those elves are making bank. I lost my wedding contract with Gigi to them and—" She cut herself off. "Forget it. Let's focus on you and your day."

"Can we get this done in two months?" Lucy bit her bottom lip.

"Yes," Callie said without a hint of doubt. "We have the venue, which is the biggest issue. Hey, Si. Can we confirm with Gus that the historical society is still available?"

"He's holding the day for us," Sirena said.

Callie opened her binder. She held up a printed-out spreadsheet. "We've got a deadline and a tight budget. We need to know how much he's charging to rent the space and pay the fee as soon as possible."

"I'll text him," Sirena promised.

Callie gave a thumbs-up. She turned to Lucy. "Now, you never gave me an answer about the mirror balls. I have a hookup with a party witch who can give us a discount."

While her sisters and cousin chattered about whether mirrors were good luck at a wedding, Sirena retreated into her thoughts once more. It had been a few days since she'd spoken to Gus, but she had texted him instead in between writing her cookbook notes and her Night Sky shifts. Sirena felt his caring and sweetness come through in his texts. He asked if she had taken a break and whether she'd gotten something to eat or drink. Gus also sent her updates on Cinder, including pictures of the cat lounging in the middle of his bed. The last picture he sent to her was lock-screen worthy: a selfie of Gus nuzzling Cinder, who seemed bored by Gus's affection. Sirena tried to hold back an "Aw," but failed.

She was never bored when she was in his arms.

Sirena refocused on the vision board, studying the pictures of models dancing and celebrating the new year with confetti and party favors. This wedding was going to be fabulous. Sirena touched the swatches of gold glitter, silver chrome, and black silk. The fabric was cool under her fingers. This entire board screamed luxe, Jersey style. Callie must have spent a fortune.

"How did you get all this stuff?" Sirena inquired.

Callie gave them a tight grin. "Don't worry about it. I'm focusing on my new clients, Lucy and Alex. Your wedding will be chic and filled with glamorous love. How do you feel about mirror balls on cupcakes?"

"I've never thought about it." Lucy tapped her chin.

"I'm a fan!" Ursula said. The glass slid against her glove, sloshing the champagne over the rim and forcing her to clutch it to her chest.

"That's it! You're paying for a new binder," Callie snapped.

"Bill me." Ursula stuck out her tongue like a little kid.

Lucy put her drink down. She eyed Ursula's left hand with a skeptical eye.

"Is there something you want to show us?"

They all turned to their cousin, whose eyes darted back and forth around the booth.

Ursula's mouth twisted wryly. "Hmm...I don't think so." She took a long sip of her drink and avoided direct eye contact with everyone at the table. Sirena joined Lucy and studied Ursula's left glove, which appeared a little bumpy. Like there was something ring-shaped hidden underneath it.

"We're already celebrating," Lucy coaxed sweetly. "Spill it, cuz."

Ursula huffed. She deposited the now empty glass on the table.

"I was going to wait to tell you, but—" Ursula slid off her gloves and tossed them on her lap. She held out her left hand, showing off a sparkly engagement ring. It was a deep red garnet stone that caught the light like a little flame.

"Xavier asked me to marry him," she said.

Lucy let out a yell of delight worthy of a warrior princess. A few diners turned their heads in their direction.

Callie sputtered. "When? How?!"

Ursula giggled. Sirena blinked. *Did she just giggle?*

"It was so adorable, y'all. He asked me on Halloween! The ring was in the candy basket, and then he waited for me to reach into it." Ursula sighed. "It's the best treat ever."

Lucy clapped her hands. "Why didn't you say anything!?"

Ursula studied her ring, tenderness in her gaze. "We're here for Lucy. I wanted to wait my turn to celebrate." She glanced up at them, her eyes filled with love and absolute joy.

"I've waited this long for this type of love. I can hold on a little longer to have my time."

Sirena blinked away happy tears. Callie cooed.

Lucy took Ursula by the hands. "We get to go dress shopping together."

A slow smile bloomed over Ursula's face. "That sounds wonderful. We're thinking about having a spring wedding in the Grove Gardens."

Callie pulled out her pocket planner. "Great. My schedule's going to be booked and blessed for the next six months. Is there anything else you want to tell us that we need to plan for?"

Ursula made a face. "Um…I'm thinking of running for mayor."

"Excuse me, what?" Lucy gasped.

"Mayor Walker wants to retire, and the Grove needs a leader who loves and understands this place. I'm going to run and see what happens."

"I better get used to calling you Madame Mayor," Callie said.

"Look at us," Lucy said, her voice filled with pride.

"All of our wishes are coming true. Nana would be so proud of us."

Those words cut Sirena right to the bone. She let out a cry that tore through her body. All she ever wanted was to take care of her family and make them proud. How was she going to do that when she couldn't even boil an egg? The tears flowed, and she couldn't stop crying. She felt Callie rubbing her back in a circular motion, Ursula took her hand, and Lucy slid out of the booth and knelt by Sirena's side.

"Talk to us," Lucy demanded.

Enough was enough. Sirena had to tell them what was on her heart and unburden herself.

"I made another wish," Sirena said carefully.

She noticed Lucy, Callie, and Ursula exchange shocked looks with one another.

"Why? When? How?" Ursula asked rapidly.

Sirena took in a calming breath, then let out everything in her heart. "I couldn't cook well after everything that happened with Helena. I felt blocked. I tried to work through it, but I ended up making everything worse. I messed up my interview with Lighthouse and . . . I failed the first time. So, on Halloween, I used the wish tea in the pantry, and it took me back in time."

"What did you wish for?" Lucy asked.

Sirena met their stares. "I wanted a second chance."

"Wish tea? We have wish tea?!" Ursula exclaimed. "Why haven't we used it before?"

Lucy clicked her teeth. "I found the recipe this summer. It took me a while to get all the right herbs. I guess the tea worked its magic."

"Literally," Callie quipped. "I knew something felt off this entire time. Start from the beginning, and don't stop until you're done."

Ursula signaled to the waitress. "We're going to need more mozzarella sticks."

Sirena briefly summarized what happened in October and the time loop.

October gave her a glimpse of what she could have if she just stayed still for a moment. If she allowed herself to stop and have fun. If she took time to become a student of her magic, rather than going through the motions.

Lucy threw up her hands in dismay.

"Hold up. Didn't you interview at Lighthouse, like, two weeks ago?"

Sirena licked her lips; a stray tear ran down her cheek. "I haven't heard from them. Since the interview, I haven't been able to cook. I'm so nervous I made an egg explode—again. I feel like my magic's stuck."

"Okay, let's get you unstuck," Callie said.

"Let's brew up some tea and wish again," Ursula offered.

Panic sparked her nerves. "I'm done with wishing. I didn't punch a clown or mess up my interview. I'm better off than I've been in a long time. I'm grateful for what I have. I'll figure out how to fix my cooking spark, again."

Even as Sirena said the words, a sense of deep weariness descended upon her shoulders. How many times was she going to keep doing this same dance?

Rule seventy: Kitchen witches fix themselves.

Her head ached trying to remember if that one was rule seventy or seventeen. Sirena couldn't keep living by the many, many rules she learned from Nana. Maybe it was time to bend them. She'd let Gus into her kitchen, and it enabled her to recall a precious recipe. Maybe it was time to make a new list of rules that allowed Sirena to forge a new path for her kitchen witchery.

She could honor the past but not be burdened with it.

Lucy's words were strong, unshakable. "You helped Alex and me, you helped all of us, and we want to help you. We're not going to wish again; we're going to help you get your spark back, for good. I think it's time you invited us into the kitchen."

Sirena picked up a napkin and wiped away her tears. "We haven't cooked together since we were kids."

"Well, that's a sign that we need to jump in and help," Lucy said.

Ursula piped up. "One for all, all for one. Let us help."

"Yeah!" Callie said gently. "Let us be there for you."

Sirena looked at her sisters and cousin, her throat tight with emotion. "I mean, what would you want to cook?"

Ursula cheered. She pulled out her phone and clicked open what appeared to be her email. "I saw a recipe for a fall vegetable soup that sounds wonderful. It's butternut season."

Callie's eyes widened. "Can we get crusty bread? I'm making a shopping list!"

"I've always wanted to host a soup party," Sirena ruminated.

"Say less. Let's get started," Lucy said cheerfully.

Ursula started listing the ingredients out loud. Callie pulled out a piece of paper from her purse and scribbled them down in a list. Lucy searched the weekly circular for the local supermarket on her phone. They worked together, throwing out suggestions and making plans to go to the supermarket after they finished their food. Sirena smiled; her chest burned with sheer love for her family. They were dropping everything to help Sirena, and she let them help. No one came around and revoked her metaphorical witchy card.

Sirena thought of her first new rule.

A kitchen witch will recognize the magic and love that their family brings into their life.

Chapter Twenty-Seven

Gus stood by the front window, golden leaves falling from the branches gathering on the sidewalk. The wind whipped up the leaves and scattered them as his neighbors cleaned their lawns and took down their decorations. By mid-November, pumpkins had disappeared from porches and were replaced with turkey silhouettes and wooden harvest-themed signs greeting impending holiday visitors. There had been an uptick in visitors to the historical society ever since Jess's show had debuted to massive streams and ratings. They wanted to see the heartsick Dearworth magician in his natural environment, away from the sequins. Visitors couldn't bring themselves to glance in his direction; anytime they did they peered at him with open looks of embarrassment or—ugh—pity. At least they signed the guestbook and left notes of appreciation for the new exhibitions. Of course, Gus defaulted to his usual mode and showed that he wasn't licking his wounds over his failed marriage. A few reporters had emailed him for a comment about Jess's impending wedding, but he had nothing to say but to offer his best wishes.

The wedding was two weeks away, and he needed to keep his peace.

He pulled his blanket close to his shoulders, fighting against the shudders that racked his body. Unable to button up a vest and his dress pants, he donned a T-shirt, sweatpants, and warm socks. Gus groaned; his head was so congested that he mixed up a Herkimer diamond with a moonstone in the mineral room. He closed the historical society early since he was so ill. He couldn't hold a simple conversation about faery rings with His Royal Highness Xavier Alder. Everything from his hairline to his toenails whined in pain. Gus dropped his blanket on the floor.

He needed soup, tea, and fluffy bread.

Gus shuffled into the kitchen, searching through the shelves for a single can or container of chicken noodle, tomato, or even lentil soup. After ten more minutes of futile searching, Gus sat down at the kitchen island and slumped over in a hacking mess.

Diane texted him, but Gus had warned her away, not wanting to get her sick. It was perfect soup weather—but of course he didn't have any soup in the house. Just his luck. He took out his phone, opened the Empty Fridge app, and scrolled for a possible restaurant. Why couldn't there be a request-a-kitchen-witch button?

Be for real; what you want isn't on this app.

He missed Sirena, but things had been odd ever since the morning after Halloween. She'd asked to push back her culinary work at the historical society until the new year and he agreed to her request. They texted back and forth, but she hadn't asked him to come over or spend the night. He didn't blame her. Ma's constant questioning about their status didn't help their fragile connection and he hadn't been very useful. Gus couldn't have agreed to go slow with Sirena and then immediately introduce her as his girlfriend. If Ma found out Sirena was his kindred, then all bets were off and all the Dearworths would want to meet her at the next reunion.

There was a loud knock at the door. Gus answered it.

Hello, chef. Sirena walked in, her breath coming out in sharp pants, black glasses on the edge of her nose. Since when did she wear glasses? There was still so much about Sirena he didn't know but wanted to learn. Her button-up shirt was slightly undone and her pants were a little wrinkled, but she was as lovely as usual. Her hair was unbraided and wavy, slightly styled, as if she quickly applied a layer of gel and then forgot about it. Desire bloomed inside him.

"Special delivery," she said. She held up a shopping bag with her unhurt hand. She shifted her crossed body with her healing hand. Her cast was covered in a few stickers.

"You've caught a leaf." Gus reached over and plucked it from her hair, savoring its softness. He put the leaf on the table. He did not know what to do with his hands.

"Diane said you weren't feeling well, so I brought you homemade soup and ice cream."

"You cooked for me," he said.

She lifted a shoulder with a grin. "It's perfect soup weather."

She took out the soup and put it on the counter.

He peered at the large tub. "I can't finish all that soup. Join me."

She gave him a brisk nod, put the ice cream in the freezer, then got a large stockpot from underneath the sink and put it on the stove burner. Gus took two bowls and spoons from the cabinet. Sirena heated up the soup. He went into the dining room with the spoons while she cooked. He lined up the candles on the table, then snapped his fingers. The candles ignited, and the room took on a pleasing glow. Sirena came into the room, holding two bowls of steaming soup, an amused smile playing on her lips.

"A good meal deserves a perfect setting," he said.

"I might have a playlist," she said.

Sirena served up the food, set up her phone, and took her seat next to him. The space filled with light jazzy music that reminded Gus of the local radio station that specialized in quiet storm music. Gus held out a spoon to Sirena. She took it from him with a smile. He clicked her spoon to his and scooped up a huge mouthful. When the savory taste exploded on his tongue, Gus gave a low growl of appreciation. How could tomato, carrots, and shredded chicken taste this good? What did she sprinkle in this? Pure dopamine? He ate for another minute, holding back from pouring the soup down his throat like a hungry bear.

Gus looked at Sirena. Her face widened in surprise. "Did you just growl?"

He gripped the spoon in his hand. He gestured to her bowl. "Have you tried it yet?"

She smiled to herself. "It's a new recipe."

"Taste it," he said firmly. Heat twinkled in her eyes. Gus couldn't wait to see the flash of pleasure that would cross her face when she had a taste. Sirena held his attention for a long beat. She maintained eye contact as she spooned and tasted the soup. Her eyes rolled slightly back in her head. Her tongue darted out of her mouth and licked the broad side of the spoon. She let out a deep guttural noise from the back of his throat that hit him right in the groin. Gus licked his lips. He remembered hearing that sound echo in his ears as she gradually spread her legs and he lowered his head and pressed his lips against the core of her. He bit back a curse.

Sirena studied Gus over the table. "That's good."

Her smile sent his blood racing. If the fires of Venus didn't burn for centuries...Gus leaned forward. She kept her eyes trained on him while she licked her spoon. Was she thinking about all the wicked things they had done underneath the candlelight?

She seemed to enjoy teasing him. Her breath grew ragged as he lapped up the broth. Inwardly, Gus greedily hoped. Pleaded. Wished. *I hope you never forget how good my body felt on your lips. I hope I never forget how you taste on my tongue. I hope you remember us together in the dark. Think about something else. Distract yourself.*

"What's in the soup? It's delicious. My compliments to the chef."

"I have to be honest. I had help."

"How many witches does it take to make a soup?" he asked.

Sirena made a face. "It takes four. One to make a playlist, two to prep the ingredients, and one to watch the soup simmer."

Gus laughed; then he sobered up. "How's your spark?"

She sighed, putting down her spoon in the bowl. "It dimmed a lot after the interview. I couldn't make breakfast without worrying I'd burn it. My confidence took a hit, but I'm working on it."

"But you've got it now."

"I'm getting better," she said lightly.

"Have you heard from Lighthouse yet?" he ventured.

Sirena made a face. "Funny you should ask, but I did get an email. The manager gave me a quick update. The chef I'm supposed to be replacing wants to stay on for another six months. The owner agreed, so they won't need a replacement after all."

Gus huffed in disbelief. How dare this fancy restaurant waste her precious time? "So, what now?"

"I'm not waiting around for an offer. I want to keep having fun. Like Nana used to say, I have a few irons in the fire, and I'm exploring my options. I'm writing a cookbook."

He blinked. "What made you change your mind?"

Sirena gave him a sheepish grin. "I've really enjoyed cooking with my family. I want to share that fun with other people, so I'm going to write it down. I'm going to share our magic."

"I'm so proud of you," he said.

Her voice dropped to a soft whisper. "Thank you."

He cleared his throat. "I didn't know you wore glasses."

Sirena touched them with a fingertip. "Ah, yes. I lost my contact lenses, and it was just easier to wear glasses. I needed to see the lace details on Lucy's wedding dress."

"How's wedding planning?" he asked.

"It's going smoothy. Ursula's helping with the flowers. I'm getting the catering together with a local restaurant. Callie wanted to know about the rental fee for the society for the wedding."

Gus waved his hand. "Consider it my gift to the bride and groom."

Sirena looked at him and her mouth dropped open. "You can't do that."

"I can and I did. I'd rather you donate to the historical society."

"You're going to be leaving this place soon."

Gus hesitated. "I don't know if I should leave."

They shared a look. A mixture of confusion and reluctance went through him as he thought about the path forward.

"Have you talked to your mother about it?" Sirena asked.

"We haven't spoken since my after-birthday brunch," he said.

They had texted about Diane's birthday in January, but that was the extent of their conversation. The responses were short and clipped. Ma was upset that he didn't have an answer for her about rejoining the tour.

He didn't want to make a commitment only to back out at the last second.

"Don't let it go too long. Talk to her about how you feel," she said.

"I've tried," Gus responded.

"Try again," Sirena said softly. He heard something like regret in her voice and paused. Life changed in an instant, and he didn't want to leave things with Ma unresolved.

They finished their soup. Gus got up and started to collect the empty bowls.

"My compliments to the head chef and her cooks."

Sirena reached for her bowl, but he moved away.

"My date doesn't clean up after me," Gus said.

Sirena's voice grew soft. "I'm not your date, remember?"

"Well, you were tonight," Gus said.

Her brow furrowed in thought, but she said nothing.

He shuffled out of the room and went back into the kitchen. If she was his date, then he would greet her with a kiss at the door and sweep her up in his arms. They would be together. It was clear. They'd order a cheesecake, crash into his room, and take nibbles off each other. Then they'd fumble upstairs, undress, and chase away the lonely ghosts that haunted them every day. Gus put the bowls in the sink with a clatter, interrupting his fantasies.

He turned away from the sink to see Sirena standing there with her purse on her shoulder.

"I should leave you to rest," she said.

"You could stay for ice cream."

Sirena peered at him. "Do you think that's a good idea?"

Gus let out a mirthless chuckle. "Haven't you heard? I'm terrible at being good."

They were going to need sugar for this long-overdue conversation. Gus went to the freezer. He took out the ice cream and grabbed two clean spoons from the drawer. Sirena went over to the table.

He sat down next to her and extended a spoon to Sirena. "I never told you about what happened with Jess."

She narrowed her eyes in reluctance but took the utensil from him. "You don't have to tell me."

Gus took off the pint's lid and scooped up a good chunk of ice cream.

"I want you to know," he said.

He let the cold deliciousness roll around in his mouth.

"I didn't think I'd fall in love with my wife. I thought it would be just fun to get married," Gus said.

"Your marriage wasn't real. But...it seemed like you loved her," she said.

He kept talking, passing the ice cream carton between the two of them.

"We decided that getting married would solve our problems without getting emotionally involved. We knew what happened when celebrities married for true love and let emotions cloud their career decisions."

Sirena made an *ah* noise. "It was a partnership."

He gave a curt nod. So far, Sirena hadn't tossed down her spoon and walked out on him. He was thankful that she was open to listening to his story. "Yes. Jess wanted to avoid that problem, so we entered the marriage with clear eyes and a plot treatment. I'm supposedly in love with the niece of my mother's rival. How romantic. How dramatic. How fun."

A light of understanding entered her eyes. "I see."

"Ma warned me not to do it." Gus heard her voice play in his head. *It's all fun and games until you have a broken heart. Tread carefully. Give it time.* "I told her 'I got this' and that I knew what I was doing. I should've watched more romance movies. I acted like a man in love, and I rushed into my marriage."

"You can learn a lot from Nancy Meyers's movies," she teased with a light smile.

He adored Sirena for trying to lighten the mood, but he couldn't keep the sense of foolishness from coming up within his chest. His gut rioted.

Gus lowered his head for a moment. "I fell in love with Jess and I fell hard. She said she wasn't interested in staying married to someone who couldn't keep a promise. I thought I could pull the greatest illusion of all and become the man she could spend forever with. I used every ounce of magic I possessed to transform myself into that person—into permanently becoming Good-Time Gus and—she served me with papers."

That fateful day was the last time Gus ever told anyone outside of his family that he loved them. He was ready to tell Sirena he loved her on Halloween, but he lost his nerve and didn't tell her. For now, it was enough that she knew that she was his kindred.

"Oh," Sirena said breathlessly.

I had no one to blame but myself for my broken heart.

"Jess was right to do it," he said. "I didn't see that at the time, but I do now. She knew she didn't love me like that, and we both deserved to find true love."

Gus would always appreciate Jess for loving him enough to let him go and end their arrangement.

"So, you never thought that Jess might be your kindred," Sirena said.

"No. I didn't believe in the idea of a kindred until—" He paused, letting his eyes roam over Sirena. *I didn't believe until I met you.*

"Until when?" she asked.

"I didn't believe until much later," he restated. "Good-Time Gus was a whole jerk. I wouldn't want to be in the same house as him. I mean, I turned my hair blond and started wearing terrible body spray."

Sirena eyed him. "Oh, Gus, no."

He groaned thinking about his platinum-blond hair and mesh top. "I smelled like a walking piña colada. It wasn't a good look for me. Diane forced me to see what I was becoming. I left the act and took a hiatus in Freya Grove to take care of myself. Ma hopes I'll come back to the stage. She hopes that I can still be Good-Time Gus."

That was the Gus that Ma knew and the version of him that she wanted back onstage with her in London. He couldn't let himself be that magician, but he didn't want to let his family down.

"Does she know this version of you, Gus?" Sirena said carefully.

Gus said nothing, unease roiling in his gut. *I'm afraid Ma doesn't like this version of me.*

Sirena finished a bite of ice cream, then spoke. Her voice was serene. "Do you want my advice or my support?"

"I'd like both, if you can give it," he said.

Sirena gestured around at the society's kitchen walls. "Show her everything that you've done here in the Grove. Don't hold back a single thing. Tell her everything, so she can see who you are. You think you can pretend behind those serious clothes, upstanding posture, and that serious beard? I see who you are."

"Tell me what you see," he said, a little too stiffly.

"You're trying too hard to be boring," she said. "Trying to be someone who demands uprightness and will be seen as a serious man. You are bad at being boring, and that's okay."

"So, you expect me to be a fool," he said. Gus drew out a curt laugh. He was never going to escape his past.

I refuse to be anybody's fool.

She dropped her spoon on the table. "Why do you think the Fool is the first card in the tarot?"

He shook his head, not trusting his voice.

Sirena gave him an assessing glance. "We are all fools before we experience life and learn harsh lessons, then lose our carefree spirits," she said sagely. "Despite everything that's happened, you've managed to hold on to that carefree magic. You've kept that ability to wonder, to play. It's such a gift, my dear August, and I wish that you never, ever lose it."

Gus swallowed down the knot of joy that rose in his throat. He yearned to give her what she deserved—a castle by the sea. He wanted to tell her what he knew in his soul—that he truly, fully loved her. But he held back. If he said the words now, then his love would become a living, dangerous event, like a wildfire. His love would do what a fire does best, and it would have the power to light his life or consume it. He yearned to live in the light.

Sirena glanced at the wall behind him, where he knew the clock was, and winced. "Look at the time. I should've been home already."

Gus stood up and walked Sirena the short distance to the back door.

He opened the door, and the hinge squeaked.

She pivoted to him, causing them to be face-to-face. "Kiss me good night?" she asked.

He nodded absentmindedly, too dazed at her simple request to realize that it was a bad, bad idea. His body droned with anticipation, but his brain yelled at him to consider his choices. If she kissed him on the lips, he might disappear into a cloud of smoke. If he kissed her on the lips, then he'd be tempted to yank her back into the house and convince her to stay with him. She leaned over into his space, mere inches away from his mouth, but he moved at the last moment. Instead, she pressed her lips, softly, gently to his neck.

Right there underneath his ear. He let out a low groan.

That was the spot, his spot, that sent shivers straight down his body and left him aching and throbbing, a delicious sensation that made his knees lock up. The spot where she had once teased the delicate skin with her soft lips and teeth while she was on top of him. Would it be wrong to moan out loud right now? Would it? He fought the urge to gather her up into his arms and carry her to the kitchen table. Craving, once buried deep within, clawed its way to the surface and took hold. His sex pulsated out a message. *Let her stay.* He hummed happily when his hand came up and stroked her arm. Finally common sense, late to the party, returned and reminded him of their friend status. He moved away, pressing his hand to his neck.

She whispered good night to him, then left. A stray thought flashed in his mind.

I could stay in the Grove forever and wish for your kiss. For your touch. For your heart.

They were indeed kindred. Now, what spell could he cast to make him speak his love out loud?

Chapter Twenty-Eight

To Sirena there was nothing more witchy and alluring than a full moon.

She stood out on the porch studying the celestial object and bathing in the moonlight. It was the Monday after Thanksgiving, so the fridge was nearly empty of leftovers. Rather than let Sirena cook the entire meal per previous tradition, everyone pitched in and cooked a dish for the dinner. The young'uns made leaf rubbings and traced their hands to make turkeys as decorations, which were taped all over the walls next to family pictures. Lucy and Ursula rallied people in their magical circle and made sure that there was enough food for all the guests and family.

Sirena cooked the huge turkey and stuffing, making sure to rub it down with the herb butter recipe Nana and Great-Aunt Winnie had handed down to her. Lucy and Alex cooked the sides: mashed potatoes, collard greens, and sweet peas. Alex even made seaweed-wrapped appetizers, which Uncle Leo devoured while watching football. Auntie Niesha and Ursula took care of the desserts, making sure to bring sweet potato pie, German chocolate cake, and coffee cake that had people going back for seconds. Xavier and his godmother, Whitney, being fae, brought vegetarian dishes that were savory and delicious.

Poe and Theo brought over paper leaf decorations and strung up banners on the walls and archways. Gus brought two coolers filled with sodas, water, seltzers, and every kind of drink anyone could request or want.

Quentin, being the ultimate organizer, helped utilize the space to pack as many people in the Caraway house as possible comfortably. All day, the house was filled with friendly conversations, screams of victory from board games being played, and magic spells being cast. People from all over the Grove dropped in and gathered with the Caraways to celebrate their community and break bread with them. With every bite of food and hug, Sirena felt the love and support of her family and friends and had to keep from weeping.

So far November had been filled with pleasant surprises and memories. Now that the month was ending, she had one last memory to make. Sirena sat on the front porch, scribbling down a few notes in her recipe book.

The front door opened, and Lucy poked her head out. "There you are. Are you ready?"

Sirena held up her notebook. "I'm ready. I got inspired by the moonlight. I was just writing down a few recipe ideas."

Lucy joined Sirena on the porch. "Are these new ideas for Lighthouse?"

"No, these recipes are all for me," Sirena said.

Lucy glanced at the stained, thick notebook and grinned. "It's almost full. I know what I'm getting you for the holidays."

"I'd like that," Sirena said.

Lucy bent her head slightly forward. "It's great to see you writing again."

Inwardly, Sirena beamed with pride, delighted that she'd

managed to get her writing mojo back. In the mornings, before she checked her phone, she reached for her notebook and wrote down any cooking ideas and magical thoughts that had come to her overnight. At night, she experimented with new dishes and had fun with making meals with Lucy and Alex. There were moments in the kitchen when she burnt toast or forgot to turn down the flame, but she laughed it off. If she cooked with love and trusted in her magic, then she'd never fail herself or her family.

Lucy held out her pinky finger to Sirena. "Let's make a promise."

Sirena laughed. "Okay."

Lucy sighed. "Promise me we won't let wishes or magic keep us from talking to each other. Husbands. Lovers. Gnomes. Jeans. No matter where life takes us—to Ocean City or Osaka—we'll always talk and listen."

Sirena hooked her pinky with Lucy's. "I promise. Always."

Lucy took her by the hand and held it. She sobered up, as though the importance of the last month had finally hit her. Lucy's voice came out in a shaky tremble. "You stayed. You fed us. You healed us. I'll always love you, Si."

And I'd do it again in a heartbeat, Sirena thought, but she couldn't bring herself to speak. She was too overwhelmed by her emotions at that moment.

Lucy took her hand back and waved at her face, as if trying to keep her tears at bay.

"Let's get inside before Ursula starts charging the crystals without us."

Sirena nodded. They went back into the house and went into the living room. Callie, in a cream sweater and jeans, was flipping through the spellbook, jotting down a few notes on a piece of paper. Ursula, in a blousy dress that reached her ankles, lined up her crystals on the mantel, polishing an amethyst as big as her palm. Her eyes went expectantly to Sirena, then to Lucy.

"Hey y'all hey. What's the plan for tonight?"

It was time for Sirena to work her magic. She took out her notebook. "I wrote a new spell I'd like to add to our book."

Callie spun around, her mouth slightly ajar. Ursula, stunned, put her amethyst into her pocket. Lucy stared at the paper as if it were a million-dollar check.

"Really? You've never added anything, have you?" she said.

Sirena glanced at the spellbook; its pages shone in response to her words. "That book's given me so much. It's about time I added to it."

Callie made a grabby hand motion for Sirena's paper, but she moved it out of her reach.

"Come on! Tell us what mischief we're going to do tonight."

Sirena held the lined paper in front of her. "I'll read it. I'm open to feedback, so let me know what you think. I'm not as talented as you all are."

Lucy snorted in disbelief. Ursula rolled her eyes, amused. Callie rolled her wrist, motioning for her to get on with it.

Sirena read off the paper. "To Invoke the Elements, by S. Caraway. To be performed during a full moon. Gather four together and sit in a circle. Light a candle to invoke the element of fire. The first person will say, 'I invoke fire to fuel my [state goal].' Each person will present a gift representing one of the other four classical elements with their wish for the first person. Once everyone has properly presented their element, then the eldest of the group will end the spell by saying, 'We invoke these elements for [state member name] to [repeat intention/ goal].' Give thanks. Extinguish the candle. Make modifications and accommodations when needed to allow those who might need to present their elements in another way, like describing the element through touch or drawing the element if gathering the element is an issue."

Sirena glanced up, meeting her sisters' and cousin's faces.

Her stomach churned. "Is that okay? Should I revise it? I want to make sure future Caraways know that you don't need money to practice your craft. That magic can meet you where you're at, no matter what."

Lucy, Callie, and Ursula traded a look, then faced Sirena.

Ursula spoke for the group. "It's perfect. Let's get to work."

The uneasiness faded from Sirena's stomach and was replaced with calmness.

Lucy, Callie, and Ursula shuffled around the room while Sirena prepped the table for their work. She brought a pillar candle and a box of matches from their stash in the kitchen. Her hands buzzed with the familiar sense of homegrown magic. She placed her items on the table, and soon they were all gathered. Sirena retrieved a match, struck it on the side of the box, and *whoosh*—the match sparked to life. She lit the pillar candle but held on to the lit match.

Sirena let it burn for a second, then spoke. "I invoke fire to fuel my heart and ignite my spark."

She stared at the flame; then with a quick breath, she blew out the match.

Lucy placed a small jar of ocean water on the table. "I invoke water to aid you and nourish your body."

Ursula presented a heart-shaped crystal stone that glittered. "I invoke earth to ground you in success and fortune."

Callie gave a cone of incense. "I invoke air to carry your talent to the right ears and minds."

Lucy turned to Sirena. Her chin trembled as she spoke, her words reverberating with the authority of a firstborn witch. "We invoke these elements to support our sister Sirena to embark on her journey. Let water nourish her body, let earth support her feet, let the air fill her lungs, and let the fire warm her soul. Let our love and magic be with you to guide you and protect you always. We give our thanks."

Sirena rose and blew out the candle. She brought in Lucy for a tight hug, and they held each other for a few heartbeats. Callie and Ursula joined in, and the four of them held one another.

They'd talk over tea tomorrow morning and many teas afterward. Her imagination conjured up a vision of her, Lucy, Callie, and Ursula sitting together at a kitchen table, showing off pictures of their respective families and friends on their phones. In that image, they were all either turning gray or had their hair dyed a fun, bright color. Their faces were covered in the wrinkles, laugh lines, and moles they'd gain through age and time. Sirena's heart rejoiced at this image of the four of them cackling like gleeful crones filled with absolute joy.

December

*If you see an oregano plant growing on the ground,
then happiness is on the way.*

Chapter Twenty-Nine

The ballroom of the Berkeley Hotel had been transformed into a full-service casino floor. Blackjack and various card tables were outside the reception hall. Flashy posters of the bride and groom outside Las Vegas and glitzy card-themed artwork decorated the wall. Roulette wheels and slot machines by the door rewarded guests with treats and small gifts. People laughed and talked over the dinging alarms and cheering of winners. Cameras scanned the ballroom, capturing the wedding and all the action. The tables were covered in personalized casino chips with the couple's names and the motto "Lucky in Love." Gus handed Sirena his cup of tokens. She still wore her half cast, with her black and red polka-dot dress. He couldn't wait to peel that dress off her later.

He smiled. "Try your luck."

"I will," she said with a wink.

Diane, looking pretty in her red chiffon bridesmaid dress, took Sirena by the arm, and the two of them went off to the wall of slot machines. Jess and Igor were taking photos outside and around the property, while the guests enjoyed appetizers from dapper waiters. A sense of melancholy went through him as he studied the ballroom. This wedding was a far cry from the little chapel he impulsively got married in. A thought zipped through his brain that made him stand still.

Next time you'll go all out.

Ma came over to him, dressed in yet another designer gold gown. She played with a token between her manicured nails, and her eyes scanned the scene with a critical glint. "I wouldn't have gone with the casino theme, but I guess it's cute."

She tossed the token to Gus; he caught it. Waiters moved between guests, holding out trays of champagne and appetizers. Ma scooped up a drink and sipped from the glass.

"I like it," Gus admitted.

"How are you really feeling?"

He patted his stomach, feeling fully satisfied in more ways than one. Gus had a beautiful woman as his date, he had reapplied for his stewardship job, and he'd completed another grant application. He even gave a friendly smile to the cameras when they greeted him at the door.

"I'm good. I've eaten way too many stuffed peppers."

Ma squawked, seemingly astonished. "Since when do you like peppers?"

"Sirena made them the other night. I never knew breadcrumbs could taste that good."

Ma watched him for a beat. "Are you two staying for the whole reception?"

"We were planning on it." He'd been looking forward to sharing a slow dance with Sirena. "Why?"

"Let's liven this party up." Ma twisted her fingers, and the token was suddenly transformed into a ring box.

Gus reeled back. *Act dumb. Pretend you don't know what's going on.* "What's this?"

"Come on, Gus. You know exactly what it is." Ma reached over and eased it open. She gestured to the camera operator who was hovering three tables down.

The ring twinkled in the overhead light, casting sparkles all over the table.

"Isn't this the perfect time to get caught up in the moment? Show them what true love looks like. Wouldn't that be fun?"

Gus let his mouth drop open to his chest. Wouldn't it be fun to propose to Sirena? Now? It should be romantic and exciting. But it should be when they were ready—if they would ever be ready—and a memorable private moment, not a viral video. Gus stared at Ma. He saw the bright light of expectation in her eyes. She wanted him to put on a show. But he would never intentionally hurt anyone else with his magic ever again. This was the moment he officially said farewell to Good-Time Gus.

"Ma. It's not the right time," he said sharply.

Surprise glittered in her eyes. "You used to be impulsive."

"I'm not that guy anymore." Gus took the box and shoved it into his pocket. Ma looked away from him, not meeting his eyes. Great. Was he going to spend the rest of his life disappointing her? The room grew hot, and he couldn't catch his breath.

"Excuse me," he said gently.

He stood and walked out of the reception and onto the balcony. The sea air rolled in, cooling his heated face. He breathed in deeply, letting the chilly air burn away some of his anger. It was exhausting. He was getting too old to pretend that he was going to turn back into someone he didn't want to be anymore. Maybe he could sneak out when the cake was being cut or when the couple had a first dance. He stayed out on the balcony for ten minutes. Gus heard the door open, but he didn't turn around.

"Gus, are you good?" He angled his body to see Sirena and Diane stepping onto the balcony. Remorse descended onto his chest like a metal weight.

He wouldn't get his dance with Sirena tonight.

"Is that a ring in your pocket, or did you steal a buttered roll?" Sirena joked.

Gus turned quietly and faced them fully. Both his sister and his date sobered up once they noticed the look on his face.

"What is it about weddings that make people…go…" He searched for the right word.

"Wacky?" Sirena suggested kindly. He gave her a hard smile. She was always trying to cheer him up and lighten the mood. He absolutely loved her for that. Gus noticed Diane gesture to Sirena, who gave his arm a gentle squeeze, then headed back through the double doors into the reception. He told Diane briefly what happened at the table between him and Ma.

"She expected me to make a scene," he said, letting irritation bleed into his voice. "It's like she doesn't know me."

How could she believe that he'd do something so thoughtless during the reception? Gus could understand why people sometimes proposed at weddings. It was easy to get caught up in the romance and love of the day, but he wouldn't steal attention from the newlywed couple. He would not do that to Jess or Igor. Nor to himself and Sirena.

Diane thought for a second, and then she spoke. "Does she know the Gus I know?"

"Which Gus is that?" He spoke carefully, trying to keep his dread at bay. If anyone knew who he'd become over the last few years, it would be his little sister. She'd been there for him and had been a source of support during his divorce and move to the Grove.

Diane furrowed her forehead. "The Gus I know volunteers to help seniors and students fill in their family trees. He takes his sister to the market to find the perfect pumpkin. He isn't flashy with his magic, but he takes delight in being able to dazzle people in small ways. He would rather dunk his head in a vat of glitter glue than ruin someone's wedding. That's the Gus I know."

Gus brought Diane in for a tight hug. "I hope you know you're my favorite sister," he said against her forehead. "Love you, Di."

She squeezed him back. "I'm your only sister, but it's nice to hear. Love you too, Gus."

Gus and Diane returned to the reception. The DJ was tuning up and getting ready on the stage in the corner.

"Ma may not like this version of Gus," he warned.

The tightness in his chest loosened. It felt good to speak his fear out loud.

"Yeah, but you do, and so does everyone in the Grove," Diane said. "I know a certain cooking witch who adores you for who you are, not who you pretend to be."

Gus found Sirena. She was at the bar, sipping on a cherry-garnished drink. Her eyes found him and mouthed the words *Are you good?* He gave her a wave and blew her a kiss. She pretended to grab it out of the air and press it to her chest for safekeeping. Yeah, that dress was going to be balled up on his bedroom floor before the night was over. He was almost done making her Yuletide gift and he really hoped that she liked it.

Gus faced Diane with a goofy smile. "We're just good friends."

"You're hopeless," Diane teased over her shoulder as she walked away toward the bar.

Ma approached Gus with clutched hands. The gold shimmer makeup around her eyes seemed to have lost its luster, as if she had been crying. His heart ached. He didn't mean to hurt her, but he wasn't sorry about what he did and how he responded.

"I shouldn't have done that," she said tightly.

"I'm trying to figure out why you did it."

Ma searched the ceiling for a moment, then met Gus's eyes. "I was trying to push you—or trying to jump-start you back into who you are or were. I don't know anymore. Pop sent me that video of you talking at the conference and...it shook me. I saw that same spark you had when you were onstage with us. Here was my son, the greatest magician of his generation, talking about primary sources and saving history! I didn't recognize you. I wasn't ready to let you or your magic go. So, I figured if I reminded you of what it felt like to perform and thrill strangers, then..." Ma's words trailed off into silence. "Maybe you'd find your way back to us."

"Ma. I'm not coming back to the act. I'm done."

A soft light of acceptance and sadness flickered in her face. "I'm understanding that now—I see so much potential in you. I don't want you to end up hiding away from the world in this town."

"I'm not hiding." *I was healing.*

Her chin trembled. "When I was in town last month, I told people I was your mom, and their eyes lit up with pride. They spoke so wonderfully about you and everything you've done for the Grove. I thought they were talking about your magic, but they were talking about *you*. I'm sorry it took me so long to see it. Honestly, I'm going to miss seeing you on the stage."

Gus considered Ma for a beat. He needed to finally close that chapter of his life.

"Everyone deserves a proper goodbye from me," he said.

He had overdue vacation time he could use, and he hadn't been to London in years. It was time for Gus Dearworth to perform for the world one last time.

Her eyes turned glassy, and her lips held back a smile. She straightened and lifted her shoulders. A tentative hope darted over her face. "You're joining us in London."

"Let's show them how the Dearworths do it," he said.

Ma embraced Gus and held him tightly to her. This time he felt her embrace all of him, including the man he'd become, and she didn't let go.

The Grove was changing right before Sirena's eyes. Gone were the turkey silhouettes and wooden harvest-themed signs; they had been replaced by white and red candy canes on doors and lit-up deer on lawns. Sirena had helped Gus decorate the historical society with rainbow twinkle lights and wreaths of plaid ribbon on the door. Even the Night Sky Bistro managed to put up fairy lights and pictures of delicious holiday drinks. Callie went all out with decorating the Caraway house this year. Old-school Christmas bulbs shaped like fireflies were hung up in the window, giving the curtains a rainbow glow. The mantel in the living room was decorated with sparkling tea lights and lush garlands. A large evergreen tree heavy with felt decorations and twinkle lights was tucked into the corner. Presents large and small were wrapped underneath the tree. Red bows decorated the staircase and every spare corner. Spicy incense of myrrh and frankincense gave the room an inviting feel. The scent of rich cocoa hung in the air.

It was the day before Yule when Sirena heard the doorbell ring and peeked out the front window. Gus stood on the Caraways' porch, clutching the wrapped present. Her heart hammered in her ears. Sirena held back a squeal and gave her reflection a quick glance in the mirror by the door. Okay, she was giving holiday movie glamour with a sweaterdress and leggings, her feet bare and toenails sparkling.

She opened the door. "Hi."

He held out the package to her. "Hey, I just swung by to drop off a gift for you."

Sirena took it from him and cradled it against her chest. "You're too kind. Come on in."

"I promise I won't stay long," he said.

Stay as long as you like.

She stepped back, giving him room to come inside. Gus wiped his feet and walked in. His cologne was different this time and he smelled deliciously mossy and cedary, like he just finished a shift at the local tree farm. She closed the door behind him, ushering him into the living room.

"You didn't have to bring it over," she said. "I'll be back working with you in January."

An unreadable shadow crossed his face, but it disappeared quickly. Sirena thought about asking him what was on his mind, but she decided she'd ask him later. Maybe she could whip up a peppermint hot chocolate and a few sugar cookies for Gus to eat before he went home. Her spark was back, and it was spectacular.

"I wanted to make sure you got your present before Yule," he said. "I was in the neighborhood. Zeke lives around the way, and I was hanging out with him."

"I didn't know he lived so close. I'll bring him some soup."

"Lucky duck." Gus grunted. She watched as he scanned the pile of mirrored disco balls, bags of lace flower petals, and mini bottles of champagne covering their living room floor.

"I'm not interrupting anything?"

A small smile of enchantment touched her lips. "No, I'm taking a much-earned break. I've been up for two days making favors. The gnomes begged to help with the wedding, so I gave them a job. Can gnomes be flower girls?"

"Gnomes are very botanical, so I think they're a perfect choice," he said. Gus glanced around the living room cluttered with wedding favors.

"You're busy. I should've texted."

"It's fine." Sirena put her gift on the coffee table, went over to the tree, and picked up a gift bag. She came back over to him, grinning. "Look what the elves left. I think you've been nice this year."

He took the gift from her.

"Okay, maybe you've been a little naughty. Open it up!"

Gus reached into the bag. He let out a gasp as he held the rich blue and turquoise crocheted hat.

Sirena lifted a hopeful brow. "It's satin lined. Your hair won't get snagged when you take it off. The artist even added a fire charm on the inside. Do you like it?"

"Sirena," he said, swallowing hard.

"I couldn't stop thinking about…that day," she said. Sirena would always hold their sweet October days in her memory, but she looked forward to their future adventures.

He ran his hands over the yarn with a slow, gentle touch. "I love it."

Gus came over and kissed her chin; his beard brushed up against her. "Thank you."

She did a little happy dance and leaned back from him. "Try it on. The maker says that you can wear this hat in any weather. It's good in snow, wind, and rain."

Another shadow flitted over his face, but this time it lingered. Gus returned his gift to the bag. He slowly placed it on the couch.

Sirena looked at him intently. "Gus, your face is telling on you. What's up?"

He met her stare. "I was told to get a sturdy hat for unexpected rainy weather."

Her belly twinged. "Okay."

"I'm going to London next month with my parents," he said. Gus briefly summarized the trip's details, making sure to explain that he was returning to the stage for a limited time. A jumble of surprise and sadness churned inside Sirena once he finished sharing his news.

"Once the theater announced on social media I was performing, they sold out tickets in three hours. They've had to add three more performance dates to accommodate the demand."

"You said you had nothing left to give. You said the well was dry."

"Someone helped me refill the well," he said, staring at her with a bright smile.

"How long will you be gone?"

His smile dipped a little. "I'll be gone until February, maybe March."

Sirena studied Gus. Pride bloomed inside her chest. There was a light of enthusiasm around him that made him radiant. He was going back to the stage, where he belonged. The Grove would miss Gus something terrible.

A question popped into her brain. "What about the historical society and Cinder?"

Gus nodded. "Diane's taking care of Cinder for me. The committee approved my temporary replacement last week. Her name is Molly and she's a history graduate student from Meadowdale College. She'll open the society for modified hours."

"Oh, that's great," Sirena said.

How was she going to support Gus while he was performing in London? Did her phone have an international plan? She didn't even want to imagine how much a phone call to England would cost her. She'd have to be aware of the time difference and not text him when it was the middle of the night. Maybe she could live-stream it or ask Ms. Anais Dearworth if she could share a recording of him onstage. Sirena couldn't wait to see him perform and bring delight to countless audiences overseas.

"Don't worry. I told Molly all about you. She's excited to meet you and she'll make sure your work isn't interrupted while I'm gone."

Sirena swallowed thickly. The truth dropped on her head hard like a cast-iron pan falling on her foot. He *was* leaving and she was staying here in the Grove.

Sirena wanted to be with him.

She hadn't even been to the Seaview Square Mall with Gus, but she was considering traveling with him overseas. Sirena couldn't drop everything and chase Gus across an ocean.

Who would watch the house? What about their cat?

It was too sudden for her to pack up and leave without telling Callie or Lucy.

Then again, if Sirena asked to join him in London, how would this trip change their relationship? She didn't want to ask him until she was sure she could trust herself to love him without a shadow of a doubt. Yes, she was his kindred, but was he her soulmate?

Until she could answer that question, she couldn't allow herself to go with Gus.

His unspoken love was so valuable to her, and she struggled to take care of valuable things.

Gus gestured to her gift bag. She noticed that he bounced on his toes, seemingly eager for her to see his gift. "Your turn."

Sirena reached for her present and opened it. She saw the glitter in the snow globe as she pulled the gift bag away. Her voice came out watery, emotional. "You didn't."

Sirena looked to him. Gus moved until he stood next to her; his jacket brushed up against her shoulder. "I went back to the store, but someone had bought it. I had to make it in my study. It took me a few times to get the glitter right, but I think I nailed it."

She tore her attention from him to study the snow globe. She shook it up. The glitter swirled around the carousel, filling her with wonder. The small horses spun around in a circle.

"You made this."

He'd given her this carousel by the sea, a beautiful fantasy wrapped up in light and sparkle. Her pulse kicked up and her hands turned sweaty.

She put the snow globe down on the table, as if it were a hot rock. "I can't keep this."

He straightened. "Why not? It's yours."

Sirena clenched her jaw. "It's too pretty. I'll break it."

"You won't," he insisted.

Gus took her by the shoulders and held her close against him.

"Even if it breaks, I'll make you a hundred more. You deserve it."

Sirena boldly met his gaze. "You trust me with something so beautiful."

His lips trembled as he fought to keep his words inside. *I trust you.* Her body singed at his proximity. Gus stared at her, as if he was hoping that somehow she could feel his sincerity through his touch. She didn't need to hear it because she knew. His hands rose up to her shoulders, up her neck, and framed her face. Absolute want zipped through her bloodstream as she studied his eyes. Sirena wanted to show him everything she couldn't bring herself to say just yet.

"Pause or play?" she asked.

Gus hesitated, not moving an inch. "Play."

She was quick, yanking down his pants in a sly motion and leaving him bare down to his ankles.

Gus stared. "How did you—" He sounded amused and turned on.

"Magic," she said.

She kneeled before Gus, dragging her full lips over every inch of his bare skin. She was desperate to drink every drop of him. He placed his hands on her shoulders, trying to keep his balance. She licked him from his base to the tip, savoring him like the last piece of candy in the entire store. Sirena looked up at him while on her knees.

He let his eyes roll closed, pleasure flashing over his face.

With every swirl of her tongue and breathy sigh from him, she felt him surrender a little bit of himself to her. *Take it all. Take my bones. Take my soul. I surrender all to you.* She continued until he was shaking, thighs quivering with tension. She could tell by the way he gripped her shoulders that he ached to move deep inside her. To watch the fire flare in her eyes as they joined together.

She pulled back, stroking him in her palm. Her lips were slick and wet. "Protection?"

"Wallet. Where do you want me?"

Sirena gestured over to the rug underneath the tree. "There."

She stood, tossing off her sweaterdress and pulling off her leggings. Gus shed the rest of his clothes and grabbed the foil packet, making sure to bring it over to the tree. She yanked her panties off with a deft move and tossed them away. They lowered themselves onto the rug, the twinkle lights illuminating his skin. She crushed him to her chest, and he pressed his mouth to hers, relishing the sweetness. He lowered his hand, caressing Sirena between her thighs, teasing her until his fingers were delightfully slick with her. She was panting and ready to join with him. Gus leaned back on his heels and sheathed himself. It was time. Sirena began to straddle him, but he gently rolled her onto her back. Previously, she enjoyed being on top, being in control and setting the pace. But tonight it seemed that he wanted to make a change.

He hesitated, meeting her eyes. "Is this okay?"

She lay underneath the lights, her chest heaving.

"Yes." She opened herself to him. Gus lowered himself until he was nestled right at her entrance. They were face-to-face. With one deft thrust he was inside her, and they were merged into one. A pleased sigh escaped her mouth. He moved delicately, surely. They rocked and moved together, the chorus of their moans and sighs filling the air. The scent of their sweat fueled her. She wasn't going to stop until he gave her everything that he had. They were creating a fire, sharing a light that would keep away the cold and warm their souls in the darkness. He reached down between them and teased her as he continued to move. She writhed against his fingers, her gasps coming closer and her back bowing. Sirena screamed out in release. He kept moving, passion rising in him like liquid fire, clouding his mind and driving him. Sirena stared up at him, her gaze clouded with bone-deep satisfaction.

She leaned up and kissed his chin, licking him and whispering, "Come for me. Now."

Apparently, that was all he needed. He soon followed her into ecstasy, yielding to his climax. Her body was electrified and turned into something new—like lightning striking a sandy beach and making glass. He'd shared her fire with him, and she transformed into something she didn't have words for. He gasped and lowered himself next to Sirena. She pressed kisses on the backs of his hands. Those hands that had crafted her a gift she'd cherish forever. She understood, as tucked her neatly into his side, why humans dared to steal fire from the gods. She'd risk the wrath of the gods for the rest of her life to bathe in his light even for a single day.

YOU ARE CORDIALLY INVITED TO THE WEDDING OF

Lucinda R. Caraway

AND

Alexander O. Dwyer

ON DECEMBER 31ST AT SEVEN P.M.

BOTH THE CEREMONY AND RECEPTION TO BE HELD AT THE

Freya Grove Historical Society

THE BRIDE AND GROOM INVITE YOU TO RING IN THE
NEW YEAR WITH THEM WITH A CHAMPAGNE OR
APPLE CIDER TOAST AT MIDNIGHT.

Let's ring in the New Year with the new couple.

Chapter Thirty

The ceremony began promptly at seven o'clock on December 31 in the library of the Freya Grove Historical Society. A string quartet version of a pop song played over large speakers as the bridal party strode down the aisle and gathered at the makeshift altar. Auntie Niesha was the officiant. The gnomes Jinxie, Herbie, and Half-Pint tossed lace rose petals down the aisle. The bride walked down the aisle wearing an off-the-shoulder cream wedding dress that showed off her shapely figure. Lucy clutched the overflowing bouquet of roses, lilies, and hydrangeas in her right hand while holding Dad's arm with her left. Mama took pictures as they came down the aisle and approached the altar.

Sirena took in a watery breath once she saw Lucy enter the room.

Lucy wore a crown of white roses and baby's breath and Nana Ruth's pearl necklace, which glowed against her skin. Her smile was radiant and seemed to reflect all the love in the room. Love was a good look for her. Alex, in a fitted tuxedo that showed off his merman build, only had eyes for Lucy, and his attention never wavered from her. Lucy and Alex faced each other at the altar, their bodies shaking with joy.

She stepped forward and stole a quick peck from Alex.

"Hold on now," Auntie Niesha chided lovingly. "Don't skip to the end yet."

Before a word had been said, people were sniffling and holding back their tears. Everyone managed to hold on until the couple exchanged vows. Mama and Papa Dwyer passed out tissues as everyone quietly cried at the beauty of Alex and Lucy's words. Even Sirena discreetly wiped away a stray tear with her thumb as Lucy spoke words of love, trust, and magic.

She caught Gus's eye and noticed he had a faraway look about him. Her heart burned, eager to know what he was thinking right then. Was he remembering their past or imagining a future? Sirena refocused on Lucy and Alex, putting off that thought until later.

The vows were finished, and the couple exchanged rings.

"I now pronounce you husband and wife. Now, you may kiss your merman," Auntie Niesha said.

"It's about time," Lucy shouted.

Alex caught her up in a movie-screen-worthy kiss that had the room cheering and hollering. Callie placed the ceremonial broom before them, and Lucy and Alex jumped over it together as a couple. They bounded down the aisle laughing, with Alex being clapped on the back by Uncle Leo and Lucy holding up her bouquet in victory to the guests. Sirena watched them from the altar. Guests filed out of the library. Sirena stood on the altar, taking in the lingering love and joy of the ceremony. Her sister was starting a new chapter to her story. It was done. She held the bouquet to her heart, bliss filling her from head to toe.

Who would think that this whole adventure had started with a simple wish?

"Hey, chef." She glanced over to see Gus dressed in his tuxedo.

Her whole being flooded with desire. "Hey."

"You sparkle like a brand-new penny," he said.

She reached out and straightened his boutonniere. "Thank you, Gus. You're looking handsome."

Gus extended his arm to Sirena. "Shall we?"

She took his arm. "Let's go."

They strolled out together to join the others getting ready for the bridal party photos.

Guests moved into the living room for the reception. The cake, ordered from the couple's favorite place, Little Red Hen Bakery Café, was three tiers of buttercream perfection decked out with candy stars that popped in your mouth when you ate them. Sirena had had the honor of sampling the cake with Lucy. Furniture was safely moved aside for a large dance floor. The dining room was set up buffet style. Once the bridal party finished their pictures, they went to complete the various jobs to help make the wedding run smoothly. Sirena and Gus organized the gift table in the study, making sure that the oddly shaped boxes didn't get knocked over.

Diane called from the study's doorway, "Gus. There's a gnome stuck under the stairs."

"Excuse me." Gus left the room. Sirena stared at the ornate glass clock on the table.

Sirena frowned. "Is this a wedding gift? I didn't know Lucy liked clocks."

Callie, in her shiny bridesmaid dress and carrying a clipboard, came up to her. "Hey, Si. I know it's not the best time, but I'm moving back into Caraway house."

Sirena pivoted. "Wait. What happened with your apartment in Meadowdale?"

Callie groaned, holding the clipboard to her chest like a shield. "My roommate's moving to Chicago. In between Enchanted Events cutting into my client list and the landlord increasing the rent in January, I can't afford the place. When did life get so expensive?"

Sirena laughed. "Don't worry. You can move back in until you get your money right. I didn't change the locks. Yet."

Callie hugged Sirena. "I adore you. Even if you did, the gnomes would help me find the hide-a-key. Thanks, sis. I didn't know how to tell you. I'm supposed to have everything figured out by now, not be moving back home. I want to make moves."

Sirena hugged her back. "One day soon, you'll be living the life you've dreamed of. When you're out there running elegant events, you'll look back on this moment and smile. Besides, you might have the house to yourself if things work out."

Callie's brow lifted in interest. She stepped back and scanned her curiously. "Did Gus...No...? Did he propose? If I must plan another family wedding, I'm going to need another binder."

Sirena laughed to combat the sudden excitement that bubbled up within her at Callie's innocent question. *Ignore the fluttering in your stomach. You still haven't felt the click.*

"Hold on to your binder. I got an email from a literary agent."

Callie squealed. "Really?!"

Sirena lowered her voice. "Shh. The agent read about me online and contacted me. She asked me if I would be interested in writing a cookbook about my culinary style. We're talking about meeting for drinks next month. I might have to travel and do research for my book."

Between last-minute tasks and getting Lucy ready for the wedding, Sirena wanted to take time to construct a clear response.

Callie squealed. "Five years from now, you could be publishing a bestselling cookbook, eating world-class food, and living your best life."

Um. Whoa. She could be living her best life, but who would she share it with?

Her inner voice whispered gleefully: *You know who. Don't act silly.*

"What did Gus say?"

Sirena winced. "Oh, he doesn't know yet. I've been so busy with the wedding and getting the house together; I haven't talked to him."

"So, great. You'll tell him on the plane ride."

Sirena had told Callie about Gus's trip to London at Lucy's bachelorette party.

"Um, I'm not going with him. I'm staying in the Grove."

Callie glared at Sirena hard, as if she had a little troll twerking on her head.

"I don't get it. Why aren't you going with your hot magic boyfriend to London? I mean, if I were you, I'd be on that plane faster than you can say 'upgrade me to first class.'"

Sirena gave her a tight smile. "I told you already. I've been busy with the house and the wedding. I haven't had time."

A deep wrinkle appeared on Callie's face. "But Lucy just got married today and I'm moving back into the house. We're okay. You can go."

Sirena blinked at Callie, her words echoing inside her head. She stayed in the Grove believing it was her responsibility to nourish and feed her family. Kitchen witches stayed where they were rooted, but her roots were growing outward. Her dreams were outgrowing the town she loved. She'd been so desperate to get that job at Lighthouse because she needed another reason to stay in the Grove. She hoped that the job would squash her desire to leave, make her happy, and keep her family close.

Callie reached over and gave Sirena's hand a squeeze. "We've got this."

Sirena nodded. She'd been there for the family, and now they were going to be there for her. Now she had to figure out how to talk to Gus.

Like magic, Gus returned, his bow tie crooked and his smile wide. "The gnomes are safe and sound. Cal, would you mind if I borrow Sirena for a dance?"

Callie waved her hand away. "Eh. Keep her. I have to figure out which one of these gifts smells like lavender and sage."

Even though Sirena hadn't felt the click with Gus, she wanted him to know that she was going to wait for him to come back to the Grove. Three months wasn't a long time to wait for her boyfriend, and they'd call and text every day.

She'd be fine. Her breath hitched. She had to be fine for him. For them.

As Gus twirled Sirena on the dance floor to a remix of a popular love song, he knew without a doubt he was going to ask her to go on a date. August Peter Dearworth was going to ask Sirena to go with him to London. No more pretending. No illusions. No charms. Gus had listened to Lucy and Alex's vows and had to fight back tears at the sincere expression of their love. If Lucy and Alex could risk their hearts after setbacks and disappointments to find their bliss, then he could find the courage to ask Sirena out on a date.

As the remix of a Janet Jackson song began to wind down and transition into a slow ballad, Sirena eased herself into his arms.

She lifted her chin, her eyelids heavy. "I'm going to sleep until February."

Gus chuckled. "You should. You and the Caraway crew did a fantastic job. I might have to hire you for my next event."

She held on to him. "You plan on getting married again?"

"It's crossed my mind once or twice."

They danced through the slow ballad, swaying together, then a new song came on. It was Jess's song, the one she wrote about him after their relationship ended. Blood drained from his face, making everything inside wonky and loose. Sirena watched him carefully. Memories of all his previous mistakes burbled up to the surface, threatening to pull him back to the past.

He breathed deeply, and for the first time ever, Gus listened to the entire song. He swallowed roughly as her sweet voice crooned about letting a good love go to find a greater love and not regretting the feelings they shared.

One line rang inside his head and slid down into his heart.

Your happy ending is on the horizon,
it's right where you can see.

Her song wasn't her kiss-off. It was a sincere goodbye. Sirena nestled into his chest, and he tucked her underneath his chin. Gus glanced around and saw Alex and Lucy swaying together on the dance floor in their own bubble. He watched Alex mouth the words *I love you, I love you, I love you* over and over to his new wife. Lucy kissed her husband and Gus looked away to give them privacy.

A flicker of hot envy went through him. Why couldn't he be that strong? He wanted the courage to be so free and open with his love for Sirena. Gus craved to stand in the middle of the town and scream out how much he loved her. His heart swelled. He was done hiding his feelings away from the world and away from life. Gus eased Sirena over to the edge of the floor, away from the rest of the crowd. Say it now. No spells. No charms. No illusions. Just love.

"I have something to tell you."

There was an eagerness in her eyes that excited him. But at the last second he pivoted.

"I'd love to have breakfast with you," he said instead. Gus clamped down the disappointment that bubbled up in his gut. Fear was one tricky bastard.

Sirena tapped her chin impishly. "I'll have to check my notebook, but I can probably squeeze you in. A New Year's Day breakfast sounds perfect."

"It's a date." His mind was spinning in hope. Maybe he'd be ready to tell her he loved her when he got back from England.

Gus licked his lips in thought. "There's a little bistro called Night Sky I know that serves the best chocolate croissants. You must give me the recipe."

Something fluttered in her eyes.

She stepped away, out of his arms. "Um...I have something to tell you."

His gut dropped. Gus forced himself to remain still and wait, to resist the urge to shape things. *She'll talk to you. No spells, no charms, no illusions.*

344

The DJ trilled, "It's time for the bouquet toss! Get on the floor, all my single peeps."

People rushed to the dance floor. Sirena was pushed to the side by one of the Dwyer women. Lucy turned her back to the crowd, shimmying her shoulders and holding the bouquet in her right hand. Cheers and shouts lifted from the crowd.

The DJ counted down. "Three. Two. One. Let's gooo."

The bouquet sailed through the air and landed right in Gus's chest, forcing him to catch it before it landed on the ground. His body burned as everyone in the room stared at him. He drew the collective attention of every merfolk, witch, and magical being in the room.

Oh snap. Half the crowd cheered, while the other side groaned in collective disappointment.

"No! He's not single!" Auntie Niesha cried out in jest. "He's Sirena's boyfriend!"

Lucy came over to Gus, her wedding dress swishing around her legs. She gave him a side hug. He could practically feel the sisterly love and encouragement through his tux.

"Let him rock, Auntie! Until Sirena puts a ring on it, he's single and ready to jingle."

Alex gave him a fist bump. "Nice catch, Dearworth."

Ursula clapped his back. Xavier gave him a slow clap. He savored the feeling of belonging as Caraways and Dwyers came over to him and embraced him as one of theirs. *I can't wait to see Sirena's face.* Gus glanced around, searching the room for Sirena, but she was nowhere to be found. His witch had vanished.

Gus listened for her familiar bubbly laughter. She was gone. He walked around the reception space, hoping that she might have slipped behind a table or bookshelf. No. She wasn't here. A ragged breath left his throat. Sirena was truly gone. Gus gripped the bouquet against his chest, scanning the crowd for her bright smile. Had the bouquet toss, with its implication that he would be the next one to get married, made her feel uncomfortable? He wasn't sure whether she was upset about the toss, but they could talk about it before he left town. Yes, he was packed, organized, and had everything he needed for this trip to London. A bitter coldness seeped into him, down to his marrow. Well, he had almost everything he needed for the trip. He couldn't just ask her to drop everything and join him. Sirena had her entire life in the Grove, and he wanted to give her the freedom to choose him. To choose them. To love him on her own terms without the pressure of their kindred past between them. All Gus was taking with him was the memory of Sirena in her champagne-colored bridesmaid dress, her beautiful eyes glowing with hope and love.

Everything around Gus dissolved away as a sudden thought raced through his mind: *Her memory is not enough for me to survive on.*

Over the years, Gus had handled the remnants of entire lives in his hands. He learned so much about a person from the items, photographs, and journals that they left behind. Life was both lovely and cruel. The people he cared for and loved could be snatched away from him through a twist of fate. Ma. Pop. Diane. Sirena. He believed in their kindred past, but their future gave him pause and kept him standing still. Gus didn't want to fear the future; he wished to embrace it.

Gus closed his eyes, letting the epiphany wash over him like a cool evening mist. Love had the power to break his soul, but it could give him the strength to rebuild and thrive in his life. Was he seriously going to let fear rob him of the complete life he wanted? Or steal the memories he wanted to make with Sirena? Love didn't have to be the fire that destroyed him. It could be the fuel that powered him to keep going, to keep getting better each day.

One thing became crystal clear: Gus didn't want to leave the Grove without telling Sirena out loud that he loved her. Terror momentarily seized his body. Even if she didn't say it back, he couldn't live with himself if he didn't tell her what was in his heart. He'd rather be a lovesick fool than a safe coward who didn't try to love again, to live fully. Yes, Sirena was his kindred, but she was so much more to him.

She was his enchanting friend. His dazzling kitchen-witch consultant. His perfect storybook love.

The coldness eased away as he pushed the terror back down into the dark. He was going to stand in the light. Gus opened his eyes and focused on the doorway. He had to find Sirena. Midnight was approaching and he wanted to start the new year in her arms. He was still a little scared, but he allowed love to lead him out of the room. Gus left the reception quickly.

His heart reminded him of his personal motto: *Everything in its right place.*

Gus knew that the right place for him was absolutely, unquestionably with Sirena.

Chapter Thirty-One

Sirena found the open study and closed the door with a snap, escaping from the music. The room, with its fireplace, couches, and plush chairs, was cozy and spacious all at once. She needed a quiet second to think and collect herself after what just happened. The instant she saw Gus holding Lucy's bouquet like he'd won an award and beaming with love for her and her family, she knew he had her heart, but wasn't her— Click.

Her jaw dropped to her chest. So, that happened.

Auntie Niesha fussed about his single status. Click.

Lucy teased Gus and hugged him. Click.

Her soul clicked. Even more, she remembered their kindred lives. Relief flooded her brain as all the memories he shared with her returned. Even though they had a past, she wanted to know their future.

Love never had good timing. He was leaving in three days.

She had made so many mistakes over the last few years, she just wanted to be right for once. She stilled her breath and peered into the flame. Was this the right path for her?

Sirena fell to her knees and studied the fireplace.

Give me a sign. The fire burned hot, warming her chilled body.

Focus. Breathe. Empty your mind. She listened to the crackle of the flame, and eventually her heart spoke clearly.

Trust.

Tears flowed from her eyes.

He'll meet you halfway. Trust. He loves the fire in you.

She had to trust that Gus would meet her halfway. He'd try to understand that this career, this job, fed and nourished a vital part of her. In turn, she couldn't feed everything—her time, her attention, and her love—to the fire. Magic was about balance. Love was about balance.

Her time in the Grove wasn't a waste, but it had taught her the first steps to balancing her life.

She didn't have to hustle day and night, but rather rest and have fun, so she could build a life she could take joy in. *Trust your love for him and your magic.* There it was. She dropped her head to her chest in realization. She loved Gus as much as she loved kitchen magic, and she didn't want either to break her heart. For a brief instant, Sirena imagined her life without both, and it was bleak and cold. A shudder went through her at that idea. She'd be safe in the coldness, but her life would lack the warmth and glow that cooking and being with her family and Gus brought. Sirena gathered herself and stood up from the floor. She whispered her thanks to the fire for showing her a way forward. The study's door opened. Gus appeared with the bouquet still clutched in his hand.

She stared at him, completely besotted.

Unease was etched on his face. "You left so quickly. Is everything okay?"

She grinned. "I needed a second."

Gus came over to her. "You said you wanted to talk."

She told him about the cookbook offer. Gus listened. He spoke when she was finished.

Gus held the bouquet to his chest, almost like a shield. "Ah. It was only a matter of time. You're too talented to be ignored."

"No one's ignoring me now."

He just watched her. "That's my girl."

There was no disappointment in his words, only pride and love. She was going to make space for him in her life. She was going to make space for him in her dreams and in her heart.

"I'm going to wait to meet with the agent. I'm going to work on the book proposal."

Gus swallowed hard and stared at Sirena, as if he couldn't believe what he was hearing.

He peered at her face. "Si, I don't want you to miss this opportunity."

"I'm going to take my time."

"I wish I could see the future," he said.

"I know what happens," she said confidently. "Your show is amazing, and you have sold-out crowds for months. We walk London Bridge, and we have afternoon tea. We see the lavender fields in Provence, and you buy me soap that makes my clothes smell divine. You ask me to marry you in the kitchen after dinner one rainy night. We make love in our library, but eventually I remember to say yes. How does it sound?"

He answered her thickly. "I'd like that a lot. No, I'd love it. That life sounds like a lot of fun."

Sirena stood before him with her heart in her hands. "I want to go with you to London. May I join you?"

"Yes," he said. The light she loved about him lit up his face.

He shined as beautifully as the morning sun. "Always. I want you with me. I love you."

The words dropped like a spell from her mouth. "I love you too."

Gus placed the bouquet on the table and took her hands in his. He pressed his forehead to hers, pinching his eyes shut in disbelief. "Say it again. Please."

Sirena told him twice, and then once more for good measure.

With each time, his smile grew until he appeared as gleeful as if he had won the state lottery.

She warned him playfully, "You're going to get sick of hearing those words all the time."

He pressed a kiss to her temple, then peered at her. "If you say those words for a hundred years, I'll never grow tired of hearing them. I love you, too. I want to spend all my days making memories with you. I'm sorry that I didn't formally ask you to join me. I didn't want to assume you wanted to go with me. I wanted to give you a choice."

Love burned stronger and brighter than any flame inside of her chest the longer she stared at him. "Ask me now. Please."

"Will you come with me to London?" he asked.

"Yes," she said. Gus swung her into his arms and twirled her around.

Sirena let out a joyous laugh. "I'll find my passport. I don't have a suitcase."

He put her down, bouncing up and down with glee. Gus paced back and forth in the room, talking excitedly. "I'll buy you seven. But let's start with two. We'll get your travel arrangements taken care of tomorrow and I'll book your ticket. Ma rented a house and—" Gus paused. He approached Sirena standing less than a foot away. Worry stirred behind his eyes. "Wait. I'm getting ahead of myself. I don't want to rush you into anything too soon. I know you wanted to go slow. Are you sure?"

Sirena tilted her head in a yes. "I'm sure. I'm sure about you and about us."

He blinked. "There's an us."

"There's always been an us. It clicked. I understand now. I *remember*. We promenaded by gaslight and watched the world transform into something new. We tracked the constellations and kept records in golden books. I kept you warm by fires under star-filled skies. We've lived this story before in different eras and places."

The worry in his eyes disappeared and was replaced with love. Sirena angled her body into his, closing the small distance between them. Gus stood before her, a glowing image of fire, magic, and, most of all, true love.

He's mine, all mine, and I'm not letting him go.

"You're telling me we're *soulmates*," he whispered.

"I believe the term is *kindred*," she suggested. "My soul has found yours across lifetimes and oceans. We tempted fate, and we've played with fire. We are destined for each other."

Sirena kissed him, and they remained embraced for what seemed like forever.

They returned to the party sometime later and danced happily with their family and friends until it was minutes to midnight. Callie held up a tablet with a live feed of Times Square. Everyone joined in once the countdown reached ten. The ball dropped, confetti showered over the party, and cups flowed with champagne and sparkling apple cider. The entire house erupted with joyful noise, and kisses were shared between friends, lovers, and colleagues in the Grove.

As Gus pulled Sirena in for their first of many, many midnight kisses and apple cider toasts, it was official.

Sirena Rachel Caraway had found her true love.

About the Author

A native of New Jersey, **Celestine Martin** writes whimsical romance that celebrates the beauty of everyday magic. She's inspired to write happily-ever-afters and happy-for-now endings starring the people and places close to her heart. When she's not drinking herbal tea and researching her next project, Celestine, with her husband, spoils their daughter in New York on a daily basis.

You can learn more at:
Website: CelestineMartin.com
X @JellybeanRae
Instagram @CelestineMartinAuthor